From the Drop of Heaven

Legends, Prejudice, and Revenge

Juliette Godot

BROWN POSEY PRESS

an imprint of Sunbury Press, Inc.
Mechanicsburg, PA USA

an imprint of Sunbury Press, Inc.
Mechanicsburg, PA USA

For information about special discounts for bulk purchases, please contact Sunbury Press Orders Dept. at (855) 338-8359 or orders@sunburypress.com.

To request one of our authors for speaking engagements or book signings, please contact Sunbury Press Publicity Dept. at publicity@sunburypress.com.

FIRST BROWN POSEY PRESS EDITION: August 2022

Set in Adobe Garamond Pro | Interior design by Crystal Devine | Cover by Lawrence Knorr | Edited by Sarah Peachey.

Publisher's Cataloging-in-Publication Data
Names: Godot, Juliette, author.
Title: From the drop of Heaven : legends, prejudice, and revenge / Juliette Godot.
Description: First trade paperback edition. | Mechanicsburg, PA : Brown Posey Press, 2022.
Summary: Based on real people. It's 1582. Martin, an accused seditionist, narrowly escapes the pyre and finds safety with Nicolas's family. Martin admits that his books are banned, but Nicolas can't resist them. He reads them to Catherine, his love. When caught with one of the books, they learn their true enemy is the man charged with saving their souls.
Identifiers: ISBN : 978-1-62006-949-3 (trade paperback).
Subjects: FICTION / Historical / Renaissance | FICTION / World Literature / France / General | FICTION / Women.

Product of the United States of America
0 1 1 2 3 5 8 13 21 34 55

Continue the Enlightenment!

For Dad

Acknowledgments

FIRST and foremost, I would like to thank Françoise Cordier for her inspiration and research without whom this book would never have been written. Many thanks to Jennifer Quinlan from Historical Editorial and Mica Scotti Kole for the developmental advice. Thanks to the Oxford Writers Group, the Butler Writers Guild, and the wonderful community of Geneanet. And thanks to the many beta readers that gave advice: Teri Meier, Anne Merrick, Elizabeth Bell, Amanda Winsteadt, Linda Harrington, and of course, special thanks to my husband for putting up with me during this adventure.

1572-1590

"HERETIC! Sorcerer!"

The shouts came from the valley. Martin crept to the precipice of a hill, crawled under a pine branch, and peered down.

Claude! His favorite professor from the University of Geneva stood shackled between an executioner and his assistants while a cleric shouted the verdict, "Sedition."

A chaplain shouted scripture above the fracas while an ornately robed judge astride a white horse led a procession to the far end of the courtyard.

Claude struggled and screamed as guards dragged him, his heels leaving draw marks in the dirt. They bound him to a stake with piles of straw and branches at the base. A hush fell over the crowd when the chaplain repeated his prayer, and the flame was set.

With shaking hands, Martin wiped the cold sweat from his forehead. *That could have been me!* Weak from revulsion, he laid his head on the ground until screaming from below erupted again. He jerked up, and his heart leapt as Claude, with clothes aflame, ran through the crowd, dragging the smoldering ropes. He didn't get far. Guards threw him to the ground to extinguish the flames consuming his clothes, carried him back to the pyre, and threw him into the blaze.

Bile rose in Martin's throat as he scrambled from under the branch, then sat motionless, trying to catch his breath. *How could the world get thrown off balance in just a month?*

Thoughts took him back to his first day at the university when Claude, philosopher of the skepticism movement, held up the Bible and said, "This book has caused more death than any disease in history. Leaders have no problem sending their soldiers to fight and die, but they themselves will change sides in a heartbeat when it comes to money or power."

As Claude's reputation grew, so did the groundswell of opinions until, without warning, a group of Calvinist fanatics raided the school, arrested him, and burned the books in the name of God. Martin and the other students fled. The master was not so lucky.

This book has caused more death . . .

Martin's horse flicked its tail, bringing him back to the present. His eyes focused on his satchel, revealing the outline of the book, Montaigne's *Theologia Naturalis*. Should he toss it under the tree? Would it make a difference? His name was on the list of heretics. If caught, he'd be a dead man either way.

Gathering his courage, Martin mounted his horse, raised the hood of his cloak, and headed toward Paris. If he could make it to his parents' home, he would be safe.

Vacquenoux, Salm
Ten years later

Catherine Cathillon turned her eyes to the heavens and grumbled, "What did I do this time?"

It didn't matter what she did or didn't do; she heard the same words a hundred times a day as if they echoed through the Vosges Mountains and came back to her. "I'm telling Mama."

Catherine's sister, Anne, was only four years older, but she acted more like their mother. All Catherine could do was silently stare at her sister's perfect complexion, perfect hair, perfect . . . Anne.

"Besides suggesting this outing? Who in their right mind would want to traipse all the way out here, in the middle of nowhere, just to pick berries? You know I hate the out-of-doors. I think you just wanted to get out of doing your chores."

Anne was right. Catherine wanted to get away from the house. She would much rather be outside than under her sister's thumb, but she couldn't say that. Instead, she settled on, "No, I wanted to get away from you. I didn't think Mémé would make you come with me."

Anne snapped her handkerchief toward Catherine's head, but she spied it out of the corner of her eye and ducked and giggled at the near-miss. "Do stop complaining. Since you are so worried about getting dirty, just stand there and look pretty, and I'll pick."

After twenty minutes of listening to Anne's complaining, Catherine's bucket was full. "Are you ready?"

"I was ready before I came."

Catherine led the way down the path while Anne carefully placed every step and quickly fell behind. "Wait for me."

"You whine like Beatrix," Catherine said, turning in time to see Anne tumbling to the ground. Panicked, Anne squealed and fluttered her handkerchief in front of her face.

Unable to stop herself, Catherine laughed aloud. "What are you doing?"

Another squeal. "Something is attacking me!"

With a smirk, Catherine said, "I told you insects are attracted to those flower sprigs, but you insist on carrying them. There are no suitors out here. Who are you trying to impress?"

When she didn't receive a reply, Catherine continued to the valley where the brook that wound through their farm fed into a small pond, perfect for a swimming hole. Brilliant sunlight dappled on the surface, so calm and clear she could see tadpoles swimming along the edge.

A naughty smile crossed her face. "Do you want to take a dip?"

Anne gasped in horror. "You fool. There are snakes in that water."

"Oh, please." Catherine lifted her skirts and skipped across the narrow inlet, but just as she suspected, her sister didn't budge.

Instead, Anne held out her pail, and her voice rose like a child's. "Take this and help me."

Catherine took it and peered inside. "There are maybe ten berries in here."

"You win the prize. Now help me."

Not usually having the upper hand, Catherine wasn't about to waste it. "You will draw the water tonight."

"Oh . . ." Anne huffed before accepting the assistance. "How much farther?"

"The road is just up that bank. Come on and stop whining."

A grove of blackthorn bushes stood between them and the road when a noise arose from the other side, just out of view. Catherine ducked and pulled Anne down beside her.

"What is it?"

"Shh, I hear something."

"Stop teasing me," Anne whispered.

Long, sharp thorns protected the sour purple fruit as though they were precious gems. Careful to avoid the barbs, Catherine moved a branch aside and peered through. Three saddled horses grazed near a rock formation just beyond the road. She stretched a little more and caught sight of three men sitting on the rocks.

Anne tugged on Catherine's sleeve. "What is it?"

"Will you be quiet? There are three men over there. Let's go back."

"Oh no, I'm not going back," Anne said, pushing Catherine as if she planned to barge out and reveal their hiding place.

"Wait! At least let me see if they're vagrants."

At that, Anne's eyes shot open, and she dropped down again.

The rocks limited Catherine's view, but when one of them turned his head, she recognized him and gasped. "One of them is . . ." She crinkled her nose. "That man from the stable. You know, the lame one with the scar. We should go back."

"Ha, I thought you weren't afraid of anything." Anne chuckled.

Catherine stiffened. "I'm not afraid of him, but . . ."

Though their mother had always told them to cover their hair in the presence of men, Anne tended to do as she pleased. She removed her coif, fluffed her honey-gold hair, and licked her lips. With her father's fine features, Anne turned heads and always seemed to know what to say.

With a disgusted frown, Anne grumbled, "Look at you." She pinched some color into Catherine's cheeks. It wouldn't help. Catherine had her mother's dark hair and plain face. Nobody ever noticed her.

"Dust yourself off and come on." Anne stepped out of the brush and onto the road. She raised her chin and approached the men with a big smile. "Gentlemen."

Catherine slipped off her coif and fluffed her hair before lowering her head and following. As they approached, she heard the scuffle of the men sliding off the rocks to stand, a rare show of respect, and she lifted her gaze. Better dressed than the average villager, these men wore embroidered doublets with long sleeves, matching breeches, hose, and leather jerkins.

The tallest one nodded. "Good afternoon, ladies. Have we met? I'm Jean de la Goutte de Paradis. This is my brother, Nicolas, and our friend Martin."

The mayor's sons. The one who had spoken, Jean, the tallest man Catherine had ever seen, went by Le-Chêne—*The Oak*. He had a strong but friendly face with thick brown hair and brows. Anne flashed him a bright smile, but Catherine thought he was married.

Martin ran the town stable. Older than Le-Chêne, he had sandy hair and a deep scar running from his forehead to his nose, then straight across his cheek, as if someone had tried to cut a slice from his face. Shorter than the other two, Martin stood about the height of her papa but had a slight frame and walked with a noticeable limp. His firm, square jawline suggested command, yet she had never heard him speak.

The youngest one, Nicolas, looked about the same age as Anne. He was long and lean with wavy brown hair like Le-Chêne, except he had a slightly crooked nose. Mischievous hazel eyes glinted as Nicolas raised an eyebrow at Catherine with an expression that made her blush. She dropped her gaze to her feet and kicked a stone.

With a small curtsy, Anne replied, "My name is Anne, and this is my sister, Catherine."

Le-Chêne nodded in greeting. "What brings you ladies out by yourselves?"

Always the flirt, Anne gave a sly grin. "If you must know, we were picking berries."

When Anne proudly held up her nearly empty pail, Catherine looked away in exasperation.

"On a Sunday?"

A gentle wind blew. Anne turned her head, and as naturally as the breeze, her hair lifted from her shoulders, billowing behind her as if she were an angel. When Catherine tried to do the same, the wind shifted, and a dark lock blew across her face and stuck to her lip.

"Picking berries isn't work," Anne told them. "Why are you here?"

With an air of excitement, Nicolas slipped a book from inside his jerkin. "We were reading."

Martin shot him a furious glance, and Nicolas stiffened.

Why was he hiding that book? What's in there that he doesn't want us to see?

"May I see it?" Catherine asked.

Nicolas held out the book to her, but Anne had already set her pail on the ground and snatched it for herself.

Although peasants were rarely educated in the Vosges, the girls' papa had been lucky to learn from their former parish priest, Father Brignon. Determined to pass along his knowledge, Papa had taught her brothers, but he didn't think women needed to learn. He made sure the girls could write their names, but Catherine thought even that was a chore. Still, these men had snuck all the way out here just to read. There had to be a reason to do something so tedious.

Anne pretended to read the book and then handed it over to Catherine. It was filled with nothing but a jumble of letters. "Why would you read in the middle of the forest?" she asked before handing it back to Nicolas.

Le-Chêne swung his arms wide. "It's such a beautiful day; we went for a ride."

As Nicolas slipped the book into his bag, he stepped back, accidentally kicking Anne's pail and spilling her ten precious berries. As if it were a great loss, she gasped. His face reddened, and he dropped to his knees to retrieve them, catching Catherine off guard. Most boys would have let her gather them herself while trying to catch a glimpse of her ankle.

Catherine bent to help Nicolas, prompting his face to light up, and he smiled at her again—a strange, crooked smile. As if the berries were valuable, he diligently collected the spoils while keeping one eye on her.

"There's one more," he said, reaching between two stones, then he flung himself backward and shouted, "It bit me!"

Something moved—a zigzag, a flash of a tail. Catherine jumped back and shouted, "Viper!"

Anne screamed and scrambled up on a rock to escape while everyone else high-stepped, but the snake was already gone.

Le-Chêne pulled Nicolas to his feet. "Let me see."

But Nicolas jumped and shook his hand furiously until Martin grabbed it and held it still. Catherine bent in to see too.

The injury looked like two minor thorn pricks on the back of Nicolas's hand. *What would Mémé do?* Catherine slipped the handkerchief from her sleeve, wrapped it tightly below his elbow, and tried to calm him. "You'll be all right. Snake bites aren't fatal."

Nicolas's eyes widened. "People die of snake bites."

"No, not that snake. Relax and breathe normally." But he didn't relax—he gulped air and staggered sideways.

Le-Chêne fetched his horse and pulled Nicolas up. "I'll take you home."

"I think he needs help now. Mémé will know what to do," Catherine said. "Come, Anne."

"But the snake," Anne screeched, refusing to budge.

Frustrated at her sister's ridiculous actions, Catherine blurted, "I think it's on the rock behind you."

"Oh!" Anne squealed again, but instead of jumping down, she pulled her legs up and squeezed her knees.

Martin reached his hand toward her. "Zee snake is gone, mademoiselle. Giff me your hand."

What did he say? Confused by Martin's strange tongue, Catherine hesitated. Aside from the scar, he didn't look any different from anyone else, but that accent . . . Whatever he'd said, it convinced Anne to take his hand, and he helped her down.

"Take Nicolas's horse," Le-Chêne said to Catherine.

Catherine swung herself up and reached for Anne, but Anne followed Martin, who stopped as if afraid to touch her. She held her arms out for him to help her onto his horse, and after a quick glance for approval from Le-Chêne, Martin lifted her to sit sidesaddle in front of him. He seemed uncomfortable, but she was all smiles.

Papa will not be happy with this stranger's arms around my sister.

"You said you know someone who can help?" Le-Chêne asked.

"Yes, my grandmother."

When he and Martin nodded in agreement, Catherine took off down the embankment and across the stream toward the farm.

Nicolas tightened his grip around his brother's waist. His hand felt as if it were on fire. Nothing looked familiar as the landscape passed by them. "Where are we going?"

Le-Chêne replied, "I'm not sure. Catherine said her grandmother would know what to do. Are you all right?"

"No, I think I'm going to faint." Nicolas's head was too heavy, and he rested it against Le-Chêne's shoulder.

"Hold on. This must be their farm."

Rolling fields and a barn appeared in the distance, and as they descended the hill, a small stone house came into view.

"Mama, come quickly," Catherine shouted.

A woman wearing a rag tied around her head rushed out of the house.

Catherine jumped from her horse and pointed at Nicolas. "A snakebite."

"Snake? What did it look like? Triangular head? How big?"

"Its head was flat. It was brown with a zigzag and smaller than my foot."

The woman dried her hands on her apron and mumbled, "An adder."

When Nicolas slid from the saddle, his head was swimming. He lost his balance and staggered against the horse. Le-Chêne dismounted and helped Nicolas to the house and, at the woman's direction, onto a massive wooden table. As Nicolas stretched out, his brother gasped, and Nicolas leaned on his elbow to see another older woman enter the room—*the witch!*

That's why he didn't recognize this part of the forest. He'd always avoided Le Petit-Courty. Everyone did. *The girls withheld their family name on purpose.* Nicolas's heart pounded, his body heaved, and he vomited on the floor. "Sorry," he sobbed as he lay back, trembling.

Though few had ever seen the witch, her description was well-known: petite, her white apron contrasting with darker skin than he had ever seen, and large, lined eyes, which were fierce, black, and knowing. He had assumed she lived in a cave or hovel. How could she be those girls' grandmother?

Calm down. Martin says there is no such thing as a witch. Besides, she must weigh less than a bag of rye.

The old woman's eyes brightened at the kerchief around Nicolas's arm. She tightened the knot and ordered the other woman, Catherine's mother, to massage down to his hand, now swollen to twice its normal size. Turning to Le-Chêne, the witch pointed to a bunch of weeds hanging above his head and said something, rolling her "R" so thickly that Nicolas could not understand. Le-Chêne appeared confused as well.

"*Qué o-rrreg-an-o,*" she repeated slowly.

"Can you reach the oregano?" Catherine said. "Snakes are sent by the devil. Mémé wants to scare the demons away by burning oregano in the fireplace. Demons are afraid of oregano."

Nicolas inhaled sharply and squeezed the wooden table. *Did she say demons?*

Le-Chêne handed the bunch to the witch, who crumbled it between her palms, mumbled an incantation, and tossed half into the fireplace. After mixing the rest with oil, she wiped it on Nicolas's arm. He tried to pull away, but she glared at him with such intensity he resigned himself to her care. *It's just oregano, just oregano.* Without a word between them, Catherine fetched a stick that the witch used to splint his arm, wrapping it with a long piece of cloth.

"Too tight?" the witch asked.

It was tight and it ached, but Nicolas couldn't think of a reply.

She pinched his fingers, appeared satisfied, and stroked his cheek, whispering, "Rrrelax child, brrreathe easily. You will be fine."

Catherine's mother patted his hand reassuringly and placed pillows under his head and knees. His breathing slowed, and he fought to stay awake.

Martin and Anne arrived, and Le-Chêne went outside to speak with him. Nicolas tried to sit up, but the old woman pushed his shoulder down and growled, "Stay still." Before Nicolas could wrest himself free, Le-Chêne returned, alone.

Then a stocky man who must be Catherine's father raced into the house and stopped before stepping in the mess on the floor. "What's happening here? Who is this?" he said.

"Sorry to disrupt your day," Le-Chêne said to him with a bow. "We're the mayor's sons."

"Humbert," the man said, nodding in greeting.

The witch ignored protocol, shooing them away from the table. "Your brother needs to rest. Show our guest outside to the bench," she said to Anne, who motioned toward the door.

As Le-Chêne moved to follow her, Nicolas panicked. *My brother is leaving me here—alone?* Nicolas's heart raced, and he tried to rise, but the iron hand of the witch held him fast. Thankfully, Le-Chêne retreated only a couple of steps and leaned against the doorframe.

Humbert took stock of the situation and called Catherine to the side. Nicolas strained to hear the exchange.

"Did I see you straddling that horse? Have you forgotten yourself? You're too old to straddle a horse."

"I'm sorry, Papa, but it was an emergency."

"Emergency or not, you'll not do it again! Do you understand me?"

"Yes, Papa."

Humbert's eyes softened, and he went to speak with Le-Chêne, but their voices were muffled. Relieved, Nicolas lay back on the pillow. He would close his eyes for just a moment . . .

2

NESTLED in a valley of the Vosges Mountains lay the town of Vacquenoux. Along the main street, the buildings were larger, mostly constructed of wood with pine-shingled roofs. Behind them stood rows of smaller houses and merchant shops, mostly wattle-and-daub with thatched roofs. But Martin barely registered these details as he rushed to fetch Nicolas's parents, arriving breathless at the La Goutte de Paradis estate in the heart of Vacquenoux.

He caught a glimpse of Nicolas's father, Jean, reading in the shade of the house. At Martin's shout, Jean dropped the book. "What is it, Martin?"

Fighting to catch his breath, Martin held up his finger. "A snake has bitten Nicolas. We took him to the Cathillon farm in Le Petit-Courty—I think you should come."

At the mention of the Cathillon farm, the lines around Jean's eyes deepened. Behind him, Nicolas's mother, Elisabeth, emerged from the house and rushed toward them.

At the sight of her, Martin whispered, "Alone."

The stiff damask of Elisabeth's skirts made her progress difficult, and she arrived out of breath amid the scent of roses. Refined brown eyes peered into Martin's as she touched her fingers to her ruffled lace collar and huffed. "Did I hear someone shout?"

Martin lowered his gaze. He had hoped to fetch Jean without informing Elisabeth to avoid upsetting her. Luckily, Jean came to his rescue.

"Nicolas has been injured, and I must go to him."

Her puffy sleeves crinkled as she grasped Martin's arm. "Nicolas is hurt? How badly? Where is he?"

Jean kissed her cheek. "We'll be right back."

Her grip tightened. "I should come too."

"There is no need for you to bother yourself. I'll not be long."

Still clinging to Martin's arm with one hand, she touched her husband's shoulder with the other. "Wait, I will join you."

Jean replied, "You can come if you promise not to get upset."

Martin winced. *Just what I had hoped to avoid.*

Worry flashed across Elisabeth's face as she nodded and whirled. "Let me fetch my cloak while you hitch the cart."

Minutes later, the wagon barreled past the last house on the edge of town, heading into the countryside.

"What kind of trouble has that boy gotten himself into now?" she asked, twisting her fingers.

Martin took Elisabeth's hand and said, "I may as well tell you. A snake has bitten Nicolas, and we took him to Le Petit-Courty."

She shivered, and the color drained from her face. "You took him where?" She ripped her hand from his. "I thought you only wanted to spare me the sight of blood." Her voice rose. "Oh, I have heard stories. Of all the places in the world to take him, why in heaven's name did you take him there? That woman is a witch."

Jean frowned. "You promised."

Shaking his head, Martin exhaled. "There is no such thing as a *vitch.*"

"You should have brought Nicolas home."

"Can *you* cleanse a snake bite?"

"Well . . . no." She rubbed her forehead. "Nevertheless, that woman does not belong here."

Jean pulled the reins, brought the cart to a stop, and turned to her. "Francisca was not born in Salm, but she is no less welcome here than Martin."

Wide-eyed, Elisabeth turned to Martin. "Yes, but Martin is—"

Martin smirked. "Pale?"

Jean's nostrils flared. "We do not involve ourselves in gossip. Now, should we continue, or shall I take you home?"

Though her face reddened, she raised her chin and folded her hands in her lap. "Please continue."

With a slap of the reins, they proceeded toward the Cathillon farm. Aside from a breeze rustling the treetops, the only sounds were the clop of hooves and grinding of wheels on the dirt path. Eventually, the trees became sparse, and fields of rye and barley replaced them.

The farm, Le Petit-Courty, shared its name with a stream that wound its way down the hillside and past the barn. Following a fencerow, the narrow path led them to a tidy house situated on the sunny side of the slope.

Most homes in the countryside were of wattle-and-daub, but this one was somewhat of a surprise. Though constructed of the same brown sandstone as the estate, it was much smaller. Diamond-shaped glass panes covered two of the windows, and the others were protected with skins.

As Martin helped Elisabeth off the carriage, she whispered, "I thought these people were poor tenant farmers."

A bright-faced woman with smiling blue eyes came to the door. A cloth wrapped her head, and an apron, wrinkled and wet as if from drying her hands, covered her dress.

"Monsieur, madame, my name is Marie. Please come in."

While Jean stepped forward to greet her, Martin stopped at the doorway with Le-Chêne.

Elisabeth pushed past them and rushed into the house, toward the wooden table in the center of the room where Nicolas lay. She brushed his hair back and said, "I am here, darling."

Just then, an old woman emerged from a back room.

Marie nodded toward her. "This is Francisca, my mama."

Elisabeth stiffened.

Clearly, Francisca was the one presumed to be a witch, but why? She had no disgusting growths on her face, nor was she hunched over, as Martin had heard. In fact, despite her age, Francisca was a handsome woman, though her dark complexion made it obvious she was not Marie's biological mother.

Jean cleared his throat, startling Elisabeth, who forced a smile. "Pleased to meet you."

"And I am pleas-ed to meet you," Francisca's French was laced with a heavy accent.

Jean bowed slightly and joined Elisabeth beside the table. "How do you feel, son?"

Nicolas awoke, leaned on one elbow, and said with a raspy voice, "Mama?" The moment his head lifted from the pillow, Francisca shoved a mug in his face.

"Drink this." Nicolas turned his head away, but she growled, "You must drink," and started to pour. Half of the contents spilled out the corners of his mouth. He coughed and gasped.

Elisabeth reached out. "What are you doing? He is choking."

The old woman was curt. "He must drink." She pushed his shoulder until he lay back.

With a whimper, Nicolas folded his arms across his stomach, but Francisca returned his swollen hand to the table. "Be still."

The old woman's sass reminded Martin of his own grandmother, and he choked down a chuckle, but when he glanced at Le-Chêne, he saw eyes brimming with anxiety. Trying to defuse the tension, Martin elbowed Le-Chêne, grinned, and raised an eyebrow toward Nicolas. Le-Chêne exhaled and softened his expression.

"It would be best if he lies still," Marie explained. "A bite from an adder could make someone sick."

Elisabeth cringed. "What do you mean, *lie still?* For how long? He cannot stay here."

Martin followed Elisabeth's gaze around the house. Bunches of dried flowers, herbs, and weeds hung from the exposed ceiling beams, reminding him of an apothecary shop in Geneva. A spinning wheel sat by the fireplace, and another smaller table separated the food preparation area. The thick wooden table where Nicolas lay stood in the center of the room, surrounded by wooden benches.

Martin's eyes lingered on Anne, who held a little girl about three years old. The child looked like a younger version of Anne, who reminded him of his former betrothed, Alix.

A middle-aged man came to the door, followed by a young boy. The stout, rugged man had sandy hair, tanned skin, and a scruffy beard. The boy seemed to be about seven or eight, with a dirty face and dark, unruly hair. His smile showed missing teeth, with those remaining too large for his mouth.

"Joseph, fetch our guests some seats," said the man.

Jean nodded. "We're fine, thank you. I'm sorry for this inconvenience. Our son is in your way."

"The boy was hurt and needed help," Humbert said.

"No need to worry, madame," Marie continued. "He'll be good as new in a day or two."

Elisabeth placed her hand on her heart. "What are you saying?" As her gaze dropped to Nicolas, tears came to her eyes. "I'll not leave my son here."

Martin wrung his hands. *Nicolas should stay. How can I help?*

He approached Elisabeth. "If it would ease your mind, and if Monsieur Humbert agrees, I shall stay with Nicolas."

All eyes turned to Humbert, who replied, "You're welcome to stay."

Nicolas raised his head, but Jean held him fast. "Lie still, son."

With a grin, Martin said, "What do you think, Nicolas? Shall we stay?"

Though the boy's eyes were wide, he didn't reply.

Jean stared at the swollen hand for a long moment while everyone awaited his decision. Finally, he raised his head and patted Nicolas on the shoulder. "I'll be back tomorrow." Jean nodded to Martin, then turned to Humbert. "Thank you for your hospitality and your kindness." Jean bowed to Marie and Francisca.

Before Elisabeth could protest, he took her by the elbow and led her toward the door. Le-Chêne nodded to Martin and mussed Nicolas's hair before taking his leave.

Martin followed them to the door and waved them off. Though he didn't believe in witches, he knew nothing about these people. He avoided social situations whenever possible, but Nicolas needed him. Martin turned to find everyone staring, and he swallowed hard. *What have I gotten myself into this time?*

chapter

3

ARTIN joined the Cathillon family for dinner in the courtyard while Nicolas slept on the table. After a pleasant meal of pottage, fresh brown bread, and rye ale, Humbert touched Joseph's shoulder. "Would you fetch the pruner and twine, son?"

The boy responded with a toothless smile and ran to the barn.

With a nod toward a ridge in the distance, Humbert asked Martin, "Have you ever seen a vineyard up close?"

Leave Nicolas? Martin glanced through the doorway. The boy was still sleeping soundly, but . . . *Would Humbert be offended if I decline?*

Joseph had returned and was waiting for his response.

A struggling farmer probably only has one or two vines anyway. Surely, they wouldn't be long. "I would enjoy that. Thank you."

But the path went on and on, much farther than Martin had anticipated, and his hip started throbbing. He must have been limping worse than usual because Humbert slowed his pace, adjusted his boot, and stopped to point at a rabbit or a bird. Joseph ran ahead to catch crickets and gather pebbles to toss at Martin, who took advantage of the pauses to rest.

At the crest of the hill, winding rows of carefully manicured vines spread down the sunny slope before them. Martin stared at them, shocked. He'd had no idea there was a vineyard like this in Vacquenoux. The men ambled through the rows and into the valley, with Humbert occasionally pausing to attach a tendril to a rail, prune a wayward branch, or touch a cluster on the twisted, gnarled vines.

"Do you make wine?" asked Martin.

Humbert nodded and pointed toward a barn in the distance. "That was my Uncle Pierre's farm, where I was raised. We tended a small vineyard, and he taught me to make wine that he sold each year at the spring fair in Senones."

"You must make a lot—"

"No."

The sharp reply caught Martin off guard. Most men would love to brag about such a notable display.

Almost as an afterthought, Humbert added, "We make preserves."

"Very impressive, monsieur."

"Humbert."

"Humbert," Martin repeated.

Upon their return to the farm, Humbert and Joseph headed toward the barn while Martin hurried inside the house to check on Nicolas. A straw mattress large enough for the two of them now lay by the fireplace, and Nicolas was sitting up on the big table. His eyes looked glazed and his skin sallow.

"How do you feel?"

"I'm not sure." Nicolas rubbed his good hand over the splint and winced. "My whole arm is killing me." With a sigh, he slid off the table. "I have to go outside for a minute."

"Lean on me."

Once Nicolas relieved himself, he gave a silly grin. "Martin, Catherine is the girl that . . ."

Martin chuckled. The boy must not be too sick to be telling another story about a girl.

". . . that barefoot girl I saw kicking around in the stream. Remember? I told you last week."

Shocked, Martin whispered, "Dare not say a word."

"I won't." Nicolas swayed and clutched Martin's arm. "I feel dizzy."

They barely made it back to the mattress before Nicolas fell asleep.

Martin's hip ached. He plopped onto a bench by the door and stretched out to rest when the rattle of horse and harness drew his attention. He leaned forward and peeked out the door.

A cart traversed the path, and Martin recognized the man driving: thin, stiff, curly hair, arrogant brown eyes, and a nose pointed like a beak. It was the parish priest, Father Michel. As he pulled up to the house, Humbert rushed from the barnyard, his face red, jaw clenched, and nostrils flaring.

"Monsieur Humbert, Madame Elisabeth asked me—" The rest of Michel's protests were muffled as Humbert dragged the priest down and around the side of the cart and out of view.

Another person who dislikes Father Michel. Martin returned to his seat, but before he settled, he heard the priest leave and the hushed voices of Humbert and Marie just outside the door.

Humbert peeked into the doorway, bowed slightly to Martin, and announced, "Pardon me, but I have to run an errand." He left on horseback.

With aprons full of their pickings, the women filed to the worktable, and while Nicolas slept, the place buzzed with hushed activity. Francisca pulled hot ashes onto the hearth to set the pot, Joseph drew water, and the girls whispered arguments over whose turn it was to dice the onions. Marie brought a piece of salted pork to the table. She smiled weakly at Martin and shook her head in resignation before picking off bits of meat and fat to season the stew.

Martin lowered his head and chuckled.

Francisca sat beside him with a huff. "These achy old bones . . . Would you like some muskroot tea before supper? It helps with the aches and pains."

Heat rose in Martin's face. *Is my weakness that noticeable?* "No, I am fine."

The old woman stood and patted his arm. "The tea helps Humbert's back. Let me give you some."

"Please do not trouble yourself."

To his surprise, her voice lowered, and her black eyes narrowed in anger. "I will make it, and you will try it."

He had not meant to offend her. "Thank you, madame."

He drank the tea, and everyone chatted, but no one mentioned Humbert's hasty departure. Though Martin knew it wasn't proper, curiosity got the best of him, and he asked, "Was that Father Michel?"

The nonchalant expression Marie returned looked forced. "Yes, but he had to leave. He probably forgot something."

Whatever Humbert had said to the priest must have made an impression, but Martin couldn't glean anything from Marie's face. Though he and Jean had often discussed the sullen little man, whom they both considered more of a troublemaker than a man of God, most of the villagers, Elisabeth included, believed everything that crossed his lips. *Perhaps Humbert is a Protestant?* Either way, manhandling a priest was not a good idea.

Humbert returned in time for supper.

After the meal, the family filed outside and knelt by the door while Marie led them in praying the rosary. Martin bowed his head out of respect for his hosts, but his mind swirled. If Humbert was not a Protestant, why had he mistreated the priest?

When nobody was looking, Martin peeked at Anne, comparing her to Alix: same soft voice, same quiet grace. Once, Anne lifted her gaze, caught him staring at her, and smiled. His face flushing, he returned an awkward grin and lowered his head.

The family dispersed. Martin stood, unsure of what he should do, when Anne beckoned him, pointing to red streaks forming in the evening sky. He followed her to a fence, where they admired the brilliant colors of the coming sunset.

"Tell me more about your travels, Martin," she said.

After not speaking with a woman since Alix, Martin swallowed hard before replying. "Well, Strasbourg is a beautiful city. The cathedral is the tallest building in the world. The pink stones seem to touch the sky. Even the air feels alive."

"Oh, I can imagine," Anne said, touching her hand to her throat. "Someday, I want to see it, and oh, I would love to see Paris."

Martin frowned—Paris—but her eyes flashed with excitement. He didn't want to destroy her dreams, so he chose his words carefully. "Sometimes a city's reputation is misleading."

Though he was standing with Anne, beautiful Anne, he thought of Alix, and that familiar pain stabbed his heart. Besides, Anne was just being a good host. Surely, his scars repulsed her.

Humbert cleared his throat behind them; it was improper for them to be alone. Though she shot her father a look, Anne nodded, and Martin followed her to a bench beside her father. They settled while Humbert enjoyed a pipe in the crisp evening breeze.

A few minutes later, Catherine joined them.

Never good at small talk, Martin struggled to think of something witty to say.

Catherine looked sideways at him. "How did you get that—"

"So, Martin," Anne cut in. "I noticed a bit of an accent."

"Switzerland is my birthplace. My father was a musician and opened a shop where he made a newer instrument called the viola for arms. The French call it a violin."

"A vio-lin?"

"A violin is like a lute, except you play it with a bow. My father was one of the first violin makers in this part of Europe."

Catherine leaned in with excitement. "Do you have one, a violin? Will you play for me?"

"Yes, if you like."

Anne remained composed, her hands clasped on her lap, her tone even, like a fine lady. "What brought you to the small town of Vacquenoux?"

Suppressed thoughts jammed Martin's mind. *Just give an overview, enough to satisfy their curiosity.* "I studied to be a professor in Geneva, but Calvinists replaced the liberal professors . . ." *They burned my teacher and were coming for me. No. Finish it, quickly.* "I had to flee."

Catherine cocked her head. "What's a Calvinist?"

Humbert shot a warning glance. "Catherine."

Martin thought of another explanation that might not scare her, but he glanced at Humbert for approval. At his nod, Martin turned to Catherine. "Calvinists are strict Protestants, and they rule Geneva."

She frowned in confusion.

He began again. "Strict Huguenots. They believe dancing, music, and drinking wine are immoral and that certain books are illegal. My father made forbidden instruments, so they accused me of Catholic sympathies, and I fled before they could arrest me."

"Well." Catherine's face pinched. "What's a Huguenot?"

With a glance toward Humbert, Martin said, "I am a Huguenot. Does that bother you?"

Humbert raised an eyebrow. "Should it?"

"No," Martin said, wishing he could take back his words.

The confused girls turned to each other and then to him. Silence hung in the air until finally Anne said, "Why did you come here instead of going back to Switzerland with your family?"

"Time for bed," Humbert said, standing and shooing the girls toward the house. Once the girls were out of earshot, he said, "I have no problem with you being a Huguenot, Martin."

At Martin's blush, Humbert touched his shoulder. "You didn't have to join our prayers if it made you uncomfortable."

Martin gave up trying to place him. "The chanting is soothing. Besides, this is your home."

"And you are our guest," Humbert said in a fatherly voice. "You needn't humor those girls with their meddling questions either."

"Thank you, monsieur."

Humbert gestured toward the house, but Martin said, "I would like to stay out here a while."

"Of course. Let me know if you need anything. Good night."

"Good night."

Martin walked to the fence where he had stood with Anne as the sun faded behind the pines. Why did he always want to debate with people? Why couldn't he keep his opinions to himself? Though it had taken years to forget Alix, Anne brought back her memory: pale blue eyes, high cheekbones, and hair the color of ripened rye.

A slight chill displaced the warmth of the day, and an icy breeze brought Martin's attention back to the present. After all these years, angry tears still burned his cheeks, and he brushed them away. With a heavy heart, he returned to the house, where a rush light had been left burning for him. Nicolas was still sleeping comfortably. Had he slept all day? Martin had promised to keep his eye on the boy, but . . .

He blew out the flame, closed his eyes, and tried to think of something else. Though he enjoyed the political conversations regularly held with his adopted family, he missed the intellectual give-and-take with his old friends and philosophers. How much more advanced the world would be if only . . .

As his mind quieted, the ache roared back into his hip. Francisca's tea had helped. He wished for another mug now. To occupy his thoughts, he tried to identify the myriad of dried greenery above his head as he drifted off to sleep. He shivered and pulled the blanket . . .

. . . *his collar, tightly against his neck. He was floating on a morning mist above the streets of Paris as the bells of Notre Dame pierced the quiet, announcing the Feast of Saint Bartholomew. As he flew around the soaring cathedral, other people floated with him. He landed on the bridge over the Seine, but the people with him were not floating in the mist, they were in the water, bobbing and turning with the current, catching in the arches of the bridge.*

"No," he moaned.

He ran across the blood-soaked ground, tripping over bodies, dead horses, and toppled carts. Lost in the fog, he ran and ran, slipping on vomit and emptied intestines. Finally, Martin found his parents' house and flew up the stairs. The door opened, and his mother was there, reaching for him. He fell into her embrace, but she was stiff. Her dress was soaked in blood from a gaping slash in her throat; her eyes were fixed and staring.

"No."

Above the fireplace, where embers still glowed, his father's head sat on the mantel, his face distorted and eyes wide open. The rest of his body hung from the chandelier. The severed head said, "Martin."

He couldn't move. Someone was holding his arm!

"Martin, Martin, are you all right?"

He awoke with a start and sat up, gasping for air, his eyes darting frantically around the room. Francisca repeated his name. His head cleared, he remembered, and he was safe.

"Let me make you a warm drink," she said, patting his arm.

A blush that began in the pit of his stomach inflamed his entire body. "Sorry that I woke you." He exhaled. "I . . . I need some air." Jumping to his feet, he stumbled toward the door. The cool night jolted him awake. He took a deep breath and squeezed his eyes shut.

Why? Tonight of all nights, why?

Francisca brought two steaming mugs that smelled like the concoction she had been forcing into Nicolas. She handed Martin one, placed hers on a bench, and wrapped a blanket over his shoulders. Her eyes were gentle, concerned.

"You are too kind, madame."

She retrieved her mug and stood beside him. The moonlight had broken through a cloud and brightened the courtyard, casting everything in muted shades of silver. Occasionally, an owl screeched over the chorus of frogs and the burbling water of Le Petit-Courty. The two stood in silence for several minutes, sipping from their mugs.

"What troubles you? I know I am a stranger," she said, "but telling me might help."

Martin turned to her. Her swarthy skin shimmered in the moonlight that intensified the lines on her face. "No. I cannot." He replied too quickly and lowered his gaze, ashamed of this weakness he could not overcome. Still, she stood there, watching him. He needed to change the subject. "Perhaps," he said, "your story could help me deal with mine a little better."

She raised her brows in surprise and gestured to the bench where they settled. She stared into the black void in front of them before saying, "My family traveled through Spain, living off the land, selling things we made."

He had no trouble understanding her—one of his classmates had the same accent.

"Mercenaries took me, my mother, and six other women from our family. They needed us to work for them, cooking, sewing, other things . . ." She stared at her hands, her voice monotone. "Whenever they needed supplies, they would steal them, and one day I was able to slip my hands from their bindings. When they attacked this farm, I saw my chance to escape. Marie was wandering alone, and when I ran to hide in the woods, I grabbed her and took her with me."

Martin nodded. Francisca had answered so quickly—perhaps too quickly, too rehearsed. "Yes, I have heard that story. I was hoping you would tell me the rest."

She adjusted her shawl and squared her shoulders. "Why do you think there is more?"

He looked into her eyes. The fiery spirit was gone, replaced by melancholy.

She tapped her fingers on her mug, stood, and stared into the distance as if watching a scene play out in her mind.

An owl called, *hoo-hoo-hooo*.

"Nothing else happened," she whispered, and she left him sitting there.

chapter
4

NICOLAS awoke at first light, his hand still swollen and throbbing. The shadow that was Humbert silently donned his boots and slipped out the door. A few moments later, another shadow came down the ladder from the loft and paused above Martin, who whispered something. From the reply, Nicolas guessed it was Joseph. Martin got up and followed him.

Nicolas remained quiet. He would wait for Catherine.

He smiled in the darkness. He had seen her before—from a distance. With her skirts pulled up to her knees, she had been kicking and splashing in the stream by the bridge near where the snake had bitten him, and those legs had filled his dreams ever since. Now he pictured her in her entirety: thick hair, brows, and lashes, the color of the dark, rich mountain earth, creamy skin, and the bluest eyes—no, more of a gray, perhaps silver. And here he was in her house.

The room lightened, and Marie came in from the back. The crisp tawny linen of her kirtle and apron matched the cloth that bound her hair.

"Nicolas, you're awake. How do you feel this morning?"

He rose to greet her. "I'm not sure. I'm not as dizzy."

"Very good."

Though he tried to raise his arm, the splint held it fast. "This thing hurts. May I take it off?"

She pinched his fingers. "The splint doesn't hurt; the bite hurts. Hold it still, and I will get you some tea to help with the pain." She nodded to a bucket and towel on the corner of the table. While he freshened up, she fetched him a mug.

Nicolas hesitated before taking a drink, then realized with amusement that he had been drinking it for quite a while now. If they'd wanted to poison him, he would be long dead.

She spread out the coals, placed an already-risen loaf of rye on the hearth, then excused herself outside. Overhead, the girls stirred in the loft.

When Catherine started down the ladder, Nicolas hid the mug behind the bucket, lay back on the pallet, and closed his eyes.

The scratching of slippers on the floor indicated she was approaching him, and he pinched his leg to keep from laughing.

She leaned over him and touched his cheek with the back of her hand. Her breath felt warm on his neck. "How do you feel?"

Opening his eyes slightly, he moaned, "I'm dying. Kiss me. I don't want to die without ever being kissed."

She checked his forehead. "You have no fever; you're not dying."

"My stomach," he moaned and rolled side to side. "I'm going to die. Please kiss me."

Soft fingers touched his arm, and she spoke in a soothing voice, "No, you'll be fine." The sweet smell of bracken and straw enveloped him as her hair tickled his neck. He couldn't help himself, and he opened one eye to peek at her when a chuckle escaped.

Blushing, she gasped and pulled away.

"Oh, come now, is that any way to treat a dying man?" He puckered his lips and leaned on his elbow.

Catherine's eyes flew open, then narrowed. "You fool!" She squared her shoulders and marched to the table, banging the wooden bowls as she set each place.

Still chuckling, Nicolas got up, smoothed the blankets with one arm, and sat back down on the pallet to watch her. Occasionally, she peeked at him from under her hair. He would smile, wink, and watch her blush again.

Francisca came and pulled the baked loaf from the fireplace. The aroma made his stomach growl. Aside from that awful tea, he had not eaten since yesterday morning.

When Humbert returned, Marie called everyone to the table, and Nicolas wasted no time seating himself in front of the warm bread. But that wasn't all. There were fresh raspberries and honey, two things that rarely graced their own table. *What a treat.*

At the sight of the honey, Humbert cast a questioning glance at Marie, who responded with a nod in Martin's direction. While Nicolas pondered the exchange, Francisca approached him.

"How does that arm feel?"

Drawing a pained face, he raised it slightly. "It's heavy, and it hurts."

Nodding, she patted his shoulder. "I will make you a sling, and you will rest today. When you finish eating, Catherine will escort you outside for some fresh air."

Catherine looked appalled. "Mémé, I—"

Ignoring her, Marie spooned some berries into the bowl and handed him a piece of bread. "You must be starving."

He was, but as he devoured his bread and berries, he glanced at Catherine, who was sulking. When she did raise her head, he winked at her. He didn't think she noticed, but her father did.

"Feeling better, I see?"

"Yes, monsieur," Nicolas replied, wiping the smile from his face.

When her father finished eating, Catherine motioned for Nicolas to follow her. He thought Martin would join them, but Martin's eyes were fixed on Anne, who was clearing the dishes.

"Are you coming, Martin?"

When Martin stood with a sigh, Nicolas rushed ahead to open the door for Catherine and bowed as she passed. She shot him a dirty look.

Once outside, Martin joined them, and the three simply stood there, staring at one another. A few moments of uncomfortable silence followed before Nicolas blurted out, "Would you like me to read to you?"

Catherine brightened. "Yes, very much."

"What happened to my bag?" Nicolas asked.

Martin's eyes widened in shock. He looked around suspiciously and whispered through clenched teeth. "What are you thinking? That book is illegal."

"Do you think anyone would know?"

As if he had been eavesdropping on their conversation, Humbert came out of the house, waving the book. "Are you looking for this? It must have fallen out of your bag." His eyes bored into them. "Who is Ronsard? Is this book banned?"

Nicolas squirmed. "I—"

Martin stepped up. "I am sorry, monsieur, it was a mistake bringing it here."

At that, Humbert seemed to calm, and he patted Martin's shoulder. "Just be careful."

Good old Martin. Always there when I need him.

"Can Nicolas read it to me, Papa? Please?"

"Daughter, you can't keep a secret. This is no game. People have been killed for less."

"No, Papa, I can keep a secret. I promise I can. Please?"

Stern eyes shifted from Catherine to Nicolas. But when they landed on Martin, Humbert sighed in resignation. "Go ahead, or she'll pout for weeks. But you can never talk about anything in that book, Catherine."

"Thank you, Papa." She kissed his cheek.

Humbert spoke over his shoulder as he turned toward the barn, "Martin, would you like to come with me or stay with them?"

Before following Humbert, Martin gave Nicolas a dirty look.

Smiling triumphantly, Catherine led Nicolas to the bench. He plopped down beside her, turned to a marked page, and read:

> "Do What Thou Wilt;
> because men that are free, well-born, well-bred, and
> conversant . . .
> break that bond of servitude wherein they are so tyrannously
> enslaved.
> For it is agreeable with the nature of man to long after things
> forbidden
> and to desire what is denied to us."

He omitted part of the passage that would be difficult for Catherine, and her reaction made him glad he did. Her eyes sparkled. He read other passages, and she asked him questions, but just as he began to feel comfortable with her, the dizziness returned. He leaned his head against the wall.

As if waiting for exactly this, Francisca appeared. "Come, lie by the fireplace."

This might be my last chance to spend time with Catherine. "But I'm fine, madame."

Without replying, Francisca eyed them and went inside, but a few moments later she was back with a blanket and a mug of tea. She nodded to a nearby oak.

Once they settled in the shade, Nicolas continued reading, noting the wonder in Catherine's eyes. With his back against the tree and the pretty girl sitting beside him, time passed swiftly. Eventually, her younger siblings wandered over, and he closed the book and told them stories from memory. By late morning, he was exhausted from speaking too much, and all four of them lay on the slope and tried to find shapes in the clouds until Marie called them.

"Lovey, have you seen your papa?"

"No, Mama, Nicolas has been reading to us."

"Come in and set the table. Joseph, find your father."

Not wanting to be left sitting there alone, Nicolas said, "I'll help you search."

While Joseph looked around the barn, Nicolas headed for a small utility building near the tree line. The back of the shed disappeared into the heavy underbrush at the base of the mountain. There were no windows, and the heavy door stood slightly ajar. He stepped inside.

"Monsieur Humbert?"

Humbert slammed the door on a closet that extended the length of the shed and spun to face Nicolas. In the dim light, Humbert's expression looked as if he had seen a ghost. "Are you spying on me?"

Nicolas flinched. "No, monsieur. Madame asked me to fetch you."

Humbert approached him with a furious expression. "Well, you shouldn't be here!"

Tensing, Nicolas backed out, "Yes, monsieur, I'm sorry."

While Nicolas was preoccupied with reading to Catherine, Humbert and Joseph showed Martin the workings of the farm, and he followed them like a child. Humbert taught him how to tan a pig's hide, scraping off the hair and stretching it on the rack. Joseph showed him how to milk the cow and *accidentally* shot a squirt his way. For the first time in his life, Martin gathered eggs, proudly holding up his full basket. Humbert chuckled, and Joseph burst out laughing when they realized Martin had collected the whitewashed wooden balls used to teach the chickens where to nest. Even as he had been picking them up, he'd thought they looked like strange eggs, but such things were not in any of the books he had read.

The midday meal came to a close when the sound of a carriage drew Martin from his seat. From the door, he said, "Nicolas, your parents are coming . . . and it looks like Father Michel is with them."

Humbert's face reddened, and he cursed under his breath as he stormed past them. Outside, though, he stopped and turned, his face bright with excitement as he shouted, "He's here!" And everyone rushed to the courtyard.

Nicolas's parents had arrived with a priest that Martin didn't recognize. Jean helped Elisabeth down, and she immediately ran to Nicolas and kissed his cheek.

"Oh, darling, I have been so worried about you."

"I'm much better, Mama."

Humbert lifted the elderly priest down and hugged him so hard he lifted the man off the ground. "Papa, you got my message. I'm so happy you could come."

The priest said, "Ah, 'Papa.' I've missed that title." He beamed and threw his arms wide, hugging Marie and Francisca at the same time.

Martin stared at Humbert. Yesterday, he had accosted Father Michel, and today . . . He whispered to Elisabeth, "Is that a priest? Did he say, 'Papa'?"

"That is Father Brignon," said Elisabeth, "our former parish priest. He arrived on the coach this morning, and Jean offered him a ride." She squinted down her nose, casting accusatory glares between the priest and Humbert. "I have no idea why these people call him 'Papa.'"

With a curtsy, Marie said to Elisabeth, "I'm sorry, we've not seen Father Brignon for a long time. Please come in."

They filed into the house and gathered around the big table.

Father Brignon sat in a nearby chair. His stark white hair and ruddy complexion contrasted with smiling brown eyes and accentuated deep crow's feet. "You must be Catherine and Joseph."

Catherine nodded, and Joseph sat cross-legged on the floor at the priest's feet. Little Beatrix wandered to them and stumbled over Joseph's leg. Joseph puckered his lips to yowl a complaint, but his mother caught his eye and he sobered.

"And you must be Beatrix." The priest lifted her to a comfortable spot on his knee and turned to Catherine. He must have noticed Elisabeth's disapproving stare, for he added, "You know, your father came to live with me after his parents died. Of course, he couldn't stay with me, so he went to live with my brother, Pierre."

Elisabeth stiffened and clasped her hands while Martin scratched his nose to hide a smirk.

"Yes, I remember Uncle Pierre fondly," Catherine replied with a smile.

Marie brought Jean and the priest bowls of raspberries, and Anne brought them ale. Martin followed her with his eyes as she poured a round for everyone and took a seat beside her mother. Laughter brought his attention back to the group. Beatrix was standing on the priest's lap, feeding him berries. The chatter continued about memories and stories from the past until Jean looked at Nicolas.

"Are you ready? The Cathillons have their hands full."

Nicolas's face puckered, and he placed the back of his hand on his forehead. "I still feel a little weak." He did look pale, but his mischievous eyes revealed his deception.

Jean rose and said, "You seem fine to me," forcing Nicolas to sigh in defeat.

Bowing to Humbert, Martin said, "Thank you, monsieur. I have enjoyed my stay."

"You're welcome here anytime," Humbert replied.

Jean motioned Humbert to a corner of the room, probably offering compensation.

While Nicolas took his leave, Anne helped Martin gather his things. Did she flirt with him? No. Why would she? He tried to think of something to say to her, but his mind went blank.

Francisca handed him a cloth-wrapped bundle. "Steep one root in water for about ten minutes to make the tea. Come back when you need more for the pain."

He bowed to her. "Thank you, madame."

When Martin climbed into the carriage, the others were already settled, and Elisabeth was fussing over Nicolas. Everyone waved goodbye.

As soon as they pulled away from the house, Elisabeth fanned herself and said, "Oh, I have been so worried about the two of you."

Jean shook his head. "Do you think Father Brignon would stay there if he thought they were doing anything sinister?"

"I have no idea." Elisabeth raised her chin. "But explain to me how he knew to come now."

Martin replied, "After Father Michel left yesterday, Humbert said he had to take care of some business and left on horseback. It was early enough that he could have sent a note with the coach driver."

As Elisabeth continued to fling reprimands, Nicolas leaned his head back against the seat and pretended to be asleep, and Martin stared at his hands, occasionally clenching his teeth. The final affront came with Elisabeth's question, "Was Francisca dancing last night? Were there any lizards or toads about the house? Father Michel told me they could be fine and crafty, and their hospitality should not fool us."

Heat rose in Martin's face. He would not take it any longer. "Would you like to see Francisca burned?"

Nicolas's eyes flew open as his mother inhaled in shock and replied, "Why would you suggest such a thing?"

Martin exhaled sharply. "Francisca has an accent. I speak with an accent. If they come for her, it will not be long before they come for me."

Jean added, "Father Michel is an agitator. Please be careful what you say to him."

Elisabeth folded her hands on her lap. "Father Michel is a man of God. I should think you would appreciate that."

Still angry, Martin said, "I appreciate your concern for Nicolas."

Her face went stiff, and he thought she would burst into tears. "There have been so many stories about her. Some of them must be true." She fingered her handkerchief. "And where do they get their money? They are poor farmers. Others struggle to survive, yet they have enough money to improve their home. Did you notice they even have glass panes in some of their windows? And that woman obviously is not Marie's mother—"

"Their money is none of our business," Jean said a little too loudly. "And I know how Francisca became Marie's mother. I was there."

Everyone turned to him. With one last glare at his wife, he began, "A week before I left for my apprenticeship, a stage driver told us about a big battle in Renty during the Italian Wars. A couple days later, we were working in the stable when a troop of the Spanish Cavalry marched through the town. They shouldn't have been this far southeast. Papa said they were deserters."

"The last cart was full of women like I had never seen before." His brows pinched. "Their hair hung loose, and they wore only torn dirty chemises with a piece of blanket wrapped around their shoulders or with their shoulders bare. Some villagers shouted at them, calling them whores, but one of them caught my gaze. I'll never forget her face—vacant. Her hands were tied to the cart, and she had a black eye. I assumed she was a criminal."

Jean's voice lowered to a monotone. "A couple of hours later, someone rode in shouting that Le Petit-Courty had been sacked, and everyone rushed to help. Those soldiers had killed everyone, even the children. The eldest boy, about my age, they'd sliced his neck so deeply they nearly cut off his head. His eyes were open and staring, and his younger brother—they'd sliced his stomach open."

Jean raised haunted eyes, reminding Martin of the horror of his own family's end. Elisabeth shuddered and slid her hand around her husband's elbow. Jean added, "Agnes and her mama had gone to sell chickens and were not home at the time."

Nicolas asked, "Agnes?"

"You know Agnes, from the inn—she's Marie's sister."

"I knew Marie looked familiar," Elisabeth whispered, almost to herself.

Jean nodded. "When they returned, well, they found everyone except baby Marie. Her mama was hysterical. She thought the soldiers had abducted her. We searched until dusk.

"What the soldiers didn't steal, they destroyed. The family was destitute. Grandfather organized donations. Papa offered a horse from the stable—my horse, Belle. He would say, 'When you give, you give your best.' I loved that horse, but he grew angry with me—they had nothing."

Though Nicolas's eyes were half-closed from drowsiness, they were glued to his father, who continued, "I was ashamed and gave them my saddle and bridle as well. That was the first time Papa said he was proud of me."

Jean's voice cracked, and he cleared his throat. "But when I took my beautiful Belle to them, I found Father Brignon trying to talk to Francisca, who was holding baby Marie amid a crowd of people. Francisca kept saying something like, '*Puede ayudar a los demás?*' Someone said she was summoning demons, and people screamed. Father Brignon said it was Spanish: *demás,* not demons. She was asking to help the others, but who—what others? Everyone was dead. Luckily, she understood a little Latin and told him she was one of the women in the cart but had escaped, found Marie, and hid in the woods." Toward Elisabeth, his voice raised, he said, "Francisca saved Marie."

Elisabeth adjusted her seat and fiddled with her fingers under the scrutiny.

The story became dreamlike. "Until that day, I couldn't wait to leave this mountain, but the massacre changed me. I realized how fragile life is and how important family is. Grandfather loved it here, called it his drop of heaven, *la goutte de paradis.* He said the phrase so often it became part of his name. Eight long years later, I returned with my beautiful bride"—Jean squeezed Elisabeth's hand—"and saw the mountain again, and I knew Grandfather was right."

Misty-eyed, Elisabeth replied, "And here we are."

"Yes, here we are." The tension left Jean's eyes, and they rode in silence for a while. He then added, "These rumors about Francisca have lingered all these years and need to be stopped. I'm glad you took Nicolas there."

Leaning his head against the seat again, his still-wrapped arm on his lap, Nicolas said, "I'm glad you took me there too. They treated us kindly."

Elisabeth lowered her head in resignation, but Martin could not let it go. "Why has no one spoken out about Francisca's bravery?" His voice was more accusatory than he intended.

Jean frowned. "Some of us have, but superstitions run deep. Francisca doesn't fit into the community. She looks and talks differently, speaks her mind, and has no patience for formality."

As she held her eyes on her clasped hands, Elizabeth mumbled. "They never attend Mass."

"They used to; I remember when Father Brignon was here—"

"Yes, we have heard that story."

They rode the rest of the way home in silence.

chapter
5

FRANCISCA watched the cart disappear down the path. After her discussion with Martin the night before, she had returned to bed but had not slept a wink. Since arriving at the farm, she rarely spoke about her past, but now the memories flooded her mind. Deep in thought, she jumped when Father Brignon placed his hand on her shoulder.

"Are you all right?" he asked.

She gave him half a smile. "Padre, it is so good to see you again." She turned away and replied flatly, "Nothing has been the same since you left."

"Oh, Francisca, you exaggerate. Would you like to talk about it?"

She lowered her gaze and allowed her shoulders to slump. Last night, she had suggested Martin relieve his burden. *What would Father think of me if I confessed?*

The priest gestured toward a bench by the barn, and she nodded. As they walked, she recalled the day they had met. Father Brignon had been her first friend in Salm, the only person with whom she could communicate. Over the years, he had visited often, watching helplessly while Marie's mother stared into space until she wasted away. He married Agnes to Sebastien, son of the local boardinghouse owner, and admitted that he was thrilled to officiate when Humbert, the boy from the other side of the mountain and his adopted nephew, asked Marie to marry him soon afterward.

At the bench, Francisca pulled her rosary from the pouch of her apron, wrapped it around her hand, and kissed the crucifix. It took her a moment to gather her thoughts, before she said, "I am not who you think I am."

He frowned. "Go on."

"My family traveled—they called us Gypsies . . . The *soldados* killed my papa, my brother, and all the *hombres* in our family, and they abducted the women who survived. These men were brutal, like animals. If we resisted, they beat us without mercy. *Mi madre* told me to do whatever they wanted—to stay alive for each other until we could escape." She lowered her head and fingered her beads.

Father Brignon placed his hand on hers. His gentle eyes gave her strength. "Trust me."

"*Mi madre* and I were . . . I was fourteen years old." She shuddered at the thought. "Many *hombres*, many different *hombres*, sometimes two at a time, abused us until we could barely walk. This continued for a long time, more than a year when they ran from a battle."

Her heart pounded as if she were still running. She had been running for so long; it was time to confess. She exhaled deeply, trying to calm herself. "I had a *bebé* . . . a little girl. A *bebé* would have held the soldiers back. They would have killed her. Madre stole her away and left her at an abbey."

A moment passed while Francisca considered her next words. She pulled her pendant from under her chemise and showed it to him: it was cross-shaped, with a heart in the middle and an anchor on the bottom. When she flipped it over, it revealed an engraving, *Fran*.

She continued, "Madre had one that said *Rita*. She left it with the *bebé*. *Mi padre* made these crosses to sell." She rubbed her thumb over the name. *Papa was so proud of these.*

The priest nodded. "Beautiful."

"Madre might have escaped that night, but she came back for me. The day before we arrived in Vacquenoux, a *soldado* beat her so badly she died in my arms. They just dumped her beside the road as if she were nothing—they would not even let me bury her."

The rosary around Francisca's hand burned like the bite of the ropes that had bound her as she watched her mother's crumpled body getting smaller and smaller behind the cart. Choking back a sob, Francisca turned to his shoulder and wept while he held her, then she pulled away, embarrassed, and wiped her face with his handkerchief. "I am so sorry."

"What sin have you committed, child?"

"I was a whore. I had a *bebé*, and I abandoned her."

"You were forced."

The trembling in her hands subsided, and he wiped a leftover tear off her cheek.

"And either way," he continued, "the abbess would never have given a single woman a baby. Surely, the sisters treated her well, or perhaps a loving family adopted her. Nothing you have done needs absolution."

Several moments passed in silence before the priest asked, "I knew you could live off the land, but when did you learn to cleanse illness?"

"While we were captives, Madre taught me. She traded remedies for food, treated the young *soldado* who helped her hide my *bebé*, and she also helped the other women, healing them, delivering their *bebés*. Occasionally, she could stop—"

She clenched her lips, having said too much.

He scowled. "Your mother taught you ways to cast infants from the womb?"

Francisca rolled her beads between her fingers in hesitation before replying, "I know the plants that will prevent them. I did not think it was a sin."

He shook his head. "It is against the pope's teachings, and I think you do know that."

Defiant, she raised her chin. "God created the plants I use. Why would He give us the ability to use nature's gifts if it were wrong?"

His eyes bore into her. "I haven't all the answers, and I'll not preach to you, but promise me you'll be careful whom you give it to. Any suggestion that you have slain an infant in the womb or hindered a woman from conceiving will surely bring an accusation of witchcraft. I cannot protect you if you get caught."

The crucifix dug into her palm, and she forced herself to loosen her grip before whispering, "Would you help me find my daughter, Padre?"

The lines on his forehead puckered even more deeply. "These people are your family. Do they know of her?"

"No, I have never told anyone."

He rubbed his chin in thought. "How old would she be now? Marie's age? What if she's married with children of her own?" He turned to her. "I will search if you want—"

Francisca looked into his eyes, then turned away. A long moment passed. "No, I cannot disgrace this family. It is best if nobody ever knows."

As if he could see into her soul, he asked, "Is she the reason you make your birth prevention? Had you taken it, do you think you would be spared this heartache?"

Another tear rolled down her cheek. *Madre thought I was too young.*

When she didn't respond, he continued, "Perhaps those terrible things happened for a reason, Francisca. If not for you, Marie would be dead, and this family would not exist—they are alive because of you." Sweeping his hand in front of them, he said, "You are responsible for all of this." He gathered her rosary and placed it in her palm, surrounding her hands with his own. "Keep this close to your heart, Francisca. If God wants you to meet your daughter in this world, you will. If not, you will be together in the next."

She gazed into his calming eyes and took a deep breath. "*Gracias*, Padre."

⚓

That evening, as Catherine combed the braids from her hair, she asked Anne, "Have you wondered how Martin got that scar?"

"Yes, but you cannot ask someone such a thing." Anne pulled Beatrix's robe over her head.

Catherine narrowed her eyes and threw her comb onto the table. "You're smitten."

The moonlight shone through the window, brightening Anne's golden hair, but her gaze seemed far away. "He's smart and sophisticated."

Catherine rolled her eyes and fell onto the pallet. "But that scar . . ."

"Hush. That scar is not important. He must have been handsome before . . . Well, it doesn't matter."

Why would Anne prefer Martin, despite his scars, when Nicolas is her age and so handsome? Catherine scrunched up her nose. "He speaks strangely."

"He's worldly." Anne combed the baby's thin blond hair, slid her under the blanket, and lay beside her. "Do you even realize Nicolas is smitten with you?"

Catherine's eyes opened wide, incredulous that anyone would be interested in her when Anne was so much prettier. She rose on her elbow to stare at her sister, considering telling her about the attempted kiss. Instead, she said, "No, he just acts the fool."

"He seemed to enjoy reading to you."

Easing herself back onto the pillow, she said, "I enjoyed it too. I'm going to ask him to teach me to read."

"Ask Papa to teach you," Anne said, fluffing her pillow.

"I did. Papa said he's too busy."

"Well, women don't read, and men like to feel important. Let Nicolas read to you."

Catherine frowned and crossed her arms. "Why don't women read? I want to—"

"Oh, you're hopeless," Anne said, rolling away from her. "Go to sleep."

Catherine studied the back of Anne's head. *What does she know? Why can't women learn to read?* But rather than falling asleep to dream of letters and pages, Catherine closed her eyes, recalling every detail of Nicolas's face—his laughing hazel eyes, crooked nose, and thin mustache and beard, barely starting to grow.

And he could teach her . . . everything.

6

THE next morning, Nicolas and Jean discussed giving the Cathillons gifts since Humbert had refused payment. Instead of Elisabeth helping decide what to give, she chose to believe Father Michel's vitriol until Jean chastised her.

Gifts in tow, Nicolas fumed as he saddled his horse and concentrated on what to say when he arrived at the farm. Though he had tried to catch Catherine's attention, she seemed indifferent to his jokes and silliness. He'd thought feigning death had been a good idea at the time, but it offended her. Now, as he prepared to see her, perhaps for the last time, he wanted to make an impression.

At the farm, the Cathillon family was finishing their midday meal when Nicolas arrived. Father Brignon slid aside to make room for Nicolas on the bench. Catherine brought him a slice of cheese and a mug of rye ale and sat across from him. He nodded his thanks and said, "I brought something for you."

Her eyes flashed. "Did you bring another book to read to us?"

"Yes, and Martin gave me this one by Rabelais."

"Did he bring it from Geneva?"

Nicolas blinked in surprise. "What do you know about Geneva?"

A smug expression crossed her face. "I know things."

He fidgeted in embarrassment, but then their eyes met, and he saw mischief before she continued.

"Martin said he attended the university, but the Calvinists forced him to flee. He said they accused him of Catholic sympathies, but I didn't understand. We're Catholic. Why do we need sympathy?"

"Oh, Martin accepts Catholics," Nicolas said. "He doesn't hate Catholics."

"Humpf," Father Brignon muttered.

She turned to the priest. "Do Protestants hate Catholics?"

He raised his scruffy gray brows. "Some Protestants hate Catholics, and some Catholics hate Protestants. Some Protestants even hate other types of Protestants." Sighing, he added, "Everyone is a heretic to someone."

Catherine breathed in sharply and covered her lips with her fingers. "So Martin could be burned like a witch? But he is so nice."

"No, he's safe here," Nicolas said, shaking his head. "The Counts of Salm don't force religion on their subjects. One of them is Catholic; the other is Protestant. They are brothers-in-law and have a good relationship."

Father Brignon nodded. "Someday, people will learn to love their neighbor as themselves."

Catherine's eyes sparkled as she turned back to Nicolas. "Teach me more."

"Now, Catherine," Marie said. "We have other worries besides the business of lords and their wars. Are there any happy stories in there?" She pointed to the book.

Without warning, Francisca jumped up and raised her hands. "Silence!" Everyone turned to her and waited. Her eyes widened in fear, and she fled into the back room with Marie and Humbert right behind her.

Nicolas's gaze caught Father Brignon's. "What's wrong?"

The priest replied with a shrug.

Marie returned in a rush, panicked. "Joseph, the water, quickly!"

The boy fetched the half-full bucket from the worktable.

Ripping it from his hand, Marie filled a canteen and disappeared out back again, reappearing without a word of explanation. She straightened her posture, readjusted her headscarf, brushed off her apron, and cleared the table as if nothing had happened. A few moments later, Humbert returned, panting and covered with sweat. He wiped his brow and announced that Francisca would not be joining them for the rest of the afternoon.

The clamor of hooves and rattle of a wagon arose out front. "Stay there," Humbert ordered them before running to the door. When Father Brignon followed Humbert, Nicolas jumped up too.

Father Michel, driving a cart escorted by five deputies on horseback, approached the house. Nicolas paled, shoved the book into his shirt, and laced his jerkin tightly.

Humbert stormed out the door. "What's going on here?" He stood firm, unflinching as the guards rushed him.

"We know that witch is here," Michel said, following the guards. "Step aside, Humbert."

"What witch?"

He pointed at Humbert and hissed, "Let us in, or they will kill you."

Father Brignon stepped between them, shouting, "What's the meaning of this?"

Michel flinched. "Father Brignon?"

When the last horseman dismounted and joined them, Nicolas's eyes bulged. It was Louis Gauthier, the provost and highest-ranking nobleman in the area—and his father's oldest friend. Nicolas pushed to the front. "Louis? What's the problem?"

Louis jerked his head in surprise. "Nicolas, I didn't realize you were here." He turned to Humbert. "I'm sorry to trouble you folks, but Father Michel has charged Madame Francisca with witchcraft for causing a snakebite, and he is insisting we bring her in for questioning."

Nicolas's jaw dropped. "Snakebite? I was the one bitten—last week." He held out his hand to show the scab.

Michel crowded Nicolas and shouted in his face, "Someone else was bitten this morning."

But Nicolas refused to budge. "Well, I've been here all morning and haven't seen Madame Francisca."

"There must be some mistake," Humbert said calmly. "My Aunt Odile fell, and Francisca went to take care of her. She left two days ago and will return via the coach on Tuesday."

Louis motioned the guards to the house. "The Lenoir boy named Francisca. You realize that if we find her, you will all be charged with obstruction?"

Humbert stepped aside and gestured toward the door. "You're welcome to look."

The group filed into the house, where the women clung together by the big table. Marie held Beatrix, who was crying. Joseph was behind her, peeking around her arm. Catherine and Anne were holding back tears. Nicolas stepped in front to shield them.

Nicolas cracked his knuckles and stared at Louis, whom he had never seen at work. A reddish tint colored his mustache and trim, pointed beard. His white lace collar contrasted with a crisp black uniform. Diagonally across his chest, a belt held a dagger that added to his powerful image.

In the loft, the clunking of toppled benches and the rustle of straw and bracken pulled from mattresses echoed through the house. The guards climbed down, and Father Brignon followed them to the back of the house. "Those are my things," he said. "Do you think Francisca is hiding under my vestments?"

They all convened before Louis, and one of them said, "We've searched everywhere. She's not here."

"She has to be here," said Father Michel, wringing his hands. His face flushed crimson as his eyes darted around the room, landing on Nicolas.

Nicolas's skin went cold, and he grasped the book in his jerkin. Realizing his mistake, he clutched his hip bag to divert the priest's attention.

"He's hiding something," Father Michel said, pointing to the bag.

Father Brignon smirked. "Do you think Francisca is hiding in that bag?"

"I demand to know what is in there."

"You demand?" Louis growled. Shaking his head in disgust, he said, "Nicolas, it's not worth an official investigation. Are you hiding something in that bag?"

Nicolas swallowed hard. "No, I'm not hiding anything."

"Let me see."

Nicolas held the bag open, and Louis pulled out the thank-you gifts. A pouch of fine tobacco for Humbert, two lace scarves for Marie and Francisca, ribbons for Anne and Catherine, and candy for Beatrix and Joseph.

"There is nothing here. Let's go, boys." Louis bowed to the women. "I'm sorry we have disturbed your afternoon."

"Wait!" Father Michel shouted and ran to the door. "That witch is hiding. They will sneak her out and say she arrived on the coach. I demand you guard them until Tuesday."

Louis clenched his jaw. "Your demands mean nothing."

The priest pointed one finger in the air and bellowed, "I'll notify the bishop."

Louis's eyebrows creased in a defiant glare. "Salm is not ruled by any church!" He turned to Humbert. "But I have been through this before. If we leave now, I guarantee he'll be back, or I can post guards for a couple of days to end the matter. Your choice."

Humbert shrugged. "Do what you must."

The group followed Louis outside, where he barked orders at his men, then turned back to glower at the priest. "This better not be another waste of my time." He nodded to Nicolas and left with two of the officers as the other two took up posts, one near the forest, the other by the barn.

Father Michel blustered to his wagon, red-faced. As he drove away, he punched his fist toward the house and shouted, "I will meet that coach on Tuesday, and she had better be on it."

Humbert bowed irreverently. As they returned to the house, his eyes narrowed in anger. He said something to Father Brignon, who whispered a reply, "Maybe, but you cannot blame the Church for the actions of one man, Humbert."

Before the dust from Michel's departure had settled, the family returned to the table with everyone speaking at once. Humbert glared at Nicolas and spoke with a hushed voice. "Why did you lie for us, boy?"

"I . . . thought I could help."

Humbert's face pinched in anger. "Did you bring another banned book here?"

Nicolas squirmed. "Well, I'm not sure." He unlaced his jerkin and pulled the book from under his shirt, placing it in Humbert's outstretched hand.

"*Gar . . . gan . . . tua* and *Pant . . . a . . . gruel*," Humbert read before looking up.

"It's delightful—about a giant and his adventures."

"A giant?" Humbert growled. "Is this book worth risking your life?"

He had not thought of it that way. "No, I guess not, monsieur."

"Think of your future, son," Father Brignon said. "Your father told me you are going to Framont soon to work as a journeyman."

Humbert raised an eyebrow. "Why not work with your father?"

Nicolas cleared his throat and tried to speak in a mature voice. "I've already completed my apprenticeship with Papa, but to get my own shop, I must work as a journeyman, then submit a masterpiece that is up to the guild's standards."

At Humbert's frown, Nicolas continued, "Papa is a blacksmith. He makes horseshoes, nails, and such. I want to open a silversmith shop to make things more intricate, like knives, rushlight holders, candlesticks, and rings. Things blacksmiths are not allowed to make."

"I didn't realize there were so many rules," Humbert replied.

"The guild has many rules," Father Brignon said.

Nicolas nodded, quietly slipped the book into his bag, and handed out the gifts that Father Michel had tossed on the table. All the recipients responded with smiles and nods.

Humbert sniffed the gifted tobacco. "This was not necessary." Humbert's usual mint herbal blend made a pleasant smoke, but Elisabeth's choice of the newly popular tobacco from the New World was a thoughtful gift.

"Yes, monsieur, it was . . . but," Nicolas whispered, "where is Francisca hiding?"

Humbert scowled. "She went to visit my Aunt Odile last week."

"But how will she get past the guards to the coach?"

The lightheartedness vanished, and Humbert spoke through clenched teeth. "She will return on the coach when she leaves my aunt's house Tuesday morning, and we'll speak no more about it, understand?"

Catherine asked her father permission to accompany Nicolas down the path. Still upset at the day's events, she could not stop her pout. "I was hoping you would read to us today. I cannot believe Father Michel ruined it for us." The minute the words escaped her lips, she realized how selfish she must have sounded. They had come to arrest Mémé!

He turned to face her. His eyes held hers longer than she had expected, and she felt her face flush. *Oh, what he must think of me.*

Nicolas said, "I will read to you again. One day, I will read only to you . . . Ronsard:

'Little nymph that I adore,
My sweet one in whose eyes reside my worst and my best.
My sweet one, my sugar, my grace, my Catherine.
You must give me peace by kissing me a thousand times a day.
Where do you flee, my soul, my diamond, my pearl?
Alas, return my sweet to my breast,
On my knees, I ask you to appease my burning heart with your kisses.'"

He'd caught her off guard. Her breath came in short gasps. "Is that a poem?"

He smiled so widely that his eyes crinkled. "It's a love poem."

A love poem . . . Catherine's heart fluttered and her mind went blank, but she forced herself to concentrate. Crossing her fingers, she blurted, "Will you teach me to read?" Her heart sank when his smile faded and he scratched his nose.

"Well, um . . ." He looked off into the distance. "Maybe if we meet once a week. Next Sunday, by the stream?"

She inhaled at the suggestion and lowered her head, her face burning. Her papa would never allow it. *Why can't he come to the farm?* She fiddled with her skirt. "I'm not sure."

He raised her chin, his eyes sincere. "I'll teach you to read."

If Papa finds out . . . But it's my only chance. She chewed her lip. Finally, she said, "I'll meet you at the ridge this side of the stream."

He nodded, mounted his horse and left, turning once to wave, then disappeared down the path.

Before returning to the house, Catherine sat on the bench outside the barn, desperately trying to think of a way to meet Nicolas without lying. While her thoughts swirled, the garbled voice of her father rose from inside the barn. She had not realized he was there.

"He was only eight years old . . . After that, my boy was a different child, angry, violent."

Violent? *Papa and Father Brignon must be talking about her eldest brother,* Jean-Baptiste.

"I am his father; I should have protected him!"

Protected Jean-Baptiste? From what? She crept to the corner of the barn to hear more clearly.

"I wanted my boy to stay with us and help me with the wine. He could have worked Uncle Pierre's farm, but he couldn't wait to get away from me."

The priest replied with surprising anger, "I'll not preach to you about getting those children baptized, but you are depriving them of their salvation."

"They were baptized—by the angels."

The angels baptized me—they are talking about me!

Father Brignon sounded furious. "You know that's not valid! There's no harm in believing it'll work for a stillborn child. Whether or not that child goes to Limbo is beyond our control, but your children are alive, and you must properly purge their Original Sin. You are compromising their immortal souls!"

"If that man represents the Church, I want nothing to do with it," Humbert snapped back.

A bang echoed through the barn. Catherine flinched. Father Brignon shouted, "He does not represent the Church! For every bad priest, there are a hundred good priests. Now you're offending me!"

Her father's voice was quieter now. "I'm sorry, I didn't mean you."

"You cannot blame the Church for one man's actions."

"I agreed to keep my mouth shut, but he's making insinuations about my family again, deflecting the attention from himself. I tried to ignore it, but when the mayor's wife believes it, I must do something."

Now they're talking about Nicolas and his parents . . . the footsteps are coming nearer! She ran toward the path, then turned, casually glancing at the men coming out of the barn. Father Brignon's hand was on her father's shoulder. She nodded and followed them toward the house as Father Brignon said, "I am so glad to see you again. Let's relax and enjoy some wine."

Immediately after breaking their fast the following day, Catherine's father summoned the family to the well, where Father Brignon, wearing a white sash embroidered with a red cross, was mumbling prayers over a bucket of water. He raised his head, smiled, and said, "Today is a happy day as Beatrix, Joseph, and Catherine will receive their baptism."

The discussion yesterday. She dared not mention it last night.

As the priest continued to pray over the bucket and then over Beatrix, Catherine recalled the day her father and Mémé had taken Beatrix, only about a week old, to Lac de la Maix to receive the Baptism of Angels. The legend says that stillborn babies were taken to the magical lake where the Blessed Mother would breathe life into them so the angels could baptize them and take their souls to heaven. Without this special baptism, their souls would languish in Limbo forever. Now that she thought about it, it did seem odd that she'd gotten one.

As Joseph stepped forward, Catherine's mind swirled. She tried to remember the conversation she had overheard. Humbert had said Jean-Baptiste was only eight years old . . .

An elbow in her back knocked her from her reverie. It was her turn. The smiling eyes of the man her father called Papa stilled her restless thoughts. He placed his gentle hands on her head, recited something in Latin, leaned her head back, and dribbled some water on her forehead.

The cold splash made her gasp, and when she straightened, she shivered.

Everyone seemed to be happy. Was she supposed to feel different? Perhaps she did. She returned their smiles and hugged the priest. "Thank you, Father."

While everyone filed into the house, Catherine stayed behind, thinking. Why did Jean-Baptiste need protection, and from whom? It must have something to do with Father Michel, and it was bad enough that her father warned her never to go near that church, but what could it be?

chapter
7

TUESDAY morning arrived. Nicolas could not get Francisca's plight off his mind. Before starting work at the forge with his father, he slipped his pistol into his girdle, saddled his horse, and tied it to the post at the coach stop outside the Auberge du Cheval Blanc, the White Horse Inn. The stable yard in front of the forge was right across the street, where he could watch for trouble.

Nothing happened until midday when Father Michel arrived, then skulked around outside.

A little while later, Jean touched Nicolas's shoulder. "Something must be going on at the *auberge*."

Nicolas turned to see Louis entering the building and two guards waiting outside.

When Humbert and Father Brignon pulled up in their cart, the suspense got to be too much. The minute Jean turned his back, Nicolas sneaked across the street and into the tavern, where Humbert, Father Brignon, and Louis were standing together at the bar, drinking ale with Sebastien, the bar owner.

Nicolas tipped his hat.

But Humbert glared at him. "Why are you here?"

"I just . . . came over for ale."

Louis's eyes ran up and down Nicolas's body, his gaze stopping on the bulge of the pistol inside Nicolas's shirt.

He squirmed and adjusted his breeches to avert the scrutiny, but it didn't work.

"Is that a pistol in your belt?" Louis asked. "Are you expecting trouble?"

Nicolas tried to think of a reply when, thankfully, the rattle of horse and harness drew Louis's attention away from him.

Father Michel shouted through the open door, "The coach is coming."

Louis led the way to the street. Humbert and Father Brignon brought their ale with them. The four-horse enclosed carriage was still rolling when Father Michel reached for the door, but Louis stepped in front of him.

A young man with greasy hair and a pockmarked face stepped out, followed by an older couple. They collected their bags from the driver and left.

The last passenger, a small woman with a veil covering her face, peered out the door. The black gown and gloves she wore were not the same as Francisca had worn the day she disappeared. The woman held out her arms for Louis to help her down.

Father Michel brushed past the crowd. "Make her remove that veil."

Humbert growled from the back. "Francisca always covers her face when she travels."

With an exasperated sigh, Louis said, "Madame, please remove your veil so I can go home."

The woman scanned the crowd before slipping the veil off her head. "What is all the fuss?"

It was Francisca! Nicolas gasped, but at Humbert's livid glare, he coughed to cover his shock.

Francisca said, "Nicolas, I am surprised to see you here."

He wiped his forehead on his sleeve and cleared his throat. "I always get ale about midday."

Father Michel pointed at her. "Witnesses saw her transform into a snake and bite that boy." He turned to Louis. "Your guards must have let her escape."

"My men are professionals," Louis shouted as his face stiffened in anger. He turned to one of the guards. "Could she have escaped the farm?"

"No, monsieur, we guarded the house night and day. Nobody came or left—except the mayor's son, who left on horseback shortly after you. She could not have escaped."

With his voice still raised, Louis stabbed his finger into Father Michel's chest. "The Count will have my full report about your witch-hunting."

The priest batted his hand away and spun to point at Humbert, his words wet with spit. "You will regret this, Cathillon."

Humbert merely raised his ale in a toast, but as soon as the priest stomped away, the amusement fell from his face, and he handed the mug to Sebastien.

As the group left in different directions, Louis turned to Nicolas. "Give your papa my regards."

Nicolas waved a reply, then, keeping his distance, followed Humbert, Father Brignon, and Francisca around the side of the building. *Martin insists witches do not exist, but how did she get past the guards to the coach? If she had been hiding in the forest, they'd have found her.*

At the cart, Humbert caught Nicolas's gaze and waved him over. "Do you realize you cast suspicion on everything that occurred today?"

"I'm sorry, monsieur. I thought if madame needed help—"

Humbert scowled. "I didn't ask for your help." He climbed onto the cart, but before he settled, a gunshot pierced the air. Humbert jerked back suddenly as blood spattered from a wound in his shoulder. With a look of surprise and pain, he jumped into the seat and grabbed the reins.

Another bang! Francisca screamed as Father Brignon gasped and fell sideways onto her, grabbing his midsection.

Humbert grated the words, "Come on, boy!" and whipped his horse into a gallop.

Instead of following them, Nicolas turned toward the sound. Something moved in the thick underbrush surrounding a storage shed behind the inn. He shouted, "Someone is in the bushes!" Nicolas aimed his pistol, but the man was gone. All he saw was the flick of a horse's tail through the vegetation.

At the side of the tavern, Nicolas's horse jittered and jerked at the noise. Nicolas leaped on its back and burst into the forest after the man, dodging trees and ducking under branches that scraped his face and arms. He considered shooting blind, but the gun was difficult to reload even when standing on solid ground, and he could never reload it on horseback.

They burst into a clearing when the assassin's horse stiffened its legs and reared. The man was thrown to the ground as the horse bolted, leaving its rider alone. He crawled on all fours, trying to hide in the underbrush, but Nicolas easily found him.

The man's clothes were tattered, and his shoes were held together with straps—not what Nicolas expected. With pleading, sunken eyes, he looked up and spoke through missing teeth, "Mercy."

Nicolas aimed his gun with shaking hands. "Who are you?"

"Please, I needed the money. I just needed money."

"What money? Why do you think they had any money?"

The sound of thundering hooves behind Nicolas tied a knot of panic in his stomach. He had never considered more than one aggressor. He circled the assassin, positioning his horse to face the advancing rider, when something moved at the edge of the clearing—more accomplices? He furiously backed his horse to get a better look.

It was a wolf, staring at him. Its yellow eyes glinting in the sunlight. Nicolas tried to swallow, but his mouth was dry. Trembling so violently his teeth chattered, he kept one eye on the wolf and waited for the approaching rider.

"Nicolas, it's me," the shout preceded Louis, who burst out of the trees with his hands raised.

The commotion caused the wolf to turn, flick its tail, and disappear into the brush.

"I heard shots. Are you—" Louis's eyes widened. "You caught the shooter?"

Nicolas slumped in relief. "Oh, Louis, thank God. This man shot Humbert and Father Brignon."

Louis scanned the clearing, then turned to face the shooter. "Did you act alone?"

The man's eyes were wide and filled with tears, and he rose to his knees with his hands in the air. "I just needed money to feed my family."

"Answer me, or I will shoot you before you have time to say an Act of Contrition," Louis said, dismounting and immediately shoving the man's face to the ground. "What's your name, and where are your guns?"

With his neck twisted and face in the dirt, the man muttered, "Lenoir. On my saddle, in the sling."

"Lenoir?" Nicolas gasped. "You're the one who lied about Francisca. Was your son bitten by a snake?"

Louis tied Lenoir's hands behind his back and pulled him up. "Why did you shoot those people?" The man simply stared at the ground. Louis thrust his dagger to the man's throat and spoke through clenched teeth, "Answer me!"

The man mumbled, "I want to speak to Father Michel."

"The priest cannot help you except to give you absolution before they hang you." Louis mounted his horse and forced the man to walk toward town.

Nicolas leaned forward in his saddle. "Is there anything I can do?"

"Yes, you could search for the horse and guns. Be careful, though—there may be others involved."

An hour passed while Nicolas patiently looked for the horse. He caught it in a clearing. The guns were in the sling like the man had said.

Nicolas was used to people charged with minor offenses coming before his father, the mayor. Still, the building on the other side of town where those charged with major crimes were housed before being transported to Badonviller for trial made him a little nervous. As he neared the building, the sound of church bells filled the air.

Louis responded to his knock. "Nicolas, I figured you'd abandoned the search."

"That man tried to kill Humbert," Nicolas replied, shaking his head in disbelief. "I would do anything to help."

Louis examined the horse and removed two expensive-looking guns from a dilapidated saddle.

Nicolas said, "You know, that man looks half-starved. How could he afford two guns?"

"My thoughts exactly." Louis eyed Nicolas. "Have you considered being a deputy? I need determined men like you. The pay is excellent, but occasionally the job is unpleasant."

"I've never thought of doing anything but being a smith." He considered it for just a moment. "Thank you, but I like working with my hands. What happens now?"

"I charged the man with murder. Father Michel refused to come. You would think he would want to hear the prisoner's confession, but he simply said to tell Lenoir that the Church will take care of his children."

"Father Brignon . . . And Humbert?"

"Just a flesh wound."

"I'd better get back. Papa's probably looking for me." As he turned to leave, he recalled the bells—the death knell. His hands began to shake again. *Father Brignon is dead.*

Back home, Nicolas found his parents in their bedchamber and peeked in the doorway. They turned to him.

"There you are!" Jean shot an evil glance, threw his starched collar on the pallet, and crossed his arms, his face pinched in a furious scowl. "I heard shots at the inn and saw Louis chasing after someone—and you had disappeared." His voice got louder with each word. "I ran to the auberge, frantic. Someone thought you were involved. Why in the hell did you go to the inn when you were supposed to be working?"

"Well, I . . ."

Elisabeth adjusted the black veil on her head, but the hairpins she held between her lips prevented her from replying. She hurriedly secured the covering so she could scold Nicolas further. "We were worried sick."

Unsure of entering the den of hostility, Nicolas remained in the doorway. "I was helping Louis."

She flinched. "Helping Louis? How did . . . Why? . . ." She turned to Jean for assistance, but his lips were still clenched.

"I chased the man I saw shoot at Father Brignon and Monsieur Humbert," Nicolas said.

Jean's eyes narrowed. "But how did you chase him? When did you prepare your horse?"

Nicolas hadn't mentioned the raid at the farm because he worried it would solidify his mother's preconceived notions. Now he shuffled his feet and told the story. The longer Nicolas talked, the more his father's expression changed from anger to concern. ". . . and Father Michel was furious and said he was going to meet the coach, so I thought . . ."

"Why did you keep that from us?" Elisabeth's voice cracked with emotion. "Louis is your father's dearest friend. How would it look if you were involved in some sort of—"

"Elisabeth," Jean said, "please remember Father Brignon is dead." To Nicolas, "Did Louis catch the murderer?"

Subduing his pride under the circumstances, Nicolas replied, "I had already caught the man when Louis arrived."

Jean's eyes widened, and Elisabeth gasped and covered her mouth in surprise before saying, "You could have been killed. What were you thinking?"

"That a murderer was getting away. I thought you would be happy."

His father crossed the room and patted his back. "We are, but we are also . . . shocked."

"Louis was so impressed he asked me if I wanted to work for him as a deputy."

Elisabeth's mouth dropped open. "What did you tell him?"

"Don't worry, Mama." Nicolas went to her and kissed her cheek. "I told Louis no."

Jean grinned. "I'm so proud of you, Nicolas. Who was it?"

Exhausted after the chase and then having to explain it, relief washed over Nicolas. "Someone named Lenoir, but I didn't recognize him."

Elisabeth checked her reflection in a highly polished piece of metal. Apparently satisfied, she said, "Well, we have to pay our respects to Father Brignon." She wrinkled her nose. "So, we have to go to . . ."

Jean frowned at her and turned to Nicolas. "He is at the Cathillon farm."

At the chance to see Catherine, Nicolas brightened. "I'll come with you."

⚓

At the farm, Nicolas followed his parents behind a stream of people shuffling past the big table on which Father Brignon's body lay. Humbert had called this kind and gentle soul "Papa."

While his parents spoke to other guests, Nicolas tried to talk to Catherine, but she was busy helping Anne with the mourners. Instead, he looked for Francisca, who was curiously absent. He found her sitting quietly, praying the rosary in the barn, blood glistening on her apron.

He sat beside her. "Are you hurt?"

After kissing the crucifix, she curled it up in her hand and turned to him with red-brimmed eyes. "No, I am fine."

All he could offer was an uncertain smile. He ached to learn how she had gotten to the coach, but before he could think of a tactful way to ask her, she said, "You captured him, then?"

His breath caught, and he forgot everything. *How did she know?*

chapter

8

HE Sunday lessons were all that Catherine had hoped.

Sneaking away from watchful eyes, Catherine met Nicolas in the field above the stream near the berry patch. They always settled on the same rock.

Nicolas's warm eyes seemed to be smiling, and though she knew she was asking too many questions, he never tired of them. At first, she was nervous, but he made her feel important, and she counted the minutes until their next meeting. He gave her a primer the first week, and she studied at every opportunity, hiding it under her pallet or tying it inside her kirtle. She spent so much time in the privy, that Marie asked if she was sick, but she had mastered the book before the next lesson. Soon, she was reading as he listened.

Words were not the only lesson, as hidden meanings gave the stories a second dimension. Now she read:

> *"Suddenly, I do not know how it happened. I did not have*
> *time to think. Panurge, without another word, threw his sheep,*
> *crying and bleating, into the sea. All the other sheep, crying and*
> *bleating in the same intonation, followed it over the side. The*
> *herd was such that once one jumped, so jumped its companions.*
> *It was impossible to stop them, as you know sheep will follow the*
> *first one, wherever it may go."*

Catherine raised her head. "This is not about sheep."

"No, it means not to follow blindly."

Proud of herself, she nodded, then she raised an eyebrow. "So I shouldn't follow Anne's orders all day."

He chuckled. "I didn't say that."

The familiarity gave Catherine confidence. "Anne told me I shouldn't ask, but how did Martin get his scar?"

"When I was a child, Le-Chêne and I found Martin and the bodies of his two brothers lying in a cart. There was blood everywhere. We thought he was dead too. Papa sewed Martin up, and Mama took care of him."

Catherine had thought Martin had fallen off a horse or something mundane. Not knowing how to reply, she waited for more.

"When he left Geneva, he went to Paris to be with his parents but found them massacred. He happened upon his brothers wandering the street. They escaped, only to be ambushed at the Donon Pass on their way to Strasbourg. The carnage was so shocking they named it the Saint Bartholomew Day Massacre." Nicolas's eyes widened with emphasis. "Possibly thirty-thousand people were murdered. At first, I was afraid of Martin—he used to scream every night—but as I grew older, he became more like a brother."

"Oh, poor Martin." Catherine inhaled and raised her hand to her lips. "That's why he cried out that night he stayed with us."

"The nightmares have lessened, but they caused him to move into Mama and Papa's little house by the stable. I have a book about the massacre if you want me to read it to you, but it's gruesome."

"I'm not sure I want to hear a terrible story." Catherine made a sour face.

"I have love stories too."

Contrasting with his tanned skin, Nicolas's hazel eyes flashed, enhancing the mischief in them. *Did he say love stories?*

Without saying a word about his plans to meet Catherine, Nicolas went through the typical Sunday mornings: Mass, dinner with the family, then off with Martin and Le-Chêne on their weekly outings.

For as long as Nicolas could remember, Martin acquired books from his printer friend in Strasbourg. Every Sunday, the trio would go off to some remote location to read and discuss Martin's latest acquisition. Though Jean knew about the books, he avoided discussing them.

When Nicolas had first sprung his arrangement with Catherine on his brothers, they balked, but to his relief, they agreed not to expose his pretense.

Catherine learned quickly, and the weeks sped past. With each meeting, Nicolas's feelings grew. One time, he brought a blanket, and they moved from the hard rock to the shade under a great oak. That became their tree. Their conversations extended to long, lazy musings until they were barely reading at all.

The appointed date for Nicolas to begin at the forge arrived, but he found excuses not to go—one week, he felt ill, the next, his arm hurt. One Sunday, pouring rain canceled the weekly outing, and despite being early June, dampness hung in the house.

Jean set a fresh fire and circled the chairs with Elisabeth and Le-Chêne's wife, Rachelle, sewing while the men read. The crackling wood echoed through the silence of the parlor. Though Nicolas held his book, he couldn't concentrate. He stared at the flames dancing in front of him, but he saw Catherine dancing in the stream, her legs glistening in the morning sun.

Was she there, waiting for him?

"Will you sit still?" Elisabeth said, nodding toward his bouncing knee.

He tapped his finger on his lap, then laid his book down, walked to the window, and watched the spattering rain. "I'm going out."

"Have you lost your mind? You will catch your death of cold."

"It's only sprinkling, Mama. You're always dramatic." He donned his cloak and an oversized hat. "After working all week, I need fresh air."

"Jean," she pleaded.

His father shrugged and turned the page. "He's not a child."

"Wait, I'll walk with you." Le-Chêne touched his wife's shoulder before following Nicolas out the door.

Rain pelted their faces as they slopped down the craggy path to the stable and stepped inside to the crisp smell of straw. Nicolas grabbed his bridle from the hook and slipped it on his gray mare before leading her into the aisle.

With his eyes narrowed and arms crossed, Le-Chêne blocked his path. He hadn't spoken since they left the house, but now he said, "Do you think she'll wait in the rain?"

Taking advantage of his brother's presence, Nicolas handed him the reins. "I don't know, but if she's there, I want to see her."

"Why not ask her papa's permission to court her? Eventually, he'll find out, you know."

Ignoring him, Nicolas took a blanket from the rack. "Mama would never permit it; she hated every minute I was at their house."

Le-Chêne shrugged in exasperation. "You should worry about her papa. Mama might complain, but she would never forbid—"

"She thinks Francisca is a witch, Le-Chêne."

As Nicolas threw a saddle over the horse's back and tightened the cinch, Le-Chêne stepped forward, trying to intimidate Nicolas with his height, like he always did. "Are you fornicating with that girl?"

"No." Angry heat rose in Nicolas's face. "You're the same as everyone else. She's not like that."

"Well, you're sneaking around for some reason."

"It's easier this way."

"Every man is afraid to speak to a lady's father." Le-Chêne returned the reins but would not back off. "What book are you reading?"

Nicolas groped his bag. It was empty. "Oh well, we cannot read in the rain anyway. I just want to make sure she's not getting soaked waiting for me."

"What should I tell Mama?" Le-Chêne asked in resignation.

Nicolas shrugged, led the horse outside, and waved. "Tell her I'll be right back." He took off, leaving his brother in the downpour.

As he climbed the hill to their meeting place, the rain slowed, and a chilly mist rose. Catherine was not there. He pushed down his disappointment and decided to follow his brother's advice and talk to Humbert. As Nicolas passed a dense grove of pine trees, something caught his eye—Catherine, soaked and standing under a thick pine branch. She waved to him, and his heart warmed. He turned his horse toward her and dismounted. "I didn't think you'd come."

"I'll not melt," she said, taking hold of the bridle.

"What did your parents say when you went out?" The carpet of soggy pine needles felt squishy under his feet. The scent hung heavy in the mist.

"My baby sister is whining with a stuffy nose, and everyone is cramped in the house. They think I went to the barn for a little peace."

"You're soaked; you shouldn't have come." He took off his cloak and wrapped it around her shoulders before putting his hat on her head. A drop of rain rolled down her cheek, and he brushed it away, his finger lingering there. His gaze moved to her eyes and the raindrops clinging to her long dark lashes. He ached to kiss her.

She's not like that.

"Let me take you home." He lifted her onto his horse sidesaddle and led her down the path. The rain had stopped, and the sun tried to pierce through a break in the clouds.

When they neared the knoll above the farm, Catherine said, "Stop here so nobody sees you."

As she slid into his arms, he considered how foolish they were. "I'm tired of sneaking around like this. I want to talk to your papa."

"Wait until next week. Papa will be furious if we go in like this."

"What will you tell him when he sees you soaked?"

Without hesitation, she said, "I'll tell them I tried to catch a stray kitten."

"Ha, you're a good liar."

She lowered her head.

A tingle of guilt gripped Nicolas. "You mustn't lie for me. Next Sunday, I'll ask your father for permission to court you properly."

All week, Nicolas rehearsed his speech, and when Sunday came, he was ready. On his way to meet Catherine, he stopped to pick a rose from his mother's garden and hid it in his bag. She was waiting for him at their spot. He dismounted and wrapped the horse's reins around a small shrub.

She smiled and said, "Shall we talk to Papa?"

This is happening too fast—I need time to calm myself. "Yes, but I thought I would read you this poem from Ronsard first."

When she nodded, Nicolas spread the blanket they had been using under the tree where he read.

"This is from the 'Ode to Cassandra':

> *'You will be old, hunched at the hearth in sorrow.*
> *For your proud scorn, for the love you willed away.*
> *Live now, I beg you. Wait for no tomorrow.*
> *Gather the roses of your life today.'"*

Laying the book aside with the page open, he took her hand.

"That was beautiful," Catherine said, her cheeks flushed.

"This passage means the girl who likes the poet is young and wants to wait, but tomorrow is not guaranteed." He took the rose from his bag and handed it to her. "We should live for today."

She nodded.

He should discuss his intentions with her father, but he could not pull away from those sparkling eyes, and he drew closer until his lips touched hers.

She didn't pull away.

Happiness swept through him like a flame. "I think about you all the time; I want you so much." *Live now, wait for no tomorrow.* He pushed the scarf off the back of her head and kissed her again.

The horse nickered, and Nicolas chuckled. "She wants the attention."

Catherine laughed nervously.

As he went in for another kiss, movement caught his attention. His horse was frantically pulling at its reins and prancing. A few feet behind it, a pair of yellow eyes stared at them.

He breathed, "Oh my God!"

She stiffened and stretched her neck to see around him. "What is it?"

He grasped the knife from his girdle. In a low voice, he said, "Climb the tree as fast as you can."

"What is it—"

"GO!"

He pushed her behind him and raised his arms just as his horse reared. As Catherine scrambled for a tree, two more wolves appeared, their lips pulled back to reveal huge white fangs. She leaped into the lower branches as all three wolves charged. The horse screamed in terror, kicking the biggest wolf in the head. It dropped, twitching, to the ground.

The second wolf leapt toward Nicolas. He swung his knife toward its throat but missed his mark. The force threw them both to the ground. The wolf's claws sliced deeply into Nicolas's side. His knife cut its shoulder before falling from his hand.

The horse reared again, shaking its head wildly until it freed itself, then galloped away, temporarily averting the third wolf's attack.

Jumping to his feet, Nicolas vaulted for the same tree and pulled himself into the lower branches as the third wolf grabbed his heel. Heaving with all his might, Nicolas slipped out of his boot and scrambled up the tree. The wolf and the boot fell to the ground.

Nicolas rested his head against the tree trunk until his pounding heart slowed to a normal pace. He turned toward Catherine, who sat next to him, hugging the trunk with her feet anchored on another branch below her. Dirty streaks marked the path of tears she had wiped away, hair tangled, bodice torn, chemise hanging off her scraped and bared shoulder.

She was a mess—but she was the most beautiful thing he had ever seen. "Ahem." He motioned toward her nakedness.

"Oh." She blushed, covered herself, and laced her dress, then grabbed the tree again.

He reached for her, but she was afraid to let go. The movement made him aware of a pain in his side. He leaned back to see a red stain spreading on his shirt. He hadn't even realized he was injured.

In a shaky voice, Catherine said, "You're hurt. Let me see."

"No, I'm all right." He covered the wound with his hand, yet blood oozed between his fingers.

With something else to worry her, Catherine let go of the trunk, tore a piece of fabric from her hem, and tied it around his chest. Leaning back against the tree, she closed her eyes. "Oh, Nicolas, I told Papa I was going for a walk. What if he finds us together like this?"

Nicolas pinched the bridge of his nose. *What am I going to do?* Trapped in the tree, his horse gone, his knife lay on the ground, guarded by the wolves. The wounded one licked the blood off its leg while the other paced and snarled. *Could this get any worse?* He took her hand and, in his most confident voice, said, "It will be all right. I will take care of you."

Time passed.

Nicolas made small talk and told Catherine stories, but she remained on the verge of tears. The sun moved across the sky. He had to do something. Maybe he could outrun the wolves. Maybe . . .

Pounding hooves! From his perch, he could see over the rocks and blackthorn scrubs by the road. "Someone's over there." He put his fingers in his mouth and let out an ear-piercing whistle. The riders waved back and rode toward them. It was Le-Chêne and Martin, going home after their outing.

Thank God.

As they approached, their horses arched their necks and pawed the ground. Nicolas shouted, "Wolves!" to warn them.

Le-Chêne loaded his crossbow and led the way up the embankment. The wolves barely had time to snarl before his brother shot the injured one. The other disappeared into the forest.

As they neared the dead wolf, the horses high-stepped, and the riders reined them in circles to calm them. Le-Chêne raised an eyebrow when he spied the blanket and coif on the ground. "What do we have here?"

Nicolas leaped down. "My horse ran off." Luckily, the boot wasn't chewed, and he slipped it on. His knife was lying next to it, and he wiped the blood on the grass. Then he raised his arms for Catherine. She fell into them, but she would not look at him. "Don't worry, it's all right now." He brushed the hair from her face and handed the coif to her.

A disapproving I-knew-it glance came from Le-Chêne before he said, "We'd better go. The other wolf is still out there. Lift her behind me."

Catherine sniffled, "I can't straddle a horse again. My papa would kill me."

"Of course." Le-Chêne slid back and helped her sit sidesaddle in front of him. She buried her face in his massive chest. Nicolas rolled up the blanket and leaped on the back of Martin's horse.

As they crested the hill above the farm, they saw the Cathillon family gathering near the barn. Humbert had his horse saddled and was comforting Marie, who was wringing her hands.

"There she is!" Anne shouted, pointing toward them. Everyone turned.

A few moments later, Catherine slid into her father's arms.

Pain stabbed Nicolas's side, and he grimaced as he jumped off the back of Martin's horse. "Wolves."

"Wolves? Oh, I knew something was wrong!" said Marie, embracing her tearful daughter.

Humbert's eyes fixed on Catherine as his brow creased. He turned to Le-Chêne. "Killing a wolf is illegal. No one can kill one except the count's *louvetiers.*"

Nicolas winced. *Illegal? Oh, no!*

"Two are dead," Le-Chêne replied.

Exhaling, his mouth a grim line, Humbert said, "We must hide them."

"I'll show you," Nicolas said.

"Wait, let me look at you," Francisca touched the bloody spot on his shirt and the makeshift bandage. She frowned, but he couldn't tell what she was thinking.

She motioned to Anne. "Take Catherine to your room and clean her wounds."

With that, Francisca took Nicolas's hand and led him into the house.

Catherine followed her sister to the loft, sat on the corner of the pallet, and tried to calm herself while Anne interrogated her. "Mémé said not to worry, but Mama was in tears, and Papa was furious. Where have you been?"

"I went for a walk."

"And Nicolas happened to pass by?"

"Yes, and he read to me, and three wolves came," Catherine replied, chewing her lip.

Anne rolled her eyes and picked twigs from Catherine's hair. "Do you think Papa will believe that? You have scratches all over you; let me get some vinegar."

When Anne left the room, Catherine fell back and closed her eyes, waiting to be chastised.

"Get up here, so I can wipe your face," Anne said.

How am I going to explain this? "It was terrifying, but Nicolas fought off the wolves until I could climb a tree," Catherine said as she pulled herself up.

Anne gave a sly smile. "You see why I stay out of the forest whenever possible?"

"Ha, you could never have climbed the tree."

"You're right." Anne chuckled. "Those wolves would have eaten me for dinner." She dumped more vinegar, pushed Catherine's skirt aside, and touched the brush burns on her knees.

The vinegar stung. "Ouch! Not so hard."

"Oh, please, Catherine, it's not that bad," Anne said, finding another clean piece of the cloth. "Let me see your arms."

"Never mind."

"We sleep in the same bed, sister. You cannot hide anything from me."

As Catherine slipped the chemise off her shoulders, Anne's eyes widened. "Catherine! You took your—"

"No!" she sobbed. "It snagged on a branch when I climbed the tree."

Anne spied the bruises and scrapes on her shoulder. "And your chemise?"

"The string ripped off. I had no time to watch where I was going, and I ripped off the bottom to wrap around Nicolas's cuts. Please let me hide it from Mama."

"Shh, I'll repair it." Anne slipped the soiled garments under the corner of the blanket. "Meantime, you can wear your spare."

chapter
9

Nicolas sat on the bench and raised his shirt, flinching as Francisca ripped off the bandage.

"Sit still, or I will make it hurt worse," Francisca growled. Without any of the gentleness she had shown when she had treated his snakebite, she cleaned his wounds, spread something smelly on a clean cloth, and tied it tightly around his chest. "You will rest."

Nicolas brushed her off. "No, I must help with those wolves."

Francisca gripped his arm. "I never would have allowed anything to happen to my Catherine."

Straightening to his full height, he replied, "I protected her from the wolves."

Those black eyes narrowed. "And who protected her from you?"

He leaped up, tipping the bench, and ran outside to find Le-Chêne holding both his and Nicolas's horses.

"She just walked in," Le-Chêne said.

Nicolas rubbed his hands over his dapple-gray mare. "What a relief. She seems fine," he said, nodding to his brother. Out of the corner of his eye, he saw Francisca whispering to Humbert before they both speared Nicolas with a piercing glare. He ducked to hide behind his horse and tried to remain calm.

"We should go," Humbert said in a guttural voice.

Le-Chêne cocked his crossbow and strapped it, along with a fresh bolt, to his saddle, mounted, and led the way. Once away from the farm, Humbert said to Le-Chêne and Martin, "Leave us. I want to talk to Nicolas privately."

As the others moved forward, Nicolas held his breath.

Staring straight ahead, Humbert said, "Catherine has been going for Sunday afternoon walks for a while now. I think she has been doing more than walking."

Nicolas nodded and fiddled with the reins. "Yes, monsieur, I had planned to speak with you today about courting her properly."

With nostrils flaring, Humbert inhaled and clenched his jaw before replying. "Oh, you planned to speak to me. Well, that's courteous of you. And what else have you been teaching my daughter?"

Nicolas's eyes widened. "Nothing, monsieur."

"And you have never touched her?"

"No, I kissed her . . . once. I never touched her."

Seething, Humbert stopped his horse. "But you considered it."

Nicolas offered a sorrowful look, but the venomous stare he received burned, and he turned away as Humbert said, "And what if you weren't interrupted?"

He didn't know how to answer. What would he have done? "I would never hurt her . . . I think I love her."

Humbert clenched his fists. "How old are you, boy?"

Nicolas's mind went blank.

"I said, how old are you, boy?"

The reply came out almost as a whisper, "Sixteen."

Humbert spat on the ground and turned to stare straight ahead.

"I'm sorry, monsieur," Nicolas whimpered.

But Humbert shook his head. "Catherine is too young. Anne is old enough to marry; you can marry her."

"No, monsieur, I want Catherine."

More spit flew from Humbert's mouth as he shouted, "I don't care what you want, boy."

They rode in silence and, after what seemed an eternity, joined Le-Chêne and Martin at the tree where the wolves had attacked. They dismounted and turned to the task.

"Did you notice any foam in their mouth?" Humbert asked, poking the body with a stick.

"No, they seemed extremely healthy."

Something white fluttered in the wind and caught Nicolas's attention—the book, open on the ground. Humbert noticed it too, and the vein in his temple throbbed.

Sheepishly, Nicolas retrieved the book, slid it into his bag, and joined Le-Chêne by the wolf's body.

"Let's drag it over there, behind those trees," Le-Chêne said, taking hold of its back legs.

Nicolas nodded, and when he bent down, he saw a flash of crimson—the wolf's body lay atop the rose he had given to Catherine. He shot a pleading glimpse toward Martin, who snatched the crushed flower and hid it in his bag.

Thankfully, Humbert was scanning the clearing and must not have seen it. "I thought you said you killed two?"

Nicolas motioned to the far side of the field where the wolf with the broken neck lay. They covered both corpses with leaves and branches and returned to their horses.

"And you said a third ran?"

"Yes, when Le-Chêne killed the second."

"Maybe you will turn into a werewolf," Le-Chêne said with a snicker.

The color drained from Humbert's face. Though Le-Chêne stood a head taller, the older man clutched him by the shirt collar and poked his finger into the big man's chest. "Never say that again, do you hear me? Never!"

Le-Chêne's eyes widened, and he raised his hands in surrender. "I was fooling."

"No fooling about such things. People are superstitious and always looking to blame someone for their misfortune. There can be no whispers about werewolves. In fact, we will never speak of this again to anyone. Do you understand?"

"Yes, monsieur," Le-Chêne replied in a child's voice.

Humbert spun, pointed his finger inches from Nicolas's nose, and growled, "And you!"

Nicolas drew in his breath. *He's going to kill me now.*

But Humbert only motioned toward his bandages. "You fell against the plow."

"Yes, monsieur," Nicolas said, lowering his head in shame.

Humbert spoke again, this time loud enough they all heard him. "Once a girl's reputation is compromised, it can never be restored. You never met with her—ever."

Silence hung heavy in the air as they rode back to the farm. Humbert was furious, and Le-Chêne and Martin were upset. Nicolas had never felt so alone.

When they neared the barn, Le-Chêne turned his horse toward the road, and Martin followed. Humbert dismounted and led his horse inside. Nicolas tied his to a fence, swallowed hard, and went in, too. While Humbert removed the saddle and blanket, Nicolas watched, trying to keep his eyes from watering while he gathered his nerve.

Finally, he said, "May I speak with you, monsieur? You trusted me. Your family helped me when I needed you. I'm sorry."

Humbert grunted but didn't reply. He fetched a brush and began grooming his horse.

"May I tell Catherine goodbye?" That unsettled feeling in Nicolas's stomach grew to an ache with every moment that passed. When it became clear that no response was coming, he said, "Will you please tell Catherine how sorry I am and give this to her?" He pulled the book from his bag and handed it to Humbert.

Without raising his gaze, Humbert snatched the book, tossed it on a shelf, and continued brushing.

Nicolas trudged outside, mounted his horse, and silently followed Martin and Le-Chêne all the way home. They returned their horses to the stable and then scaled the hillside. Martin touched Nicolas's shoulder and handed him the rose he had hidden from Humbert. The crumpled flower lay in his open palm as he stared at it. It had been perfect and beautiful, like his love for Catherine. Now it was crushed. He couldn't bear to look at it and let it fall from his hand.

Through the loft window, Catherine watched the men go off to hide the wolves. Nicolas had said he was going to ask her father's permission to court her, though, after today's events, she hoped he would wait, at least until they got back.

Left alone with her thoughts, Catherine sat on the pallet, worrying. Anne was the world's biggest tattler, but she had promised . . .

When the men returned, Catherine ran to the window. Humbert disappeared inside the barn, and Nicolas followed, but only a few moments later, he rushed out and raced away, and her father stormed toward the house with his lips pursed into a grim line.

"Catherine!" he roared as he entered the house.

Not knowing what to expect, she climbed down and turned. Her mother and Mémé stood behind Humbert, whose eyes were wild.

"You defied me?"

The words hit Catherine like a shot, and she suddenly felt like a child. "No, Papa."

"Then why have you been lying and sneaking around behind my back?"

Her words came out in a whisper. "I asked Nicolas to teach me to read."

Humbert flung his arms in the air, pacing. "You asked Nicolas to teach you to read?"

Tears came to Catherine's eyes, and she retreated a step. "Yes, Papa."

"Why didn't you ask me?"

"I did ask you."

He flinched before lowering his gaze and his voice. "Why did you tell us you were going for a walk when you were actually running off to meet Nicolas? What were you doing that you were ashamed to admit?"

Catherine had never thought her father would believe such things about her. "Nothing."

"Then why did you lie to us?"

The tears spilled over. "I was afraid you wouldn't let me go."

"And why did you think we would not let you go?"

Her mother's disappointed eyes seared into her, and she didn't know how to respond. "I asked Nicolas to come here, but . . . his mother would not let him because of . . ." She choked and glanced at Mémé. Catherine couldn't say it aloud, so she slumped on the bench, buried her face in her hands, and cried silently.

The room went quiet. A long moment passed, and then something thumped on the table, and she heard Humbert leave without another word.

A gentle hand touched her shoulder, and she raised her head. Mémé was there with a mug of tea. "Go and rest."

As she walked to the ladder, Marie handed her Nicolas's book.

It felt heavy in her hand.

When Anne climbed into the loft with Beatrix that night, Catherine pretended to be asleep, not wanting to be chastised further. She must not have been very convincing, however, as Anne said, "Do you think we will ever be free of the cloud over us?"

Catherine opened her eyes. They felt dry and swollen, and though she thought Anne would be smug, her sister also looked as though she could cry. "What cloud?"

"Rumors, accusations."

Another tear ran down Catherine's cheek, and she turned her head and stared at the rafters.

"If not for Mémé," Anne continued, "Nicolas wouldn't have had to—"

"It's not Mémé's fault," Catherine snapped, roughly wiping her face.

After sliding their baby sister between the blankets, Anne crawled into bed and leaned on her elbow. "I love Mémé, but sometimes I wish I could go somewhere nobody knows."

"And how are you going to do that?"

"Maybe Aunt Agnes knows someone from the inn."

Catherine turned her back and closed her eyes, angry with everyone. "Perhaps."

Mémé had done nothing wrong; Nicolas had done nothing wrong; Father Brignon had done nothing wrong, and he was killed, and Humbert blamed it all on Father Michel.

The fading orange sunlight glared through the skin-covered window, casting long shadows in the loft. Nicolas had taught Catherine that things were not always as they appeared. Why had Father Michel done this to them? She decided to find out, one way or another.

HE next day, Nicolas trudged to work. Wanting to be alone, he
mucked the stalls. The autumn air was heavy with humidity, and
chaff stuck to his skin, but Catherine crowded his thoughts until
Martin peeked into the stall. "Time for dinner."

Without saying a word, Nicolas ate his bread and pottage. When the cook
placed the cheese tray in front of him, Nicolas could only stare at it.

"What's wrong with you?" Elisabeth asked.

"Nothing. I was thinking. Maybe I could start my journeyman appointment."

Jean's eyes bored into Nicolas. "You've been delaying for weeks now. You
left me in an uncomfortable position—I thought you had changed your mind
about owning your own shop."

"I've not been feeling well, but I'm ready now."

"The apprentice supposed to take your place has found a new position. His
father told me this morning—he was not happy."

Nicolas whipped up the most sorrowful look he could muster and said,
"But I thought—"

Elisabeth scowled. "Don't you think we should have told Le-Chêne that
you were coming? And we must find a new apprentice first." She placed her
napkin on her plate, signaling the end of the discussion.

"I can help until you find someone," Martin said.

Good old Martin.

Thankfully, the cook spoke.

"Excuse me, monsieur. Would you consider my son, Quentin, as your apprentice? He's a good boy and would be a fine worker."

Jean smiled at her. "Magdalena, I didn't realize. How old is your boy now?"

"He'll be ten next month."

His smile faded. "Boys must be at least twelve to obtain an apprenticeship."

The woman slumped her shoulders, and for the first time, Nicolas noticed her. Though he'd thought she was only Rachelle's age, lines around the woman's eyes made her appear much older. Besides being dreadfully thin, her hands were red, and her hair was dry as straw. Patches held her dress together, leather straps bound her shoes, and she wore no hose. She had been working for them for about a week, but he could not even remember her name—Magdalena.

"Yes, monsieur." She curtsied. "I understand."

Jean tapped his finger on the table. "But I am desperate with Nicolas leaving, and it would be a great help if your son could start right away. Could he come to the forge early tomorrow morning?"

She brightened and replied with a cracked-lipped smile. "*Merci*, monsieur."

Jean used his bread to sop up the last broth, but instead of eating it, he simply stared at it. Finally, he said, "And you know, since Quentin is so young, perhaps he could live with you. I would pay him a salary."

Papa is paying a nine-year-old a salary?

Tears came to her eyes. "Yes! Oh yes. That'd be wonderful. *Merci*, monsieur."

Later that day, Nicolas packed a bag, and Jean drove him to Framont, a nearby industrial village rich with iron deposits and home to the largest forge in the county. A surprised Le-Chêne greeted them at the door and showed Nicolas to his room in the attic—a sweltering crawlspace with a pallet, a table, and a single window.

Nicolas wanted to be a silversmith, but to own a shop, he had to put in his time at the forge with Le-Chêne, a master, glaring over his shoulder. There was much to learn: to use box bellows, to reduce iron, and to cast it for things like cannons, fireplaces, and bed warmers. Though he liked the work, his arms felt like jelly by the end of the day. In fact, Le-Chêne worked Nicolas even harder than his father ever had.

Amid the clamoring hammers, the roaring fire, and the sizzling water, Nicolas dreamed of Catherine, her lashes wet from the rain. "Teach me," he could almost hear her say.

Catherine raised her face and allowed the warm autumn breeze to lift her hair. The path she had taken to meet Nicolas almost seemed to beckon, and she wondered what he was doing now.

"Still waiting for that kale," Mémé shouted out the door.

Catherine fumed. *Carry this for me. I'm waiting for that kale. Bring some water.*

"Did you say something?"

Catherine fidgeted with the laces on her skirt. "No, Mémé."

"I did not think so, but I was thinking of going to Lac de la Maix today, and I need your help."

Though Catherine was tired of following orders, she loved the lake and jumped at the chance to see it again. She filled the canteens, donned her shoulder bag, and enthusiastically accompanied her grandmother.

The walk was long, through dense forests and grassy meadows, over streams, and up rocky slopes. Along the way, Mémé gathered certain types of mosses but left other varieties. She collected nuts and stripped bark from different trees. As Catherine helped her pick hips from a wild rose stalk, she asked, "Why doesn't everyone know how to heal themselves?"

Francisca shrugged. "Nobody taught them."

"Will you teach me?"

"Yes, Lovey," she replied with a smile.

"Who taught you?"

"*Mi madre*, when I was your age. I taught your mama, but she usually defers to me. Aunt Agnes learned, but she does not have the time since she works at the tavern."

"Why doesn't Auntie have any children to help her?"

"Agnes's first child did not survive, and your aunt almost died. She cannot take the risk to try to have another child."

"Oh, poor Aunt Agnes, I didn't know."

"Sometimes things go wrong," Mémé said, "and precautions must be taken to maintain a happy marriage."

Precautions? Catherine must have made a sour face because Mémé stopped abruptly. As she slipped the canteen over her head, the strap caught in the old cross pendant she always wore. She tucked it under her chemise and said, "Your mama has been lucky."

Catherine nodded. She wanted to ask about the precautions, but Mémé continued down the forest path. At the crest of a ridge, they stopped to rest on a fallen log. The sky was clear, and on the mountaintop the two women could see miles of sweeping tree-covered valleys and open fields spread below them. An eagle soaring above cast a shadow on the treetops, as if they were on top of the world.

"Your friend Dimanchette lives over that ridge, and the iron mine where your brother works is in the valley," Mémé said, pointing.

Catherine recalled the day several years ago that her eldest brother, Jean-Baptiste, had stormed out of the house. He was a handsome man with his father's muscular build and sandy hair, but his mother's gray eyes. The similarities to their parents ended there, however. Jean-Baptiste could be kind and considerate, but he drank too much and had a quick temper. Anne said he had taken the job to spite their father.

"Why did Jean-Baptiste leave home for the mine if he hates it?"

"Your brother thought that by moving away he would leave hardship behind him."

Working on the farm was a chore, but— "What hardship?"

Mémé frowned and pointed to a group of stones jutting out from a circular rock formation.

She's ignoring my questions again.

"That is the abandoned castle of Salm," Mémé said. "Those flat stones have the centers cut out of them. Some say an ancient tribe of Gauls used them for human sacrifices to their gods."

A cold gust caught her, and Catherine chewed her lip. "Human sacrifices?"

"Oh, you are not scared, are you?"

"I'm not scared. I'll go with you anytime."

Mémé nodded and pointed at a rock in the shape of a cat ready to pounce. "That one is La Chatte Pendue."

Catherine stood to get a better look. "Why is a stone called the Strangled Cat?"

"Once, a woman accused of witchcraft disappeared from the village. The next day, the villagers found a black cat dressed in the woman's clothes hanging by the neck from that rock, confirming their suspicions—she was a witch!" Mémé laughed, waving her fingers beside her head before saying, "Come on."

About halfway down the elevation, Francisca pushed a large pine branch aside, and there was the lake, shimmering in the sun. The water, rippling, and black at the edges, reflected the dark green hue of the surrounding pines. The translucent wings of dragonflies skimmed the water's surface, causing ripples to stretch its entire length.

Beside the lake, a wooden statue representing the Virgin rose from a grove of wildflowers. The figure radiated strength and drew Catherine close. "Who placed the robe on her?"

"People come on pilgrimage from all over the county to this holy place, bringing clothes as an offering." Mémé stepped to Catherine's side. "We must start our collection before it gets too late." She pointed to the inlet. "We will dry the bark of those white willows to treat pain, and those reeds will make a nice basket . . ."

As winter approached, Catherine learned to pulverize eggshells into powders, to recognize leaves of linden and plantain, which mushrooms were edible, and which ones to avoid.

Of the many who came to Le Petit-Courty looking for remedies, Magdalena, a widow from town, visited most often. Catherine would help Mémé gather remedies to common ailments for her to sell. One day during their collection, Magdalena asked, "Do you know how to make birth prevention powder?"

Precautions . . .

Francisca scowled. "No, it is too dangerous."

Nodding, Magdalena replied, "While the money I receive for selling remedies for aches and pains has helped, people are willing to pay a small fortune for birth prevention powder, and I need the money." When Mémé didn't reply, she added, "My children need shoes for winter—"

"I'll not make it for you," Mémé cut in. "I promised Padre Brignon, and I'll not break my promise to him."

"If you teach her how to make it, you will not break your promise," Catherine said as she tied a string around a bunch of dried willow bark.

Mémé shot her a furious glare. "Lovey, please understand. This is not pain medicine. Padre said it is a crime against nature. The Church charges women with this knowledge with witchcraft . . . they are burned!"

Witchcraft? Catherine murmured, "Is it illegal?"

"It's not illegal, but they can charge anyone with witchcraft. You cannot defend yourself against it!"

"Please, Francisca," Magdalena begged. "Some women are not able to carry a child. Do you want them to die?" She paused, waiting for a response. When none came, she continued, "No one knows I come here. To be safe, I'll not come back—ever. And I promise I will never tell anyone."

Mémé's eyes darkened. A weight seemed to hang over the room, and a terrifying chill raced down Catherine's spine. She squirmed, wishing she hadn't said anything.

Finally, Mémé said, "I will show you—once. You must remember it well."

She turned on her heel and left the house with Magdalena close behind her. As Catherine followed them past the rye fields to an open meadow, she considered—how could using a plant make you a witch?

Mémé stopped, picked a wildflower, and showed it to them. "This is the plant. It grows about waist high. The flat white blossoms resemble lace with a red spot in the middle. Do you see its hairy stem?" She rubbed her finger along the stalk. "Remember, hairy legs are safe. There is a poisonous plant with a similar flower, but its stems are reddish and smooth, so be careful. When the flower curls, it is ready to harvest, but make sure you scatter some seeds to help ensure future plants. After your customers . . . lie together, the woman simply swallows a pinch of seeds. To be sure, she should eat a sprig of rosemary the next day."

Magdalena nodded. "And this will also *provoke the menses*?"

Mémé's eyes narrowed in anger. "I have already stretched my promise to Father Brignon. I will show you no more." She turned on her heel and led them back to the farm. Before going into the house, she turned and said, "Please, Magdalena, remember my warning—because if you get caught, they will vilify you and nobody will be able to help you."

ICOLAS sat on the pallet and stared out the little window of his room
in Le-Chêne's attic. A burst of yellow daffodils brightened the gray
landscape. Nicolas had survived both the bitter winter in the un-
heated attic and his brother's iron hand at the forge.

With spring, Le-Chêne's wife, Rachelle, contracted some disease and started vomiting every morning. It got so bad that Martin began bringing Elisabeth
every day to fix their midday meal, but no one mentioned Rachelle's sickness.
When Nicolas learned the reason, he confronted his mother.

"With child? I thought Rachelle was gravely ill. Why the big secret?"

"It is not a topic of polite conversation."

"But women have babies every day."

Elisabeth gasped in horror and folded her hands on her lap.

Exasperated, Nicolas silently pushed a pea through the broth left in his bowl.
Upon realizing the room had gone quiet, he glanced up to see all eyes on him.

Elisabeth's face pinched. "I said, the tanner's wife knows a girl who would
be perfect for you—the miller's daughter, Salomé. They say she is lovely; you
should meet her."

"If she needs a friend of her mama to find her a suitor, the girl must be
breathtaking," Le-Chêne said with a chuckle.

Rachelle smacked his arm. "It wouldn't hurt Nicolas to meet the girl."

"I'm not interested in meeting anyone," Nicolas grumbled. "Why is everyone so concerned about me?"

That night, the heavy beams supporting the roof seemed to push down on
him, trapping him in the cramped attic. He closed his eyes but could not close
his mind to the swirl of the pale-gray eyes of his love. But did he love Catherine?
Then he remembered Francisca's fierce black eyes, and uneasiness swept over
him as he remembered her words.

Who protected her from you?

Five months later, Nicolas took off his hat and knocked on the door of the little house in Le Petit-Courty. Humbert answered.

"Sorry to disturb you, monsieur," Nicolas rushed out. "I know you don't want me—I mean, I know I'm not supposed to—"

"What do you need, boy?"

"My brother's wife gave birth a couple of days ago, and everything seemed fine . . ." Nicolas ran his fingers through his hair. "But today, when we came home for our midday break, the baby looked funny, yellowish. Rachelle is crying. Mama asked me to fetch the priest, but he was gone, and the midwife wasn't home, and I thought, perhaps—"

"Impossible. Francisca never leaves the farm until after dark. Bring the infant here."

"Please, monsieur, by the time I ride back to Framont—"

"I can hear you talking about me," Francisca said, peeking around Humbert and swinging the door open. "Of course, I will help your brother's child."

"Later," Humbert insisted.

Through the open doorway, Nicolas looked past them and saw Catherine standing beside the big table. Her dark hair was loose and fell about her shoulders. She smiled at him, and a stab pierced his heart. *My God, she is beautiful.*

Humbert stepped into his line of sight and growled, "We will come after dark. Where does your brother live?"

"In the timber-framed house across from the forge."

The door closed in his face.

As Nicolas walked away, an incomprehensible tirade of Spanish spewed inside.

At Le-Chêne's house, Nicolas retreated to the corner and buried his face in his book. Though he never heard the knock, the change in tone of his brother's voice caught his attention.

Curiosity brought Nicolas to the kitchen. Elisabeth wore a forced smile. Francisca was there, dressed similarly to the day Father Brignon was killed. Her face covered by a veil, her gown decorated with lace, and her hands clad in delicate gloves. Even her skin color appeared lighter.

Then Catherine stepped in, and Nicolas's breath caught. In the year that had passed, she had become taller, her cheeks thinner, her body fuller. Though she stood right before him, he missed her more than he could bear.

Humbert followed them in and cleared his throat. His glare cut through Nicolas. "Don't you have somewhere to go?"

Conscious of Elisabeth's staring at her, Francisca couldn't help but feel smug: funny how a fancy dress and a little face paint could change one's opinion. Elisabeth's greeting was stiff but without the same frightened expression she'd had at the farm.

"Thank you for coming," Elisabeth said. "Whenever I saw this yellowing before, it was not this bad, and it always faded."

Le-Chêne bowed to them and stumbled over his words. "I'll fetch Rachelle, or, uh . . ." He rubbed his hands together. "Would you rather come into the bedchamber?"

Francisca patted his arm. "Relax, child—everything will be fine. Where is the babe?" She followed him through three main rooms, their high ceilings and huge windows making her feel small.

Rachelle sat on a carved wooden bed under a beautiful white quilt, holding the sleeping baby. The sunlight streamed through the window, brightening her blond hair and making mother and child glow. Tears welled in her lovely green eyes.

The child appeared healthy. Francisca touched its head, no fever. "When did she eat?"

"We've let her sleep to boost her strength."

"No, she must eat every two hours. Feed her now."

"Well, I . . ." Rachelle's face turned crimson.

"*Vamos*, feed her now," Francisca said, clicking her fingers.

Smiling nervously, Rachelle set about nursing the baby, but within a few moments, the infant fell back asleep.

"Wake her and make her suck. Food will get her body working." Francisca smacked the bottom of the baby's foot, but the little girl would not rouse. "Give her to me; I'll wake her." The others moved aside as Francisca carried the baby to the front room. There, she took off her gloves and laid them beside a bucket. "Is this clean water?"

Le-Chêne could only nod.

She undressed the baby, found a rag, and washed the child. The cold water triggered loud wailing. Relieved, Francisca smiled, ran her fingers through the baby's sparse peach fuzz, and tickled her belly. "That's better. Catherine, fetch me the healing."

The little pot pulled from her bag contained bluish powder. Elisabeth's face drained of color. "What is that?"

"Smashed eggshells," Catherine explained. "It helps those who feel tired or weak. Mémé says the blue ones are the best."

Francisca mixed the powder with water and dropped some on the baby's tongue during one of her shrieks. Immediately, the wailing ceased; the child puckered, squeezed her eyes shut, and stuck out her tongue.

Catherine giggled; Elisabeth gasped; Le-Chêne and Rachelle stared.

"You must get the babe moving, eating, and going." Francisca pointed to the baby's bottom. "If you must bathe her five times a day, do it."

"You mean we just needed to wake her?" Rachelle said with tears in her eyes.

"Sit by the window. Give her lots of sunshine, fresh air, and food."

As Rachelle scooped up the baby and returned to the bedchamber, Le-Chêne gestured to chairs by the table. "Have a seat, ladies. Mama, would you fetch us some ale?"

Elisabeth prepared two mugs. "I'll take these to Papa and Monsieur Humbert," Le-Chêne said. He went out with the ale but returned with Father Michel.

At the sight of the priest, Francisca lowered her eyes, dipped her hands unseen under the table, and gestured to Catherine to fetch the gloves beside the bucket. She slipped them on quickly.

"Father has come to bless the baby," Le-Chêne said.

"Father, thank you for coming," said Elisabeth, pouring another mug. "Would you join us for some ale?"

"Yes, thank you," he replied to Elisabeth, but Francisca felt the priest's eyes boring into her.

"Have we met?" he asked.

The priest apparently didn't recognize her or notice Humbert sitting outside. Good thing Anne had suggested lightening Francisca's skin with face paint. Still, her accent would give her away, so she remained silent.

Along with the silence, tension grew until Le-Chêne exclaimed, "She is my auntie."

Oblivious, Elisabeth turned to the table with two more glasses of ale.

"Your auntie?" Father Michel gawked at Elisabeth and turned back to Francisca. "I don't see any resemblance."

Elisabeth paled, halting in her tracks. Her hands shook, and one of the mugs she held fell from her grasp, spilling on the table and knocking over the pot containing the blue powder.

The priest's eyes bulged, and though Catherine reached for the pot, he snatched it and jumped to his feet. His eyes narrowed in suspicion. "What's this?"

Le-Chêne took it and returned it to the table. "That's mine. I use several types of powder at the forge."

The priest pursed his narrow lips. "What's in there?"

"Why do you ask?"

"Do you know how witches make their powders? They grind the bones of babies."

With a smirk, Le-Chêne replied, "There are no witches here. Do you honestly think I have ground baby bones in a little pot on my table? That is the most absurd—"

Rachelle appeared in the doorway. "Did I hear something fall?"

Everyone stopped and turned to her. Her eyes darted around the room in confusion.

Le-Chêne rushed to her side. "No, my heart. Father Michel is leaving."

"Oh." She ducked behind her husband and smoothed her hair. "I will fetch the baby."

Le-Chêne kissed her forehead. "He cannot stay. Go back to bed." Then he laid his hand on the priest's shoulder and ushered him toward the door. "Thank you for stopping by, Father."

The priest shot one last evil glare over his shoulder as he left.

Nicolas stepped outside. Heat radiated from the forge across the street where pillars of smoke blackened the sky. It was early afternoon, and he should return to work, but he was already late. Besides, his brother was the master, so he might as well take advantage of that fact and take a ride to the country for some fresh air.

The temptation to follow the path he used to meet Catherine was too great. He paused at the swimming hole—*oh, those legs*—and with a sigh, proceeded to *their* rock, dismounted, and stared into space, trying to think of a path to redemption.

After a while, Nicolas heard someone talking—no, it was singing. Turning toward the sound, he waited until a boy came into view. It was Joseph, walking the pigs. He must have herded them to the oak grove to eat acorns. Occasionally, he tapped one with a stick to keep them moving. *Oh, to be that carefree.*

At the swimming hole, Joseph undressed and waded into the water, wearing only his breeches while the pigs happily wallowed in the mud at the river's edge. The pigs scattered when a yelp pierced the air. The boy thrashed wildly, then went under. Nicolas stood, gaping. The inlet was not even waist-deep. Surely, Joseph could stand with his chest out of the water, but the boy went under again.

Nicolas dashed down the embankment, slipped out of his boots, jumped headlong into the pond, and grasped Joseph's arm. But the boy punched Nicolas in the eye with his other hand. When he tried to catch that arm, he received a bloody nose and scratches to his neck. Finally, he caught Joseph from behind and dragged him to the bank, where they both collapsed, out of breath, on the grass.

"It's all right, Joseph, you're all right."

Joseph's trembling body racked with coughing and ragged gasps of air. "Where are the pigs? I've lost the pigs!"

"Rest here. I'll find them."

Nicolas wiped his bloody nose on his sleeve and followed the hoofprints to a shady grove of oak trees where all four pigs, covered in a muddy crust, huddled together, grunting and crunching on acorns. Taking a wide berth, he circled them, found a stick, and herded them along the water's edge toward the swimming hole.

A cold chill went up his spine. He stopped in his tracks. There was no breeze. The trees were still. Not even a bird sang. All his senses sharpened. *Someone is watching me.* He held his breath and heard . . . something. Moments passed as he stood motionless. His eyes darted, trying to determine why his nerves were on edge. A hot breeze blew up the valley, and the gust carried away the feeling as suddenly as it had come. He exhaled, feeling rather silly. With a nervous chuckle, he pushed the pigs onward.

When Nicolas returned, Joseph was dressed. The boy scraped his boot in the mud and looked up sheepishly. "Sorry about your eye."

"What would have happened if I had not seen you? You shouldn't swim by yourself."

"But I swim here every day. This time I just lost my footing." He lowered his head again and wrung his hands. "Please don't tell Papa, or I'll be in so much trouble."

I understand how it feels to make Humbert angry. "I'll not tell, but never do it again."

Back at Le-Chêne's house, Nicolas worried if Humbert might still be inside. To be safe, Nicolas decided to sneak in the back door, maybe get a glimpse of Catherine on his way to the attic. But his father was sitting on a bench in the shade. Nicolas lowered his head, hoping to get past without notice, thankful that the heat of the day had dried his hair. Maybe nobody would notice his damp clothes.

"What happened to you?" Jean asked.

Before Nicolas could explain, Humbert appeared at the back door. Stopping abruptly, Nicolas closed his mouth and swallowed hard while Humbert turned sideways to allow Nicolas to enter. Inside, everyone was sitting at the table. Francisca's glare sliced right through him, and uneasiness swept over him again.

Jean followed Nicolas into the house. "Son, what has happened to your face?"

If he told the truth, he would have to break his promise to Joseph, but maybe Humbert would forgive him. With every eye on him, he sighed. "I . . . was in a fight in the tavern."

Le-Chêne stood and banged his ale on the table, his face filled with fury. "Fighting in the tavern instead of going back to work? Damn it, Nicolas! You know we have enough on our minds without fretting about you."

Humbert walked away, shaking his head in silence.

Nicolas caught Catherine's gaze before she sighed, slumped her shoulders, and lowered her head. "I'm sorry," he muttered, heading toward the stairs.

Francisca followed him. "Nicolas, let me see your wounds."

"I'm fine."

"Nicolas, stop."

The stern tone stopped him in his tracks. "Sit," she growled, and he could do nothing but comply. She grabbed his chin and moved it from side to side.

"Why did you say you were fighting in the tavern?"

"Because I was fighting in the tavern."

That look again, Francisca's eyes so intense they could surely read his thoughts.

"*Hohamno,*" she said under her breath.

What does that mean?

She gave him that sinister grin and replied, "People don't usually swim in taverns."

The color drained from his face as he remembered the sensation with the pigs, as if someone were watching him, and when she had asked who protected Catherine the day the wolves attacked. *How did she know? The stories must be true!*

He gulped before bounding up the stairs, wanting only to hide in his bed. He glared at the clouds through his one tiny window, remembering the afternoon he spent with Catherine at the farm. He flung his arm over his eyes to banish the thought.

At some point, Martin fetched the cart, and Nicolas sat up. The Cathillons were leaving.

"Thank you, dear ladies," Le-Chêne said. "How can I ever repay you?"

"That's not necessary," Francisca said with a blush.

"I want to give you something—something you would never get for yourself."

"A favor, then, for another day?"

Le-Chêne nodded and kissed the old woman's hand—and then he kissed Catherine's cheek.

Through the window, Nicolas fixed his eyes on Catherine. He couldn't get near her, but his brother could kiss her. Nicolas couldn't hear what she said as she climbed onto the cart, but her father's reply rang loud and clear.

"No, daughter, you can do better."

chapter

12

Instead of getting ready for work the following day, Nicolas burrowed into the sheets. Le-Chêne's call to breakfast went ignored, but then his brother clomped up the steps and pulled the pillow out from under Nicolas's head. "Why aren't you dressed?"

As his head bounced off the pallet, he grumbled, "I have a headache."

Le-Chêne ripped off his blanket and threw it across the room. "Get out of that bed now."

"No. My eye is swollen, and it hurts."

Not showing any pity, Le-Chêne crossed his arms and glared. "Well, Nicolas, I guess you shouldn't have been fighting."

Should I tell him about Joseph? What's the point? Le-Chêne will never believe it.

Grumbling, Nicolas got dressed and snatched a crust of bread on his way out the door. At the forge, he stood in the back as his brother handed out assignments.

Le-Chêne pointed to a young man about Nicolas's age, but a little shorter and stockier, standing in the crowd. ". . . and this is Balthazar Osché. He will shadow someone this week. Who needs a second pair of eyes?"

Though Nicolas tried to crouch behind the men in front, Le-Chêne was out for blood. "Nicolas, you look like you could use one good pair."

The other workers laughed at his expense until Osché turned to Nicolas and gave him half a grin. Nicolas sneered. "He loves to make me the butt of his jokes. Come on."

The coming of spring meant a resumption of deliveries of butchered rabbits and chickens to the White Horse Inn, the tavern owned by Catherine's Aunt Agnes and Uncle Sebastien. Beneath a giant wooden replica of a white rearing horse, the inn stood across the street from the stables owned by the La Goutte de Paradis family. The coach connecting Salm to the industrial power, Strasbourg, in the east, and Lorraine's capital city, Nancy, in the west, stopped at the stables twice a day to transfer fresh horses. Travelers wearing unusual clothing or hairstyles and speaking different dialects bustled to and from the inn.

One Saturday, Catherine persuaded Humbert to allow her to join him on one such delivery. Much later than usual, the Angeles bells were already tolling as Humbert pulled the cart up to the tavern. A crowd of people passed them, pushing through the doorway while others looked in the window.

As soon as Humbert disappeared around back with the goods, Catherine crept over and peeked inside the open door. The tables had been pushed against the wall, and people piled on them or stood shoulder to shoulder, leaving the center of the room open. The dozens of candles and lanterns cast an eerie light on their faces. She had never seen so many people in one place.

A round of laughter erupted as a troubadour appeared and skipped around the room, making gestures her father would not appreciate. Catherine had heard of troubadours, of course, but entertainment in her small town was rare. And this man was beautiful, with strange golden skin and a wiry frame. He wore a bright green velvet doublet with matching breeches, and, to top it off, feathers in an oversized hat over long black curls that hung halfway down his back.

When two lute players struck up a tune, he sang to female patrons in a rich tenor, touching a cheek or hand, causing the glassy-eyed women to fan themselves with their handkerchiefs. Catherine giggled at them as he bowed and passed his hat to collect donations.

A group of latecomers pushed beside her, and when the troubadour waved them in, he caught sight of Catherine hiding in the doorway. He beckoned to her, but she could not enter the inn at this hour.

Prancing toward her, the troubadour extended his hand and sang:

"Come to me, my darling . . ."

The clearest emerald eyes she had ever seen met hers, and for a moment her heart stopped beating. Her hand lifted toward his as if it had a mind of its own.

"Catherine!" Humbert shouted. "Get back here."

Oh no! Inhaling sharply, she looked over her shoulder. Humbert stood beside the cart with his hands on his hips, scowling. When she turned back to the troubadour, he was dancing off. The magic had vanished.

⚓

Nicolas and Balthazar became fast friends, and after work every day, the pair headed for the Framont Tavern. Today, taking an alley as a shortcut, they passed a maze of crates that smelled of rotting food. When they turned the corner, someone tossed a bucket of dirty wash water through an open door, hitting Balthazar in the face.

Nicolas jerked back in time, but his feet went out from under him, and he found himself sitting in a puddle. He looked up to see Balthazar's wet hair clinging to his forehead with little pieces of food dangling in front of his ear. As Nicolas wiped his face with his shirt, he burst out laughing. He stood, shaking the mud from his hands.

"Oh—oh, stop it, please," a shrill voice rose behind him. He spun to see two lovely young ladies. One with unnaturally red hair had soiled, gloved hands in front of her face. Her dress had a splash of mud across the front.

His cheeks burned. "I am so sorry."

Flecks of amber in her brown eyes shot sparks as she shouted, "You stupid clod! What have you done to me?"

He couldn't help but stare. She wore no partlet or ruff, and her full bosom overflowed the square neckline of her green silk gown. Nicolas forced his eyes away and pulled out his handkerchief, but she was so perfect he was afraid to touch her. "Let me reimburse you."

Her skirts whirled. "Oh, forget it." While the brunette smiled shyly at Balthazar, the firebrand grabbed her elbow and dragged her up the street.

Nicolas turned back to his friend and laughed again—a piece of eggshell was stuck in his wet hair. Balthazar's face reddened, and he combed through his hair with his fingers.

"Did I get it?"

Nicolas brushed the shell off Balthazar's shoulder. "Yes, you got it. Let's get that ale."

"No, I stink like yesterday's soup."

"In that tavern? You'll still smell better than half the people in there."

In August, Nicolas found himself dutifully stuck between his brother and father, parading up the street behind the bishop toward the church to celebrate the Feast of the Assumption. While they sang and prayed to the Blessed Mother, Nicolas was more interested in the food carts, jugglers, and games of chance. When he spied Balthazar in the crowd, he decided to make his move.

He tapped Le-Chêne on his opposite shoulder, and when his brother turned away, Nicolas ducked and ran.

Minutes later, they were tossing coins on a board of painted squares, trying to win a knife. Balthazar elbowed Nicolas and pointed. Following his friend's gaze, he found the same two women they had met the week before. The one he had sprayed with mud once again wore a low décolletage with a small ruff and winged collar, contrasting her companion's demure high neckline.

"Let's talk to those ladies," Balthazar said.

With a sour expression, Nicolas replied, "You go ahead."

"Come with me. I'm just a journeyman; she's too classy for me."

"But she flirted with you the other day."

"Well, I'm not going without you." Balthazar dragged Nicolas, and as they approached the women, one beamed and the other scowled.

Balthazar tipped his hat. "Ladies, we meet again. My name is Balthazar Osché, and this is my awkward friend, Nicolas de la Goutte de Paradis."

The scowl immediately brightened as the one with henna-colored hair extended her gloved hand toward Nicolas. "De la Goutte de Paradis? Why, are you the son of our mayor?"

Nicolas took her hand and bowed. "The same."

"My name is Salomé Müller, and this is my friend, Claire."

Müller? Is this the girl Mama wanted me to meet?

The crowd erupted behind them as a skinny troubadour wearing a hat with ridiculous green feathers pranced toward them. He knocked off Nicolas's cap and—while onlookers laughed at his embarrassment—sang a love song to Claire and Salomé.

> *"For little coin, thy heart; and grace,*
> *Sweet stars, be kind to my desire,*
> *Because on earth ye did not scorn my fire,*
> *Bethink ye, now ye hold your angelic face."*

Fuming, Nicolas picked up his cap. *That charlatan is singing a Ronsard poem!* When he turned to glare at those laughing at him, he spied a peddler's cart. While the women were swooning over the singer, he slipped away and returned with a cloth tied by narrow blue ribbon. He presented it to Salomé.

Her eyes widened. "What is this?"

"Open it and see."

Nimble fingers pulled the ribbon and unfolded the cloth. "Oh," Salomé cooed, lifting a delicate pair of gloves.

"To replace the ones I ruined."

She touched her throat in surprise, and again his eyes drifted to her bosom. "They are beautiful," she said.

Yes they are . . .

She removed her gloves, handed them to him, and tried one on, raising her hand for Claire to see. "It fits perfectly." Before putting on the other one, Salomé ran her ungloved hand along Nicolas's open palm. His skin tingled.

Churchgoers flooded the street; the service must have ended.

The ladies excused themselves. Nicolas and Balthazar, while snacking on apples, bonbons, and ale, wandered past vendors selling leather crafts, embroideries, baked goods, and produce. Eventually, Balthazar had to leave, and Nicolas sought out his parents, finding them in line for the feast.

"Good to see you, son," Jean's voice was laced with sarcasm, and Nicolas braced himself for a tongue lashing for missing Mass. Instead, his father handed him a bunch of lavender before shaking out his arms. "Your mother has been shopping."

Elisabeth, preoccupied with the flowers she was carrying, must have forgotten his absence at the service. "Smell it."

Fragrance enveloped him. He held in a cough, nodded, and joined them in line.

Jean said, "Louis's supper is Saturday; are you coming?"

"And sit around all day?" Nicolas must have made a sour face because his mother gave him one of her looks.

"It will do you good to meet the local citizens. The Müllers will be there."

"Stop pushing him," Jean said.

The Müllers. Nicolas sighed with feigned exasperation, but his thoughts turned to Salomé's low-cut bodice and full lips. "If it makes you happy, Mama, I'll go with you."

Louis's stone chateau, the largest in the area, overlooked the river and sported several buildings linked by balustrades and formal gardens. When they entered the courtyard, Elisabeth herded Nicolas toward the Müller family. Nicolas bowed politely at the introductions, pretending indifference.

Salomé flashed a dazzling smile. "I had hoped to meet you today."

The host's daughter, Louise, and Salomé's friend, Claire, joined them in a flurry of embraces and kisses. Compared to the flamboyant Salomé and the elegant Claire, Louise looked plain and immature but anxious for the older girls to accept her as their peer. Nicolas had known her forever.

After a few minutes of small talk, Salomé said, "Oh look, Nicolas, the river." She stood on her toes, but a wall of hedges circling the garden partially obscured their view. "See how the water glitters in the sunshine."

Beyond the cobblestone entryway, a marked footpath led through a field of waist-high grasses to the river, La Grande-Courty. "Would you like a closer look?" he said to all three girls.

Salomé's eyes brightened, and when Nicolas offered his elbow, she slipped her gloved hand through. As they ambled through the crowd, she appeared to push her bosom out even more, if that were possible. At the ogling glances from other male guests, Nicolas abounded with pride to be with such a desirable woman.

Assuming the other girls were following them, he spoke over his shoulder, but there was no reply. He turned—he was alone with Salomé, but she didn't appear worried about her reputation.

"Shall we go back?"

She pouted. "Nobody noticed us leave. I thought you were going to show me the river."

Not sure what to do, Nicolas continued along the path, passing the time with small talk. "I trust my peace offering persuaded you to forgive me."

"Oh, you are just a little clumsy."

At the water's edge, they stopped to watch a line of ducks parading toward and then into the meandering river. When the ducks' heads disappeared underwater, Nicolas pointed and laughed at their bobbing rear ends.

Salomé rolled her eyes. "You are such a child." She leaned against him, looked into his eyes, and ran her finger across his lips. "But a handsome child." The soft touch of her gloved fingers made him feel light-headed. She smelled like sunshine and wildflowers.

The next thing he knew, he was kissing her, but she pulled away, blushed, and lowered her lashes in embarrassment.

"You make me forget what is proper," she whispered, looking around nervously.

"I am sorry, I—"

Before he could stumble past the first few words, she pointed to an old outbuilding not far from the path and clutched his hand.

"Come," she whispered.

He followed her to the shed. The door hung off its hinges, cobwebs blocked the entrance, and an overpowering musty smell saturated the air. Wide-eyed and slightly nervous, he asked, "You want to go in there?"

"Yes."

A stick lay beside the door, and he used it to scrape down the cobwebs. Inside, the windowless room was dark and dank, its only décor an old table and some broken tools. As Nicolas considered his next move, Salomé pulled him toward her—

And touched him through his pants.

If the earth had opened and swallowed him, he would not have been more surprised. She stepped back and unlaced her bodice and chemise.

"Salomé?"

She pulled his mouth against her neck and flung her head back. He ran his lips across her neck. She blew in his ear, and a tingle raced down his spine. Before he knew what had happened, she shoved him back and wrested the buttons of his jerkin open, then she tossed it on the table and sat on it. "Come closer," she commanded in a rush of breath. She tugged the laces of his pants loose and rucked up her skirts.

His heart pounded in his ears, and pent-up desire flared. As powerless as a fly caught in one of the spiderwebs he had brushed down, he went to her, and she clamped her legs around his hips, pulling him in. He thrust deep and groaned. She was warm. Wet. She sighed and arched her back as he pulled her tighter against him again and again until an earth-shattering spasm left him breathless.

But it was over much sooner than he wanted it to be. He panted and stepped back, the ramifications overwhelming. "What if you become with child, Salomé? I'm not ready for—"

"Oh hush," she said as she rearranged her skirts. "I would never embarrass my family with a bastard child. I know what I am doing."

Nicolas folded his vest inside out. They returned to the party and found their parents sitting together.

Salomé kissed her mother's cheek. "Sorry we are late, Mama, madame. Nicolas was kind enough to show me the river."

Elisabeth smiled at Salomé and then shot Nicolas one of her looks. "They are serving the food. Where is your jerkin?"

Heat rose in his face. *Could Mama know what I have done?* Before he could think of a reply, Salomé intervened.

"It's my fault, madame. I'm sorry, but I spilled my drink on him."

chapter
13

ANOTHER year passed uneventfully. Though Mémé kept Catherine busy learning to forage, she wondered what her life would be like if not for those wolves.

Anne also seemed to be getting desperate in her situation. No respectable boy would court her, and she took her frustration out on everyone. One morning, a particularly loud disagreement sent Catherine rushing out the door. She joined her father on his way to the inn.

"You should have more patience with your sister," Humbert said, helping her onto the cart.

"She treats me like a child," Catherine huffed.

"You are a child."

She turned to glare at him, but the gentle look in his eyes changed her mind, and she laid her head on his shoulder. He put his arm around her, and they rode in silence.

At the mill, he unloaded his sacks of grain and disappeared inside while she waited. The swirling water reminded her of the story of Panurge, and she thought of that summer almost two years ago and sniffed back tears.

Humbert returned with sacks of flour, and they proceeded to the inn.

Inside, Uncle Sebastien boomed over the clamor of mugs, bowls, and conversation. "Humbert, Catherine, welcome."

The first person everyone noticed upon entering the White Horse Inn was Uncle Sebastien. Though average height, the paunch he carried over his girdle made him appear much larger. Thick, unruly hair heavily sprinkled with gray seemed to float above him as if his head were in the clouds, and his deep voice resounded to the street. He had opinions on everything and was not shy about sharing them.

"What's going on between the bishops and counts now?" Humbert asked as they joined Sebastien on a bench.

"The counts want to regulate everything: wine, grain, and meat, all except the bumpy roads. If we want them fixed, they will charge another tax."

"If they would fix the road, I wouldn't mind a tax," Humbert grunted.

Uncle Sebastien shouted, "*Vingt Dieux!* Only peasants pay taxes—nobles and clergy pay nothing." He banged his ale on the table to emphasize his discontent, flinging his arms as fast as his words, the gray rag he used to mop the bar throwing droplets of fishy-smelling water through the air. "We need salt to keep our meat, so they force us to buy it from the granaries and pay an exorbitant tax. If we buy it directly from the source, the bailiff will fine us for not having bought our ration of salt."

Aunt Agnes peeked out of the kitchen and glared at her husband. "Sebastien! Your words!" She turned to Catherine, and her face softened. "Would you like a piece of tart?"

Like Marie, Aunt Agnes was quiet and reserved, the opposite of her animated husband. Despite working in the tavern morning, noon, and night, she was heavy, with permanent bubbles of sweat on her forehead. Her chin disappeared into her thick neck, and her apron would wrap around Catherine twice.

Tart? Yum. In the kitchen, Catherine sat on a tall stool beside a thick worktable aged with scratches and burn marks. "Why does Uncle Sebastien speak of many gods?"

Lifting her chins, Agnes pointed at her. "Catherine, you'll not start cursing. Your uncle speaks without thinking."

Catherine shrugged while Agnes gave her a small piece of custard-filled tart, saying, "The baker outdid himself with these."

While Agnes gossiped about who did what, Catherine closed her eyes and let the rare delicacy melt in her mouth. She understood Agnes's weakness for sweets.

As the door opened and Sebastien came in with more dirty bowls for the pile, the sound of music entered the kitchen. Catherine would know that voice anywhere—the man of her dreams, the emerald-eyed troubadour. She rushed over and stood in the doorway.

"That's Sir Guy," Agnes said with a smirk. "His troupe played here this spring on their way to Nancy, where he performed for the duke—or rather, his daughters. Rumor has it he had to flee, and fast."

The troubadour looked exactly as Catherine remembered. He raised those emerald-green eyes and sang, "*Catherine, how I dream . . .*"

Her jaw dropped, and she gawked at her aunt. "How did he know my name?"

"Oh, he saw you the other day when you came in with your father," Agnes said, waving off the comment. "He asks about every pretty girl." But then she frowned, and her tone changed. "Stay away from him, Catherine! He has no real employment, plays for tips, and refuses to give his real name. 'Sir Guy,' indeed."

Catherine could barely contain herself. *He asked about me!*

Suddenly, her father was there, taking her sleeve and dragging her through the door, but she peeked over her shoulder as the man sang:

> *"And I lie awake at night,*
> *The wind whispers her name,*
> *My dreams full of melancholy."*

That evening, Martin returned to his one-room house after supper with Jean and Elisabeth. His little place beside the stable had everything he needed. Shelves of books from floor to ceiling covered an entire wall behind a desk; an upholstered chair sat in front of a fireplace; and along the back wall sat a chest for his clothes, a pallet, and a table with a bucket and washbowl. Under the pallet, removable floorboards stored a cache of books he kept hidden.

Though Jean and Elisabeth wanted Martin to stay with them at the estate, he preferred his little house. He gave them a weak excuse—he could kick his shoes off or leave his blankets a mess if he wanted, but he never did those things. No, he stayed alone because of the shame of the nightmares that he could not overcome.

He stoked the embers and added another log to the fire, lit his lamp, and leaned back with his book when screaming and pounding on the door interrupted the quiet evening. He rushed to find the young apprentice, Quentin, trembling and hysterical.

"My house is gone," Quentin cried, falling in and wrapping his arms around Martin's legs. "Burned to the ground, and Mama and my family are gone."

Martin brushed the unruly mop of blond hair from the boy's tear-streaked face and said, "They are probably at a neighbor's house."

"No, I asked all the neighbors, but nobody would open the door. They told me to go away, so I ran the whole way back."

"And nobody tried to put out the fire?"

The boy wiped his nose on his sleeve and sniffled. "No, nothing is left but a pile of ashes."

Not knowing what else to do, Martin said, "Let's talk to Jean."

Raising the lantern, Martin searched the evening mist for loose stones as they rushed up the hill. The moonlight slanting through the trees and across the rough stone of the estate gave the manor a sinister air.

Elisabeth answered the door in her nightclothes, a bedside candle in her hand. "Martin. Is something wrong?"

Martin nodded and entered the house, dragging Quentin who clung to his leg.

Elisabeth shouted for Jean before wiping the boy's tears with a dishrag. "Poor boy, I will fetch you something to eat," she said, helping Quentin onto a chair at the kitchen table. Jean, wearing his nightshirt, joined Martin in the pantry, where they discussed the situation.

"Maybe he was afraid in the dark. I'm sure we will find her tomorrow," said Jean.

"No, master." Behind them, forlorn and desperate, Quentin wiped his nose on his palm and said through tears, "Mama's gone. I looked everywhere." Elisabeth held the rag to his nose and told him to blow. She gave him a leftover crust of bread and a slice of cheese that he gulped down. She led him to a chair in front of the fireplace, but when she sat down, he abandoned his chair and climbed on her lap. She laid his head on her shoulder and rocked him until his tears stopped and he fell asleep.

In the morning, Martin, Jean, and Quentin crossed the Framont River to the hamlet where the boy lived. Clusters of wattle-and-daub houses lined the dirt street where chickens roamed freely. The sounds of barking dogs and bleating sheep filled the air as Quentin led them to his house, but all that remained was a pile of rubble, as if no one had attempted to extinguish the fire.

As Quentin had reported, no residents answered their knocks or shouts. Mystified, they rushed to the provost's house. Although Louis worked for Salm and had no jurisdiction in another country, he agreed to investigate off the record.

The next day, with no word and little more they could do, Martin kept Quentin busy, keeping one eye on the road for the provost, who arrived in the afternoon, looking pale. Martin sent Quentin to muck the stalls so they could talk openly. The boy's shoulders slumped as he plodded toward the barn.

With a shaky voice, Louis said, "I found them. Magdalena was caught selling birth prevention."

Martin started. "Is birth prevention illegal?"

"Frowned upon, but not illegal . . . yet. However, they accused her of being a demon and forced her to confess to witchcraft. If found guilty, she will be burned—alive."

"Oh my God," Jean moaned. "What about her children? Are they in an orphanage? I will—"

Louis shook his head and cut in. "They were arrested as accomplices."

"No," Martin gasped and reached for support from Jean, who had clutched the fence.

Louis closed his eyes and scratched the whiskers in his perfectly trimmed beard. "I have spent all day arguing, but they fully intend to burn his siblings for helping to gather the herbs. The youngest is only five years old. The thought sickens me, but even bribery would not sway them."

Minutes passed in silence as they absorbed the information until Martin composed himself and asked, "Should we tell Quentin?"

Jean wiped his eyes and replied, "We have to tell Quentin something. Eventually, the boy will learn the truth, but I'm not sure how to soften the blow."

That same evening, Nicolas and Salomé joined Balthazar, Claire, Louis's daughter Louise, and the notary's son, whom Louise had begun courting, at a gathering at the Gauthiers'. The provost had been called away on an important case, and Louise's mother seated the guests without him. The entrée was served amid laughter and blushes when suddenly the door burst open. Louis looked confused, as if he had not expected guests. His wife jumped up, but he brushed her off and turned to Nicolas.

"You may not be aware of this, but your father's cook and her children have been arrested for witchcraft." Louis tossed his coat over the back of his chair and pinched the bridge of his nose. "They will all be burned alive." He slumped and leaned on the table for support. "I cannot believe they will burn little children."

Nicolas leaped to his feet. "Oh my God—Magdalena. What about Quentin?"

"Luckily, he was at your father's shop when they arrested the others. He's safe here, but he can never cross that river."

"But witchcraft? What did she do?"

"She has been accused of selling birth prevention."

At that, Salomé paled and fanned herself. "This is so upsetting; I need some fresh air."

Nicolas helped her stand. "Are you all right?"

"I will be fine, thank you." She turned to Louise. "Will you help me?"

"Of course," Louise said, taking Salomé's elbow. "Follow me."

The provost slumped beside Nicolas and recounted all that had happened. As Salomé and Louise returned, Louis shook his head. "There is nothing anyone can do. I'm physically sick; I cannot join you for supper."

"Yes, I've lost my appetite as well," Nicolas said. He turned to Salomé, expecting her to show some emotion, but she smiled coolly and kissed Louise's cheek. By contrast, Louise looked as though she would faint. Nicolas took Louise's arm and helped her to her seat. "Did you know Magdalena?"

"Yes," Louise replied, her eyes wet with tears. Then, curiously, Salomé cleared her throat and shot what looked like an angry glance at the girl, who stiffened. "I mean, no, I don't know her. I'm just upset."

"We are all upset," Louis said.

As Nicolas escorted Salomé home, he felt as though he could wretch, yet she excitedly discussed the new dress her mother was having made for her.

She must be so upset that she is diverting her attention to happier things.

One week later, on his way to the stable yard, Martin spied Jean and Louis deep in conversation. Magdalena had heard their political conversations. Perhaps she'd said something under torture that could be misconstrued. Martin sent Quentin to the house, then paced the stable, worrying, waiting. When Jean returned, pale and unable to raise his eyes from the ground, Martin held his breath.

"Magdalena is dead," Jean said.

"Already? With no trial? What about the children?"

Jean shook his head. "Louis couldn't find any information about the children, but Magdalena has been murdered."

Not knowing how to reply, Martin stared at Louis.

"The official report says she threw herself on a knife."

"Where did she get a knife in prison?"

chapter
14

THE winter of 1584 came early, the second since Catherine had last spoken to Nicolas. Chilling winds swept through the valley, plucking the remaining leaves from the trees and howling under the door and through the skin-covered windows. Sheets of freezing rain pelted against the walls of the farmhouse. In the evenings, Catherine heard wolves howl. Her family stayed inside except to feed the animals, bring wood, or draw water.

The women passed the time doing needlework, making clothes, and embroidering lace to sell. Catherine helped her grandmother pound dried grass and herbs to fill pots, Humbert taught Joseph to read and tally, and Beatrix played with her doll. Occasionally, Catherine read aloud from the book Nicolas had left for her, but some stories made no sense. If neither she nor her papa knew the hidden meaning, she would mark the page to ask Uncle Sebastien.

One morning, Jean-Baptiste arrived to break the monotony, and everyone settled around the big table as Francisca and Marie fussed over him.

The chatter was lively until Humbert asked, "Son, are you still thinking about leaving the mine for the forge?"

"At either place, all I would be doing is shoveling."

"But you could work for Le-Chêne with Nicolas," Catherine said. "Do you ever see him?"

"Yes, I see him sometimes at the tavern."

"Does he speak of us? When will he return to his parents? Because he still has things to teach me . . ." At Humbert's frown, she added in an indifferent tone, "Stories to read."

Though Jean-Baptiste's eyes looked glazed with drink, they filled with pity. "Probably next summer. Nicolas's parents want him to marry Salomé, the miller's daughter, but he only likes her for—" Abruptly stopping mid-sentence, Jean-Baptiste turned to his mother, red-faced.

The words hit Catherine like a shot. Barely able to breathe, she lowered her head and studied her fingernails.

He cleared his throat and continued, "It's a good match. The father of Salomé Müller is respected—they have money."

Humbert's expression flashed with fury but softened almost immediately. "That boy has no respect; you can do better."

Marie rubbed Catherine's back. "Lovey, tradesmen's sons marry daughters of the tradesmen, lords marry noble ladies, and peasants marry other peasants. It has always been this way."

"Sister," Anne added, "who is that boy from the village with chubby cheeks and little legs? He has loved you for a long time, plus his parents have two cows."

"A short guy with a big face?" Jean-Baptiste snickered. "Still, the two cows are appealing." He hesitated as if waiting for a sharp retort but Catherine couldn't think, and she pinched her leg to hold back tears.

Anne chewed her lip before touching Catherine's shoulder. "Oh, Catherine, I beg your pardon. As Jean-Baptiste said, Nicolas might not love the girl. Wait to see if he will obey his father."

"You girls are setting your sights too high," Marie interrupted. "There's nothing wrong with a hardworking farmer."

Wanting to change the subject, Catherine raised her head. "Who said I want to marry Nicolas? I wanted him to teach me to read, and he did, nothing more." But her words came out a little too loudly.

"Well, the reason that I came . . . I . . . well . . ." Jean-Baptiste said, shifting uncomfortably and clearing his throat. "Dimanchette and I will marry in the spring."

Catherine came to her senses, and her eyes flew open. "Dimanchette? When did you start courting? She would have told me."

He shrugged. "We've been courting for a while."

"What a strange way to announce it," Marie said. "You should have spoken to your papa first."

"Humpf," Humbert grunted.

"Mama, I came all this way in a snowstorm to talk to Papa." Jean-Baptiste turned to his father as if waiting for a tongue-lashing.

Eyeing him suspiciously, Humbert said, "Why did you come today?"

"We are hastening our plans, unless you want to be a grandfather before being a father-in-law."

Everyone gasped and spoke at once. Humbert jumped to his feet and paced as he shouted, "Young people of today, no respect! Do you at least love the girl?"

Before Jean-Baptiste could reply, Marie's voice rose over the others'. "Her father will be furious. Does he know? Have you spoken to him?"

With his head lowered, Jean-Baptiste clasped his hands in front of him and replied, "I spoke with her father last week."

Marie continued, "We love sweet Dimanchette and are happy she will join our family, but we would have preferred you not celebrate Easter before Palm Sunday."

"Mama, we're not the only ones to . . . celebrate, as you say, and I do love her, Papa. We will marry in the spring. I wanted to let you know."

Humbert turned and stared into the fireplace. "Dimanchette is too young; she's Catherine's age."

Catherine opened her mouth to reply, but her mother shushed her.

Jean-Baptiste continued, "Soon to be sixteen, Papa. The same age as Mama when I was in her belly."

"Two different situations!" Humbert's face contorted as he roared, "When Aunt Agnes married Sebastien, Francisca and your mama were alone. They needed someone to take care of them." Humbert rubbed the pucker from his forehead. "And she was not with child when I married her either."

Though Catherine had never seen her father so angry, Jean-Baptiste merely shrugged.

Marie stood and motioned toward the door. "The deep snow will make your trip home tedious. I think you'd better go now, son."

Jean-Baptiste nodded and went around the room, taking his leave with hugs and kisses, but Catherine couldn't even blink when he kissed her cheek. "I'm sorry, sister."

She moped for the rest of the day and went to bed early, but sleep wouldn't come as her brother's words echoed through her mind. *Nicolas is fornicating with that girl.* Crushing sadness filled her one minute, anger the next.

The following day was sunny. Despite the deep snow, Marie asked Catherine if she wanted to go for a walk. She jumped at the chance at a diversion. They layered their wool cloaks and stockings and knotted skins on their boots to brave the descent to the village. Snow-laden hills and trees covered in icicles sparkled in the sunlight as they entered the frozen woodlands. The sun was warm and the crisp air refreshing as they trudged down the road, sinking, slipping, and laughing.

When they arrived at the inn, Aunt Agnes greeted them with a hug. "The bottom of your dresses are soaked. Come, get dry before the fire and tell us what's happening on the farm."

The women sat by the large brown sandstone fireplace that dominated the center of the inn. Open on both sides, it provided heat for the customers and a place for Agnes to cook her bread and pottages. There was a back room too, where she would wash the dishes and slice vegetables on a thick wooden table. Above it, bread pans, skillets, pots, and stack upon stack of wooden bowls lined shelves. In the main room, Sebastien stood behind a bar that separated his barrels of ale and wine from the dining area.

Snow on the Donon Mountain left no passable trail for a coach, so diners were rare this time of year. Of the few in the room, Catherine recognized Jacques, the peddler. Each month, he came to the village with his mule to sell his haberdashery. Two other men, probably merchants, sat behind their soup and ale.

"Everyone is well," Marie laughed, "except the days are boring and the nights are long."

Aunt Agnes nodded toward the peddler. "You'll not believe what happened to Jacques's cousin from Fouday. A couple of years ago, her husband died. They had no children. Her neighbors wanted her vineyards. When the old woman refused to sell, the neighbors accused her of throwing green powder on their cows, which died a few days later, and black powder on their parents, who died of a stomach ailment."

Catherine brushed her off. "Oh, those are only stories trying to scare us."

"Possibly, but when she denied the charges, they tortured her until she confessed. If convicted, the neighbor may redeem her property as a reward."

"They wanted her vineyards and invented the whole story!"

"If that's not enough to upset you, this surely will," Uncle Sebastien added. "The calendar has changed—ten days were cut. *Vingt Dieux!*"

"Sebastien!" Agnes scolded.

"Stop nagging," Sebastien growled before turning back to Marie. "Next week, we go straight from Sunday, December ninth to Monday, December twentieth."

"How can that be?" Marie replied. "Who decided this?"

"The pope said there is an error in the old calendar, and he authorized a new one. They call it the Gregorian calendar. I didn't know the calendar had a name, but Jacques said the previous one was the Julian calendar, after Julius Caesar."

Catherine asked, "Who?"

"I asked the same thing," Agnes whispered. "Jacques said Julius Caesar was the emperor before Charles V."

Catherine nodded at the explanation while Marie continued, "But rye will not grow ten days faster to meet the schedule, and the beasts will not bear their young any quicker. How does it change anything?"

When Sebastien shrugged, one of the merchants, soup and ale in hand, approached them. "For most, not much, except your taxes will be due ten days earlier. For us merchants, everything is upset—our order dates, the deadlines for our bills. The German and English Protestants are complicating matters by refusing to comply with the pope. They're keeping the old calendar, and France has asked permission to delay."

"And here in Salm, what will we do?" asked Marie.

"The counts will do whatever the Duke of Lorraine does. Next month, I'll have new calendars, and you can buy one."

Marie smirked. "Yes, I could buy one."

He nodded. "And Christmas is coming, time to cut the trees and shine the apples."

Catherine turned to him. "Why cut the trees?"

The merchant took a bite of soup. "Is it true the custom hasn't come this far? In Alsace for Christmas, every house is decorated with fir."

Wide-eyed, Marie said, "They bring the whole tree into their house?"

"Yes, the fir is the tree of life, so they hang apples from the branches—red ones, fruits of temptation, to signify the fall from sin."

As they trudged home, Catherine considered what they had heard. "Is it possible they would accuse someone of witchcraft just to steal her vineyard?"

"Yes." Marie nodded. "Good wine can bring good money. It can make people crazy."

"We make wine. Is it as good as ours?"

"Well, Sebastien said ours is the best he has ever tasted."

"Why is ours better than any other? Does Mémé throw in magic herbs?"

Marie's eyes narrowed, and she clutched Catherine's arm. "Never say that about Mama."

It was the first time Marie had ever lost her temper in Catherine's presence, and it caught her off guard. She teared up and cried, "I was just fooling."

"Never fool about things like that—ever." Marie released her arm, but the sting of her words remained. "Remember what happened to Magdalena? They will take Mama away—is that what you want?"

chapter
15

THE book Nicolas had given to Catherine lay on her bedside table, ignored. After reading it over and over, she knew the stories by heart, though some hidden meanings were beyond her and her father's comprehension. Disheartened, she looked out the window. *Why learn to read if you cannot understand the stories?*

She wanted to learn more, but there was no school; even if there were, it would only be for boys. Below her, she focused on Humbert harnessing the horse to make a delivery to the inn. She slipped the book into her bag and joined him. Unfortunately, the inn had no patrons, and Uncle Sebastien read less than she did.

Catherine wandered to the front door, gazed down the dusty street, and sighed at people with exciting lives: A fishmonger pushed a smelly handcart toward the square. A man lugging a bundle from the supply shifted his load and tipped his hat to a milkmaid carrying two heavy buckets toward the baker. The girl returned his toothless smile. Across the street, Martin emerged from the stable, filled a pail from the trough, and disappeared back inside.

Of course, Martin!

Her papa was talking to Uncle Sebastien, and Aunt Agnes was slicing vegetables—this was her chance.

Creeping out of the inn, Catherine boldly approached Martin and opened the book to the page she had marked, but his face drained of color, and he dropped the bucket, water splashing their legs. He glanced around, snatched the book, and shoved it into his shirt.

"You should not have zis book," he whispered through clenched teeth.

Tears stung Catherine's eyes when she realized her foolishness. "Please give it back; I just wanted to learn what those stories mean."

"They mean we will both be arrested."

Arrested? She scanned the street; nobody was watching. She turned back to him, trying not to appear childlike and pushed. "Could we go somewhere safe where you can explain the stories? Nicolas used to meet me by the swimming hole."

"Oh no," Martin gasped. "I cannot meet you. How would that look?"

"You could say you needed more herbs to help your hip."

"If word got out . . ."

"We could meet in that old barn, beyond the bridge—behind the tree line?"

Still, he gaped at her, wide-eyed, his mouth open. She had to think of something. "Maybe we could . . . you could . . . bring Quentin. Please, Martin, it'll not take long."

While Martin lowered his head and shuffled his feet, Catherine crossed her fingers and waited. Finally, he replied, "Very well, I will discuss it with your father."

Smiling triumphantly this time, she returned to the inn and peeked into the kitchen. Agnes looked up from her slicing and asked, "Where have you been?"

Catherine whispered her reply, "I asked Martin about those stories."

Agnes paled, dragged Catherine in, and closed the door. Pointing the knife at the book and speaking through clenched teeth, Agnes snapped, "Does your father know you have that?"

"No, but—"

Flinging her flabby arms into the air, Agnes exhaled loudly and raised her eyes to the heavens before glaring at Catherine. "Oh, Catherine, you must be more careful, especially since you are accompanying Mémé. Martin has a cloud of suspicion over him too."

"What does Mémé or Martin have to do with my book?"

"In case you are being watched," Agnes whispered.

Catherine rolled her eyes. "Come now, who would watch me?"

A bead of sweat rolled down Agnes's temple, and she wiped it with the back of her hand. "Mémé is a stranger to this land. People don't trust her."

Catherine giggled. "Mama said your real mama thought Mémé was the devil because of her dark skin."

But Agnes was not amused. "Please take my words seriously. When my family died, people from all around the county came to help, bringing food and supplies. Some demanded to have Mémé burned as a devil. She spoke a language no one understood. Father Brignon sprinkled holy water on her.

Mémé smiled and made the sign of the cross, but the look on his face—I think he expected her to shriek in pain."

When Agnes suggested their good friend Father Brignon may have originally been suspicious, Catherine listened more seriously.

"Father Brignon said that her dark skin made him think Mémé was a Gypsy. She showed him her devotional scapular, and he held it up for everyone to see the face of St. Francis, her namesake. He told us not to be afraid. Nevertheless, the next time we came into the village, children threw stones, and adults shouted to me to stay away from her."

"But I thought everyone loved Father Brignon. Why wouldn't they believe him?"

"Father Brignon was a good man and well-respected, but superstitions run deep. When Mémé and I learned to communicate, I told her what the townspeople had said. Why do you think she only leaves the farm at night?" Though Agnes stopped as if waiting for an answer, she received no reply and continued, "The story of Nicolas and the snake has reminded them of their old ideas. The serpent is a transformation of the devil."

"That was two years ago, and nothing has happened since."

"Just because you haven't heard a rumor doesn't mean one isn't being spread. You're an adult now, and I will tell you as I told Mémé and your parents," Agnes leaned in to whisper, "be careful whom you trust. I understand why your parents are upset with the Church, but people talk, especially after a couple of drinks—I hear it every day."

"But I have no accent. What would happen to me?"

Agnes took Catherine's hand. "Travelers discuss terrible cruelty between Catholics and Protestants. Think of poor Magdalena and her little children, tortured and killed. Some have told tales of children as young as two being tortured and burned."

"Why don't we go to church? There are festivals and celebrations—but we never do anything."

"Your papa—" Agnes stopped abruptly, and her eyes widened before she covered her mouth.

Aha! Keep pushing, maybe Auntie will finally tell me. "Papa wasn't mad at the Church when Father Brignon was here, and Papa hated Father Michel before they came to arrest Mémé. Something happened after Father Brignon left. What was it?"

There must be another reason.

Agnes just stood there, unable to answer, so Catherine continued, "Jean-Baptiste and Anne were baptized, but then . . ."

A guilty look crossed Agnes's face before she lowered her gaze. "I knew it! Tell me, Auntie."

Pointing with her knife again, Agnes replied, "You know nothing." Shifting her weight, she leaned on the table toward Catherine. "Lovey, if your papa will not tell you, I'll not tell you. I'm only informing you now so you'll heed the danger." Agnes gave Catherine a warm hug. "Now go home and be careful."

They left the kitchen together to find her father waiting at the door. "Come, daughter, it's getting late."

As they left town, Martin glanced at her from across the street, but she was preoccupied with her conversation with Agnes. So many things to consider. Why had Humbert come to hate the Church? He would never tell her. Was it possible that the snake which had bitten Nicolas was a devil? That was ridiculous, but Elisabeth did seem afraid. Father Michel had suggested their eggshell powder was ground baby bones. Did people grind baby bones? Catherine shivered and tried to think of something else.

At supper, her father's mood seemed light. Catherine crossed her fingers and said, "I saw Martin today; he offered to teach me—"

Humbert's glare cut her off. "Why, today of all days, did Martin offer to teach you?"

Catherine wrung her hands and mumbled, "I asked him."

"What did you ask him?"

"I asked him what the hidden meanings were."

Humbert's eyes bulged. "You took that book into town when I expressly forbid it? I knew I should have never given it to you in the first place. Did anyone see you with it?"

"No, Papa. And you know Martin; you trust him."

Humbert stared at his bowl for a long while before replying. "Well, you'll not be meeting with anyone, young lady. We've been through this once."

"Please, Papa, it's been two years. Besides, Martin already agreed to meet with me if you allow it, and I'll not be alone. He'll bring their apprentice, Quentin."

Anne cleared her throat and put down her spoon. "What if I accompany her?"

At her sister's suggestion, Catherine crossed her arms. "Anne, you have no interest in learning to read."

"But I've often considered learning."

"No, you have often considered how to get Martin to like you."

Anne's eyes narrowed. "Hush, Martin has nothing to do with my desire to better myself."

"Women have no need to learn to read," Humbert grumbled.

"Well, maybe not," Marie replied. "And I know you are too busy, but if Martin is willing . . ." She nodded suggestively toward Anne.

"All right," Humbert sighed. "As long as you stay together. I'll have no whispers of impropriety in this house. I'll discuss it with Martin tomorrow."

Catherine jumped from her seat, wrapped her arms around her father's neck, and kissed him atop his head. "Thank you, Papa. You'll not regret it, I promise."

"Perhaps you could give me a few lessons before meeting with Martin?" Anne asked.

Catherine smirked. "I will. But we must walk through the forest to meet him."

"You're so wrong about me, sister." Anne bit her lip. "I have no problem with the out-of-doors."

Martin anxiously awaited for Saturday, and it arrived bright and sunny. As he and Quentin rode toward the meeting spot, knots tightened his stomach. Though Martin had taught Elisabeth and Rachelle to read, this time he would be teaching Anne, beautiful Anne. He had ached to ask Humbert to court her, and Humbert probably would have agreed, but Martin couldn't bear the thought of disappointing either of them with his failings. He pushed down his insecurity and concentrated on what he would say.

Tall weeds and woodlands surrounded the partially burned barn about a half-hour's ride from the estate. Only two walls and part of the roof remained; they should be safe there.

When Martin and Quentin arrived, they found Catherine wiping down spiderwebs with sticks while Anne stomped brambles. They had even piled old straw for seats.

"Papa would not allow me to come without Anne as a chaperone," Catherine complained.

"I hope you don't mind," Anne added, looking upward from under long lashes.

The memory of Alix had left him. Now, when Martin looked at Anne, he saw Anne. "Not at all," he replied. "I spoke with your father. Shall we begin?"

Bright sunlight fell through the leaves as they took their places on the straw with Catherine on one side of him, Anne on the other, and Quentin sitting before him on the dirt. Martin explained the confusing words and hidden lessons from Catherine's book.

"The meanings are so obvious now," Catherine said. "Thank you, Martin."

"Look behind the words," he said with a nod, alternating glances between the girls.

Anne said, "We were hoping . . . if you have the time . . . perhaps you could give us a few more lessons."

Their pale blue eyes shone with enthusiasm. Such lovely girls. "Why do you want to learn?"

Catherine's eyes flashed. "I want to learn about the world."

"I want to be more than I am," Anne added, holding his gaze much longer than normal.

His heart leaped. Could he—scarred, outcast—offer her something she might accept?

"Contrary to local belief, women do read—Elisabeth, Rachelle." He untied his satchel from his saddle, pulled out another book, and returned to his seat.

"In case you asked, I brought you this book, *The Monument of Matrones*. Everyone should learn to read and continue learning their whole life." Handing the book to Catherine, he said, "This book is safe for you to read because it contains prayers and meditations written by women for other women. Would you like to start now?"

Two meetings passed, and Martin found himself thinking about them often. Not only were the students making remarkable progress, but he was sure Anne's actions were coquettish. Once, she dropped her handkerchief, and when he retrieved it for her, she ran it across her lips before folding it and slipping it into her sleeve.

He decided to ask Humbert to court her formally, even practicing a speech, but at the next lesson, Martin lost confidence. How could Anne ever be happy with him and all his scars? Besides, his home was one room, and he shared that with Quentin, who insisted upon staying with him despite the cramped quarters. After dutifully teaching the lesson, Martin went home, kicking himself.

Sitting dejectedly on his pallet that evening, he spied his violin in the corner. Playing used to give him confidence, but he hadn't played since his father died. Martin took the instrument from its case and ran his fingers across the strings, and then he lifted it, gently rubbed the bow with rosin, and played. He decided to take it to the next lesson.

As he had hoped, his music captivated the students. Anne closed her eyes and swayed gently, and when she opened them, her face lit up when their eyes met. His heart skipped. She was as refined as any woman he knew from his past life of luxury and privilege—delicate, sensitive, charming—and he was falling in love with her.

Though he didn't want to be deceptive or upset Nicolas or Jean, Martin kept quiet about where he was going on Saturday afternoons. The next week, when Jean asked Quentin to help repair one of the stable doors, Martin set off alone. The girls would have each other as chaperones. It would be all right.

When he arrived, though, he found Anne alone, hiding in the corner of the barn. She nervously peeked out when he approached. "Catherine has a fever," she said, wringing her hands. "She wasn't allowed to come."

"Quentin had to help Jean."

Her anxious expression softened into a shy smile. Should he stay here with her, alone? Nervously, he sat beside her, but before he could begin the lesson, storm clouds swirled above them. As the wind tossed loose straw around them, a lock of Anne's hair pulled free from her coif and blew against his cheek. They backed into a corner of the shelter to stay dry, and when a crack of thunder startled her, she buried her face in his chest.

She was so close. The scent of lavender radiated from her. As rain fell all around them, he raised her chin and gazed into her eyes. She traced the scar down his forehead and across his cheek, and he considered pulling away. Surely, his appearance repulsed her.

But then she kissed him.

The warmth of her breath spread through him like a flame.

He turned away from her. "Anne, I am not . . ."

She ran her lips across his cheek and whispered his name, and this time he pulled her close. The air was heavy with the smell of wet straw as he slid to the floor and pulled her down beside him. He removed her coif, allowing her blond tresses to fall about her shoulders. She untied her bodice and slipped it off, then helped him remove his jerkin and shirt. While he touched her bare shoulder, she traced the scar across his chest with her fingers and followed with her lips, kissing all his flaws until he moaned, "Anne."

He pushed her back, lay beside her, and raised her skirts. As he threw his leg over hers, he froze, and his hip exploded with pain. In anger and embarrassment, he squeezed his eyes shut and rolled away from her as an excruciating spasm rocked his body.

I should have known—

"Let me make it feel better," she said, running her hand down his back.

But he bristled at her touch. "Please leave me alone."

"It's all right."

"Please go."

"Martin," she said with a sob.

"Leave me alone!"

He felt her movements as she pulled on her clothes and bound her hair. Through it all, he lay there wishing the rain would wash him into a crevice in the earth. Why had he dared to dream of a future? He should have known better.

He couldn't bear to face her again, so the next day, he asked Quentin to deliver a message that they could no longer meet for lessons. However, to Martin's surprise, Anne appeared at his door a few hours later, her face mottled and eyes red. Unable to look at her, he limped to the window. Although the day was bright and sunny, he saw a gray sky, a gray fence, and a gray courtyard.

"Please look at me, Martin."

He turned but stared at the floor instead. "Anne, I cannot give you what you want."

Her normally quiet, controlled voice was laced with anger. "You have no idea what I want."

"Please, Anne, leave me alone."

"Whatever happened to you is in the past—you are alive. Why are you afraid to live?"

He raised his head and shot her a furious glare. "How could I provide for you, Anne? I cannot even provide for myself." He swung his arms wide in his cramped house. "If not for Jean, I would have starved to death years ago."

She reached for him, but he stepped back. Undeterred, she said, "You can teach, Martin. You are smart and talented."

"Teach? Whom will I teach—a couple of young girls to read? As you starve to death, you will come to hate me."

"But we could leave Vacquenoux. We could . . . we could go to Paris."

"Paris?" Martin gasped. "I can never go to Paris! You are a naïve country girl, and you have no idea what you're suggesting. Now please leave."

"I thought we . . ." She flinched, her eyes brimming with tears, but she clenched her jaw and raised her head proudly. "Very well, I will leave. Soon, I will leave Vacquenoux for good. My uncle has secured a servant position for me in Ban de la Roche." She turned and strode to the door but hesitated and turned back. "If you change your mind, let me know."

With a whirl of her skirts, she left him, his heart shattering with the slam of the door.

chapter

16

Spring 1585

CATHERINE used to long to be away from the tattling; however, only a week after her sister left, she missed Anne deeply. Uncle Sebastien had pulled some strings to find a service position at the home of Baron Herbert de la Roche. The baron and his family employed eight servants in one of the largest houses on the square of Senones.

The minute Humbert collected Anne's letter from the inn, he rushed home to read it to everyone.

Dearest family,

I have settled into a room with the cook and two other servants who help her. For now, I slice vegetables and stir sauces. Besides having our own meals for the servants, we get to eat the baron's family's leftovers—delicious and wonderful dishes—and tarts. I received my first pay yesterday. It was so exciting to go into the supply with my own money. I received a new dress to wear to Mass, and I will get another for Christmas! Every week, we attend High Mass as a group, and then I have Sunday afternoon free until supper.

I miss you all.

Love, Anne.

After they had been courting for a year, Elisabeth joined Salomé in pressuring Nicolas to commit, but the more they pushed, the more he pulled away.

When Salomé announced that her aunt was sick and she had to rush off to Strasbourg to help her, he was relieved to have some time to himself. Elisabeth worried that six weeks was too long a time to be nursing someone and suggested Salomé had found someone else. The thought did not upset him the way he thought it should.

Now that she was back, though, she looked lovelier than ever. Arm in arm, they walked along the river that flowed behind the mill. The gurgling water reminded him of one of his legends. "Did you see Lorelei on the Rhine?"

"Who is Lorelei, and what is the Rhine?" The look she gave him reminded him of his mother's scalding glance.

"There is an old legend of a girl named Lorelei whose sweetheart accused her of witchcraft. Instead of sentencing her to death, the bishop sent her to a nunnery. On the way, she became so distraught she jumped off a rock to her death and is said to haunt the Rhine River."

Salomé rolled her eyes. "Only you would tell such a harebrained story, Nicolas. Why do you say such stupid things? You're a grown man."

He picked at his fingernails and mumbled, "I like legends." An awkward silence followed before Nicolas continued. "Did you see the Notre Dame Cathedral? It's the tallest building in the world. They started building it nearly six hundred years ago."

"Oh." Salomé sighed, raising her eyes to the heavens and shaking her head. "Now that is ridiculous. Do you honestly think a building can stand for more than five hundred years?"

Clenching his jaw, he stared at her. The bright sunshine lit her hair and made her painted lips glisten. She was so lovely. Perhaps he was being petty. He stepped behind her, put his hands on her slim waist, and nibbled on her neck. "I missed you."

"Not today, Nicolas. It's my time." She pushed him away.

Exasperated, he sighed and plopped on a rock. "Come, sit beside me. What did you do in Strasbourg?"

"That is none of your business."

Shocked, he frowned. *She's always been gruff, but now she's treating me like a fool.* "I might as well go home."

"Typical. If I refuse to lay with you, you get angry." She crossed her arms and huffed.

"This is the first time I have seen you in seven weeks. In the last ten minutes, you have called me stupid twice and told me to mind my own business. I've always wanted to see Strasbourg."

He turned away from her and gazed into the distance. One big puffy cloud shaped like a cat caught his eye, and that afternoon with Catherine and her siblings—almost three years ago—popped into his mind. He closed his eyes and sighed. Something as simple as gazing at the clouds was a pleasure with Catherine. She would never call him stupid.

"Why do we even bother?" he mumbled.

"What does that mean?" Salomé's voice was shrill.

As his eyes drilled into her, her demeanor immediately changed to the coquette he knew so well. "Oh, Nicolas, I'm sorry. I've missed you." Salomé ran her gloved finger down his arm. It tingled. Cocking her head to the side, she said, "Maybe you should walk me home."

He offered her his arm, and they walked in silence. At her door, he remembered to invite her to supper next Sunday. Though he wasn't thrilled about it, he said, "Mama is hosting a May Day fête next week. Would you like to come?"

Seven days later, Nicolas stepped aside as Salomé burst into the house and greeted his mother with a spirited air. This dinner was not a good idea. The pressure to marry would start again.

Twenty minutes of inane conversation followed before Elisabeth called everyone to the table where, thankfully, the talk soon turned to politics.

Martin scooped a bite of meat pie, but instead of putting it into his mouth, he held it high. "Oh, you'll not believe this," he said, his eyes widening. "Finally, Mary, Queen of Scots, was caught trying to overthrow Queen Elizabeth."

"I forgot you went to Strasbourg this week," Nicolas said, popping a crust of bread into his mouth. "But I thought that happened years ago?"

"She's been in prison for years on suspicion, but now she was caught with a red hand," Martin said, the food still on his spoon.

Waving off the conversation, Jean said, "England is a mess."

"Well, France is worse," Martin replied. "Mary's uncle, the Duke of Guise, is plotting to have King Phillip of Spain's daughter be named ruler of France. They're preparing for war."

Jean set down his goblet. "At our meeting last week, Louis said that King Henry is thinking of choosing Henry of Navarre as his heir to the throne."

"Yes," Martin added. "But Henry of Navarre is a Protestant, so Guise is planning a war to keep France Catholic."

Elisabeth nodded toward Salomé. "Why does any of this affect us?"

"Of course it affects us; we do not live in a bubble," Martin replied. "Our Count Jean is Catholic and is easily swayed. They might draw us into war. Hopefully, Count Frédéric, a Protestant, will be able to keep the peace in Salm."

The meal came to a comfortable close. Nicolas and Salomé joined Le-Chêne and his wife in the carriage ride home. Uncharacteristically, Salomé was quiet, pouting, and staring at her gloves as she sat beside Rachelle and the baby.

Nicolas said, "Is anything wrong, Salomé?"

Without raising her eyes, she replied, "Your political debate did not interest me; I prefer to discuss relevant things."

"Yes, we should have deliberated hairstyles," Rachelle said, but her eyes revealed mischief.

Nicolas couldn't stop his chuckle, but the amber flecks in Salomé's eyes cut into him as she said, "I am not amused."

About halfway to Framont, the wind picked up and brought with it a driving spring rain. The partially covered carriage offered little protection against the downpour.

"My dress will be ruined," Salomé huffed.

"I'm sorry," Nicolas replied. "We'll be home in a few minutes."

Le-Chêne scowled. "Why are you apologizing? Are you responsible for the weather?" This prompted an even more obvious sneer from Salomé.

The farther they traveled from town, the thicker the mud became. As the coach struggled, it suddenly jolted violently to the side, knocking the women from their seats. Baby Marguerite shrieked.

"The wheel," Nicolas said, jumping out into the pouring rain. "It doesn't look broken, it just slipped off the axle, but the pin is gone. Do you think we can fix it, Le-Chêne?"

With a shrug, Le-Chêne said, "We must try." He tied off the reins and jumped into the slop. Reaching for his wife, he said, "I'm sorry, my heart, you're going to get wet."

Rachelle tucked the baby inside her cape and adjusted her hood, then reached out to Le-Chêne, and he carried them to shelter under a tree.

"You too," Nicolas said, reaching for Salomé.

"That rain will ruin my dress for sure. I'll not add much weight." She turned her head to dismiss him.

Nicolas's mouth dropped open. He turned to Rachelle, with her cloak offering little protection, her curls flattened and stuck to her face. Le-Chêne winked at her, she returned it, and the day Nicolas spent in the rain with Catherine flooded his mind. He turned to Salomé—to the back of her head. This was too much.

The wheel easily slipped back onto the axle, but the pin was lost in the mud. Rachelle shouted and pointed, but they couldn't see it. She sat Marguerite on the wet grass, and sloshed to them. She handed it to Nicolas and wiped her brow, leaving a dirty streak across her forehead. While the rain continued to pour on them, Le-Chêne removed his wet handkerchief, wiped the mud from her face, and kissed her, and all the while, Salomé glared at Nicolas.

A pang of jealousy struck him.

The following Wednesday dawned bright and clear, the first after several days of mist and downpours. In the stable yard, Martin held a horse while Jean taught Quentin to file its teeth. Though everyone had tried to convince the boy that he would be more comfortable up at the estate, he continued to live with Martin in his little house.

Midmorning, Father Michel bustled into the team-exchange area. Martin nudged Jean, who went to greet the priest. Father Michel climbed off his cart, rushed to him, and snapped, "I need to discuss something with you privately." He turned and glared at Martin.

An uneasy feeling swept over him. "Come, Quentin," he said and led the horse into the barn, leaving Jean alone to speak to the priest. A little while later, to the sound of the departing carriage, Martin looked out the door. Jean was running toward him, pale and sweating.

"Is something wrong?"

"I must talk to Louis." Obviously shaken, Jean sprinted for their fastest horse while Martin went for the tack. Jean jumped on its back.

Martin tensed. "What is it, Jean?"

Dread was apparent in his reply. "I'll tell you later." He bolted up the street.

As he awaited Jean's return, every passerby drew Martin's attention. He cracked his knuckles so many times his hands hurt. To pass the time, he decided to let Quentin practice his riding skills.

When Jean finally returned, Martin lifted the boy down and asked him to help Elisabeth with dinner. "We'll be there shortly."

As soon as Quentin left, Jean's face turned somber, and an ominous mood filled the air. Martin held his breath and waited.

Nervously running his hand through his hair, Jean said, "Father Michel is accusing you of sedition."

Martin's jaw dropped as a thousand thoughts ran through his mind. The words he eventually settled on were, "I must pack."

"I went to see if Louis could do anything."

"Oh, Jean, you should not have done that. You'll ruin a lifelong friendship. There is nothing anyone can do."

"No, Martin, you're like a son to me. I'll not sit by and let this happen."

Humbled by the words, Martin lowered his head. "Thank you. I feel the same way, but I've been through this before. Will you take care of Quentin for me?"

Instead of replying, Jean scratched his eyebrow and frowned. "Well, he's the reason you cannot go just yet. The priest is after him too."

Disbelieving, Martin raised his hand to cover his mouth. "No, what has that boy done?" Martin paced around the yard.

"The child is trapped. If he returns to Schirmeck, he'll face charges of witchcraft, but he may not be able to stay here."

Both men stood in silence until Jean said, "When Father Michel advised me of his plans, I told him that I know what he did, and I am going to report him to Count Frédéric."

Confused, Martin asked, "What did Father Michel do?"

"I have no idea, but he must have done something because he paled and left, so Louis said to wait and see if the priest presses charges. In the meantime, we are to continue with that charade and act as if we are not afraid of him. If they come for you, Louis will warn me in time for you to flee, but you must prepare."

Jean patted Martin's back. "Come on; I'm starved."

As they walked toward the house, Martin said, "What should we tell Quentin?"

"I'm not sure. He has just begun to feel safe here," Jean said with a sigh.

"I wonder . . . why now?"

The week dragged along as Martin tried to remain focused, but the gravity of the situation weighed in the air at La Goutte de Paradis. As they were finishing their dinner at the estate on Saturday afternoon, Louis surprised them with a knock at the door. They settled by the fireplace in the parlor while Elisabeth hovered over Martin, placing her hand on his shoulder.

"Join us, Elisabeth," Louis said. "I have good news. Father Michel has not pressed charges yet, and I am beginning to doubt he will. I made up some excuse to see him today, and he never mentioned a word about it."

Tears of relief stung Martin's eyes, and he lowered his head quickly.

"Perhaps your bluff worked, Jean," Louis continued. "The priest must be afraid of something he has done, but I have not found what it is. Do any of you know who may have an issue with him?"

Martin said, "Did you talk to Humbert Cathillon?"

Everyone turned to him, waiting for more.

"While Nicolas was recovering, Father Michel came—"

Elisabeth's eyes widened in remembrance. "Yes, I had asked him to give Nicolas a blessing."

Martin nodded. "Humbert had words with him, and Father Michel left immediately."

Louis flattened his beard and stared at the fireplace thoughtfully. "Father Michel had threatened Humbert before Father Brignon's murder, but the murderer confessed. I will speak with Humbert. In the meantime, attend Mass tomorrow and act normally."

SINCE Jean-Baptiste's wedding, Catherine made weekly visits to the newlyweds. In mid-May, she found her sister-in-law's face swollen, eye blackened, and lip split, injuries inconsistent with her explanation of falling into the door. Catherine prodded her until Dimanchette admitted Jean-Baptiste had beaten her, and to Catherine's dismay, this was not the first time.

"It's my fault," Dimanchette added. "After work, he stopped for ale, and I fell asleep waiting for him." She dabbed her tears with a handkerchief and twirled it in her fingers. "I let his supper go cold."

Struggling to understand, Catherine stared at her friend's swollen belly. Jean-Baptiste had always had a quick temper, but she never suspected he would beat his wife. Dimanchette lowered her head, trembling in fear, and Catherine embraced her. "Papa will speak to my brother."

"No, please, he will beat me again."

"Papa will not let him beat you."

"My husband is better than most; he only beats me when he drinks."

"How can you defend him when he treats you like this?" Catherine said angrily. "Why do you want to live like this?" The house, supplied by the mine, was little more than a shack with paper-thin walls. The thatched roof needed replacing, where birds, searching for insects and seeds, had damaged the straw. The leaks turned the dirt floor into mud.

Dimanchette dabbed her eyes. "I know he loves me, but he hates his job, and his overseer mistreats him. Besides, all men beat their wives."

"No, Papa has never . . . Stop defending him!"

Mémé's words popped into her head; Aunt Agnes almost died with her first child. "Please, Dimanchette, have Jean-Baptiste bring you to our house so Mémé can take care of you."

"I will."

As Catherine walked home, she was so disappointed in her brother that she didn't notice the three men staggering toward her until it was too late. Her breath caught in her throat, and she leaped behind the blackthorn scrubs growing along the road—but they saw her.

"Come out of there, baby. We'll not harm you," one of them called.

Alone and defenseless, her heart pounded. She broke off a limb, bending it with a large thorn sticking out of her fist before peering through the branches. She sighed in relief at the sight of Sir Guy, the emerald-eyed troubadour who had occupied her dreams so many times. She moved out of the bushes, hoping he recognized her too.

The man to his left sneered, revealing decaying teeth. "Hey, she likes you."

Those striking green eyes narrowed. "Yes, I remember—you are the niece of that fat pig who kicked me out of his inn." Sir Guy seized her arm.

A cold chill coursed through her veins, and Catherine swung her fist, holding the thorn toward the singer's face. He shrieked and jumped back, but his accomplices threw her down, knocking the wind out of her.

Dazed, her head swimming, she tried to stand. She heard shouts, a scuffle, and as she struggled to catch her breath, someone took her arm. She sprang at him, swinging, but he spoke to her softly.

"Whoa, it's all right now. You're safe."

Trembling so hard that her teeth chattered, Catherine raised her gaze. The drunks were gone. She must have passed out. She touched her forehead and tried to calm her breath.

It took a moment to realize what had happened and to recognize Nicolas. She had never seen him like this, dressed in finery. He was taller, more muscular, his hair was much longer, and his face was chiseled and mature. For three years, she had practiced what she would say to him if this moment ever came. But now, her mind was blank. "Nicolas?"

Recognition registered in his eyes. He whispered, "Catherine?" and raised his hand toward her skinned cheek. But someone pulled him away—a beautiful woman. Her copper hair flashed in the sun, and her lips were the deepest red Catherine had ever seen.

The woman looked down her nose. "Catherine? Is this your peasant girl? Why, she is cute."

Slowly coming to her senses, Catherine gaped at the woman. Her green damask gown's square neckline almost reached to her underarms, her breasts overflowing and looking like they would choke her. She had pearls around her neck and gloves on her hands.

Catherine peered down at her own kirtle, wrinkled and dirty from the scuffle, and clutched the coarse folds of linen. Though she had chosen her best dress to go to Framont and visit Dimanchette, it looked like rags beside this woman's clothes. Suddenly, she realized her place, and her mother's words echoed in her mind. *Tradesmen marry daughters of tradesmen, and peasants marry peasants.*

With her cheeks burning, she pulled away from Nicolas's grasp, lowered her head to hide the tears, and curtsied. "Thank you for your assistance," she said as she jumped off the bank by the bridge and slid down on her bottom, splashing through the stream without even trying to step on the rocks. The water stung her scraped legs and elbows.

Nicolas shouted something, but she let the wind carry his words away. *Don't turn around, don't turn around . . .*

At the crest of the hill, with as much dignity as she could muster, she raised her head, squared her shoulders, and walked on.

As Nicolas watched Catherine run from him, he slumped. She was even more beautiful than in his dreams.

Salomé pulled out her kerchief, grabbed his chin, and wiped the blood from his split lip. "Come quickly, my darling; we're late."

The ride through the countryside was a blur, his mind numb. Though he knew Balthazar and Claire would be happy together, Nicolas dreaded this betrothal party. Salomé chatted on and on about her dress, her hair. *Do you ever talk about anything but yourself?* That irritating voice was impossible to ignore. By the time they reached Claire's house, he realized he had been clenching his teeth the entire trip, and he had a pounding headache. He scarcely raised his eyes to greet his host and retreated to the corner with a goblet of wine. Besides Balthazar refilling Nicolas's drink and speaking to him occasionally, his cup was his best friend for most of the evening.

After what seemed like hours of incessant gossip, Balthazar asked about his swollen lip.

"The poor boy risked life and limb for his peasant girl," Salomé said, fanning herself.

"Please," Nicolas muttered, "I have a headache."

Trying to drum up support, she looked around the room. "Peasants always find themselves in these situations, then whine about their lowly circumstance."

Through clenched teeth, he said, "Salomé, I'm warning you."

"Oh, come now, Nicolas, your little peasant was alone with three men. It was no accident; things simply got out of hand."

He could not stop his anger. "You know nothing about her, and you'll not talk about her like this." His voice was louder than he'd wanted.

Salomé responded with a flutter of eyelashes. "Why are you shouting at me in front of our friends?"

Pompous, insincere, shallow . . . "I need some air."

Balthazar followed Nicolas to the courtyard. "Girl problems?"

"That's putting it mildly." Nicolas sighed. "I'm sorry to cause a scene at your celebration."

"Don't think twice about it. Come back inside; we have enough wine to make you forget all your problems."

The trip home was unbearable, the silence deafening. At Salomé's house, Nicolas handed the reins to the groomsman and helped her down. Following a stone path lined with rosebushes and lit with lanterns, he escorted her across the manicured courtyard to the door. There, Nicolas tried to remove her hand from the crook of his elbow, but she pulled him inside. Brown eyes, soft and pouty, flickered with the lamplight.

"I'm sorry, Nicolas. Come have a drink with me, and we can talk. My parents have gone for the weekend."

But Nicolas remained rooted in the doorway. "I have nothing more to say to you."

"Oh, darling, are we going to allow one little misunderstanding to come between us?" She took off her cloak, threw it over the back of an upholstered chair, and ran her fingers down her long, slender neck, pulling her bodice off her shoulder.

He stared at her nearly exposed breast. He'd drunk too much wine. She pressed herself against him and touched him through his slops. The scent of her perfume fogged his mind.

"Come in and close the door."

Is her tongue forked and hissing? "That's your way, Salomé. Take off your clothes—"

Her face mottled crimson, and she slapped him, opening his lip again. Stunned by the taste of his own blood, he clenched his jaw, inhaled deeply, and turned on his heel.

"If you go out that door, it will be over between us."

His mother's disappointment crossed his mind briefly, but he didn't care. He went out into the night. Not wanting to go home to that sweltering attic, he rode aimlessly, regretting the wine he'd drunk. Catherine's tear-filled eyes flooded benumbed thoughts; his eyelids grew heavy.

When he came out of his stupor, darkness had fallen. The moon hung high in the sky. The landscape glowed in every shade of silver. His horse stood at the side of the road eating grass, and Nicolas realized it had wandered all the way to the road to Vacquenoux. At the bridge, Nicolas stared at the rock formation. As if on cue, a wolf howled in the distance.

Catherine used to look at him as if he were someone special. He had to see her.

Steering his horse off the bridge and down the embankment where she had fled earlier that day, he stopped near the swimming hole where she had danced barefoot. He paused at the oak tree—what would he have done if the wolves had not interrupted them? He was not even sure he knew what to do back then, but he'd have figured it out if given a chance. Still, he'd never have hurt her. Continuing the path, he argued with himself the whole way to the knoll above the Cathillon house.

Moonlight brightened the courtyard in a silvery glow. The night had never seemed so clear. The flowery smell and homey feel of the dried herbs hanging from the rafters in the quaint little house filled his mind—but what was he doing here now?

With a heavy heart, he decided to go to his parents' house tonight and miss work tomorrow. At this point, a few hours' sleep would be worth his brother's wrath and his mother's lecture.

Halfway home, Catherine collapsed in the grass, sobbing until no tears were left. Had Nicolas ever loved her? He'd never said the words. She rolled onto her back and stared at the clouds. Though Nicolas had said he wanted her, Anne claimed the two things were not the same. Catherine missed her sister so much. Anne would know how to make her feel better, but she was gone.

All Catherine wanted was sleep. She trudged home, brushed off her mother's concern at her soiled clothes and skinned cheek, and went straight to bed without supper.

The heat from the chimney made the loft oppressive, waking her in the middle of the night, and she kicked off her blanket and lay awake while everyone else slept. The air brimmed with the sweet smell of bracken and straw.

Branches tapped against the roof, too quiet to cover the sound of her brother snoring on the other side of the room. She rolled over to find her younger sister hogging her pillow and breathing in her face.

The oiled skin covering the window had partially fallen, blocking the fresh air. Catherine rose and stuck her head out the window. The moon hung silently amid a million stars while the distant cries of wolves drifted in the darkness beyond the barnyard. A cold breeze caught her, and she shivered.

On the knoll above the house—a man on a white horse, wearing a white shirt, sitting there, motionless. Transfixed, she stood there, watching him. He faded in and out as clouds rolled over the moon. How long had he been there? She squinted, but all she could see was the outline of the white shirt. Occasionally, the man's sleeves and the horse's long tail billowed in the wind.

Then, for no apparent reason, he turned and disappeared into the darkness.

She watched for a while, and when he didn't return, she went back to bed. Was he real or was she dreaming?

When the sky lightened, Catherine dressed and went to the barn to help her father, who flinched at her bruised cheek.

"Who did this to you?"

Her eye felt swollen, but she'd thought it was from crying. She touched her cheek lightly before brushing him off. "Oh, I'm fine. But you need to check on Dimanchette."

He took her arm. "Your eye is blackened. Who did this to you, Catherine? Tell me. Why were you crying?"

She didn't want to tell him and pulled away. "I'm not hurt. I saw Nicolas."

"Nicolas!" Humbert's eyes filled with fury, and he started toward the horse tack. "I'll kill him."

She grasped his arm. "Papa! Listen to me! It was three drunkards—Nicolas saved me. One was Sir Guy, that troubadour from the inn."

He straightened and gawked at her. "The troubadour?"

"He's gone, Papa, please. Dimanchette is not well, and I'm worried about her. Jean-Baptiste beat her. I should have said something last night, but she begged me not to tell."

His expression changed to disappointment and disbelief. "He . . . beat her? Are you sure?"

"She admitted it. She's afraid of him."

chapter

18

THE midday sun shining through Nicolas's window woke him from a deep sleep. His eyelids were swollen and heavy, and his head throbbed from the wine. It took a moment to remember the previous day's events. His mouth tasted fuzzy, and he flinched when he ran his tongue over his swollen lip. He crawled out of bed and slogged to the kitchen.

"Good morning, Mama."

Elisabeth smirked. "Morning? I thought you needed an incentive to get out of bed." She cut into a warm loaf of bread and handed Nicolas a slice. "You startled me when you came in last night. You should have said you were coming. What were you doing out so late?"

Instead of answering, he kissed her cheek, snatched another slice, and looked out the door. "Is Papa at the forge?"

At her nod, Nicolas stepped outside, where the intensity of the sunlight burned his eyes. As he walked down the hill, the craggy path seemed to be moving under his feet. He found his father alone, heating a horseshoe in the flames. Nicolas added some charcoal to the fire. "Where's Quentin?"

"Helping Martin muck the stalls. I'll be just a minute."

Jean grasped the white-hot metal with a long pair of tongs. Sparks flew as he pounded the shoe around the anvil's horn. Satisfied, he placed the shoe in a bucket of water, and immediately a loud sizzle and a puff of steam filled the air. He took off his heavy gloves.

"What's on your mind, son?"

"I broke off the courtship with Salomé."

Jean paled. "When? Why?"

Of all the reactions Nicolas had expected from his father, shock was not one of them. "Last night. I couldn't stand her for one more minute. Did you hear about the carriage wheel?" Not waiting for an answer, he continued, "And she called Catherine a peasant."

"That Cathillon girl?"

"She's not a peasant."

"There is something you need to know, son." Jean motioned to a bench in the shade, and his forehead creased with concern. "We need to talk."

"What's wrong, Papa?"

"Martin has been accused of sedition," Jean said, tapping his fingers on his knee. "The issue may have passed, but Louis believes Salomé was the instigator."

"No, Salomé is spoiled and selfish, but . . . Why do you think she betrayed us?"

"There's no proof, son. We suspected her since she was here just before the accusation."

Jean continued to tap his fingers nervously. Nicolas stared at them. *Could Salomé have acted so maliciously behind his back?* He stood, folded his arms, and thought furiously. Monsieur Müller railed that all Protestants were heretics, but would she? With his back to his father, Nicolas said, "Those rumors might have been brewing for a while. Perhaps it was—it could have been—well, it could have been someone else."

"Yes, you're right. It might have been a coincidence, and since you have ended the courtship, it doesn't matter."

Nicolas turned to face his father. "What will happen to Martin?"

"We can only wait and see, but Louis wants to talk to you."

Nodding, Nicolas returned to the bench. "I'll stop by his house on my way home."

A long silence followed before his father said, "And how is your masterpiece coming along?"

The rest of the morning flew as Nicolas worked with his father, but to avoid his mother's lecture on commitment, he left at the midday break. At Louis's house, Louise greeted him with red-rimmed eyes.

"Papa's down there," she said, pointing to the same path Nicolas and Salomé had once strolled.

Obviously, Louise had been crying, and Nicolas shifted uncomfortably. "Thank you," he said without letting on that he noticed.

A twinge of guilt swept over him as he passed the abandoned tool shed where he and Salomé . . . Was that the only reason he had stayed with her for so long? Was he really that shallow? He didn't want to think about it.

The glare of the afternoon sun burned his eyes, and he promised himself he would never drink that much wine again.

At the river, Louis was sitting on a large rock, flicking his line.

"Are the fish biting today?" Nicolas asked with a smile.

The furious glare Louis returned softened when he recognized Nicolas. "Oh, Nicolas. I want to talk to you, but I rarely spend time at the river. Do you mind?"

"Of course not."

"Good." He cast his line.

Nicolas settled beside him and gazed at the rippling water. "I heard about Martin. Papa thinks Salomé is behind the accusation, but I cannot believe it. Have you found anything more?"

Still angry about something, Louis clenched his jaw before saying, "I'm not sure who made the allegations, but I did a bit of checking, and there is no way to say this gently . . ."

At his hesitation, Nicolas turned toward him. "Should I be worried?"

"Did you know Salomé bought birth prevention powder from Magdalena?"

The weight of the air pushed down on him, making it hard to breathe. He turned away and inhaled, burning with embarrassment. "She . . . she said she knew what she was doing, but I . . . I never asked her." A long moment of silence passed as his heart pounded.

Louis turned his gaze back to the river and said, "Salomé was lucky Magdalena did not live to testify."

"Magdalena," Nicolas whispered.

Without turning his eyes from his line, Louis said, "Do you know why Salomé visited Strasbourg?"

What does one question have to do with the other? "Strasbourg? To nurse her sick aunt."

Another pause with Louis staring at his fishing line, ignoring that it was moving erratically with a hooked fish. The silence gnawed at Nicolas until he said, "Maybe Louise could tell you more; they're good friends."

That furious look again. "Not any longer," Louis said through clenched teeth.

Louise was crying. Nicolas squirmed.

Calming just a little, Louis added, "Do you love this girl, Nicolas?"

"No, monsieur, we're not together any longer."

Still staring straight ahead, Louis said, "Did you break off the courtship before or after Strasbourg?"

Nicolas swallowed hard. "I broke it off yesterday. Do you want me to talk to her? Salomé probably hates me now, but if it would help Martin and Quentin, I could ask her."

Finally, Louis exhaled, releasing the creases on his forehead. "No, that will not be necessary. Thank you."

With his thoughts swirling, Nicolas nodded and hurried away. Salomé had bought her product from Magdalena. What if Magdalena had testified? That poor woman only wanted to feed her children. *Oh my God, Salomé might have been arrested—and burned.*

By the time he reached his brother's house, his stomach had flipped. There was no one he could confide in; he had to live with this. He went straight to the attic and fell onto the bed.

The next day after work, Nicolas debated with Balthazar whether to stop for ale on their way home. "I came to work yesterday while you slept in," Balthazar complained. "I'm going home; I need a nap."

"Yes." Nicolas touched his still tender lip. "Tomorrow." They started to walk away when someone whispered, "Nicolas."

"Pardon?"

"Huh?"

Nicolas turned, looking behind him. "I could swear someone said my name." He scanned up and down the street. "But it must have been the wind."

"There's no wind today."

Suddenly, his mouth went dry. "Let's get that drink."

Sighing in agreement, Balthazar followed.

To their surprise, only one patron was inside, sitting in a dark corner and concentrating on his untouched mug. Nicolas recognized the man.

"Jean-Baptiste?" Catherine's brother was a regular and usually had a few too many. Sure enough, his eyes were bloodshot, but as Nicolas approached the table, he noticed those eyes were not glazed from drink, but they held the most sorrowful air he had ever seen. "Are you all right? How long have you been here, my friend?"

"I've killed him," Jean-Baptiste whispered. He lowered his head and closed his eyes.

"Killed? What did you kill?"

Two burly men entered the tavern and flanked them. Nicolas recognized the pair as Jean-Baptiste's friends. Both had chestnut hair and freckles.

"There he is—I should have known he'd be in here," the taller one hissed.

The innkeeper pointed toward the door. "Take it outside."

The two men ripped Jean-Baptiste out of his chair.

Nicolas jumped up. "Leave him alone; he's drunk."

Jean-Baptiste shook Nicolas off. "Stay out of this, Nicolas. I deserve whatever they give me."

Nicolas watched in dismay as the men dragged Jean-Baptiste to the street, where he stood with his arms at his sides, taking punch after punch without even trying to defend himself.

"What are you doing?" Nicolas demanded, stepping between them.

But Jean-Baptiste again pushed him out of the way. "Stay out of it, Nicolas."

Another blow to Jean-Baptiste's face. Blood and spit flew. He staggered but regained his footing until another bone-shattering blow to the ribs knocked him to his knees, and the two men kicked his face until he lay motionless in the dirt.

Nicolas grabbed the tall one's arm, shouting, "Stop it, you're going to kill him!"

The man spun and landed a sharp blow to Nicolas's face, the other man, on Balthazar, who had jumped into the fray. A crowd gathered and the instigators raised their hands in surrender. The two men spat on Jean-Baptiste as they left.

With his face swollen and covered in blood, Catherine's brother was unrecognizable. Nicolas and Balthazar pulled him up, slipped their arms around his waist, dragged him to his shack, and helped him onto his pallet.

Nicolas asked, "Where's your wife? We cannot leave you here like this. Let me take you to your father's house."

"No, please," Jean-Baptiste moaned. "I'm no good. Let me die."

"Will you sit with him while I fetch the wagon?" Nicolas asked Balthazar.

"Of course."

Suddenly, the door swung open, and Nicolas spun and sighed in relief. "Monsieur Humbert, thank heavens."

Humbert brushed past them to his son on the pallet, then stood and stared furiously at Nicolas and Balthazar. "What is going on here? My son has enough problems, and you get him into another fight?"

Nicolas flinched. The accusation infuriated him. He clenched his jaw. "You misjudge me, monsieur. Again."

"Papa, no," Jean-Baptiste moaned.

Balthazar approached Humbert and said in dismay, "Monsieur, we found him—"

But Nicolas grasped his arm and bowed mockingly.

"Don't bother, Balthazar. Monsieur Humbert knows everything." He pushed his friend and followed him out the door.

THE next day, Nicolas's headache had returned, and he was surly all day. Though the other workers teased him about his fat lip and fresh black eye, he ignored them and went straight home after work. He had no sooner flopped on his pallet than Le-Chêne called him from the bottom of the stairs.

"Come here, please, Nicolas."

"I just got home. Can I get a little rest?"

"Now," came the command he dared not refuse.

Le-Chêne met him with a scowl and led him into the parlor, where Humbert Cathillon, hat in hand, stood staring into the fireplace. Nicolas crossed his arms and glared.

Humbert met his gaze and said, "I must speak with you, monsieur."

When has Humbert ever called me "monsieur"?

"Excuse me," Le-Chêne said and turned to leave.

"You should hear this too, Le-Chêne," Humbert said. "Jean-Baptiste told me what happened yesterday. When I spotted your battered face, I jumped to conclusions. Perhaps because of what I had seen, right here in this room." Lowering his eyes, Humbert paused before continuing, "However, I was wrong then too. Joseph admitted that he asked you to lie. I wanted to thank you for what you did for Catherine as well, but with everything else going on . . ." Humbert sighed and shook his head. "I did misjudge you, and I'm sorry."

He turned to Le-Chêne. "Nicolas lied the last time I saw you, but he had a reason. He wasn't fighting, he was saving my son from drowning, and Joseph repaid Nicolas by asking him to lie—which he did, placing himself in an unflattering light. Then he saved my daughter from three drunkards, and yesterday he saved my eldest son. You should be proud of your brother. I am proud to say that I know him. That's all I came to say."

Humbert turned to leave. Stunned, Nicolas stared at his back but pulled himself together. "Wait. Does this mean I can call on Catherine?"

Humbert shot him a sideways glare. "You mistake my intentions. Catherine will not see a betrothed man."

"Me? I'm not betrothed. There is no contract."

"Jean-Baptiste said you were to marry the girl."

"No, he misunderstood. I would like permission to court Catherine."

Humbert's stern eyes glanced at Le-Chêne, who nodded, then lowered until a smile spread slowly across his face. "You are welcome in our home."

Disbelieving the change of events, Nicolas beamed at Le-Chêne and shook Humbert's hand. "May I go now?"

Humbert stared at him for a long moment. "Go."

Without hesitation, Nicolas rushed toward the stable for his horse, then rode toward Le Petit-Courty, where he found Marie in the courtyard, rubbing laundry on a washboard while Francisca carried a bucket to her.

The old woman stopped and turned, but this time when those black eyes bored into him, her gaze was soft. She spoke to Marie, who wiped her hands on her apron and approached him, wincing at his bruises. "Nicolas, what a surprise."

"Yes, a pleasant surprise."

Small lines had appeared beside Marie's pale blue eyes. More importantly, Marie gave him a warm smile and didn't appear angry with him.

"You came to see Catherine?"

"Yes, madame."

She led him toward the house and shouted through the doorway, "Lovey." Then she patted his arm and returned to the laundry.

"Coming, Mama," came a voice from inside the house.

Half-hidden behind an armload of dirty laundry, Catherine appeared in the doorway. The bruise on her cheek had darkened to a purplish green. Her worn apron covered her faded work dress, her hair pulled back in a simple bun with stray strands sticking out everywhere.

She gasped, "Nicolas," and her gaze dropped to the floor.

"Nicolas?" Jean-Baptiste shuffled up behind her. One of his eyes had swollen shut, and he held his back as he limped past her, grasped Nicolas's arm, and led him inside toward the big table.

"Do you remember my wife, Dimanchette?"

Nicolas nodded in greeting to Jean Babtiste's wife. She looked pale, and a yellow shadow darkened her right eye. *She was heavy with child the last time*

I saw her, but now . . . He saw no baby things and felt the tinge of sadness in the air. He forced his attention to Jean-Baptiste, then to Catherine, who disappeared out the door.

"Of course," Nicolas said, forcing his attention back to them. "Good to see you again."

"I want to apologize for the way Papa mistreated you yesterday," Jean-Baptiste said, holding his middle and letting out a moan as he lowered himself to sit beside his wife.

"I spoke with your father, and he invited me here. How do you feel?"

"Much better. I'm sorry to get you caught up in the middle of . . . my mess." Jean-Baptiste grimaced through a swollen lip, and his eyes glistened. "I'm really sorry."

"Don't worry—I'll heal."

"Well, I owe you one."

"Someday, I might collect." Nicolas chuckled. "But who were those men? I have seen them with you a dozen times; I thought they were your friends."

Dimanchette shifted uncomfortably. Her chestnut hair was the same color as the men who had beaten Jean-Baptiste—they must be her brothers. *And she has a black eye? But . . . did he kill someone?*

Speaking more to his wife than Nicolas, Jean-Baptiste said, "Yes, they are my friends, my good friends."

Nicolas fidgeted. He shouldn't be prying. "I came to speak with Catherine. Would you excuse me?"

Without waiting for a reply, he hurried out the door and found her in a heated discussion with Marie, who nodded in his direction. This meeting was not going as he had thought, but what had he expected? That Catherine would rush into his arms, take his hand, and they would run through a field of flowers, fall to the ground, and make love—like in his books? She didn't even want to talk to him.

"May I speak with you, Catherine?"

With an irritated sigh, she gestured toward the bench under the big tree where he had read to her while recuperating. Without lifting her eyes from the ground, she sat primly and folded her hands in her lap. She acted so differently than he had remembered. He sat beside her, and an awkward silence followed until she spoke.

"Why are you here, Nicolas?"

Stung, his reply came out as a whisper. "I wanted to see you. I've been worried about you since the other day."

"I'm fine, thank you," she said, rubbing a stain on her apron with her thumb.

His heart pounded in his ears. "I felt awful when Salomé called you a—" He stopped and inhaled. "I know she hurt your feelings."

"Why would being called a peasant hurt my feelings?" Catherine's concentration shifted from the stain to a bumblebee as it moved from clover to clover. "I am a peasant, and that is all I will ever be." Catherine turned away, but not before tears filled her eyes.

Knowing he was responsible for them, Nicolas frowned. "No, you are not a peasant, Catherine."

Angry now, she lifted her apron. "Look at me, Nicolas. These are peasant clothes." She pointed to her mother draping the laundry over the fence. "These are peasant chores."

"No, you are a farmer's daughter. Even if you were a peasant, I wouldn't care. I love you."

She caught her breath.

Humbert's reaction popped into Nicolas's mind, and he realized she might also think he was betrothed. He took her hand, and she pulled it away.

"Catherine." He knelt before her. "I am not betrothed; I have never made a promise to marry."

She stared at their clasped hands and whispered as if she hadn't heard him, "She's so beautiful."

"No, it's just hair dye, face paint, and expensive clothes. You're more beautiful than she could ever hope to be." This time when he took her hand, she didn't move, and he stroked it with his thumb. "Salomé and I are not courting any longer. I asked your papa for permission to court you. Your papa said yes."

Nicolas leaned forward and looked up at her until she turned to him.

"I love you, Catherine. I've never stopped loving you."

When she remained silent, he struggled to think of something else to say that would convince her.

"You used to look at me as if I were special, even smart."

"But you are smart." The tears in her eyes spilled over, and he wiped them away.

"You're the only person in the world who thinks so."

He raised her trembling hands to his lips. When she didn't pull away, he stood and helped her to her feet, gently removed her coif, and smoothed her hair, looking deeply into those beautiful silver eyes. She held his gaze.

Burying his hands in her long dark hair, he kissed her forehead and trailed his lips over her cheek. He cupped her face with his hands and kissed her with such passion and longing she went limp in his arms. She clung to him, and he held her head tightly against his chest, hoping she could feel his heart pounding as loudly as he could hear it in his ears.

He sensed someone standing behind him and turned to find Joseph quietly waiting. "Mama wants to know if you're staying for supper, but Mémé said the Wild Hunt of the Demon Hellequin would start soon, and you should come back another time."

"The Hellequin?" Nicolas chuckled. "Now there's an old legend. Will the demons be flying tonight, searching for souls, Joseph?"

The boy's eyes were serious. "Yes, as soon as it gets dark. You cannot outrun them. You must be inside before dark, monsieur."

Since the last time Nicolas had seen Joseph at the swimming hole, he had matured and had grown into his teeth, but he still had that childlike twinkle in his eyes.

Though Nicolas turned back to Catherine, he replied to Joseph, "Tell your mama thanks, but Madame Francisca is right. I'll come back tomorrow after work."

"That is a long ride for a short visit," Catherine replied.

"But it's worth it."

He took her arm, and they slowly walked toward the gate. The evening air chilled, and the sun hung low in the sky when they arrived at the road.

"If the rose is life, pick me," Nicolas whispered against her cheek as he left.

HE Sunday visit to Nicolas's parents' house was a blur. He needed nudging when it was time to stand and kneel during Mass, and at dinner he picked the peas out of his pie and ate them one at a time, paying little attention to the conversation.

His mother touched his hand, rousting him from his reverie. "Nicolas? Your father asked you a question."

"Pardon?"

An irritated smile preceded Jean's reply, "I said, Salomé denied being the accuser, and Louis thinks the issue has passed."

Hoping to dismiss the conversation, Nicolas shrugged. "I told you it wasn't her."

"No, Louis didn't say she didn't do it; he said she denied it, and he found something he thought would scare her. It must have."

"What's she hiding, Nicolas?" His mother's tone was stern.

Magdalena . . . "How should I know?"

"That is none of our business, Elisabeth," Jean said, but his eyes widened, and he chuckled. "Oh, Louis also told me something else—his wife is having another baby."

"Ha, she's too old." Nicolas snickered.

Elisabeth stiffened. "That is not a subject for you to—"

"She's as old as—"

"Nevertheless, she is with child," Jean cut in, clearing his throat. "But Louis is worried about her age, and they have decided she should go to Strasbourg, where she will have access to a physician."

The glare Elisabeth shot Nicolas stopped the rest of his debate.

"A city as large as Strasbourg probably has many physicians," Martin said.

"I thought it was a good idea," Jean added. "And Louise is going with her."

Perhaps Louise was crying because she didn't want to go.

"Well." Rachelle set down her spoon, smiled widely, and nodded toward her husband. Le-Chêne winked at her. "Speaking of babies . . ." He lifted his goblet in a toast. "Another one is on the way."

Everyone raised a glass at the news.

Then, Le-Chêne added, "And I almost forgot we have a hero in our midst. Nicolas, are you going to enlighten everyone about your little lie, or should I tell them?"

Elisabeth scowled. "What lie?"

Indifferent, Nicolas shrugged. "Go ahead and tell them."

"He thinks what he did was insignificant," Le-Chêne explained. "Remember the day Francisca came to our house to care for Marguerite? Nicolas got a black eye and said he had been fighting at the tavern? In truth, he saved the young Cathillon boy from drowning."

"Why would you let us think the worst of you?" Elisabeth touched his arm. "You finally did something to make us proud."

"Finally," Nicolas mumbled.

"Not finally." Jean shot her a scalding glance.

"That is not what I meant. We are proud of you, Nicolas, but why would you not tell us?"

"Oh, that's not the whole story," Le-Chêne continued. "Apparently, Monsieur Hero also did something to save two others in their family, but I didn't understand Humbert's explanation, nor will little brother elaborate, as modest as he is."

"It was trifling."

"Well, it doesn't sound trifling, son." Jean raised his goblet in salute before taking a drink. "And how is your masterpiece coming along? Almost done?"

"Ummm," Nicolas replied. "Well, I've not worked on it lately because I have been working on this." A flash of light glinted off the metal of the ring he pulled from his bag and laid on the table. "I bought the silver and worked on it during breaks. I hope it will fit her."

Rubbing the ring in his palm, Jean replied with dismay, "It's beautiful."

Unable to contain his smile, Nicolas said, "I'm going to ask Catherine to marry me."

Incredulous, Elisabeth's jaw dropped, and she stared at him. "You cannot be serious. Last week you were upset after breaking off your courtship with Salomé, and this week you are—"

"No, Mama, ending the courtship was my idea."

Jean handed the ring back to him. "Well, I'm glad you and Salomé are not together, but you've not seen Catherine in years. People change. Your first goal must be your masterpiece."

Martin said, "Nicolas, are you sure you are not, as Ronsard suggested, *desiring what was denied you?*"

"No," Nicolas snapped.

Eyes wide and fingers on her lips in shock, Elisabeth stared at him. "Why are you rushing into this? Your brother courted Rachelle for two years before they married. Is Catherine . . . with child?"

"That's enough!" Nicolas stood and threw his serviette, his face burning. "No matter how hard I try, I will never live up to my big brother."

As if singed, Le-Chêne rose and pointed toward him. "One minute I praise you, and the next you criticize me? The only person comparing us is you. Now sit down and discuss this like a man."

Wide-eyed, Jean stood. "Elisabeth! Why would you pit your sons against each other? Nicolas, your mother did not mean to compare you. Forever is a long time. We want you to be sure." Calmer now, he continued, "I respect Humbert, and Catherine is a nice girl. I would welcome her into our family, but you must finish your masterpiece so you can provide."

Nicolas turned his gaze from his father to Le-Chêne. "I overreacted, I'm sorry, but Catherine certainly is not with child. You always think the worst of her."

Gently, Elisabeth took his hand. "I am sorry, Nicolas. I did not mean to suggest Catherine is not a nice girl, but people do not usually hasten into marriage unless . . ." Elisabeth's face reddened, and she lowered her gaze. "Well, never mind. Like your papa said, forever is a long time. I would never forbid you to marry someone you love. If you are sure this is what you want, she is welcome here. This is a big house."

That afternoon, Nicolas headed for the Cathillon farm, practicing what to say. When he arrived, the family greeted him warmly and invited him to join them at the big table. They already treated him as if he belonged. There was just the matter of getting Humbert alone.

As if Humbert had read his mind, he excused himself, fetched his pipe and pouch, and disappeared out the door. Nicolas saw his chance. Outside, Humbert leaned against the wall, packing the herbs into the bowl. He smacked the flint several times, but it wouldn't light. "Eehhh," he muttered in frustration, then stared at Nicolas. "Do you want something, boy?"

All his preparations and practice scenarios forgotten, Nicolas stammered, "I am sorry, Monsieur Humbert, I wanted to ask you properly—"

"Ask me what?"

Nicolas looked inside, and his eyes met Catherine's. She motioned for him to join her on a bench. Instead, he turned his attention back to Humbert. "Well, ummm . . ."

"If you want to say something, boy, say it."

Nicolas gathered his courage, raised his head, and spoke firmly, "Monsieur Humbert, I would like your permission to ask Catherine to marry me."

For the first time, Humbert smiled at Nicolas. He laid the pipe on the bench and embraced Nicolas with both arms. "I'd be proud to call you my son."

As Marie and Francisca stood to clear the table, Nicolas asked Catherine to join him for a walk. Arm in arm, they strolled to *their* tree by the stream, but before they settled, he scanned the field. "No wolves this time." He chuckled.

Catherine sat on the rock, and Nicolas knelt in front of her. Before he lost his nerve, he asked, "Will you marry me, Catherine?"

"This feels like a dream," she whispered.

"It is a dream, something I have dreamed of for a long time." He gazed into her eyes. *"If the rose is life, pick me."*

She pulled him up and jumped into his embrace. "Yes. Of course, yes."

That night, Catherine lay awake, trying to listen to her parents discuss her impending wedding. "Nicolas's parents are citizens," Marie said.

"Yes, they will expect a large dowry, and I want to give at least as much as Salomé's parents would have offered. I'll visit the mayor tomorrow and discuss the contract."

Catherine focused on the rafters. What was she doing? The tradesmen married daughters of the tradesmen, but she was not the daughter of a tradesman. How was she supposed to act in the presence of citizens? What should she say? She squeezed her eyes shut and prayed that whatever magic had brought them together would last forever.

Early the next morning, Jean came to their door, and Marie welcomed him with a curtsy.

"Bonjour, madame," he said, but instead of entering the house, he motioned to Humbert. "Would you walk with me, monsieur? It is a beautiful day."

Dread gnawed at Catherine. She positioned herself at the chair nearest the window to listen, but her mother looked at her sternly and set her to knead the bread.

When Humbert returned alone, he looked pale, and her stomach flipped. "What's wrong, Papa? Has Nicolas's father rejected me?"

"No, daughter," Humbert said with a forced smile. "Your wedding will take place. No need to worry."

Marie replied, "Why the look?"

Flopping on the bench, Humbert closed his eyes and pinched the crest of his nose as if in pain. "Yesterday, after Mass, Monsieur Jean heard Madame Müller ranting to the priest in front of everyone. She suggested Catherine is learning to be a witch from Francisca."

The air went out of the room. Catherine sank beside her father, who was staring into space. "He said Martin has been under investigation too."

An uncomfortable silence hung in the air. Humbert shifted his weight before turning to his daughter. "So you will be married as soon as possible. I still have Father Brignon's catechism, and I'll teach you everything you need to know. Monsieur Jean's brother is a priest and will perform the ceremony."

HAT Sunday, Catherine prepared for supper with Nicolas's parents, fretting over what to wear and her constantly unruly hair. Her hands shook so badly from nervous anticipation that Francisca made a calming tea.

The sky shimmered when Nicolas arrived in his parents' fine carriage to collect Catherine. On the way to his home, he discussed his progress on his masterpiece, proposed a betrothal party, and went over the wedding plans, all while Catherine wrung her hands.

"Is something wrong? You look pale." He lifted her hand to his lips.

She pictured Salomé in her gloves and pearls and swallowed hard. "No, I'm just a little nervous."

"Why? Nobody will be there but my family—you know everyone."

Perhaps, but aside from sharing a cup of ale at his brother's house when baby Marguerite was sick, Catherine had never spoken directly to any of them but Martin. "Yes, I do. I'm fine, thank you."

At the estate, everyone kissed her cheeks. She smiled but spoke in a voice barely above a whisper. When Martin and Quentin arrived, she relaxed a little, though she blamed Martin for breaking her sister's heart. The table was set with fine linens; meat pies were served on plates of tin, not wood; there were tin cups for wine; and they even had the curiosity they called "forks." Catherine watched the others for cues before taking a bite.

After they passed the food, Martin said, "A couple of young men stopped at the stable today on their way to Lorraine to enlist in the army. They say war is imminent."

Le-Chêne poured the wine and said, "I think the Duke of Guise is becoming too dependent on Spain. I mean, what will stop Spain from annexing France if they succeed in defeating Henry of Navarre?"

"Well, that is exactly what worries King Henry," Martin replied, "but Guise is so worried about a Protestant succeeding the throne, he will risk France's sovereignty. Another war is coming, and we will be caught in the middle again."

Never having been part of such a conversation, Catherine hung on every word, repeating the names to herself to help her remember them.

Jean added, "I should warn the neighboring farms to keep their families and animals close. Soldiers use Salm as a shortcut to France, and they steal whatever they want. Your family can testify to that, right, Catherine?"

Everyone turned to her, and she swallowed before replying, "Yes, monsieur."

"Don't be so formal, Catherine. Call me Papa."

"Yes," Elisabeth said, "we are all family here." She passed a tray of bread. "Tell us a little about yourself."

Catherine fiddled with her skirt. "There is not much to say; Nicolas taught me to read."

At that, Nicolas winked at her, and she blushed. "And Mémé is teaching me to treat illness. It's fascinating how plants growing by the road or in the forest can cure so many things."

Though Elisabeth's forehead creased in anger, her mouth turned up in a fake smile. "Well, once you are married, you'll not be able to accompany Francisca. You will have a house to care for and soon children."

"I enjoy helping people, madame."

The smile vanished, and Elisabeth's tone became sharp. "Think of the scandal. Can you imagine if Louis came here to search for heaven knows what? He is Jean's oldest and dearest friend. It would place us in an unpleasant situation."

"It might be best, Catherine," Martin added, "if you avoid putting yourself into a circumstance where you might be persecuted, whether for an honorable cause or not."

"Why do the authorities care if I try to heal someone?" Catherine replied, almost in a whimper.

"We are not uniting against you," Le-Chêne said. "Nobody appreciates what you do more than my family." He gazed at his sleeping toddler and turned back to her. "But you must realize superstitions run deep."

"And next week, you will join the religious community," Elisabeth said, finishing with the butter and handing it to Nicolas. "And the betrothal celebration afterward will introduce you to many more people who will see how sweet you are, and the rumors will cease."

All the wind had gone out of Catherine, and she lowered her gaze to her plate and pinched her leg to stop the tears. "Yes, madame." She felt like a child who had spilled the milk.

Elisabeth smiled again, another fake smile.

"Was that so bad?" Nicolas asked as he drove Catherine home.

Without raising her head, she replied, "No."

"What's wrong?"

The pitch of her voice rose. "What should I do, turn my back on a sick person?"

"Of course not, but remember when Louis came to arrest Francisca? The whole event was based on a lie."

"Nothing happened."

"What if you rushed into a stranger's house and it turned out to be a trap?"

"What are we doing that's so wrong?" Her reply sounded childish. Catherine corrected her posture, folded her hands in her lap, and stared at them.

"Martin has recently been under scrutiny. What did he do wrong? This is the way of the world."

Filled with desperation, she blurted, "Your mama doesn't like me."

Nicolas looked puzzled. "My mama doesn't know you. Give her time." He stopped the carriage and took her hand. "Would it bother you to live with my parents? I'll complete my project soon and will be able to afford a house."

Oh, he must think I'm a fool. Perhaps his parents were genuinely concerned about her well-being. "I shouldn't have said anything."

"Louis once offered me a job as a deputy. I will talk to him. I could probably start right away."

"Why would you do that? You are talented, and you love to make things."

He shrugged. "But I enjoyed chasing that murderer, and I wouldn't mind doing it for a living. Besides, I could still make things in my spare time." He kissed her hand. "I love you, Catherine, and I'll not be happy making things without you beside me."

She squeezed his hand. "You enjoyed chasing him, but what if the murderer had shot back? I was nervous and overreacted today. I'm sorry."

The last streaks of light led Nicolas up the mountainside toward his parents' house. A rabbit ran through the yard and drew his gaze across the field to their abandoned barn, unused since his grandfather had built the town stable. Looking critically at the building, Nicolas noted the beautiful stonework, wandered over, and went inside where the smell of old straw filled the air. Cobwebs hung from the rafters, nesting birds complained at his disturbance, and dust danced in the fading sunlight. Outside the back door, a natural spring flowed into a small pool where the horses used to drink. Smiling, he continued home.

"No son of mine is going to live in a barn," Elisabeth said. "What will people say?"

"It's not going to look like a barn."

"What did Catherine say?" Jean asked. "Women are fussy about where they sleep."

"The idea hit me on the way home, but Catherine will love it. I know she will."

"Well, her dowry is more than enough to make it livable, but you cannot even think about it until you complete your masterpiece."

"Yes, Papa. I'm almost done."

Everyone from Vacquenoux attended the betrothal party at La Goutte de Paradis, except Francisca and the Müllers, of course. Throughout the day, Nicolas stayed by Catherine's side while Jean and Elisabeth introduced Humbert and Marie through the guest list.

After everyone had left, Elisabeth rested on a chaise. "Whew, what a day. I must admit I was worried, but it turned out to be wonderful."

"Not the boorish, uneducated peasants you had expected?" said Nicolas.

She ignored the comment and added, "Their gowns were beautiful, and Catherine's sister, Anne, is stunning. Has she been gone for a while?"

"Yes, she left about a year ago and just came back for the wedding."

The empty wine barrels were stacked in Jean's cart. When Nicolas delivered them to the inn, Sebastien explained that his storeroom was full and asked if he would take them to Humbert's farm instead. While they rolled the barrels into the barn, Nicolas tried to pass the time with small talk but with little success.

"Thank you for buying the wine for the celebration. Everyone loved it," Nicolas said.

Humbert nodded.

"Martin told us about your vineyard."

As if stung, Humbert froze.

Nicolas wished he would learn to keep his mouth shut. He forced out, "I just wondered if you have ever made any wine?" He fidgeted and picked at his fingernails. Humbert lowered his gaze to the hay-strewn floor.

Time passed and Nicolas considered taking his leave, but then Humbert raised his eyes and said, "Walk with me."

Nicolas followed Humbert toward the tree line to the shed where he had been chastised for spying. Humbert opened the heavy wooden door, and they stepped inside. The shelves lining the back of the building were bare. A hammer and ax lay on a rickety table that stood against the wall.

"Lock the door behind you," Humbert said.

Tightness grew in Nicolas's stomach as he slid the bolt.

Humbert removed the shelves from their supports and handed them to Nicolas, who leaned them against the wall. Next, the back of the cabinet was removed in the same manner. Cool air burst into the shed, and anticipation swept over him as a dark passageway came into view.

With a determined stare, Humbert said, "I hope you realize you can never speak of this."

Anxious to see what lay hidden in the gloom, Nicolas blurted out, "Yes, monsieur, thank you for trusting me."

Humbert brought out a large lantern and struck his flint, bringing the wick to flame and brightening the damp shadows. "Be careful. The floor is slippery."

Nicolas followed Humbert into the dimly lit cave, where heavy, moist air sent a shiver down his spine. It took a moment for his eyes to adjust to the murkiness, but eventually he could make out barrel upon barrel lining the walls, ending about thirty feet away by a pile of rocks and dirt.

"This is an abandoned mineshaft. My uncle, Pierre . . ." Humbert hesitated and began again. "My parents died when I was ten years old. Father Brignon took me in, but I could not stay with him and went to live with his brother on the neighboring farm. I called him Uncle Pierre. At harvest time, they would help us, and we would help them. When we finished working, Marie's brothers and I played hide-and-seek, and our mangy old dog would follow us. Marie's father hated that dog. I can still hear him yelling, 'Take that dog with you,' whenever we left." His eyes crinkled, but the crinkling quickly faded into a melancholic frown.

"Then one day, we were visiting, and the dog took off as usual. We chased it deep into this thicket, moved the brush around, felt the cool air, and found the opening, but we couldn't investigate because Uncle Pierre was ready to go home. We had planned to explore it the next time, but the soldiers came. After I discovered this cave, I often thought if only we had found it earlier, it might have saved their lives."

A pick mark in the stone caught Nicolas's attention, and he rubbed his finger along the indentation. He had not known the family but sensed the loss.

"Francisca, Agnes, and I decided it would be our refuge in case of any future attacks, and we agreed never to tell anyone." As Humbert lifted his lantern, illuminating a dark corner and revealing a small hole in the rock not much bigger than a wine barrel. "Would you like to take a walk?"

There's more? Nicolas's breath caught, and he nodded, dropped to his knees, and, following Humbert, crawled through the opening. Once on the other side, the shaft opened, and they could stand.

"Francisca found this tunnel; she was always fearless. We increased the opening so the barrels would fit."

The dim flicker of the lantern lit up a wheeled cart holding a barrel and a torch leaning against the wall. Using the lantern flame, Humbert lit the torch and handed the lantern to Nicolas. The additional light revealed a huge shaft ending in black nothingness. "At first, we were afraid to follow this path"—Humbert nodded toward the void—"but curiosity got the best of us."

They walked in silence for a while, the only light coming from the lantern and torch, the only sound the scratching of their feet on the stone floor.

"So, this is how Francisca escaped," Nicolas said.

"Not the magical disappearance you had expected?"

Suddenly, Nicolas felt very small. "I almost believed the rumors."

"I saw the expression on your face." Humbert chuckled.

"But why do you hide your wine in here?"

"When Uncle Pierre died, I sold his farm but kept the fields of grapes. I brought the barrels home, planning to sell them at the spring fair, but there was no room in my barn. Leaving them outside all winter would ruin them, so I rolled them into this shaft and forgot about them until we needed vinegar a year later. When I opened a barrel, it wasn't vinegar. It was the best wine I had ever tasted. The longer I store it in here, the better it becomes. Occasionally, I rack and refill the barrels, but I do nothing special to the wine."

"And you sell it to Sebastien?"

Eyes flashing with excitement, Humbert explained, "Nobody knows this except Sebastien, Marie, and Francisca. Eventually, I will tell my children, but Jean-Baptiste cannot be trusted yet, and Joseph is not old enough. What I tell you must remain with you."

"Of course, monsieur, you can trust me."

They started walking again, Humbert gesturing with his hands as he spoke. "Sebastien was selling my wine in the tavern when a steward from the Duke of Lorraine stopped in. He liked my wine so well that he bought a whole barrel for the duke, and then he came back a month later wanting to buy as much as I could make."

Nicolas stopped and gawked at Humbert's shape in the darkness. "The Duke of Lorraine? You sell your wine to the Duke of Lorraine?"

Humbert stopped. The flicker of the lantern lightened his face. The usually stoic expression was gone, and he smiled ear to ear as he shook his head. "Not anymore. The duke has a new steward, who probably gets it from some relative—probably not as good." Humbert winked.

"How long did you—"

"A year or two."

That's where they got their money. "But you could be rich and famous . . ."

"Perhaps, but if anyone knew that I made it, they would want to know how I made it. My family's safety is more important."

Humbert walked away, and Nicolas stared at his back, shocked. Considering what happened to that woman from Fouday who had refused to sell her vines, Humbert was smart to be cynical. After all, he had seen his friends massacred. Nicolas ran to catch up and walked with Humbert until they came upon some additional barrels and a wooden plank wall barring them from continuing.

"Where do you think we are?"

At his shrug, Humbert moved a plank. Between the boards, Nicolas could see the inside of a tool shed. "I noticed a shed behind the inn, just sitting in plain sight, but have we walked that far?"

Humbert nodded. "Instead of going around the mountain, we've cut through. When Agnes married Sebastien, they bought this property, partly because of the location, across from the stable, but mostly because of the tunnel. It offers them safety as well as a place to store the wine."

Shaking his head, Nicolas added, "And Agnes gave Francisca her change of clothes."

Francisca cannot disappear—but those all-knowing eyes still haunt me.

A WEEK later, with the wedding date fast approaching, Catherine stood on the bench while her mother and grandmother made the final alterations to her wedding gown. To occupy her time, she quizzed her papa on gardening and farming tips from the almanac.

"Do you see why I didn't want you to learn to read?" Humbert laughed, adding, "Sebastien suggested I take the wine to Jean's today so it can settle before the celebration. Come, Joseph, help me with the barrels."

"No, he cannot go. I still have to finish his breeches," Marie said.

Joseph groaned. "Oh, must I? I should help Papa—"

"Mind your mama," Humbert replied. "I'm sure I'll find someone to help me."

"I want to come too," Catherine said. "Martin offered to play his violin at the ceremony and asked me to choose the songs."

As the cart neared the final stand of trees before the road, a large dust cloud rose ahead of them. Humbert stopped his horse. "Must be a large group."

Catherine shrugged, but her father's furrowed brow and rapid breathing concerned her.

"What is it, Papa?"

He quickly tied off the horse's reins and hopped down. "Probably nothing. Help me cover the wine."

With the canvas hiding their cargo, they returned to the cart and waited, giving the group ample time to move ahead of them. No sooner had they pulled onto the main road, however, when another smaller group of men wearing military uniforms passed them, trying to catch up.

Suddenly, Jean's warning about keeping close to home popped into Catherine's mind, and she leaned toward Humbert and whispered, "Papa, Monsieur Jean said to watch out for soldiers on their way to France."

"Keep your head down, daughter."

The first group passed without turning, but the soldiers trailing behind took note of the cart and made Humbert stop. The story of Mémé's abduction flashed in Catherine's mind, and she shook uncontrollably. *Oh, why didn't I remember earlier?*

One of the men removed the canvas, revealing the wine barrels and salted meats. "Whoop. Look here—celebration tonight."

"Take it and let us go," said Humbert, lifting Catherine down and pushing her behind him.

The one in charge motioned for assistance, his eyes traveling down Catherine's body as a slow, terrifying smile spread across his face.

Catherine clung to her father's back.

"Take the wine and meat," said Humbert. "We'll not stop you."

The man thrust out his hand. "Give me your purse too, papist."

Without hesitation, Humbert handed the man his poke. "I have little money. I'm making a delivery. Sell the wine—it's worth a fortune."

"Sell the wine?" the man jeered. "No, but that sweet one can help me drink it."

Cruel and sneering eyes bored into Catherine, and he nodded to another soldier, who seized her arm and pulled her toward him.

"Papa!"

Lunging at them, Humbert shouted, "Run."

Caught off guard, the leader fell against the cart, his head slamming into the wooden seat.

Catherine whirled toward the soldier holding her. With as much strength as she could muster, she kicked him between the legs, pulled herself free, and dashed into the forest without looking back.

Tomorrow, Nicolas would present his masterpiece silver chandelier to the guild for approval and recognition as a master smith. After work, his brother reviewed it one last time.

A clamor of horses, carts, and shouting arose outside, and they ran out the door.

Immediately, dozens of soldiers brandishing guns and swords surrounded them and forced them back against the wall. The director of the forge staggered into the street, his arms held high, pushed by men dressed in military uniforms.

In a shaky voice, the director mumbled, "They have my wife and children. Give them whatever they want."

A soldier pulled a knife on them. "Come here, papist."

Le-Chêne said, "Papists? Are you Huguenots? What are you doing here?"

The leader said, "We want to live in peace, so we need weapons. We'll not hurt you, and we'll pay you a fair price."

Amid the chaos, Nicolas noticed a smaller cart in the rear of the procession led by a single horse. A tarp in the back took on the shape of a wine barrel. He elbowed Le-Chêne. "I think that is Humbert's cart."

Le-Chêne squinted and whispered, "I'm not sure."

Nicolas's heart pounded. "Where did you get that cart?"

The leader waved him off. "We do not steal—"

One of the men in back yelled, "We found it abandoned along the roadside, sir."

"That's Humbert's cart," Nicolas shouted and lunged as terrible images flashed in his mind. But Le-Chêne caught him and struggled to hold him fast. "There are hundreds of them, Nicolas. Don't be a fool."

Once the last of the weapons were loaded onto the carts, the group left in a cloud of dust. The director ignored the coins tossed in his direction and hurried back to his house.

Nicolas jumped on his horse and thundered toward Vacquenoux with Le-Chêne on his heels. As they neared the town, the now-familiar sound of the church bells pierced the air.

Oh God, no.

"Check the inn, and I'll ask Papa," Le-Chêne shouted.

Closing his eyes, Nicolas said a quick prayer, not for intercession but for a miracle. At the inn, he found the door locked. He considered obtaining a fresh mount from Martin, but it would take too long, so Nicolas raced his big gray toward the farm, leaning forward and flattening himself against its back.

As he neared the house and the ground leveled, several horses and wagons came into view. A crowd of people stood by the door, Louis Gauthier among them. Francisca was openly weeping, leaning against the great tree in the courtyard. His heart sank. Nicolas threw himself off the nearly dead horse. As he staggered through the doorway, his father caught him.

He frantically searched for Catherine but found only Humbert's lifeless, blood-covered body lying on the big table, exactly like Father Brignon's. "Monsieur Humbert."

Father Michel stood over the body, his eyes bright and cheerful. Marie was there, sobbing, with his mother comforting her. In the corner, Anne held Beatrix beside Jean-Baptiste, his wife on one knee, and Joseph on the other.

But where is Catherine? Panic tightened his stomach as a voice screamed in his head. *Where is she?*

Aunt Agnes stepped forward, her eyes rimmed with red. "Come, Nicolas—she's upset, but maybe she'll respond to you." In a back room, Catherine sat on a bed, pale and forlorn amid blankets and pillows, staring into space.

A tear ran down Agnes's cheek as she said, "The same thing happened to my mama."

He rushed to the bed and sat beside Catherine, pressing her hand to his lips and searching her face for a sign of recognition. He whispered, "Catherine?"

He turned her face toward him, his hand lingering on her cheek, a blink and an incomprehensible murmur her only response. Sliding closer to her, he kissed her cheek, gazing into her blank stare.

"Catherine?"

She focused on him, let out a gasp, and wept. He drew her into his arms, feeling her tremble against his chest. "Papa's dead," she cried. "They called us papists and killed him—they killed him for no reason. Papa's dead! He's dead!"

Nicolas gently held her, rocked her, whispered to her, and she finally went limp and fell asleep in his arms.

24

THE next morning, while her mother and grandmother wrapped her father's body for burial, Catherine sat in the corner, staring at them. This was her fault. Monsieur Jean had warned her, but she was too preoccupied with her wedding and had completely forgotten—and now her father was dead.

At the inn, the mayor's family waited, and as church bells called the townspeople to participate, Uncle Sebastien drove his fine cart, carrying the body. Catherine wanted to walk with Nicolas, but he and his father led the procession, carrying crosses while Jean-Baptiste and Joseph held torches behind them. Anne carried Beatrix and held Catherine's hand as they slogged behind Elisabeth, Aunt Agnes, Marie, and Mémé.

This was the first time Catherine had ever attended a service inside the church. Though she had asked dozens of times why they never joined in community events centered around it, Humbert had been adamant about her never stepping foot in the door, as if it were a place to fear. Now, as she stepped inside, her heart pounded at the soaring height, the way the light danced through the stained-glass windows, and the pungent smell of the incense.

Anne regularly attended Mass at Ban de la Roche, and so Catherine followed her lead, dipping her hand in the bowl of water by the door and crossing herself with it, bowing before filing onto the bench, and kneeling on the floor instead of sitting on the seat. Jean-Baptiste, who had followed behind her, also seemed to know exactly what to do.

Before the service, a smiling Father Michel proclaimed, "A violent death is a sign of the devil's interference. This man has paid the ultimate price for his many wrongdoings, and he will suffer in Purgatory for a long time—but if you want to shorten his sentence, you may purchase indulgences after the committal ceremony."

When two young boys dressed in white joined the priest on the altar, Jean-Baptiste pinched the bridge of his nose. He was pale and sweating, and even his lips drained of color as if he were going to faint. Catherine wrapped her arm around him, and he placed his hand on her shoulder and closed his eyes.

"Are you all right?" she whispered.

"No, I can't breathe," he replied, sinking to the bench and burying his face in his hands.

The service passed swiftly, and they followed Father Michel to the graveside, where he lit incense to consecrate the body, sped through a couple of prayers, threw holy water all around, and left.

As two helpers lowered her father's body into the hole, Catherine fought to remain standing. Just as her strength waned and her knees buckled, Nicolas was there.

"I'm here," he said. "I'll help you through this." And then he whispered, "I told Papa that I would report Father Michel for trying to sell indulgences, but he told me to let the issue drop. He will make a donation in your father's name."

Martin attended the funeral Mass, and though he considered returning home to avoid the crowd—he hated crowds—he followed both families to Le Petit-Courty, trying to be helpful. Together with Le-Chêne, they found Nicolas sitting with Catherine.

"It's time to go to the guild meeting, Nicolas," Le-Chêne said. "Martin has agreed to stay with Catherine."

Crossing his arms, Nicolas replied, "I am not leaving her. The guild will understand the circumstances and give me another opportunity to exhibit."

Le-Chêne sighed. "Why take the risk? It won't take long, and Martin will stay with her."

"Yes, I am glad to sit with her," Martin replied.

Catherine cast a disapproving glare at them. "Stop talking about me as if I weren't here. Go ahead, Nicolas. I'm not a child."

With a motion for Nicolas to move, Martin settled beside her, saying, "I deeply respected your papa."

"Thank you. He liked you too," Catherine said, dabbing her handkerchief to her eyes.

Not knowing what else to do, he took her hand. She stared at it and then turned to him.

"Why would Huguenots kill my papa? He never judged you or thought what you believe to be wrong."

"Just as Catholics did not kill my family, Catherine, Huguenots did not kill your father. Murderers killed them. Evil people think they can get away with their wickedness by hiding behind religion, but they are not religious—they are just evil.

"It took me a long time to accept what happened to my family. Truthfully, I am still not sure I have put it behind me." The weight of the air pushed down on him, and he mumbled, "I have closed myself off from the world, but no one could have hurt me as much as I have hurt myself. You could not have changed what has happened, and though it's hard, you must learn to live with it. At least you still have your love."

"Was your love killed too?"

Sighing, he looked away. "No. Perhaps that is why it hurt so badly." Martin had never spoken of Alix to anyone, but if his story would help Catherine . . .

"When I fled Geneva, I was betrothed. On my way to Paris, I wrote to her with my plans, but when I got there, I found them . . ." He cleared his throat. "It was too late to help my family." Disbelieving, even after all these years, he shook his head. "When I found myself in Vacquenoux, I wrote to her again, asking if she would go to England, where Huguenots can live in peace. When I did not receive a response, I wrote to a friend." Martin clenched his jaw. "Within three months, her father had pronounced me a heretic, kept the dowry, and she . . . she had already married someone else."

"Oh, Martin, I'm so sorry."

He narrowed his eyes. "At first, I hated her—I hated everyone, even Jean and Elisabeth. I wished they would have let me die, and I retreated into my self-made prison." Suddenly, he felt old. "But I do not hate her anymore. I remember how much I loved her. The time I spent here with your family helped me. Your papa helped me, and I considered him my friend." Martin's voice broke, and he lowered his eyes.

Nodding, Catherine replied with a pale smile, "Papa thought the same of you, Martin."

The two sat on the bench, holding hands until Nicolas returned, a full-fledged master smith.

At the betrothal celebration, even though he had ached to speak with Anne, Martin had avoided her, but he needed to talk to her now. He found her standing at the fence where they had watched the sunset, looking out over the fields of rye. She had aged more than the two years she had been gone. He looked into her beautiful, melancholy eyes. "How are you, Anne?"

Raising her head proudly, she clasped her hands in front of her. "I'm fine, Martin, thank you. You look well."

"I am sorry about the way our last meeting ended."

"There is no reason to explain. I understand." Her thoughts seemed far away, and she turned her gaze from him. "I know what people say about our family. Papa never noticed how everyone avoided him—he never saw evil in anyone." Tears trickled down her cheeks. "Did you notice how few people were at the funeral? Even the priest raced through the prayers."

Wait, she thinks she is not good enough for me?

"These townspeople wouldn't even pay their respects, though Papa would have given his shirt to anyone who needed it. Catherine is lucky that Nicolas can look past—"

"No, Anne, you are so wrong. I never meant—"

She turned her back to him. "I want to be alone now."

His heart ached for the pain he had caused her, and he tried to think of something to say. She deserved so much more than he could ever give her; she deserved to be treated as a fine lady, and she deserved children. Considering what had happened the last time, he probably couldn't . . .

Though he wanted to hold her, to wipe her tears, it was better this way.

Louis filed a complaint with Count Frédéric, who was furious that Huguenots had sacked his forge, but Humbert's murder remained unsolved.

According to custom, Nicolas postponed the wedding for mourning and used the time to renovate the barn. Jean made the nails and hinges, and as they were installing a new front door a week before the revised wedding date, Martin arrived with a message from the coach driver and handed it to Jean.

Taking advantage of the break, Nicolas sat in front of the newly constructed fireplace on one of the upholstered chairs delivered that morning, a gift from the Gauthiers. The other two sat on the matching divan.

"It's from my brother, Antoine," Jean said after scanning the page. "Pope Gregory has died, and the cardinals have gone into the conclave. The bishop needs him next week—he cannot perform the ceremony. He says he will be happy to come later but understands if you want to ask the parish priest."

"Oh no," Nicolas said, rubbing the creases from his forehead. "That leaves us with Father Michel. I know Catherine will not want him."

"But will she want to postpone again?" Martin asked. "Perhaps you should speak to the priest before getting her upset."

At that, Nicolas and his father went to the church. As they entered the vestibule, a boy with a tear-streaked face burst out and ran headlong into Jean, knocking him back a step. "Pardon, monsieur," the boy said without stopping.

Nicolas asked, "Who was he?"

"The Lenoir boy—son of the man who killed Father Brignon."

"Father Michel had promised to care for his family," Nicolas said.

As they entered the back of the church, shouting arose in front. Father Michel was shoved through the door of the sacristy by Louis Gauthier.

Shocked, Nicolas and his father stood in silence for a moment before Jean said, "Louis, is something wrong?"

"Yes, something is very wrong," Louis growled, pushing the priest again.

Stumbling but catching his balance, Father Michel raised his fist in the air. "I'll notify the bishop."

"Shut up and move," Louis growled.

Walking backward, the priest banged into a bench and fell to one knee. "You saw nothing!"

But Louis didn't ease up. "I know what I saw, and it will haunt me the rest of my life." He turned to Jean and said through clenched teeth, "Father Michel will not be available for a while."

The priest regained his footing and shouted, "I'll be back by this evening."

Louis pushed the priest out the rear door and growled, "We'll see about that," and they disappeared up the street without explanation.

Dumbfounded, Nicolas asked, "What do we do now, Papa? What does this mean?"

"I have no idea, but we'd better tell Catherine."

At Le Petit-Courty, they found Jean-Baptiste and Joseph struggling to carry a trunk into the house. Nicolas grabbed one end while his father helped Joseph with the other.

Jean-Baptiste let them take it, rubbing his back. "Thank you."

"I told him not to carry that heavy trunk," Francisca said. "His ribs still have not healed. Will you please bring it in here?" She pointed toward a back room where Marie was coming out, carrying women's clothing.

Smiling, Marie said, "Jean-Baptiste and Dimanchette are moving in with us."

Catherine waited by the big table, and her face brightened when their eyes met. He hated to destroy that smile. He rubbed his hands together and glanced at his father for support before saying, "Uncle Antoine expresses his regrets, but he cannot officiate our wedding."

The smile faded.

Jean shuffled his feet. "And Father Michel had to . . . go somewhere. He did not explain."

"What do you mean he went somewhere? What will we do?" Catherine asked, her eyes wide and anxious.

"We will wait," Nicolas said, taking her hand. "It'll be fine."

On the way home, Jean said, "I spoke with Marie. I tried again to return the dowry money, but she said Humbert saved the money for the girls' dowries and she would not spoil his legacy."

After adjusting his hat against the glaring sun, Nicolas replied, "Marie is tough, but I'm glad Jean-Baptiste and his wife are moving back home. He'll take care of them. Maybe he'll take better care of himself as well."

Two days later, responding to a knock, Francisca opened the door to find a twinkling pair of brown eyes staring back at her from under thick brows. Tall, thin, dimples. As she took in the young man's garb, he energetically introduced himself. "Bonjour, madame, my name is Father Edmond, your new parish priest."

New parish priest? "Welcome, Father. Come in. Marie, Catherine, come meet our new priest."

Francisca motioned toward the big table. "Would you like some ale?"

"Yes, please."

As they sat around the table, Francisca could not help herself and asked him about Father Michel.

The young man replied quickly before changing the subject, "I know nothing about my predecessor, but I will work hard to make my parish the best in Salm." He nodded to Catherine. "You must be the bride. I'm happy to perform your ceremony."

"Yes, I am. Thank you." She sighed in relief.

The priest folded his hands on the table and added, "I cannot seem to find your baptismal record. Were you baptized elsewhere?"

Francisca exchanged glances with Marie. The records. Had Humbert delivered them to the abbey with Padre Brignon's personal effects? "Our former priest, Father Brignon, performed the ceremony. The records should be at the abbey."

"Oh, Father Brignon, I knew him from the seminary. He was known for being fastidious. I'm sure the records are there."

25

THE next morning, Nicolas leaned against the doorframe of his very own smithy and raised his face to the sunshine. Tomorrow he would marry the woman he thought he had lost forever. Today, he wanted to relax, but his mother's incessant nagging drove him out of the house. As he entered the stable yard, he noticed Martin peeking over a horse's back at the new priest they'd met yesterday and a woman talking with Jean. When Martin ducked his head to steal a look around the horse's rear, Nicolas went to investigate.

As he approached the group, Father Edmond's face lit up, and he said to the woman, "This young man is getting married tomorrow. It will be my first time officiating a wedding."

"This is my son Nicolas," Jean said.

Father Edmond nodded. "Nicolas, this is my childhood nurse, Madame Laville. She would like you to make a pendant for her."

The woman nodded. "Bonjour and congratulations."

"Thank you," Nicolas replied with a nod.

Dark hair lightly sprinkled with gray, covered in a simple scarf. Olive-colored skin. The shape of the woman's face looked familiar, and there was something memorable in her eyes— striking. "Pleased to meet you, madame. Have we met?"

"Have you ever been to Strasbourg?"

"No, but I—" He caught himself staring. "I'm sorry, you'd like me to make something?"

"Yes. A pendant to replace the one my mama gave me. Recently, I gave mine to my son, but I feel lost without it."

Father Edmond turned to her with a surprised look. "You have seen Guillaume?"

"Yes, he's come home," the woman said with an unmistakable expression of sadness. "But . . ." She lowered her eyes without finishing her thought. Edmond squeezed her hand while an uncomfortable moment passed.

Jean broke the tension. "Nicolas, why not show them your shop?"

Nicolas gestured, and they followed him.

While Nicolas would use his father's furnace and anvil to make his wares, he had built a small office attached to the side of the forge where he would create his designs. Box bellows hung on the wall beside his heavy leather apron, and stacks of metal lined the floor beside a table with mandrels, chisels, files, and hammers of different sizes.

"Could you draw a likeness?"

Taking a piece of parchment and quill, she drew a cross sitting on an anchor with a heart on top. At his questioning glance, she said, "The abbess said it means *God's love is an anchor to the soul.* I've had a pendant like this all my life, and this may sound unusual, but I think it was made of nails. The arms of the cross were narrower than the corners, and the metal was dark, almost black."

"Made out of nails, you say?" Nicolas rubbed his chin. "I've never seen anything like this."

"Yes, nails. I have never seen another. Can you make one for me?"

"Well, yes, I can make it. Let me get some nails." He scurried to his father's shop, returning with a handful of horseshoeing nails. He laid them in a pattern on the table with the pointed ends overlapping in the middle. "Like this?"

Her face brightened. "Yes, exactly like that, but much smaller."

"Well, I have smaller nails at my house. How long will you be staying?"

"Nounou is staying for a couple of days," Father Edmond replied, "then I will drive her to Etival. She has decided to become a nun."

The woman's eyes beamed. "Shall we wait?"

"This will take a while. I will bring it to the rectory—this afternoon?"

As they were leaving, she jumped as if stung. "Oh. I almost forgot, could you engrave my name on the back?"

Engrave a name on that little nail? Nicolas forced himself to nod.

"The name is Rita. R-i-t-a."

They left and Nicolas forced all the distractions out of his mind. Several hours later, he laid his hammer on the table and took a relieved breath. When he leaned back, he found Jean, Martin, and Quentin watching him. He had never noticed them come in.

A look of pride filled his father's face. "You did it, son." But then he furrowed his brow. "But is that a cross?"

"Yes. Have either of you ever seen anything like this?"

"There is the cross of St. Clement with an anchor," Martin said. "I've never seen the addition of the heart."

"Impressive handiwork," Jean chimed in. "How will she wear it?"

"Oh, we didn't discuss that."

Martin raised his index finger and said, "Humbert gave me a strip of hide that I helped him tan. I want to keep some as a remembrance, but this use would make him proud."

While Nicolas polished the dull metal on a soft cloth, Martin fetched the leather. When he returned, Nicolas said, "Did you recognize that woman?"

"Indeed, she looked familiar."

"I swear I know her."

"She looks like that old lady who used to visit us," Quentin said.

When everyone turned to the boy, he lowered his head and bit his lip.

"Tell us," Martin said, touching his shoulder. "What was the lady's name?"

The boy looked as though he could cry. "I'm sorry, I cannot remember, but she brought me these boots. She said her grandson had grown out of them."

"Thank you, Quentin," Martin said, rubbing his back. "You have been very helpful."

The boy's pout disappeared, replaced by a shy grin.

The boots were barely worn and looked a little too large, but Nicolas put the thought out of his mind and turned back to the task. "The woman said she had a pendant like this her whole life, but she gave it to her son, and she is going to take her vows to become a nun. Strange."

"Why is that strange?" asked Martin.

"How can a woman with children become a nun?"

"I should think that is a common occurrence. Perhaps her husband died, and she has no means of support."

The cord slipped easily through, and Nicolas held it up. Sunlight reflected off the dull metal.

"Who would have thought nails would make such a nice ornament?" Jean said.

Nicolas was filled with pride. He did it! He was a professional. But then he frowned. "How much should I charge a nun?"

"That is your decision now that you are the master," Jean replied.

The next morning, Martin met the Cathillon family at the inn and played his violin behind the bridal procession to the church of Vipucelle. Curious townspeople, having never heard the instrument, came out of their homes and quietly watched them pass.

Anne walked with Joseph. If only Martin could have offered her the life she deserved, he would be beside her.

Long streamers of white and blue flowers adorned Catherine's waist-length hair. The subtle scent of her bouquet wafted along the slight breeze.

At the church, Martin was filled with a sense of pride. He had watched Nicolas grow from a mischievous boy to standing proud and tall beside his father and brother. Jean-Baptiste placed Catherine's hand in Father Edmond's open palm, then took his place beside her. The priest joined Nicolas's and Catherine's hands and led them through their vows.

"With this ring, I espouse you. With my body, I honor you; my goods I give you . . ."

Their parents and witnesses signed the register and proceeded inside for Mass. The couple knelt before the altar, and Father Edmond covered them with a white veil while saying a blessing over them. When the ceremony was complete, they kissed as the guests cheered.

The celebration followed at the inn, where Le-Chêne stood and asked everyone to raise their glass. "May the little birds that Martin and I helped pluck from the tree find happiness in their new nest."

Martin laughed aloud while the other guests tried to figure out the joke.

Catherine had held her nerves in check throughout the day. Both Marie and Francisca counseled her about what to expect that evening, but Catherine wasn't worried about being intimate with Nicolas. She was concerned about disappointing him. She was, after all, just a peasant.

Tied to a fold in her dress was a pouch of *precautions*. She didn't want to deceive anyone, but she had enough to worry about becoming a tradesman's wife with all the duties that entailed. She couldn't think about becoming with child immediately.

Mémé understood. Mémé always understood. Together they decided that Catherine could take the precautions for about six months without causing any harm.

With the wedding celebration over, moonlight lit their path. Arm in arm, Nicolas led Catherine toward the beautiful house he had prepared for them. She couldn't help but pinch herself. Everything she had dreamed of had come true. Her new name, Catherine de la Goutte de Paradis. Befittingly, Catherine from the drop of heaven.

With so much activity in Vacquenoux, Martin had not been able to purchase any new books all summer. Autumn was fading fast, and before the heavy snows left them isolated, he decided to take a quick trip to the Strasbourg printer.

He stepped off the coach to the familiar sounds of the bustling city—the throng of carts on cobblestone streets, groups of people gossiping amid others pushing to get past them, and peddlers bellowing their wares with shoppers haggling prices.

His empty satchel over his shoulder, he followed the alley to the boarding-house he frequented not far from the print shop. A thickset woman with sweat on her forehead answered his knock. She wiped her hands on her apron, then threw them in the air.

"Martin. What a surprise. Your room has been waiting," she cried with a heavy German accent, pulling him into the house, where he immediately recognized the smell of cabbage soup.

"Good to see you, Madame Somer. Yes, since spring."

She wiped her brow with a handkerchief pulled from her sleeve. "You have been busy in your stable?"

"Yes, my . . . brother recently married."

"Ah." She patted his hand and led him toward the stairs. "What about you? I have a niece who would be perfect for you."

He could do nothing but agree with her. "Thank you, madame. I would like to rest a while before supper."

"Of course. I will ring the bell."

The next day, after a breakfast of warm bread and a small beer, Martin took the alley to the bookstore. With Madame Carolus's help, he chose his new purchases, then packed his bag with as many books as it would hold. He lugged the bag to the street and looked for a boy for hire to carry it back to the room.

As he waited, a small group of women walked up the street toward him. He stepped back into the portico to let them pass. Louis's wife, Madame Gauthier, and their daughter, Louise, were among them.

Martin remembered that, as a woman advanced in age and with child, Madame Gauthier had come to Strasbourg to be nearer to a physician. He was about to step forward to speak with her when he noticed Louise was obviously with child while Madame Gauthier . . . was not.

Turning his head quickly to hide his identity, he ducked back into the shop.

chapter
26

A YEAR passed quickly. Nicolas's business slowly became successful, and his shop grew crowded with brass, tin, and silver for special orders. Le-Chêne and Rachelle welcomed another girl into the family, while Catherine's brother, Jean-Baptiste, and Dimanchette came to terms with the death of their unborn child.

One Sunday in October, sunlight brightened the colors of the changing season, and as Nicolas took it in, Catherine stepped beside him and asked, "What would you say to a long walk? I need to gather reeds for a new basket and would like to go to Lac de la Maix."

"Yes, I've always wanted to go to the lake," Nicolas replied.

The walk was long but pleasant. Eventually, the couple sat on an old stump by the spring-fed lake and soaked their feet in the water.

Taking Nicolas's hand, Catherine said, "Do you know why I asked you to walk with me today?"

Though Nicolas had learned the signs from Rachelle, he did not want to ruin Catherine's surprise and returned a confused look.

"We are going to have a baby," she said with a smile as wide as the hills.

During that time, Anne and Catherine continued their correspondence, sharing the most mundane occurrences, family matters, and updates about her pregnancy. Sometimes Anne's news was so exciting that Catherine had to rush to the farm to share it with their mother.

"Dearest Sister,
You will not believe what happened to me today. The staff went to the abbey, and I was to clean the library. It was incredible. Books covered the

walls from floor to rafters, with moving staircases providing access to those on high shelves. The steward said scholars from all over the world go there to read.

Stacks of books were everywhere, but he said I was only there to dust, and I shouldn't move the books. When I read a title aloud, he was shocked and said I am welcome to come and read anytime. I am so glad I convinced you that we should learn to read."

"Oh, now it was her idea," Catherine grumbled.

"Hush." Marie glared and pointed to the letter. "What else does your sister say?"

"While I was dusting, a young girl entered. She had jewels in her hair and rings on her fingers—it was Chrestienne of Salm."

"OH!" Both women gasped. "The countess!"

"The countess picked a book, but when she laid it on the table, she cut her finger on the metal corner. Blood was everywhere. I wrapped it with my handkerchief to stop the bleeding.

She was embarrassed that she had ruined the kerchief, but I told her not to worry, because I would just make another. She was so impressed by the stitching that she asked me to come to the castle in Badonviller to sew for her. I will not raise my hopes because she probably has forgotten me. Nevertheless, I met the countess!

Love, Anne."

As the date of Catherine's ordeal approached, an unexpected visitor knocked at her door.

"Anne!" Catherine squealed as they ran into each other's embrace. "Oh, it is so good to see you, but what are you doing here?"

With eyes flashing in excitement, Anne pulled a letter from her bag. "I asked Baroness Henrietta for a couple of days off, and she said yes. It seems the abbey's steward had asked about me, and ever since, the baroness has been afraid to deny me anything. She doesn't know about this."

Catherine unfolded the note and read it aloud.

"Dear Anne,

Thank you for rescuing me. The hurt has healed.

I hope you have considered my proposal to join my embroiderers. As we would not want to offend our loyal subjects, as soon as you obtain the agreement of your current employer, you may introduce yourself to the castle.

Sincerely, Chrestienne de Salm."

"The castle," Catherine shrieked, and they embraced again.

Anne chewed her bottom lip. "I'm not sure I'm as excited as you. Moving all the way to Badonviller worries me. I thought Jean said he lived there for his apprenticeship, and I wanted to ask his opinion."

"But this is your lifelong dream."

"It is, but I'm nervous. At Ban de la Roche, I'm not that far away, and I can always take the coach home if work becomes unbearable." She fingered the lace on her bodice. "The castle in Badonviller is far away, and I won't know anybody except Countess Chrestienne, and she'll certainly not have time for me. Besides, I don't know how to act in front of royalty."

"How many people did you know when you went to Ban de la Roche in the first place? Of course, this is your decision," Catherine said, touching Anne's hand and trying to stop her nervous fingers. "But if you miss this opportunity, you'll regret it. Talk to Jean if you want."

"Yes, I was hoping Jean could ease my mind. He's met the count. I'll be right back."

As Anne scurried up the hillside, Catherine placed her hand atop her bulging stomach. Both of their lives were about to change forever.

Embroideress of the countess! Imagine that. Papa would be proud.

As Catherine's due date approached, Marie came to stay with her and discussed her upcoming ordeal in private. Elisabeth apparently caught wind of their plan, even though the topic was not open for polite discussion, and she brought up the subject over supper.

"People will talk if you do not use the village midwife."

"Well, Mama delivered my seven children, five of whom survived," Marie replied.

"The previous midwife was excellent as well." Elisabeth nodded. "But Father Michel replaced her before he left—"

Catherine sat quietly as they discussed her as if she weren't involved. Finally, she asked, "What does a priest have to do with birth?"

"In a town as small as this, there are no licensed medical practitioners," Martin replied. "The Church has always feared midwives may hold knowledge they do not understand. In their fight against witchcraft, they favor a pious woman over one with more experience."

"Of course, any woman vital to society must be a witch."

Elisabeth's jaw dropped. "You must not say things like that, Catherine."

"Well, it's true."

"Even if it is true," Nicolas whispered, "think it, but don't say it."

"There is a rational reason as well," Martin added. "If a baby may die, these appointed midwives have been given the power to baptize." At Marie's grunt, he continued, "The priest feels that the child's life in the hereafter is more important than his earthly life. If not baptized, the baby cannot be buried in the consecrated graveyard and is doomed to languish in Limbo forever."

"While I realize Francisca is competent," Elisabeth said, "having the midwife would be preferable to me."

I'm the one having the baby, so I will do what is preferable to me. But this time, Catherine held her tongue.

When the time drew near, Nicolas rushed to fetch Francisca, who arrived with a basket full of remedies. Outside, he and his father paced and read and paced some more.

Long hours later, when Nicolas heard the cries of an infant, they hurried inside but were stopped at the bedchamber door by Francisca, who was carrying a towel with the umbilical cord. "It's a boy, and all is well. You can see them both in a bit," she said, throwing her bundle into the fireplace while mumbling something under her breath.

Nicolas turned a questioning glance at his father, who only shrugged. His mother, who had not said much all day, shot him one of her looks before returning to the bedchamber.

When the door swung open for him, instead of following his first inclination to bound in, he entered cautiously. Marie and Francisca left, carrying armloads of sheets and towels, while his mother lingered. Catherine was sleeping with the baby on her chest.

Nicolas pulled a chair beside her and touched the soft fuzz on the baby's head.

"Do you want to hold him?" Elisabeth asked.

"Umm. No."

"There is no better time to learn." She moved his arms into position, gathered the baby in a bundle of blankets, and gently handed it to him. "Relax," she whispered, squeezing his shoulder and leaving them alone in the twilight.

He stared at the sleeping child, both pleased and terrified at the same time. Catherine opened her eyes and smiled. Though he wanted to be nearer to her, he was afraid to move.

"What do you think of little Nicolas?" she asked.

But Nicolas had thought the name was obvious—a family tradition. His grandfather, papa, and oldest brother were named Jean. "No, we must call him Jean."

"But Le-Chêne will name his son Jean. If not Nicolas, we should name him Humbert, after my papa."

"Le-Chêne and Rachelle have two girls now. What if they are not blessed with a son? And Jean-Baptiste has already said that he is hoping for a son that he will name Humbert . . . or our next boy will be Humbert."

"All right. Little Jean."

⚓

Over the next couple of weeks, Catherine often found herself near tears. She had thought the baby would make her happy, but she found herself thinking of her father all the time. This would have been his first grandchild. And though she had taken care of Beatrix, Catherine had no idea what she was doing.

When the family again gathered around the supper table weeks later, Elisabeth asked Catherine if she had considered what she would wear to her churching. Having never heard of churching, Catherine turned to Nicolas, who sighed, closed his eyes, and lowered his head. When she turned back, she found Elisabeth looking down her nose.

"After forty days, you must go before the church with the baby. The priest blesses you both, and you are thus purified and again have the right to enter and receive the sacraments."

"Purified?"

"To remove the impurities of birth, of course—and to give thanks for your survival." Elisabeth sighed in exasperation.

"Impurities of birth?" Angry now, Catherine glared at Nicolas, who raised his head but did not come to her defense. With a huff, she said, "If women did not become impure, there would be no more people on Earth. And if we try not to have children, this is a sin also . . . a mortal sin, so we must be a witch that deserves to be burned alive."

Trying to calm her, Nicolas touched her arm while the others stared at her in silence. "If I'm impure, you've made me so." She pouted.

"Yes, I did," he said, raising an eyebrow.

Horrified, Elisabeth gasped and covered her mouth with her serviette as the others chuckled.

Catherine searched the faces—her mother's pursed lips, Martin's empathetic frown, Nicolas's silly grin. Perhaps she was overreacting. *What harm is a little blessing?* "Will you help me pick out something appropriate?"

After the ceremony, the family gathered outside the church. Louis and his wife joined them, carrying their toddler, a sturdy boy with thick curly hair and a wide smile sporting a single tooth.

"Look at those curls. He's adorable." Catherine pinched the boy's cheek.

"The apple of his papa's eye," Nicolas said.

Louis beamed.

"He is such a good baby," Madame Gauthier said as Louise and her long-time suitor, the notary's son, joined them.

"Nicolas told me you were betrothed. Congratulations," Catherine said to .Louise, kissing her cheeks.

"Yes," Louise said. "We'll be married in the spring." The child reached for her.

"Your little brother looks a lot like you," Catherine said to Louise.

"We both look like Mama," Louise said.

27

1588

THREE years passed swiftly. As Little Jean grew, Catherine became more comfortable in her role as wife and mother. When Nicolas asked her to keep the accounts of his rapidly growing shop, she threw herself into the job with zeal and immediately discovered one excessive cost. Dropping Little Jean with Elisabeth, Catherine strolled down the hillside to discuss it with Nicolas, finding him in the stable, backing his horse between the shafts of his cart.

Nicolas glanced up but returned to the task. "I am on my way to fetch charcoal, and a storm is coming." He nodded toward the ominous clouds forming in the distance.

"Charcoal? Exactly what I wanted to discuss. Perhaps you could negotiate a better price since you are now buying enough for both forges."

"Don't worry about that."

"But I think you could—"

In an irritated voice, he replied, "Catherine, please. Just keep the accounts."

Deflated, she said, "Sorry that I bothered you."

But then his tone changed. "Wait." He scratched his ear. "Would you like to come with me?"

She brightened. *Maybe he doesn't think I'm stupid after all.* Little Jean was safe with Elisabeth. "I would love to go."

⚓

Following the main trail to Donon, they turned onto a path barely wider than the wagon. Deep ruts marked the passage of previous carts. Weeds as tall as the wheels grew on both sides, sometimes hitting their legs.

"This is a small operation, so the road is poorly maintained," Nicolas said. "They frequently move to stay close to the lumber supply."

The clouds rumbled, and as the first drops of rain fell, a vast plateau opened before them. Large mounds of earth, some smoking, others half-destroyed, rose among countless tree stumps. The air, thick and heavy with soot, flashed with lightning, giving the place an even more sinister appearance.

"You see?" Nicolas pointed to the piles. "They stack cut wood intertwined with twigs and cover it with dirt, leaving a chimney at the top, set it on fire, and let it burn for about ten days. When the dirt mounds cool, it's charcoal."

As heavy rain began to fall, two broad-shouldered men covered in soot with matted beards and hair came toward them. Nicolas lifted Catherine down and whispered before the two could hear, "They appear rough, but they're good people, tenderhearted. I've known them for a long time." They followed the men into a primitive work shelter made of planks, no bigger than Nicolas's shop, built on the bare ground.

Inside, Catherine felt the presence of other people, but there were no windows, and the few candles did little to lighten the shadows. Once her eyes became acclimated, she distinguished a goat standing in the corner and several people sitting on piles of bracken on the floor in the absence of furniture. A haggard older woman and another, much younger, gave her the same toothless grin. Two filthy children dressed only in tattered shirts of coarse cloth hid themselves from the intruders, then two larger boys entered; they too were filthy, dressed in simple shirts and wearing rags on their heads as protection from the rain.

This shack must be their home!

Catherine nodded greetings around the group, her gaze stopping on a boy about the size of Little Jean. She held her hand toward the child, but he screamed, prompting a slap that made him wail even louder. Trying to break the tension, she said, "We have a boy about three who's also afraid of strangers."

The young woman said, "Well, he's more'n four." She nodded toward a sleeping baby beside her. "This'n must be three years."

"All these children are yours?" As soon as Catherine said it, she touched her hand to her mouth, wishing she could take back the question.

"No, they're my sister's. She died having this'n, and she lost two others when there wasn't enough work to feed'm. I lost one last winter'n another a couple of months ago. I've only those three still alive'n soon another, but I'm only eighteen, so I've still time to replace'm."

Replace them? Catherine inhaled sharply, then scratched her nose to hide the shock. She offered a handkerchief to the child, whose runny nose was about to drip. "I think he has a cold."

"M'lady, we all get cold. Some live and some die. That's how 'tis."

"Fortunately, God gives us more," the old woman said, then whispered to the younger. "This is Francisca's granddaughter."

Catherine overheard her. "You know Francisca?"

The old woman sobered. "No, I don't know her."

Catherine stared at them. *That woman just said Francisca's name. Why did she deny it?*

The thunder stopped, and the sound of the rain diminished, emphasizing the uncomfortable silence that followed. The young man lifted the crying child on his knee, sat on a block of wood, and beckoned Catherine to sit on another.

Before taking a seat, she scanned the room. A small table held a basket of berries, a picked-clean slab of ribs, and a loaf of bread. A pot hung on a tripod over a pile of unlit twigs underneath a hole in the roof in the middle of the cabin. When a flock of chickens sheltering from the rain approached her, the young woman chased them off with a kick.

"They'll peck at anything, but we rarely find any eggs."

One of the men looked out the door. "The rain's stopped."

With a nod to Catherine, Nicolas followed the men but returned almost immediately with a slab of salted pork and several loaves of bread.

"How good ye are," the old woman said. "The last slab held us until the fruit and crops were ready. Thankee again, and your family." She took his hand to her lips, and Nicolas's face flushed. He cleared his throat and paid the elder man, who accepted the money without counting.

To Catherine, Nicolas said, "I will help load."

Catherine sat quietly as Nicolas steered the cart through the muddy ruts. He said smugly, "You came to tell me something?"

She kissed his cheek. "I had no idea. Thank you for showing me. I could never imagine such misery. Those poor people. But they show no emotion about the children dying."

"They care, they just cannot do anything about it, so they build a wall."

"And the meat? We've not killed a pig."

"Yesterday, when Joseph visited, he brought it to me. The bread too. Francisca is friends with the old woman we saw, but no one can ever know, as a safeguard."

"A safeguard?"

"The matron has a reputation as a witch, and these days it's not good to say you know her."

"But why? What has she done?"

Nicolas frowned. "Catherine, both Martin and I have told you. The prelates do not need a reason. These people are poor—that's why they want rid of them."

"So that's why she said she didn't know Mémé. If she were a witch, though, she'd take her family from this misery. We must take them more things—clothes, shoes. I'll go with you from now on."

But Nicolas's frown turned into anger. "No, you will not. It's not safe. I only go when we need charcoal."

"But they need help."

"And we are helping them as much as we dare."

chapter

28

1591-1597

THE pouring rain slapping the side of the house woke Nicolas earlier than usual. Next to him, Catherine slept, and Little Jean, now six—who had joined them in the middle of the night—was curled up between them. In a cradle beside the bed, their three-year-old daughter, Marie, blew a tiny bubble in her sleep.

Life doesn't get any better than this.

When the rain stopped, Nicolas got out of bed and glanced out the window. The morning sun, muted by thick fog, barely lightened the sky. An illuminated mist appeared to skip across the courtyard. He shuffled into the parlor and added another log to the embers.

As he filled the pot for chicory, the door flew open. Le-Chêne, soaked and disheveled, collapsed against the doorframe.

"She's dead," he breathed.

Nicolas helped his brother to a chair as Catherine appeared, wrapped in a blanket. They both stared at Le-Chêne.

"Rachelle is dead." The big man buried his head in his hands.

"I'll fetch your parents." Dropping the blanket, Catherine ran out of the house barefoot, wearing only her nightgown. Nicolas fetched a towel and grabbed the fallen blanket for his brother. Within minutes, Jean and Elisabeth appeared in their bedclothes wrapped in cloaks.

Elisabeth knelt before her son, her eyes already wet with tears. "What happened?"

"Yesterday, Rachelle said she felt weak and dizzy and went to bed early. She got up to use the chamber pot and collapsed. Blood was everywhere. I carried her to the bed and sent Marguerite and Marie to the neighbor for help. The midwife came quickly. Rachelle delivered the baby, a boy, but she . . ." Le-Chêne gulped. "It happened so fast."

While Jean tried to comfort Le-Chêne, Elisabeth sobbed and collapsed on the floor. Nicolas pulled her and Catherine into his arms and held them. *Not Rachelle. Oh God, not Rachelle.* He pulled himself together. "Where are the children?"

Dazed, Le-Chêne stared straight ahead. "The neighbor's eldest daughter, Claudette, is watching them. I had to get out of there. Everywhere I look, I see Rachelle's face, her beautiful face. What am I going to do?"

Months passed with Le-Chêne existing in a daze. Elisabeth stepped in and began planning. The neighbor was a respected business owner in Framont, and his daughter Claudette was of age. Le-Chêne and his children would benefit from such a union. "Most marriages are based on economics, not love," Elisabeth said.

Nicolas tried to reason with his brother, who offered no resistance to his mother's urging. "Remember when Mama introduced me to Salomé? You know how Mama is, always trying to run everyone's lives."

Le-Chêne stared past Nicolas and mumbled, "I'll never love anyone else. Claudette is as good as any other."

"She's only sixteen, Le-Chêne, almost half your age."

"Well, I can't take care of three children by myself." Le-Chêne slumped in the chair and turned toward the window to dismiss him, but Nicolas pressed him further.

"Hire someone to take care of the children until you get back on your feet."

When no response came, Nicolas left, shaking his head.

Four weeks later, Nicolas stood beside his brother in front of the church next to Claudette. Without lifting his head, his voice barely above a whisper, Le-Chêne repeated after the priest.

"I do."

Every Saturday, peasants and farmers flocked to the market in Vacquenoux, selling or exchanging livestock and produce or merely coming to meet. The aroma of freshly baked goods, the stench of goats and raw fish, and the shouts of vendors, hagglers, and sheep charged the air.

Catherine loved the animation of the market, meeting friends or searching for new products, but a week after Le-Chêne remarried, she was still behind on her housework and arrived a little late. At the square, she found a crowd gathered around a feed merchant from the Alsatian Plain. He stood on a crate, his arms as animated as his face. She craned to see above heads and backs, noting the hushed crowd, and listened intently as he said, "Several German cities are closed for fear of the contagion. The gates are guarded by sentries who refuse entry or exit with orders to shoot anyone who tries to break the blockade."

"What contagion?" Catherine shouted from the back of the crowd.

Staring directly at her with eyes so fierce her skin crawled, he bellowed for all to hear, "Victims get a fever and abdominal pain before developing black spots on their nose, fingers, and toes and swollen pustules in their groin, neck, and armpits. There is no cure."

"The plague!" She gasped in horror. Shopping forgotten, Catherine hurried home and rushed to the farm for advice. To her disappointment, Mémé replied, "I know of no cure. My only advice is to stay away from strangers."

The next day, church bells called the townspeople to the square. Approaching with dread, the children in tow, Catherine rushed to meet Nicolas and Jean, who were listening to an officer of Salm reading a document to the crowd that had gathered.

The counts, worried about the danger of the influx of transients, had published orders for police regarding the contagion. It required the town to ban gatherings, kill stray animals, and prohibit passage between the German states and the County of Salm. When the officer finished reading, he hung the document on a post and turned to leave.

People shouted questions at his back. "What do you mean we can no longer cross between Vacquenoux and Wackenbach? And what about Schirmeck?" But the officer mounted his horse and left.

Panic swept through the crowd. Catherine looked to Jean, as mayor, who stood on a step and raised his hands to address the people. "This decision is to prevent refugees from bringing the contagion with them. Movement between neighbors from Wackenbach and Vacquenoux should not be affected. As for Schirmeck, stay away, or you'll be arrested at the toll station."

Despite the precautions, the disease soon spread to the other towns in the parish of La Broque. Rich citizens rented countryside homes whose owners moved their families into makeshift shelters in the forest.

A few days after the melee in the square, as the evening meal was ending, Le-Chêne rushed his cart to the estate without his new wife and dragged his children into the house. "Framont is bordering on lawlessness; everyone is leaving town."

Elisabeth took the squalling baby from Le-Chêne's eldest daughter, Marguerite, but held the child away from her. "He is soaked."

After sending Little Jean to fetch a clean clout, Catherine asked, "Where is Claudette?"

"Claudette is a child," Le-Chêne replied, his eyes flashing in anger. "No responsibility, screaming, crying, and scaring the children; she wouldn't even watch them so I could secure the forge. I told her to flee with her parents."

A guilty look crossed Elisabeth's face before she left to change the baby.

Nicolas traded a look of disgust with Catherine before fetching his brother a glass of wine and sliding a chair to him. "Thank heavens you got out," Nicolas said.

"No, I'm the master; I have responsibilities. Would you watch the children until I get back?"

"Surely, you're not going back. If things are that bad in Framont, why would you return? The forge isn't going anywhere."

"I must secure the building from looters."

"Of course we'll watch them," Catherine said. "But I wish you'd reconsider—"

"No," Le-Chêne said, "I'll be right back."

The next morning, Nicolas looked out his shop window. Father Edmond and two nuns were talking to Jean in the stable yard. Nicolas went out to greet them.

"Bonjour, Father, Sisters," Nicolas said as Jean secured the horse to the cross ties and examined its foot.

"Bonjour, Nicolas," Father Edmond replied. "The Sisters are on their way to Framont before the quarantine to try new remedies. I'm going with them."

"Quarantine? My brother is in Framont."

The priest's thick eyebrows accentuated his frown. "I'll warn Le-Chêne to flee while he still can."

Nicolas ran his fingers through his hair in frustration. *Why didn't Le-Chêne stay here yesterday? Protecting the forge from the plague?*

One of the Sisters spoke, breaking his distraction. "Bonjour, monsieur, do you remember making my necklace?" She pulled the pendant from under her habit and looked at him with familiar eyes and olive skin.

"Of course, I remember. How are you, Sister . . . Rita?"

"Fine, thank you. Your kindness has given me much happiness over the years." She tucked it back under as Catherine rounded the corner carrying a bucket of fresh milk she had just bought from the supply.

Nicolas waved her over. "This is Sister Rita, my first customer. Sister, my wife, Catherine."

Catherine's jaw dropped. "You look exactly like my grandmother."

"Yes, Francisca," Nicolas blurted out. "I knew she looked familiar."

Father Edmond nodded. "Since you've mentioned it, Nounou does look like Francisca."

A pasty-faced nun with a nose much too large interrupted with a scowl. "Sister, this is not a social visit. It will be getting dark soon." She turned to Nicolas. "We've been traveling the countryside, creating relief areas in churches, and treating plague victims."

"Oh, Mémé is knowledgeable about using plants to treat all kinds of things," Catherine said. "Perhaps on your way home, you could meet her."

"Yes, I'd like that very much," Rita said. "But we really must go now."

The horse's shoe reset, Jean helped the sisters board the cart.

After they had gone, Nicolas said, "Le-Chêne needs to get out of there."

chapter

29

FRANCISCA thrashed in her sleep. *Did someone call my name?* She sat up in bed, panting.

Marie stirred beside her. "Mama? Did you hear something?"

"Quiet." Sitting in silence, she listened before replying, "Jean is sick."

"Who? Jean-Baptiste?"

"No, Jean Le-Chêne. He has the pestilence."

She pushed the blankets back, but Marie grabbed Francisca's shoulder. "What are you saying? Mama, you cannot help him."

Brushing off the hand, Francisca jumped out of bed. "Yes, I must go; I must try." After lighting the bedside candle, she dressed, fetched her bag, and packed it with dried weeds and herbs.

Helplessly watching, Marie followed her. "Are you sure? There might be guards at the city gate who will shoot you if you try to enter."

Jean-Baptiste peeked through the doorway, squinting. "What's going on?"

With tears in her eyes, Marie said, "Le-Chêne has the plague, and Mama insists on going to him."

He paled. "How do you know? Mémé, you cannot—"

The curt response Francisca gave surprised even herself. "I'm going. Either you will take me or I'll walk." She sat on the bench and slipped on her boots.

"Stubborn old woman," Jean-Baptiste grumbled, combing his hand through his hair. With a heavy sigh, he said, "I'll take you to talk to Catherine and Nicolas."

"Why? Le-Chêne is sick, not Catherine or Nicolas."

"Le-Chêne is Nicolas's brother, and he deserves to know."

Francisca picked her shawl from the hook by the door and tapped her foot impatiently. "Well? Get dressed."

As the sun brightened the horizon, Francisca waited while Jean-Baptiste pounded on his sister's door. Shirtless and still tying the laces on his pants, Nicolas answered.

Jean-Baptiste rushed out, "I'm sorry to bother you this early, but—"

Pushing him aside, Francisca wasted no time relaying the news as Jean-Baptiste came in and closed the door. As expected, Nicolas paled and dropped onto the bench by the table.

"No, he cannot have it. How do you know?" He raised his eyes to her. "How could you know?"

She sat beside him and took his hand. "I'm sorry, child."

Catherine appeared in the doorway, wrapping her shawl over her night-gown. She searched the faces before standing behind Nicolas and placing her hand on his shoulder. "Mémé—what is it? What's wrong?"

"Lovey, I'm afraid Le-Chêne has the plague. Where are his children?"

"With Elisabeth. How do you plan to help them? You said there is no cure."

A question Francisca had asked herself. "Well, I brought a bit of everything, and I will try each, one by one."

Jean-Baptiste paced, flinging his arms. "Even if you can cure him, you're not as strong as you once were, and you'll die."

Such insolence from a grandchild. She ripped her hand from Nicolas's grasp, stood, and poked Jean-Baptiste's chest with her finger. "If it's my time, I'll die. No matter what you say, I'm going."

While Jean-Baptiste took a step backward to avoid the wrath, Nicolas grasped Francisca's hand midair. She spun, ready to give him a tongue-lashing as well, but calmed when he asked, "What do you have in mind?"

"In case the road is blocked, I need someone to keep the guards busy until I can sneak past them.

Nicolas glanced at Catherine, still standing beside the chair. "What do you think?"

Though Catherine opened her mouth, no words came out. Nicolas embraced her and turned to Jean-Baptiste. "He's my brother. I'll take her."

Exhaling loudly, Jean-Baptiste crossed his arms and leaned against the fire-place. "Please consider your children. Let me take her." When he received no response, he added, "At least wait until this evening, right before dark. You'll have a better chance when the shadows are long."

"Yes, I agree with Jean-Baptiste," Catherine replied. "Wait until this eve-ning. If you get caught, you won't be able to help anyone."

"If you're determined to go," Nicolas added, "you must take precautions. I've seen a drawing of a mask doctors wear—looks like a bird head with the beak full of herbs. And they wear gloves, boots, and an outer cloak."

The suggestions made sense. Francisca studied their faces and rubbed her chin. "All right, I will wear my apron and gloves, and I have lavender in my bag. I'll wear it under my veil."

"You can take my leather apron," Nicolas said.

"I could not lift your apron, let alone wear it." She smiled and patted his arm. "I appreciate your concern, but I'm not worried."

Early that evening, Nicolas drove Francisca to Framont, arriving near the city at dusk, stopping the carriage by the last stand of trees where the road bent sharply. She dressed in black with a veil over her face, a wreath of lavender around her neck, and two sacks of herbs flung over her shoulders. She quietly slipped off the cart and disappeared inside the tree line, hopefully unseen.

Nicolas continued to the city gates to try to keep the guards busy until Francisca could sneak past them. Two men lounged on the grass, and a third man, slightly better dressed with a badge on his sleeve and a pistol at his side, sat on a tree stump. Nicolas recognized him as one of Louis's deputies. Though his heart pounded, Nicolas casually nodded to them and turned his attention back to the road.

The deputy motioned toward the two guards, who scrambled to their feet, brandishing swords. One raised his hand and spat before shouting, "Stop."

Pulling the reins, Nicolas leaned toward them. "Is there a problem, monsieur? I want to get to my brother's house before dark."

The deputy remained seated, his face rigid as he barked, "You can't go into the city—Framont's been quarantined since yesterday."

Perhaps he doesn't recognize me. As if hearing the news for the first time, Nicolas leaned forward and widened his eyes. "Quarantined? Why?"

The guard spat again and wiped his mouth on his sleeve. "The Great Mortality. Where have you been, under a rock? Notices have been posted for miles."

Scratching his nose to hide his identity, Nicolas shuffled nervously. "Well, I saw signs, but I'm in a hurry."

A twig snapped in the trees. The deputy stood. "Somebody's over there." He motioned with his pistol, and the spitter took off with his companion into the underbrush. Then he turned the gun toward Nicolas, who inhaled sharply and raised his arms above his head.

"Whoa! I only wanted to see my brother before dark."

A few seconds later, the guards came crashing out of the woods, their faces flushed. They ducked behind the wagon and pointed toward the thicket, screaming, "Wolf!"

The deputy joined them but kept his gun on Nicolas.

Does Francisca have a pet wolf? They seem to appear at just the right time. Despite the desperate situation, he fought to keep a straight face. To the guard, he said, "I didn't try to sneak a wolf into the city. Please turn that away from me."

The spitter turned and laughed at his companion. "I've never seen you move so fast."

"You ran first."

"I did not—"

The deputy lowered his gun, waved off the others, and returned to the stump, leaning back against the tree and pulling his hat down over his eyes.

"Can I go now?"

The guard spat again. "I told you, Framont's quarantined. Now get out of here before I arrest you."

With an exasperated sigh, Nicolas turned the carriage.

By the time Francisca arrived in Framont, darkness had fallen. The moon crept over the horizon, and a million stars dotted the sky. The city was deserted; acrid smoke floated in the air. She tiptoed silently to Le-Chêne's back door and knocked.

"Le-Chêne?"

It was too dark to see inside. Francisca found a rock, climbed onto a bench by the door, and broke a window. Pale moonlight shone through shards of broken glass and lit the way through the house.

"Le-Chêne?"

She found him in the bedchamber, sitting on the floor, leaning against the wall, his eyes bloodshot and his breath coming in ragged gasps. "Francisca? Why are you . . . Get out of here."

She touched his forehead; it was on fire. "I came to help you." She took his arm.

"Too late. I'm a dead man."

"Come, lie by the fireplace."

"Go away."

"Le-Chêne, you owe me. Remember that day?"

"Oh, you fool."

"Come," she said, tugging his arm.

With a relenting sigh, he reached for the bed frame and tried to stand, but he didn't put forth much effort. "I can't." He fell back against the wall. "No strength."

"Oh, lean on me and stop whining."

"But I'll crush you if I fall on you."

"Then don't fall on me."

She pulled his arm and refused to let go until he dragged himself up. He took a few steps, lost his balance, and clutched the doorframe, took a few more, and staggered into a table. For a moment, she thought he *would* fall on her, and then what would she do? But finally, he made it to the parlor. Gulping for air, he tumbled to the floor and passed out.

chapter 30

IMMEDIATELY, Francisca set to work. She started a fire and fetched a fresh pot of water to boil, opened her bag, and spread her bounty on the table. Throughout the night, she peeled horseradish, ground herbs for poultices, boiled leaves for ointments, and steeped roots for teas using every combination.

By morning, she was exhausted and plopped down next to the hearth. Why did she think she could cure the plague? Everyone knew there was no cure. Was it purely arrogance? She had dreamed about Le-Chêne and sensed his need so strongly. There must be a reason.

A knock at the door roused her. Father Edmond was there with two nuns and two men behind them, all wearing heavy cloaks, gloves, and handkerchiefs over their faces.

"Father," she said in relief. "Come in."

"Francisca? How did you pass through the blockade?"

She touched her throat in surprise. "Oh, Padre, I am so glad you came."

The nuns rushed past them and knelt by Le-Chêne, still lying beside the fireplace.

"Nothing I've tried will reduce his fever," Francisca said, kneeling beside them.

The taller nun removed Le-Chêne's shirt and replied. "Do you see this swelling?" She fingered a red spot under his left arm. "This is how the disease progresses. When this bump turns into a black blister-like pustule, a bubo, we will lance it. The pus and the smell are poisonous, so we wear heavy gloves and try to avoid the miasma with the scarves. This one is not ready yet."

As they stood, Father Edmond said, "The men will bring Le-Chêne to the church."

"No, I will take care of him here," Francisca replied.

"But he would be better off in the church, where someone will watch him constantly."

"I will watch him constantly right here."

The shorter of the nuns spoke. "Edmond, I will check on him after we finish today."

The other replied, "Yes, it's on the way back to the church."

Father Edmond said, "Nounou, you cause more work for yourself."

The taller one spoke to Francisca. "My name is Sister Grace, and this is Sister Rita."

For the first time since they had arrived, Francisca looked directly at them. When she took in the shorter one's eyes, she saw her own looking back. As if struck, she staggered and clutched the wall to keep from falling. "Sister . . . Rita? Please stay for a while."

"No," Sister Grace replied. "We'll be back in a couple of hours. In the meantime, try to get him to drink."

And they were gone.

Drained, Francisca fell to a bench near the door, trembling. She had prayed so hard, and now . . . Could that woman be her daughter? No. Besides, there were probably many nuns named after the Blessed Rita.

Nervously, Francisca bounced her leg and tapped her fingers. To keep busy, she returned to the pantry and pulled together a pottage. Every so often, she would glance at the sky, wishing the sun would make its way toward the west a little faster so she could talk to Sister Rita again. At last, a knock at the door. The two nuns had returned as promised.

Francisca invited them in, led them to Le-Chêne, and lifted the drawing poultice to reveal the spot under his arm. "Is this what you meant about the pustule being defined?"

"This is exactly what we meant," Sister Grace replied. "If the disease has not progressed too far, we have had some success." She removed a canteen of vinegar. "The smell of the vinegar helps with the miasma." When she poured it on the blade of her knife and onto Le-Chêne's armpit, he awoke.

He thrashed his head and moaned, "Rachelle . . ."

"Lie still," Sister Grace whispered as she lanced the bubo. Le-Chêne gritted his teeth as rancid blackish liquid oozed from the cut.

After Sister Rita cleaned his arm and the knife, she threw the rag into the fire. "The more poison released, the better." Then she covered him with the blanket, and he fell asleep.

Francisca showed them a cloth pack from the mantel. "I've been feeding him candied horseradish and using this periwinkle drawing poultice. Should I continue?"

"Yes, I should . . ." Sister Rita wobbled as she stood, "think so." Grabbing the mantel, she steadied herself. "Oh, I stood too fast. I feel a little light-headed."

Francisca helped her to a chair. "Are you all right, Sister?"

Rita removed her veil and slipped her coif off the back of her head, revealing soaking wet hair.

"Sister, you're drenched," Sister Grace scolded. "How long have you been ill?"

"I got a headache this morning. I tried to ignore it all day."

"Let me help you to the church."

"I don't think I can make it to the church," Rita said as her eyes brimmed with tears.

Francisca took her arm and led her to Le-Chêne's bedchamber. "Stay here. Come, rest on the bed. I'll make you some tea. Perhaps it will help."

A thousand thoughts crowded her mind as she ladled some boiling water into a mug and threw in some crushed willow bark and muskroot, reappearing at the door as Sister Rita removed her robe.

A pendant caught on the laces and glistened as it fell against her chest.

Francisca gasped at the sight and dropped the mug. It shattered on the floor, the hot liquid dancing on the cold wood, spattering her skirt.

The two nuns whirled. "Are you all right?" they said as one.

Ignoring the mess on the floor, Francisca tried to calm her racing heart. "Yes, sit down, my child."

Grace turned back to the task and touched Rita's arm. "Oh no. Not you too, Sister."

"I'm sorry," Rita cried, fingering the bubo under her armpit. "I have probably infected you and everyone at the church."

"All for the greater honor and glory of God," Grace said, crossing herself.

Francisca pulled back the blankets. "Lie down."

A moment of quiet followed before Grace collected Rita's clothes, and on her way out she said, "I will tell Edmond."

"You will be all right, child," Francisca said. "God has brought you to me." She wanted to dance and sing, but her daughter's pale, sweat-covered face terrified her.

"Yes. He has." Rita sighed, closed her eyes, and crossed herself as she resigned herself to the bed. A single tear rolled down her cheek.

"Do you feel well enough to talk?"

The nun's red eyes narrowed in pain and disappointment. "Yes, please stay with me. I'm ashamed to say that I'm afraid." She slid over, allowing more room on the bed for Francisca to sit beside her.

Taking her hand, Francisca said, "I want to tell you about my life."

"Of course." Rita sank into the pillow.

Where do I start? "When I was about twelve years old, my mama gave me a necklace . . ." Francisca's hands shook as she pulled out her necklace at the end of the story. "I have prayed for this day since the last time I saw you. Ever since the day you were born."

With her eyes wide and staring, Rita lay motionless while tears poured down both cheeks. "Mama?" She tried to sit, but a quiet moan escaped her lips, and she fell back.

Francisca patted her hand. "Let me fetch you some more tea; it will help with the pain. God has sent you to me. He would not be so cruel as to allow us to be together just for you to die."

"Thank you, Mama," Rita said with a shaky voice.

While her two patients slept, Francisca sat beside Rita's bed, holding her hand. In the morning, Grace returned and examined Le-Chêne's armpit. She lanced the bubo under his arm again, commenting on the lessening amount of black fluid drainage.

"I've kept it moist with poultices all night," Francisca said, "hoping to draw the poison."

Grace nodded. "It appears to be working."

As they moved to the back room, Francisca said, "Rita's fever seems high. She speaks, but I cannot understand her."

The cloth from her daughter's forehead was warm, so Francisca dunked it in a bucket of water before replacing it. The cool water awakened the patient.

"How do you feel, Sister?" Grace asked, taking Rita's hand.

Though her breathing was shallow, she managed to say, "Fine, thank you."

Grace kissed her forehead. "Let's see how you're doing." She pulled back the blanket, and upon finding another bubo on Rita's groin, Grace closed her eyes and sighed. "There's another one on your leg, dear. Let me lance them both for you."

As the knife cut through her daughter's rotting flesh, Francisca cried silently. The foul stench indicated the severity of the infection.

After praying together, Francisca followed Sister Grace to the door. "Sister is declining rapidly. I will return as soon as possible with Father Edmond to give her Extreme Unction."

Unable to stop the tears, Francisca pleaded with her. "No, Rita will recover."

"Her nose is darkening, and her fingers are turning black. I'm sorry, but we must be strong and know that whatever happens is God's will."

The weight of the words made it hard to breathe.

"Mama?" Rita called.

Francisca realized Grace was gone and she was standing in the open doorway. She rushed to her daughter's bedside. "Yes, my heart."

"I want you to know that I have been happy."

"We will talk about this later when you are well."

"I may not be able to speak later. God, in His infinite mercy, has sent me here as an answer to your prayers, so we could meet before I die." With a heavy exhale, Rita closed her eyes.

"No, my treasure, you will not die."

"I love you, Mama," Rita murmured as she slipped into unconsciousness.

The air was thick and sweltering. Francisca stood in the corner, staring at her daughter's dead body, praying for her own demise.

A young boy swung the thurible back and forth as the smoke from the burning incense floated through the room, clung to the rafters, and drifted toward the open window. Father Edmond leaned over the body, reciting prayers. *". . . quam semper optaverunt, piis supplicationibus consequantur . . ."*

A vague sense that everyone had left the room brought Francisca back from her melancholy. The service must be over. Two men came in, wrapped her daughter in the blanket on which she lay, and carried her out the door. Another gathered the bedclothes, pillows, and even the window coverings.

Francisca slogged to the doorway, where Father Edmond was speaking to Le-Chêne.

Le-Chêne? He was sitting on a chair with a blanket wrapped around his waist. The cuts the sisters had made on his underarm had dried into scabs.

Sister Grace touched his forehead and asked, "How do you feel?"

"If the room would stop spinning, I'd be fine. Is Francisca all right? And I remember another nun—"

Father Edmond replied. "Francisca is fine." He teared up, and his voice cracked. "Nounou— *ahem*—Sister Rita did not survive."

The thought cut through Francisca like a knife. *My daughter . . .*

Le-Chêne breathed in sharply. "Oh no, she died saving me?"

"No, she gave her life willingly and saved many." Edmond's tears spilled over, and he turned his head and wiped his eyes. "She inspired us all."

Upon seeing Edmond cry, Francisca began again.

Le-Chêne must have heard her and turned. She tried to smile, but the tears wouldn't stop, and he held out his arms. "Come here," he said and doubled the blanket over himself before pulling her to sit on his lap.

She laid her head on his shoulder, and he held her while she wept until she had no tears left. By the time she composed herself, everyone had gone. Embarrassed, she pulled herself from his embrace and stood.

"You must be starved. Let me fetch you something to eat."

When she returned from the pantry, carrying a crust of bread and a mug of spruce tea, he pushed a chair out with his foot. "Sit with me. Have you eaten?"

"I'm all right."

Le-Chêne ripped a piece from the crust and stared at it.

"Are you in pain, child?"

"Physically, no." But she could see the worry in his eyes. "I took my children to my parents. What if they carried the disease with them—I may have killed my entire family and the whole town of Vacquenoux."

Francisca patted his arm. "Your family is fine."

"How do you know?"

"They're safe. I'm sure."

He stared at her intently. "Do you know how foolish you were coming here?"

Tears stung her eyes again. "This time has been the most fulfilling of my life." She dabbed her handkerchief before adding, "I will cherish it forever."

Inside the guarded city, food became scarce. Francisca foraged what she could but trapped in quarantine, with few fields or gardens, pickings were slim. Once Le-Chêne had regained his strength, they set out to see what they could find.

The burning smell that had enveloped the region since the epidemic began grew more pungent, stinging their eyes. A morose silence had settled over the town—no inhabitants, no animals, nothing except the distant sound of wailing and the putrid odor of death and smoke.

In the shadow of the church, Francisca saw a figure crouching on the steps. It was Father Edmond. As she and Le-Chêne approached the priest, he raised his head, his eyes sunken and glazed in exhaustion, as if he did not recognize them. "Are you sick?" he asked in a tired voice.

"Father Edmond. What happened to you? Are you all right?" Le-Chêne asked.

Father Edmond allowed his head to fall back against the door of the church and stared at the sky. "They brought the sick and just dropped them off, like sacks of flour. All I could do was quench their thirst, give them a little comfort, and bury their bodies in pits to keep the disease from spreading."

"What of the sisters who were helping you?"

"There's only one left—Sister Grace. She's sleeping inside the church."

"Shall I take you somewhere to rest?" Le-Chêne said.

"No." He hung his head. "This is my parish. I must welcome and give comfort."

Le-Chêne looked up the street. "We're going to the supply to buy food. I'll bring you back something."

"Supplies were supposed to be left at the gate. At first, they brought enough food, but nothing has come for days. When villagers left, they took everything with them."

Francisca scanned the desolate town. "You look half-starved. Have you eaten?"

Father Edmond smiled weakly. "No, but I'm fine."

"Come to the house this evening. I'll make us something to eat."

Surely the plague was the work of demons. Attempting to scare the devil away, the formerly sensible people of Salm burned cats or signed allegiance to the Prince of Darkness. Catholic churches multiplied their processions, burned incense, and sprayed holy water while Protestants gave accusatory homilies blaming Catholics, heretics, and sorcery. Both sides meticulously recorded accusations filed by parishioners against neighbors and even members of their own families.

Amid all this fear and frenzy, from his shop window, Nicolas glanced at a carriage that pulled into the stable yard.

Le-Chêne and Francisca!

Dropping everything, Nicolas ran to them, shouting for Martin and Jean as he went.

While Quentin rushed to tell Catherine and Elisabeth, Le-Chêne embraced his brother and father. Nicolas ran around and pulled Francisca into his arms.

He spun her in circles, but she smacked him on the head with her bag, and he put her down and kissed both her cheeks.

"We were so worried about you," Jean said.

"Papa, Papa," Le-Chêne's children shouted as Elisabeth led them down the path. He touched the baby's head, then knelt for the older girls to hug his neck.

At the estate, he recalled the events. At the end of the account, he said, "After I recovered, Francisca invited Father Edmond to supper, and he told us of the other villagers plundering vacant homes for food." Le-Chêne kissed the old woman's cheek. "She scolded the weary priest for not inviting everyone."

Francisca smiled half-heartedly and lowered her head, but she was not as jubilant as Nicolas would have expected, and he decided to watch for signs of the sickness.

"So," Le-Chêne continued, "the priest brought about ten people and a dozen orphans. There was barely any food, so Francisca sent us out to find something, anything. The children were to search for acorns and nuts, dandelion greens, or purslane. One man returned with a couple of onions, another with a bunch of kale. She made enough soup to feed all those people. We ate only once a day, but nobody starved."

"Did you see Balthazar and Claire?" Nicolas asked.

Le-Chêne's breath caught. "No, I never thought to check on them."

Nicolas paled. "Is it safe to go into the city?"

"Yes. I will come too."

"No, you're half-starved," Nicolas said, jumping to his feet. "I'll be right back."

Nicolas entered the city warily. The wind blew dust and leaves across the street before him, punctuating the desolation.

He stopped his horse in front of his friends' house and dismounted. "Balthazar, Claire?" No response. Nicolas tied the horse to the pole and ran through the open door. "Balthazar, Claire?" Complete silence. Above the fireplace, where Balthazar had proudly displayed his papa's silver sword, dangled a small piece of twine. Remnants of curtains hung in tatters by the windows, and furniture lay on its side.

"Come back here," someone shouted outside.

Through a broken window, Nicolas saw two shaggy youngsters untying his horse, and he shouted, "Hey!"

The urchins abandoned their target and ran as Father Edmond chased them. When Nicolas rushed out the door, the priest stopped, bent to rest his hands on his knees, and panted.

"Father. Should I catch them?"

Raising his arms in exasperation, Edmond replied, "Let them go. They'll be back by suppertime. They ran away from the orphanage, but there is nothing left for them to steal. Have you seen your brother?"

"Yes, thank God. Do you know Balthazar and Claire Osché?" Nicolas nodded toward the house.

The priest slumped. "I'm sorry. Were they your friends?"

Nicolas's breath caught in his throat, and he stared into the distance as he listened.

"Their baby was one of the first to get sick, and Claire contracted the disease soon after he died. I told Balthazar to allow us to take her to the church so he could escape with the other children before the quarantine, but he refused to leave her side and caught it within a few days." The priest lowered his eyes. "But I must confess: I killed him."

Confused, Nicolas focused on the emaciated priest.

Father Edmond clasped his hands. "The Sisters were instructed how to drain the poison, but they asked me to lance the men's groin area. Balthazar was my first patient and—I'm afraid I made the cut too deep." Father Edmond swallowed hard and added, "We couldn't stop the bleeding."

Though his heart was breaking for his best friends, Nicolas placed his hand on Father Edmond's shoulder. "You risked your life to try to save them. Then you must have also saved my brother?"

"The Sisters did. They gave their lives . . ." His voice cracked. "Excuse me," he muttered and shuffled away.

31

Dearest Anne,

I have wonderful news and shocking news. The shocking first—
Le-Chêne has survived the plague. Though Mémé said she had nothing
to do with it, he credits her for saving his life. However, his new wife,
Claudette, is gone. Her father decided it was best to run from the disease,
but they have never returned, and after Le-Chêne and Nicolas have
searched everywhere, they have not found her. We are all heartbroken,
and Le-Chêne blames himself.

Why not come home for a while and see if you could create a spark?
He is an attractive man with a good job and a beautiful house; he needs
a beautiful wife—and I miss you. As for the wonderful news, you are
going to be an aunt again. If it is a girl, we will name her Claudette,
but we are hoping for a little Humbert. Either way, Le-Chêne will be
the godfather.

Consider my suggestion. Now is a good time to come home.
Love, Catherine

Dearest Catherine,

Thank you for thinking of me, though I am not desperate enough
to prey on a man in mourning. Give Le-Chêne my address, and if he is
interested, he can come to see me or write to me.

You will not believe what is happening here. Rumors flew that
Countess Chrestienne would marry the son of the Duke of Lorraine, but
then the duke tried to secure an alliance with the Emperor of the Holy
Roman Empire and asked for the hand of Marie de Medici for his son.

We were all offended for Chrestienne; however, the humiliation inflicted on the Salm family became even greater for the duke when the Italian spurned him.

After countless talks, the hand of Marie de Medici, who is Catholic, was denied by the Catholic duke and given to his enemy, the new King of France, Henry of Navarre, which is unbelievable since Henry is a Protestant—and already married. Not only is he getting a divorce—I mean, an annulment—he has a mistress who has several children with him, and she is pregnant again!

Now the wedding between the countess and duke's son is back on. As soon as they ratify the contract, Chrestienne will be off to Nancy. Her father, Count Paul, and uncle, Count Jean, must first dispossess all their assets. In addition to the land, the dowry was set at an incredible 100,000 francs.

I am not sure where that will leave Salm.

Love, Anne

Baby Claudette came into the world in 1595. On the day of the christening, Marie hosted a gathering at the farm, and Nicolas enlisted Little Jean, now ten years old, to circulate among the guests, filling goblets. One guest stood alone, gazing at the gardens. Nicolas approached him.

"Father, would you like some wine?"

The priest turned, revealing eyes lined with worry.

"Is something wrong, Father?"

Clasping his hands in front of him, Father Edmond nodded before waving to Le-Chêne to join them. "May I speak with you?" The brothers exchanged worried looks and followed the priest away from the crowd.

"I've just returned from a disturbing trip to Badonviller," Edmond said. "I had expected to report on the treatments of the pestilence or the status of the orphans." The priest rubbed his brow and frowned. "Instead, they interrogated me about Francisca."

With a gasp, Nicolas said, "Francisca? Why?"

"At the abbey, the Sisters swapped stories of their experiences, and Sister Grace mentioned the drawing poultices Francisca had used. One of the bishops took an interest."

Le-Chêne flinched. "A bishop?"

"Yes, Bishop Michel."

"Bishop Michel?" Nicolas repeated. "What did he look like?"

"Thin, curly hair, close-set brown eyes—"

"—and a nose like a beak?" Le-Chêne finished his sentence.

Father Edmond sighed. "It did resemble a beak. Do you know him?"

"The provost led Father Michel, our former parish priest, away a few days before you arrived, but we never heard the reason. Why, what did *the bishop* say about Francisca?"

"He suggested she must be a witch since she didn't get sick."

The priest held up his hands to the immediate protests. "I told them that neither Sister Grace, nor I, nor many helpers got sick and that I'd have starved if not for Francisca. It took a while, but I convinced the other bishops to drop the issue. Do you think I should advise her of his accusations? I don't want to scare her."

"Thank you for telling us," Nicolas said, refilling the priest's goblet. "Let's not alarm the guests. We will tell her later."

"I thought that little weasel was out of our lives," Francisca murmured.

Jean-Baptiste stood, slammed his fist on the table, and yelled, "I've had it with that priest. I will find out once and for all why he hates us." Swearing under his breath, Jean-Baptiste walked away.

"Wait," Nicolas said to his back. "Father Edmond didn't make the accusations; he just informed us of them."

Marie inhaled as if to say something but pursed her lips.

The look of panic in her eyes prompted Nicolas to follow Jean-Baptiste. "Wait, I'll come with you."

At the church, Jean-Baptiste ripped the door open and stormed into the vestibule. Father Edmond was at the altar, replacing burned-down candles. He waved to them and said, "Let me put these away. Would you wait for me in the sacristy?"

The small room beside the altar was cluttered with crates, and the air was heavy with the scent of candles, faded incense, and sacramental oils.

Upon entering, Jean-Baptiste lowered his head and dragged his feet. "It's been a long time since I've been in here."

Nicolas leaned against the doorframe, waiting for the priest, but Jean-Baptiste backed against the wall and stared wide-eyed at the stained-glass window, his face as pale as a ghost's. "S-s-something's wrong here," he said, sliding down the wall.

Nicolas snatched a stool and slid it under Jean-Baptiste, who dropped on it, then laid his head on his knees. "This smell is oppressive. I think I'm going to be sick."

Father Edmond joined them. "Thank you for waiting."

"No problem, Father," Nicolas said. "We have come to discuss—"

Jean-Baptiste raised his head and squinted at the glare of light streaming in the window, raising his trembling hand to shade his eyes. Without warning, he shouted, "Never again, you bastard!" and he flung himself at the priest with such force that they both fell against Nicolas. All three tumbled to the floor with Jean-Baptiste on top of Edmond, pummeling his face.

Wriggling from under the pile, Nicolas pulled Jean-Baptiste off the priest.

"Let me go," Jean-Baptiste shouted as he struggled to get free.

Nicolas dragged his brother-in-law into the church and threw him onto the first pew. "What in the hell are you doing?" Nicolas shouted through clenched teeth.

Sweat ran down Jean-Baptiste's face as he glanced around the church as if he couldn't remember where he was. He stared at the blood on his hands. "Something came over me." He whispered, "I thought he was . . ." His eyes darted around until they stopped on Father Edmond, who remained near the door, holding a handkerchief to his nose. "I . . . I didn't mean to hurt you. I thought you were . . . someone else. I mean, I thought . . ." Jean-Baptiste glanced at Nicolas, then back to the priest before hanging his head.

Edmond approached cautiously, his forehead pinched. "Who did you think I was?"

Nicolas brushed the wrinkles from the priest's clothing and adjusted his collar.

Without replying, and before either man could stop him, Jean-Baptiste bolted from the church, jumped on his horse, and flew up the street.

Father Edmond ran after him. "Son, stay here and talk to me."

There was nothing to do but assume Jean-Baptiste had gone home, so they went there. Marie met them at the door, and when she saw Edmond's battered and bruised face, she paled. Taking her hand, Nicolas asked, "Marie, where is Jean-Baptiste?"

"He left with you." She raised her hand to cover her mouth as tears came to her eyes.

Father Edmond helped her to the bench by the door. "Marie, tell us."

Removing a handkerchief from inside her cuff, she touched it to her eye and began, "Humbert never told anyone except Father Brignon. You knew Humbert; he thought he could handle all our problems alone."

"Trust us, Marie," Nicolas said.

"A long time ago, when Jean-Baptiste was a child, Father Brignon was our parish priest." She fumbled with the kerchief before raising her gaze and continuing. "We enjoyed church activities, and we loved Father Brignon. Humbert called him Papa."

Nicolas nodded in acknowledgment.

"Jean-Baptiste learned to be an altar boy, and he enjoyed serving. We thought he might even become a priest someday, and if things had worked out differently . . ." She sighed heavily. "We were so proud of him."

"But Father Brignon was reassigned, and Father Michel replaced him. Of course, things were not the same, and when Jean-Baptiste came home crying . . ." The tears she had been trying to contain spilled down her cheeks.

Father Edmond touched her arm. "Go on, Marie."

"Humbert worried what people would think—he's going to haunt me for telling you." She dabbed her eyes again. "In the laundry, I found blood in Jean-Baptiste's braies. When I asked about it, he burst into tears and refused to tell us what had happened until Francisca gave him one of her drinks and got the truth. He told her everything. The poor boy was so angry and afraid, and we didn't know what to do, so Humbert wrote to Father Brignon, who came immediately." She blew her nose and continued to wring her handkerchief.

Though Marie's voice wavered, she continued as if relieved to get the weight off her. "Father Michel denied everything, of course. He called Jean-Baptiste a bad boy who simply didn't want to serve, but Father Brignon knew better. The authorities said the bloody pants were not enough evidence by themselves and they'd not believe a little boy's word over that of a priest." She shook her head in anger and disbelief. "We hid our shame and stopped going to church. Once away from the situation, our boy forgot, but his anger remained. Father Michel has hated our family ever since."

Everything finally became clear: Humbert's hatred of Father Michel, why Catherine had not been baptized as a baby, why they seemed so pious but never went to Mass. Nicolas remembered the boy who had run headlong into his father before the wedding. Louis must have caught Father Michel with a red-hand, which explained his sudden disappearance.

Father Edmond said, "I want to talk to your son, Marie. Do you know where he is?"

"No, but he used to hide in the loft of the barn."

Nicolas led the way, climbed the ladder, and found Jean-Baptiste standing amid a cloud of dust and chaff as he rammed the rake around the loft, scraping so hard scratch marks appeared in the wooden floor. As Father Edmond stepped onto the platform, Jean-Baptiste spun and dropped the rake. He opened his mouth to speak, but no words came out.

"Are you going to hit me again?" Father Edmond asked.

"No, Father," Jean-Baptiste replied, his face haggard. "I thought—I mean, you reminded me of someone else. I will go with you to the provost."

"Why would we go to the provost?" Edmond stepped forward, but Jean-Baptiste jumped back.

"Don't touch me."

Father Edmond frowned and went to the corner to sit on a crate, leaned his head against the wall, and motioned for Jean-Baptiste to join him. "Tell me what happened when you were a child."

How can I get out of here? I don't want to hear this! Nicolas shuffled his feet. "Maybe I should go?"

Jean-Baptiste's eyes narrowed. "Please stay. I'm not comfortable alone with a priest."

Edmond shifted his weight before replying, "We're trying to help you."

But Jean-Baptiste just clenched his fists. "I'd rather not talk about it." He turned to stare out the vent window.

"We spoke with your mama," Nicolas said.

Jean-Baptiste spun, red-faced, his eyes shooting sparks. "She had no right."

Waiting for another attack, Nicolas tensed, but Father Edmond remained seated, his hands folded in his lap. His eyes were swelling and turning purple, yet his voice was steady. "You must come to terms with this, Jean-Baptiste. This anger is ruining your life." Edmond opened his palms. "Know that this was not your fault; you were just a little boy."

Without replying, Jean-Baptiste turned back to the window and angrily wiped a tear on his sleeve.

"I've never dealt with this before," Edmond continued to his back, "but perhaps if we talk about it—"

"Please leave me alone."

Desperately trying to think of a resolution, Nicolas pinched the bridge of his nose and remembered his father's answer to most problems. "Let's go fishing. Tomorrow at noon—the three of us."

"Great idea," Father Edmond replied. "I can come right after I ring the bell."

"I'm busy," Jean-Baptiste said with a sniffle.

Nicolas scowled. "You will make time. We'll ride together."

Jean-Baptiste glared, but Nicolas held his ground. "Remember the day I kept Dimanchette's brothers from killing you? You owe me."

In the rural counties of the Vosges, the price of rye or the construction of a new blast furnace in Framont dominated conversations. One morning, about three years later, that all changed.

On a bench in the shade of the stable, Martin oiled the leather on a harness while Quentin buffed it and polished the brass. While they worked through the pile of tack, Provost Louis Gauthier approached them.

"Bonjour, Martin," Louis said. "Is Jean here?"

"Bonjour. He's at the house," Martin said before turning to Quentin. "Would you fetch Jean for us?"

As Louis took Quentin's seat, Martin asked, "Are you here about the division of the county?"

Louis grinned. "You're always the first to know everything. I just got confirmation yesterday."

"Coachmen listen, and they also talk." Martin winked. "Oh, and I heard Paris is worth a Mass—" At Louis's dismayed look, Martin continued, "I heard that King Henry has become Catholic, hoping finally to end the Wars of Religion, and that's what he said, *Paris is worth a Mass*. I wish he would have kept his convictions."

"Well, I heard he has just survived another assassination attempt. I think he's a good king and is working toward a chicken in every pot. He will come up with an edict or something so everyone is free to worship as they wish. I don't blame him for switching. Wouldn't you?"

But before Martin could consider it fully, Jean came up beside them and said, "What have you heard, Louis?"

Louis replied, "Countess Chrestienne's wedding to the future duke has caused major changes to the borderlines of the county. They have split Salm into two equal parts. The half ruled by Rhingrave, Count Frédéric Sauvage, will continue as Salm, while the half ruled by Count Jean IX will become part of Lorraine."

"Where does that leave Vacquenoux?"

"Thankfully, it will stay Salm—under Count Frédéric."

Louis raised his gaze, scrutinizing a passing horse and rider before turning back to the group.

Martin smiled, always working.

"The mine and forge will still be shared with the abbey," Louis continued. "However, they cut the cities in half, using income as the dividing line. In Badonviller, sixty houses for one, sixty for the other. In La Broque, twenty-three houses remain Salm, and twenty-three will go to Lorraine."

Silence followed while everyone absorbed the information.

Martin said, "Help me to understand, Louis. Some people awakened this morning living in Salm and will go to bed this evening in Lorraine?"

Louis nodded and replied, "Rumor says those going to Lorraine must convert to Catholicism and change their names or go into exile."

"But they may have lived here quietly their entire lives," Martin said, almost to himself.

Jean said, "Thank God we are on the Salm side. Count Jean has always fought with the Catholic Abbey, but he would follow the Catholic Dukes of Lorraine in a heartbeat, and Chrestienne's marriage is proof."

After Chrestienne's wedding, Catherine waited to hear from Anne. Instead of receiving a letter, Anne surprised Catherine with a visit in time for Little Jean's twelfth birthday and Confirmation celebration.

The sisters sat outside, watching the children play while Anne told Catherine of the grand wedding gown she helped make for Chrestienne. Then she showed a coin struck for the occasion given to the staff with a profile of Chrestienne on one side and François de Vaudémont, the future duke, on the other.

Catherine ran her thumb over the images and flipped the coin over and over before giving it back to Anne, worried she may never see her sister again. "So you are going to Nancy with Chrestienne?"

Claudette brought them a bouquet of dandelions. Anne took the flowers and kissed the child on the cheek before replying, "No. The castle is too big, too crowded, and too far from you."

"Will you stay in Badonviller?"

"Now that Chrestienne is gone, her mother went to live with her family, so the castle will only house the garrison and a handful of servants."

"Then you will come back to us," Catherine said with excitement, raising her arms for an embrace.

Anne shook her head. "Sorry to disappoint you, but I am going to Pierre-Percée."

Shocked, Catherine grasped her arm. "To the castle of the Savage Count?"

"The village at the foot of the castle." Anne shook her head and returned that superior look that Catherine knew so well. "The count is not a werewolf, Catherine."

"Have you met a man there?"

Anne's face lit up as it had when they shared a room in the attic at the farm. "Yes, his name is Henri, Captain of the Guards."

Catherine's jaw dropped. "Captain? A nobleman. Will he marry you?"

"Of course not. He dares to go to war, but not to defy his papa."

"Why would marrying you defy his papa?"

"He cannot marry me, Catherine. Henri is nobility, and I am just—"

"You're not *just* anything, Anne." But then Catherine's gasped when she realized what Anne meant. "You're going to be—his mistress? Is that the kind of life you want?"

Anne wrung her hands before replying, "It'll be fine because his family's lands are far away in the south of France, so nobody will surprise us. We're going to build a beautiful stone house in the village. Everyone already thinks I am his wife. Imagine me bearing descendants to the noble family of Puyloubier."

Catherine stared at her graceful, beautiful sister. "I don't think you're putting a proper value on yourself."

Anne lowered her head, the glint in her eye gone, and Catherine regretted saying anything. She took her sister's hand. "But if you're happy, so am I. I wish you a life full of love and children."

chapter

32

1598-1605

STILL reeling about Anne's revelation a week later, Catherine barely listened as Nicolas complained about one of his customers. Over-whelming nausea brought the realization that she had been lax in her *precautions* and was pregnant with their fourth child. The girls were growing out of their dresses, the garden was full of weeds, and all her husband could think about was someone's silly complaint.

Little Jean wasn't helping matters. As he ran past Catherine on his way to the table, she reached for him, hoping for a quick hug, but he slipped out of her grasp. He'd grown too fast and was tall for his age, taller than she was, and since his confirmation declared him an adult, he hated the title "Little Jean." Though he had helped Nicolas since he learned to walk, now his apprenticeship became official. He worked with great enthusiasm for the first couple of weeks, but his excitement waned quickly. At supper one evening, he was unusually quiet.

As Catherine dished out the stew, she asked him, "Is something wrong?"

Sad blue eyes turned to Nicolas. "I don't want to let you down, Papa."

With a confused glance, Nicolas cocked his head. "I'm so proud of you, son. Why would you let me down?"

Little Jean squirmed before replying, "I don't like working in the forge, and I cannot imagine doing it for the rest of my life."

Stunned, Catherine waited while Nicolas spoke, "I thought you enjoyed working with me."

"It has nothing to do with you, Papa."

"What's on your mind?"

"Well, Martin mentioned that his friend from the Strasbourg print shop takes in apprentices. Perhaps I could learn to be a printer?"

Incredulous, Catherine stared alternately between her husband and her son. The air hung heavy over the meal. As she gathered the bowls, Nicolas said, "I'll talk to Martin tomorrow."

She froze. "Surely, you're not going to allow our child to move far away when he is so young?" The look Nicolas shot her burned, and she flinched.

"Martin would never suggest it if he had any concerns, and I've not given my permission yet. I said we would talk to Martin, nothing more."

Frustrated with his wife and son, Nicolas had nothing to say the rest of the evening or at the table the next morning. At work, Little Jean lingered by the door of the shop, his face brightening with anticipation when Martin emerged from his house.

"Sharpen those boring bits for me." The tone of Nicolas's voice was harsher than he'd intended; however, he needed Martin's honest opinion without sorrowful eyes swaying him. Sorrowful eyes always persuaded Martin. Little Jean's shoulders slumped as he set to the task.

As Nicolas approached the barn, he considered alternative careers for his son, though he had instilled the love of reading in him, and what better choice could there be?

He swallowed hard and stepped into the coolness of the barn, where chaff and hay dust floated in the air. A wheelbarrow full of manure came out of a stall, and then Quentin appeared, pushing it.

"Good morning, Uncle," Quentin said.

Nicolas chuckled.

At twenty-two, Quentin had grown into a fine young man with fair hair and a freckled complexion. Though Jean had offered more than once to sponsor him at the Framont forge, Quentin always declined, opting to divide his time between the forge and stable. He was happy with the simple life. Why couldn't Little Jean be more like—

Martin poked his head out of a different stall. "Is something wrong, Nicolas? You look like you just lost your best friend."

The irony. "I have a favor to ask of you."

"Of course," Martin replied, motioning to a grain bin, where they sat together.

"Well . . ." Nicolas fidgeted while gathering his thoughts. "It seems Little Jean hates working with me."

Martin nodded. "Yes, I saw this coming."

Am I the only one who didn't see it?

"How can I help you, Nicolas?"

"Little Jean wanted to know if you could ask your printer friend if he has some type of publishing apprenticeship available."

Martin raised his eyebrows. "And what do you want?"

I want my son home with me.

Nicolas stared blankly up the aisle of the barn, wishing he could get out of this entire conversation. Quentin returned with the wheelbarrow and disappeared into another stall. The sound of the shovel scraping the dirt echoed through the empty barn. Nicolas pulled himself together. "I guess I want Little Jean to be happy."

Martin appeared satisfied. "Then I will ask Johann."

"But is it safe in Strasbourg? Little Jean is so young, and—"

"Is it safe anywhere?"

Nicolas couldn't think of a reply.

"Come with me next week and decide for yourself."

"I guess Mama could stay with Catherine . . ."

"Look, you've always said you wanted to see Strasbourg. It will ease your mind."

Nicolas always wanted to go to Strasbourg but had never taken the time. Now he was almost as excited as Little Jean, who sat across from him in the coach. Beside them, Martin dozed despite the bumps.

Once they passed Russ, farther than Nicolas had ever been, vast plains opened before them, and he peeked through heavy curtains and pointed at the passing landscape. At Lutzelhouse, Martin parted the curtain and motioned toward a stone.

"This is Schneeberg, where women suspected of infidelity suffer the judgment of the rock."

"What judgment?" Little Jean asked.

"An unfaithful woman must walk across the unstable rock. If she can cross, she is freed of suspicion. If she slips and falls into the gorge, it means she must have been guilty."

Nicolas flinched. "What if she's just clumsy?"

Martin replied with a sour face that prompted a gasp from the others.

A little while later, at the ruins of the castle of Mutzig, the coach changed horses, allowing the riders to stretch their legs.

"I never thought I could be so shaken," Nicolas said, rubbing his back.

"The rough journey is worth it," Martin said. "Once you see the sights, you'll not regret being abused."

There were many more hours of shaking to endure and several more stops to change horses before reaching their destination. Along the way, the appearance of houses changed to lime-washed, multistory dwellings interspersed with dark beams. On the top of a few pointed roofs, huge birds rested on large nests made of sticks.

"Those are storks," Martin explained. "They spend the summer here and return to Africa in the autumn."

The language of those they passed gradually changed too. Throughout the valley of the Bruche, Nicolas recognized French or Welche, but the farther they traveled from the Vosges Mountains, the language became mostly German, especially the Alsatian dialect.

When they finally arrived, the cobbled streets of Strasbourg were a mishmash of passengers alighting from coaches and carts laden with vegetables, wood, or barrels, driven by men who shouted at them for getting in their way. On one corner, Martin stopped and pointed upward.

The gigantic pink cathedral rose toward the sky. Awestruck, Nicolas whispered, "Notre Dame. The tallest building in the world."

"Let us drop off our bags first, then we can see it more closely," said Martin.

At the boardinghouse, a heavy-boned middle-aged woman with a warm Alsatian accent greeted Martin with kisses.

"Bonjour, madame," Martin said, showing none of his usual inhibition. "This is my good friend Nicolas and his son, Jean. We are hoping to secure an apprenticeship."

Her face lit up. "Vonderful, I have three students sharing a flat right now. There is plenty of room for one more with them."

The old woman preceded them up a small wooden staircase separated from the main room by finely cut spindles with a leaf design. At the top, she dabbed the sweat from her forehead, panting, and pointed to a room lit by a narrow yellow stained glass window, the same as the White Horse Inn in Vacquenoux, furnished with a large bed, table, and cabinet.

"Zis is your room, the same size as the one upstairs. You see? Plenty of room for four."

The bed barely looked big enough for the three of them, but Little Jean would stay at a group home provided by the master if he secured an apprenticeship. Nicolas nodded and smiled at her.

"Can we meet Master Carolus now?" Little Jean pulled Nicolas's sleeve like a child.

Nicolas shot him a stern look, and the boy straightened his posture and lowered his eyes. *He doesn't act old enough to be on his own.*

Nicolas and Little Jean followed Martin through the narrow streets to a workshop with a wrought-iron sign representing a book. The thick carved wooden door was propped open. They stepped inside, immediately surprised by a strong smell of leather mixed with glue, where the silence contrasted with the bustle and cries of the street.

"This is the bindery," Martin said. "Now we will see the print shop."

A few doors down, another much larger workshop bustled with activity. Young boys with bundles of paper ran in all directions. Two men were busy around a large press. Another called to invisible people at the bottom of the staircase, who responded by shouting to overcome the general noise.

A hefty figure dressed in a long red velvet cloak appeared before them. His booming voice rose above the noise, "Martin, my friend!"

As the big man approached with his arms extended for an embrace, Nicolas recalled that Martin and Johann had been friends for a long time. Johann supplied the books they had enjoyed for all these years.

"Nicolas, Jean, this is my friend Johann Carolus, master of this place and the bindery where we began." To Johann, he said, "We were hoping to discuss some business with you."

"Certainly." Johann nodded toward a distant doorway.

Inside, a large desk and several tables were stacked with piles of printed sheets. A clerk sat at another much smaller desk in the corner, looking up from a ledger as they entered. He stood but returned to his seat with a wave of the master's hand.

Johann offered them chairs and closed the door to the chaos. He went around his desk, sank into an upholstered chair with a sigh, and glanced at Martin. "I got those books for you." He handed a sack taken from under his desk to Martin.

Martin's eyes lit up, and he held the books as if they were fragile.

"I think I found the other ones you've wanted too. Hopefully, I can get them for you next month."

"Oh, thank you."

Johann leaned back and clasped his hands across his hefty waist. "Now, how can I help you?"

Martin gestured. "My nephew Jean is hoping for an apprenticeship in the printing industry. He is a smart lad and is eager to learn."

Little Jean's face lit up with excitement as he looked up at the big man, who was probably inundated with these types of meetings.

"Your nephew, eh?" Johann turned to the clerk. "Would you hand me the calendar, please?"

Running his finger down the page, Johann mumbled names and dates to himself while Nicolas crossed his fingers that nothing would be available.

"I was hoping for editor or proofreader," Little Jean said.

Turning from Martin to Nicolas, Johann frowned and explained, "I would not recommend either. Authors try to avoid prosecution for illegal books by blaming it on the proofreader or the editor. Sometimes they are successful, but I refuse to print anything that could be misconstrued."

Nicolas exhaled. "Thank you for warning us; I would never have thought of that."

Johann lowered his head again, mumbling. "Binding." He raised his gaze to Jean. "Every book needs to be bound. What do you think?"

Little Jean turned to Nicolas. *This happened so quickly. How can I say no?* Nicolas swallowed hard and forced himself to smile. "Thank you." He bowed to Johann, knowing Catherine would not be pleased.

"Very well, then. I will have a position in about six months. I will draw up the contract, and you can stop and sign it before you leave." Johann handed the calendar back to the clerk and stood, signaling the end of the conversation.

Before Nicolas could open his mouth, Johann motioned to the door, and Martin followed him.

But I have so many questions.

"Thank you, Johann," Martin said. "We will come back the day after tomorrow?"

"Very good. See you then." He turned and disappeared into the shop.

While Little Jean chattered all the way back to the boardinghouse, Nicolas barely raised his head. In the room, a young girl brought a fresh bucket of water to share. While Martin sat on the pallet near the window, Little Jean plopped on the other side.

"Binding. I never even thought about the binding."

"You saw the boys running with heavy piles of paper," Martin said. "You will have many years of working hard before you have a career."

"I don't mind. This is where I want to be."

Nicolas went to the window and looked through the rippled glass at the distorted shapes of the city. He never thought they would secure an apprenticeship at their first meeting. Although as tall as Martin, Little Jean's voice had not changed yet. He was skinny, and he acted childishly.

The rumble of footsteps on the stairs announced the arrival of the students lodged on the top floor. Martin said, "Time to eat. Who wants to wager we will be having cabbage soup?"

They followed the racket to the dining hall, where Madame Sommer had indeed placed a steaming bowl of cabbage soup on the table. Little Jean elbowed Martin and giggled. The young men greeted them with nods, took their place at the big table, and served themselves. Nicolas quietly listened to their stories of living in a big city while Jean and Martin compared them to their quiet lives in the Vosges Mountains. When the meal was over, everyone tired from the long journey or a week of work or study, the entire company went to bed early.

Nicolas tossed all night. *Though Johann has a stellar reputation, he acquires Martin's questionable books.*

33

I N Strasbourg, with no agenda, they spent the next morning at the cathedral. The turrets pierced the sky overhead, and Nicolas gazed at the soaring heights and rose-colored stones as he stood before the bronzed double doors.

Martin pointed upward. "See how those stained glass windows play with the light? This Saint Christopher window is four hundred years old, and those over there are five hundred."

"Oh, look at the scenes in each window," Little Jean muttered.

Roaring music seeming to come from heaven pierced the air. "The melody comes from a great organ," Martin shouted, leading them inside and pointing to a beautiful cabinet painted in various colors with rows of pipes of different sizes. "Perhaps I could ask if we can see how the organist plays. Meantime, let us climb to the top of the tower. The three hundred eighty-two steps will seem much higher than our little mountains."

Martin led the way as a crowd of people climbed the stairs. They arrived on the platform panting, and the view took what remained of Nicolas's breath away. Tiles of all colors arranged in patterns adorned the expanse of roofs. At this height, only a few major arteries separated blocks of houses.

"Son, come here and look at this," Nicolas said over his shoulder.

"There is the Rhine River, and the dark mass over there is the Black Forest," Martin explained. "And there are the Vosges, but our valleys are beyond what you can see from here."

Nicolas took in the scene, aware of other people joining them on the platform. Far below, a priest and bishop approached a young man studying the windows. "From this height, you cannot even tell who those people are."

One of the others near them said, "Sure, you can. That is Father Mark, and that is Bishop Michel. I don't know the boy."

Nicolas's skin grew cold. *Bishop Michel?*

The bishop pointed off into the distance, then put his hand on the boy's shoulder and began to lead him away from the priest.

Nicolas quickly scanned the crowd. "Jean? Martin, have you seen Jean?" The shrill tone of his voice caused several people to glare at Nicolas.

"I thought he was right behind us."

"He was!"

"What is it, Nicolas?" Martin asked.

"Is that Jean?" Nicolas shouted, straining to identify the boy following the priest.

"Oh my God, it's Jean!"

Nicolas shook with panic and shouted, "Jean! NO! JEAN!"

The boy could not hear him.

He pushed through the crowd and bound down the stairs two and three at a time as one name reverberated in his head.

Jean-Baptiste.

When Nicolas finally reached the ground, he ran through the church, pushing pious visitors out of his way. Some tripped, but he never hesitated and burst out the door to the courtyard.

His son was gone.

The priest he had seen from above was speaking to three women. They were in Nicolas's way, and he shoved the women aside and grabbed the priest by the collar. "Where is my son?"

A blank stare. "Who is—"

Nicolas took a deep breath and forced out, "Bishop Michel?"

The priest pointed to a building on the other side of the courtyard. "They went to look at—"

Without waiting to hear the rest, Nicolas turned and ran, his chest burning as he struggled to catch his breath. *If he so much as touches my son, I will kill that bastard. I will . . .* Up three steps to the door, he gripped the knob.

It was locked.

He pounded and shouted, "Jean! Are you in there, Jean?"

He stepped back and kicked the door. It didn't budge. "JEAN!"

As Nicolas raised his foot to kick it down, the door suddenly opened. "What's going on here?" Thin, curly hair, arrogant brown eyes, and a nose pointed like a beak—it was Father Michel.

Nicolas barged in, ramming the bishop, who tripped and clutched a table skirt, pulling statues on top of him as he fell amid a loud crash of ceramic and metal.

Little Jean appeared from a back room, his eyes wide. "Papa, what are you—"

"Are you all right, son? Did that man touch you?"

"The bishop wanted to show me—"

"Show you what, his bedchamber?" Nicolas roared. "What are you thinking?"

Martin burst in, gasped, and helped the bishop to his feet. "We are sorry for any misunderstanding, Your Excellency." Livid, Martin turned to Nicolas, seized his arm, and pushed him toward the door.

Ripping himself from Martin's grasp, Nicolas pointed at the bishop. "There has been no misunderstanding."

Michel brushed himself off, shouting, "What is going on here? Who are you?"

Hatred as Nicolas had never felt before flowed through his veins, and the words came out without a second thought, "I am Humbert Cathillon's son-in-law."

Michel paled and staggered back against the wall before Martin threw Nicolas out the door. Little Jean followed.

Nicolas stormed across the churchyard toward the boardinghouse, so angry that he could barely breathe. Thinking better of it, he crossed the street toward the river and sat on the bank. Eventually, Martin sat beside Nicolas, while Little Jean, apparently trying to get as far away as he could, took his place on Martin's other side.

"What were you thinking?" Martin said after a long silence. "You know how dangerous that man is. Why would you provoke him?"

Nicolas closed his eyes and rested his head in his hands.

Little Jean said, "He was simply going to show me—"

"Don't say a word, Jean," Nicolas snapped. "You have no idea the danger."

The air felt heavy with trepidation until Martin stiffened and said, "Did he—I mean, were you . . ."

With a sigh, Nicolas pinched the bridge of his nose. "No, not me. A good friend of mine."

Martin's mouth gaped open before he replied. "I had no idea. Why didn't you warn us?"

"By the time I found out, Father Michel was long gone. I thought he was out of our lives forever."

"Did you report it to Louis?"

Fury rekindled within Nicolas, and he clenched his fists. "Louis arrested Michel. But then, the next thing we knew, he was increased to a bishop."

Little Jean whined like a child. "What did he do? He's a bishop. I thought I could trust—"

"Will you please act your age?" Nicolas shouted louder than he had wanted to. Then he mumbled, "This trip was a mistake."

Tears came to Little Jean's eyes. Martin glanced from one to the other before putting his hand over his mouth and focusing on the river.

Nicolas lowered his eyes to his clenched fists and forced himself to relax them. In a quieter tone, he said, "Son, you cannot trust—"

"Anyone," Martin finished his sentence. He turned to Little Jean. "You cannot trust anyone." To Nicolas he said, "I just hope you have not focused the evil on your family. Losing your temper does not help anyone, and provoking someone that you know is dangerous—"

"Oh God, I never thought . . ." Pulling himself up to sitting, Nicolas focused on his son's tear-filled eyes. "What did you say to that bishop, Jean? Tell us everything that you discussed."

"I don't know, Papa."

"Think, Jean," Martin said. "If Michel thinks you were just visiting, then perhaps you could still take the apprenticeship, but if he knows you will be living here, he might come after you."

Little Jean wiped his nose on his sleeve. "What do you mean, come after me?"

"That bishop will demonize you. Say he saw you casting spells or something ridiculous. Years ago, he tried to have Francisca and me arrested before Louis ran him out of town. If Michel knows you will be here alone, you will not be safe."

Tears spilled down the boy's cheeks. "You mean I cannot be a printer?" He sounded like a five-year-old.

"No," Martin replied. "There are other printers. I could speak to Master Carolus. Does the bishop know you might be moving here?"

Little Jean sniffled, but before he could soil his sleeve again, Nicolas handed the boy his handkerchief. "It will be all right, son. We will find you an apprenticeship. Just think about what you told the bishop."

Sorrowful blue eyes looked toward the river. *Catherine cannot know any of this.*

"I was looking at the rose window. Each section has its own scene. The bishop said he had the artist's original drawings." He looked up. "I'm sorry, Papa."

"Did you talk about anything other than the window?"

"No, I'm sure," Little Jean said, blowing his nose. "I didn't mention anything else."

Nicolas rubbed the crease between his brows and sighed. "What do you think, Martin?"

"I think the bishop would look in Vacquenoux. Jean might be safer here."

"Oh, I wish I had more time to think about it, but I have to sign the contract tomorrow, and I would have liked to see the living quarters."

With his forehead crinkled in confusion, Martin said, "Did any of the apprentices look neglected? Master Carolus has a stellar reputation."

Nicolas lowered his eyes and studied his fingernails. Just yesterday, he was sitting in his dimly lit bedroom with a newborn Little Jean in his arms, afraid to move. His son leaving home was bad enough, but because of his outburst, the boy's life might be in danger.

"And you can never go anywhere near that church." As soon as the words left his lips, Humbert's stern face flashed in his mind. Nicolas clenched his jaw.

"I do not think Michel will look for you here, hiding in plain sight. Perhaps we could change your appearance, though, just in case," Martin added.

NE day, about a month later, Nicolas stared out the forge window. As expected, Catherine was unhappy with Little Jean leaving home for his apprenticeship. Of course, Nicolas had not told her about the confrontation with Father Michel. Nevertheless, she had been arguing since their return. Nicolas's only relief from the vitriol was work.

A stranger leading a horse up the street caught his attention. The bearded man wore a tall black hat with a drooping brim and a huge green feather pinned to the front that bounced with every step. Though slight, the man had an air of confidence befitting his ruffed collar and embroidered doublet with matching shoes.

Curious, Nicolas leaned against his doorframe and watched while the man approached his father in the stable yard. After a short discussion, Jean lifted the horse's foot and wiggled its loose shoe, nodded to the man, and led the horse to the cross ties.

While Jean worked, he asked, "Just passing through?"

The character, who was intently staring across the street at the inn, turned when Jean spoke. "No, I lived here before I made my fortune and have returned to finish some business."

When Jean finished, he wiped his hands on his apron and said, "Oh, will you be staying a while?" He nodded at the inn. "There are clean rooms and good food just across the street."

Nothing to see here. Nicolas returned to his desk, and later in the day, Jean came and stood before him.

"Who was that?"

"Name of Laville, said he lived here years ago," Jean snickered, "before he made his fortune."

Nicolas crossed his arms and leaned back. "Did you recognize the man?"

"Not at all. The hat covered most of his face, and he wore a patch over one eye, but he had a distinctively quiet voice—spoke barely above a whisper. I surely would have remembered him. He looks about your age. He bought the former bailiff's estate and is remodeling and furnishing it at great expense."

"With all that money," Nicolas added with a chuckle.

The stranger did not attend Mass, but afterward, he paraded through the congregation, who typically mulled around outside, chatting with friends. His huge hat partially hid the patch over his eye. The man's oversized mustache, peppered in gray, curled at the ends above a perfectly manicured beard. Nicolas was sure he had never met the man.

Louis and his family joined Nicolas's group, and together they watched Monsieur Müller hurry to introduce himself and his daughter to the man.

"Another rich husband for Salomé?" Nicolas said with a smirk. "At least this one isn't quite as old as her grandfather."

"No, Laville says he is rich and earned his fortune in Strasbourg." Louis shook his head. "But I've done some checking, and I'm having trouble finding anyone who knew him. Don't trust him."

Strasbourg. The word hit Nicolas like a slap in the face. Was the stranger's arrival a coincidence? He shot an uneasy look at Little Jean, who nodded.

"What's the matter? You look pale," Catherine said, placing her hand on her bulging belly.

Since they had returned, Catherine had been distant. Perhaps Nicolas was worrying too much, but she was the one who looked pale. He originally blamed Little Jean's leaving, but Mémé had noticed it too and ordered Catherine to bed for her confinement, though she insisted on coming to Mass.

"Headache," Nicolas replied, offering her his elbow. With a nod, they took their leave and went home.

Ever since Nicolas had broken off their courtship, he avoided Salomé. To his relief, she had married quickly and moved to a neighboring town, but she was back within two years, widowed. He thought she was gone for good when she married the second time, but again, within a couple of years, she was back, twice widowed.

With Catherine's pregnancy coming to term, Nicolas originally refused an invitation to a supper at the tanner's house, but when Martin offered to take the children, Catherine insisted Nicolas go with his parents. One of the first people Nicolas recognized among the guests was Salomé, who approached him easily, as if they were still courting, then she maneuvered to sit at his table. She looked even more beautiful than he'd remembered.

"My darling Nicolas, you look wonderful. How long has it been? Ten, fifteen years? I think you've been avoiding me."

"Frankly, I'm surprised you came back to our small town. Besides, I imagined I was the last person you wanted to see."

"Oh, Nicolas, you're so silly. Come. Walk with me."

"No, I should join my parents." He turned to walk away.

Salomé snatched his arm. "Nicolas, walk with me!"

Disapproving stares at her shrill tone shot his way, and he glanced at his mother for help, but she remained seated. Not wanting to cause a scene, Nicolas followed Salomé outside to the gardens, where she stood before him. He didn't know what she had in mind, but he knew it wouldn't turn out well.

"Nicolas, I still think about you. Do you remember how we were?"

"Of course I remember, but that was a long time ago. I'm happily married."

"Really? That's not what I've heard," she said, raising an eyebrow.

He withdrew a step and stared at her. "What does that mean?"

Instead of answering, Salomé pressed her body against his and kissed him. Shocked, he pulled away. Angry? Aroused? Perhaps a bit of both.

Between worrying about Little Jean and Catherine, Nicolas found a few moments of diversion thinking of Salomé. He would close his eyes and see her fiery hair and those full lips, remembering the day he followed her to the shed . . .

Martin peeked into his office. "I am back."

Caught deep in reverie, Nicolas started, heat rose in his face, and he took a quick drink.

Oblivious to Nicolas's preoccupation, Martin reached for his bag. His eyes sparkled with excitement as he handed Nicolas a large book. "See what Master Carolus has unearthed for me—two volumes of *La Fabrica* by Vesalius."

"*De Humani Corporis Fabrica,*" Nicolas read.

"The fabric of the human body, if you have forgotten the little Latin that I taught you. Finally, after a twenty-year search."

Gently opening the other one, Martin inhaled. "Look at these illustrations—all the bones here." He turned to a separate section. "And this, all the muscles."

The drawings were disturbing. Nicolas rubbed his fingers along the picture of a human's bones. "How could this doctor draw things inside the body?"

"He cut it open," Martin said casually as he turned the page.

Shocked, Nicolas's jaw dropped. "But that's forbidden!"

Without taking his eyes from the book, Martin replied, "The pope had to relax his regulations—too much pressure from doctors to the high court. While he has authorized autopsies on the dead, he still prohibits surgery on living patients." Turning another page, Martin continued, "This way, doctors can view the perfection established by the Creator, but they should not try to understand it since it is divine.

"Vesalius lost his life over these books. Never in my life have I owned anything as prestigious. The printer who originally published them was burned. For all these years, I had hoped to get at least one volume, and here I am with two. I want to revel in them first, and then I will lend one to Catherine."

"Well, Catherine often talks about how herbal remedies can heal the body; she will marvel at this."

Martin returned to the book. "Oh, look! Here's the explanation of the lungs and the resuscitation of a person who has ceased breathing."

"It explains how to breathe for someone who has died?"

A few days later, Martin brought a volume of *La Fabrica* as promised. Like a treasure, he laid it gently on the table in the back room of Nicolas's shop.

"I finished this one."

"Martin," Nicolas frowned, "I'm not sure I want this book in my house."

"Oh, right, I understand."

"No, leave it, thanks. Catherine has been so irritable with Little Jean leaving and waiting on this birth. Maybe this will take her mind off it. I'll bring it back in a couple of days."

That evening after Martin left and Little Jean went home, Nicolas finished putting the final touches on a silver candlestick. Satisfied, he hung his apron on the hook and wiped the sweat from his brow. Still overheated, he dumped the pitcher over his head and let the cool water run down his neck. Refreshed, he dried his face and hair and entered the back room of his workshop, where he froze.

Salomé stood beside his desk, flipping through the pages of Vesalius, turning her lips in disgust. Looking up from under long lashes, she said, "You were too busy at your fire to notice me pass, so I figured I would wait in here. Tell me, what is this horror?"

Throwing the towel over the book and grabbing her hand, he hissed, "What are you doing?"

Rather than reply, she pressed herself against him.

"Salomé!"

"Nicolas," she whispered, blew in his ear, and put her arms around his neck. He began to pull away, but then he remembered the fragrance of her hair, her mouth so red and full. She kissed him, and he didn't pull away. She closed her eyes and threw her head back, and he let his lips graze her throat, but he quickly realized what he was doing and pulled back abruptly, glaring into her eyes.

"Why are you here?"

"Well, I heard your wife is not doing well." Salomé ran her finger down his arm, drawing circles on the back of his hand.

He shivered.

"Just know that if anything happens, I'm here for you."

Shocked, he said, "Catherine is having a difficult pregnancy, but nothing will happen. If you're waiting for me, please stop; I've loved Catherine since we were children."

"How could you; she is so plain—a peasant!"

"Salomé, you're a beautiful woman—you deserve happiness, someone who will love you."

With that, her eyes narrowed. She lifted her hand to slap his face, but he caught it midair. She ripped herself from his grasp, raised her chin, and walked out of the shop, talking over her shoulder, "You have no idea what I went through for you!"

"What you went through?" he followed her, speaking through clenched teeth. "Don't you feel at least a bit responsible for Magdalena? She died selling you birth prevention powder—you should've told me!"

Salomé spun and met him eye to eye. "How did you know?"

"Because Louis asked me about it when he was investigating Magdalena's death. I was so embarrassed!"

"Oh, please, you were embarrassed? You never cared where I got . . ." Salomé looked around. The street was vacant, but she lowered her voice. ". . . my powder. You act all high and mighty now, but I never heard you complain. You knew it was illegal, but you were fine with it because nothing would have happened to you! Only the woman is punished for trying to stop nature."

"I deserved to know. What if Magdalena would have testified?"

Salomé took the handkerchief from her cuff and, with her little finger extended, touched it daintily to the corner of her mouth. "I made sure she did not testify."

She's delusional. A drop from his wet hair ran down the side of his face, and without acknowledging her deranged comment, he reached in the shop door and retrieved the abandoned towel.

"And you have never wondered why I went to Strasbourg for six weeks?"

He shrugged and dried his hair, wishing she would leave. "To visit your sick aunt."

She rolled her eyes and snapped, "You are so stupid, Nicolas!"

Dropping the towel around his neck, he said, "You know, Salomé, in all these years, Catherine has never called me stupid."

Salomé's eyes pierced into Nicolas, and she said with an exaggerated curtsy, "I was with child, Monsieur Honorable."

He laughed. "Oh, how you lie—you wanted so badly to marry me you'd have danced with bells on your ankles."

"Don't flatter yourself, Nicolas." She crossed her arms, cocked her head, and sneered. "You weren't even curious as to why I had to go when I did, were you?"

He tried to think back. *She said her aunt was sick.* The realization hit him like a shot, and he grabbed the door to keep from falling. "What happened to the baby?"

"You really are a stupid fool! Do you seriously think I would bear your bastard? I'd never have embarrassed my family. Besides, I shouldn't have had to force you to do what was right."

Horror-struck, Nicolas whispered, "You . . . killed it?"

She laughed at him.

"Why are you telling me this? You could be put to death for this!"

She waved him off. "You act as if you are an important person, but you're nothing but a village smith who lives in a barn." She spun, raised her chin, and left.

With his head swirling, Nicolas fell to his knees and gagged. *Salomé carried my child?*

That strange interview when Louis asked why Salomé went to Strasbourg came to his mind, and bile rose in his throat. Did Louis know? *Oh, God!* Did his papa know? He sat on the street with his back against the wall and held his head in his hands.

Catherine stepped outside and lingered in the shadow of the house, enjoying the cool, quiet evening. *A couple more weeks and this child will come.* Though she was not looking forward to the ordeal, she wanted to be done with the discomfort.

Muffled voices rose from the forge, but it was too late for a customer, and Little Jean had come home a while ago. She held her breath and strained to listen. "You never wondered why . . ." but she couldn't make out the rest. A man replied. Was it Nicolas? She stood on her tiptoes. "Catherine . . ."

It is Nicolas. Did he say my name? All she could see was the top of—a red head? It could be none other than Salomé! And she was laughing. They were standing close together. What was he doing?

Catherine staggered back and leaned against the house, wanting to collapse right there on the grass, but the children . . .

She forced herself inside, holding on to the wall for support through the kitchen to the bedchamber, and fell onto her pallet, too devastated to cry.

Nicolas gathered his senses, grabbed the book, and went home. When he opened the door, his girls rushed to him and clutched his legs. He laid the book on the table and lifted the giggling children over his head while Little Jean barely registered his arrival. Then he peeked into the bedchamber to check on Catherine, trying not to appear upset.

She lay on the bed, chewing on her lip, her expression unreadable. She didn't even look at him. "Is something wrong, Catherine?"

She stared at the rafters. "Were there any customers in your shop this evening?"

He hesitated.

She glared at him, and her eyes widened. "You have lip stain on the corner of your mouth."

Oh, God! Nicolas recoiled and wiped his lip with his finger. "Catherine, nothing happened."

"I saw you!" She swung her legs over the side of the bed, but her heaving belly made getting up difficult. He reached out to help her stand, but she pushed him away.

Her eyes narrowed, and she screamed, "I saw you together!"

"What are you suggesting?"

She stood too fast, and her eyes glazed. He reached for her, but she fell—hard. "Catherine!" He dropped beside her. She gasped and clenched her teeth. Tears came to her eyes as she looked down and saw the blood stain spreading on her dress. She leaned convulsively forward and moaned in distress.

He cradled her shoulders, shouting, "Jean, fetch Mémé—now!"

The girls rushed in. "Mama! Mama!" They ran to hug her, but her face distorted in pain, and they stood there, crying.

Trying to speak calmly, Nicolas said, "Marie, honey. It's all right. Fetch Grandma quickly. Take Claudette with you."

Once the girls left the room, he carried Catherine to the bed and tried to keep her calm until Elisabeth burst in a moment later. The look in her eyes terrified him. He stood, hoping for instructions. "Little Jean went to fetch Francisca," he said.

Nicolas's voice brought Elisabeth back to the moment. She focused and touched his arm, speaking calmly. "The baby is coming. Get some towels and a fresh bucket of water."

Soon, Mémé and Marie were there, and he was banished, pacing through the darkest of nights while Catherine's screams cut through him like a knife.

What have I done? This is my fault.

As the sky lightened, the screams stopped, but the silence was worse.

The same as Rachelle.

With his stomach tangled in knots and his mind racing, he pushed into the bedchamber. The dimly lit room smelled of candle wax and suffering. Catherine's face appeared as pale as her pillowcase, her dark hair soaked in perspiration, her lips white and indistinguishable. Her breath came in shallow gasps. Blood-soaked towels littered the floor.

Elisabeth shouted at him to leave, but he dropped to his knees beside Catherine and touched her cheek. It was cold.

Mémé sat at the bottom of the bed, pleading, "It's in position now; you are almost finished. Push, Lovey. Push!"

Catherine tried, but it was clear she had no strength left. She flung her head from side to side, moaning, "I'm not good enough, not good enough."

"Please try, Catherine," Nicolas begged, then everything became a blur.

Marie raised Catherine's shoulders, and with one more groan and a relieved gasp, a baby girl was born. But it didn't look real—it was bluish, soaked, and limp. Nicolas stared at it. *Is it alive?*

The women worked around him as if he weren't there. Francisca wiped the baby's mouth and nose, then flipped it over, rubbing its back until it made gurgling noises and turned pink. She handed the baby to Marie, who washed and swaddled her.

"It's a girl," Francisca panted.

A girl? She is alive . . .

While his mother pushed and pushed on her stomach, Catherine lay motionless. Mémé caught the afterbirth, which she carried into the parlor and again tossed into the fireplace before collapsing into the chair with a heavy sigh.

He stood there helpless as the women cleaned his silent wife. When Catherine didn't move, Marie gathered up the shrieking infant and carried her from the room.

After the others left, Nicolas moved back to kneel by Catherine's bedside; eventually, he fell into a fitful sleep on the floor. Several hours later, sensing movement from her, he sprang up and touched her cheek. He laid his head on her chest, said a silent, thankful prayer, and whispered:

> *"Little nymph that I adore.*
> *My sweet one in whose eyes reside my worst and my best.*
> *My sweet one, my sugar, my grace, my Catherine."*
> *He held her until she fell asleep.*

OTHING more was said about Salomé, but jealousy and inadequacy ruled Catherine's thoughts. Since that day, Nicolas seemed quiet. Perhaps he planned to leave her. Baby Mougeotte grew rapidly, and Catherine cared for her, but the tenderness she had felt with the other children would not come. Instead, emptiness filled her until she could barely bring herself to eat.

As the seasons changed and the days grew short, so did Catherine's strength. Her sister Beatrix, now eighteen years old, who had been visiting daily, suggested Catherine come to the farm for the upcoming grape harvest to help with the meal. She reluctantly agreed.

On the first day, while Nicolas helped the men in the fields, Catherine sat and chatted while the women fluttered about the kitchen, cooking, cleaning. An occasional sideways glance was shot her way, but she was too weak to help. The next day, she settled by the fireplace and laid the baby in her basket. Marie took the older girls to work in the garden while Mémé started the bread.

"Lovey, take this ale to the workers," Mémé said.

"I'm too tired." She leaned back and closed her eyes.

With her hands covered in flour, Mémé took the baby's basket and propped it by the big table. "Take this and go."

Catherine's mouth dropped open. "With everything I've been through?"

"That was months ago. You are fine now." She pointed to the door. "Go."

Grumbling, Catherine took the jug and trudged outside. *Mémé still treats me like a child.*

After pouting for a while, Catherine decided to try to walk to the field and watch the others work. Halfway up the hill, she tripped on a root, and as she flailed to the ground, she heard herself cry out. She pulled herself up, recalling the day Anne had whined when she tripped on a vine on their way to pick berries. Back then, Catherine had thought her sister pathetic. Now she sat, quietly considering her situation as the sun warmed her back against the chilly autumn breeze.

For a moment, the vision of Nicolas with lip stain on the corner of his mouth flashed in her mind, but instead of filling her with sadness and grief, she thought how ridiculous he looked. He was smarter than that. If he had been unfaithful, he'd have covered his tracks better.

She had survived the worst of ordeals and would no longer feel sorry for herself. She stood, squared her shoulders, and joined the others in the field.

Long hours later, with a cart full of grapes, they returned to the farm and crowded around the big table to await the evening meal. The conversation drifted from the crops to the weather to local gossip.

"Little Jean left last week," Nicolas announced to the group. "The house feels empty now."

A lump formed in Catherine's throat. Little Jean had changed so much since his trip to Strasbourg. When he'd come home with an apprenticeship, she was furious, but she couldn't ignore her son's new attitude. Without nagging, he had taken responsibility for the girls while she recuperated, finished projects for her, and helped in the garden all evening after working with his father all day. His voice had changed, and he began mimicking some of Martin's strange pronunciations *to fit in*. But the strangest thing of all, Little Jean had asked her for odd types of clothes to take with him, and though the style was outdated, he had grown his hair long and tied it back with a string.

Forcing it out of her mind, Catherine stood and motioned to Beatrix. "The bread smells done." While Catherine dished out the stew, she asked, "Anything new with you, little sister?"

Looking up from slicing the warm loaf, Beatrix smiled. "Yes, I'm going to move into the tavern to help Aunt Agnes full-time."

Shocked, Catherine turned to her mother, who nodded. "Yes, Sebastien is getting too old, and Joseph—"

From across the room, Joseph replied, "I'm not spending my life in that tavern."

"Well, sister. That's wonderful," Catherine said. "Then I'll see you more often."

The chatter continued through the meal, after which Jean-Baptiste opened the door, leaned against the frame, and lit his papa's pipe. Catherine hadn't realized her brother had taken up her father's habit, and she wasn't sure how she felt about it.

Exhaling a puff of smoke, he said, "Nicolas, I heard that girl you used to court is marrying that pond scum Laville. She must be desperate to marry that one-eyed bastard. Probably for his money."

Nicolas tapped his foot nervously and replied, "I wasn't aware."

A sudden twinge of anger stung Catherine's heart, but she clenched her jaw and fetched Mougeotte. She wrapped the baby in blankets, gathered the girls, and took their leave. On the way home, Catherine concentrated on the tasks she needed to finish that night, trying not to think of *that* woman.

Halfway home, Nicolas broke the silence. "Catherine, I need to tell you something."

Without raising her gaze, she wiped the drool from the baby's chin.

"Before Salomé and I ended our courtship, we—"

"Nicolas, please—the children."

He stopped the carriage, turned to her, and said, "I must tell you. I want to be honest with you."

Afraid of what he would say, she tensed. She knew what he had done, and she didn't want to hear it. After all, he had bragged about it to her brother. "Have you been lying to me for all these years?"

"No, I swear to you. I love you and have never lied to you."

She couldn't bear to look at him. "If nothing will change between us, I'm not interested in hearing your confession simply for you to clear your conscience. Can we go home?"

Though his stare bored into her, he remained silent and snapped the reins.

The rest of the evening was spent in silence, and the next day at work, Nicolas tried to put his failures out of his mind. Trying to keep busy, he cleaned his shop. Late in the morning, two young men wearing filthy rags, their faces half-hidden under mats of uncombed hair, rushed toward him from the street, shouting, "Nicolas, Nicolas!"

When his father stepped out of the forge, Nicolas rushed to join him and asked the men, "Do I know you?"

Confusion obvious on their faces, they stopped. "We work in the charcoal," said the taller of the two.

"Oh, I've never seen you in the village. Is something wrong?"

The older one spoke, "They took Gran, and they say they're gonna burn 'er!"

Nicolas gasped. "Who took her?"

"Nancy accused Gran of spreading the plague."

Turning to Jean, he said, "Surely, Louis would have told us."

Aghast, Jean dropped his gaze, searching for words. "Well, if they said Nancy, it was the duke. The Lorraine courts need little evidence to send someone to the stake."

The boys gawked at each other, and the younger spoke. "Lorraine?"

The mountaintop people did not read nor write, never left their encampment, and were rarely apprised of current events. Nicolas asked them, "Did you move your cabin into Lorraine?"

"I don't know what you mean, but we're not in the same place. We moved farther back into the forest, closer to the wood."

Jean rubbed his forehead and closed his eyes before saying, "Let's talk to Louis."

However, their hopes faded when Louis said, "My friend, I cannot do anything for this poor woman any more than I could help Magdalena. The location you specified is in Lorraine, so her case is not in my jurisdiction. I'm terribly sorry."

On the way home, Nicolas's mind raced. *What if they torture the old woman? What if she mentions Francisca's name? She knew Catherine's name that day as well. What if . . .*

Then he felt guilty, worrying only about his family when this poor woman faced an unimaginable fate. The boys were quiet. He would find them jobs. Jean had not spoken since they left Louis's house either, his face ashen. Nicolas lowered his head and closed his eyes.

One week later, Martin had just finished a coach exchange when he received an urgent summons from Louis Gauthier. Martin gathered Jean and rushed to the provost's home.

Louis greeted them with a look of dread and led them to his office. "The last time I saw you, we discussed the old woman of the coal. A friend who works at the Nancy court said she has confessed."

Martin exhaled loudly.

But Louis continued. "He gave me a transcript of her trial. They tortured her, and the poor woman confessed to witchcraft, like all the others. Unfortunately, I need to tell you something I read in the transcript."

Jean's expression dire, he said, "What is it?"

"She named accomplices. Though she invented many of them—she didn't know many people—she mentioned Francisca."

All the air left the room. "No," Martin moaned.

"Francisca will be arrested, Jean, and I cannot do anything—you must hide her. Take her to Strasbourg to live with your grandson. They will not seek her there. The villagers will be questioned until they find enough evidence, but you have little time to act."

While Jean paced, Martin held his head in his hands, trying to make sense of it all.

Jean's voice rose, "The old woman was not a witch, and Francisca even less! She risked her life to save Le-Chêne and has gone in the middle of the night to help someone, never asking for anything in return. How can these same people condemn her?"

"People need to blame the plague on someone," Louis said, shaking his head. "They demand something be done to prevent it from happening again. Witchcraft is an easy solution."

Coming to his senses, Martin leaped to his feet. Arguing with Louis would not help, and they were wasting precious time. "We had better hasten, Jean. Francisca is stubborn, but she might listen to Catherine and Nicolas."

Louis led them to their horses. "Good luck. I will stall as long as I dare."

At home, Catherine and Nicolas absorbed the news and, at Martin's urging, pushed down their fear. Worrying would not help Francisca.

At the farm, Marie invited them to sit and have a cup of tea. Obviously not understanding the magnitude of the situation, Francisca brushed off the whole business. "Oh, they have been saying these things for years."

"This time, it is different, madame," Martin said, taking her hand. "This has gone beyond rumor. The only chance you have is to flee."

"I will go neither to Strasbourg nor elsewhere," she said, pulling her hand away from Martin's grasp. "I regret not believing in the devil, as I would ask him for a curse."

Nicolas knelt before her. "Mémé, you know your friend would never have given your name willingly. They tortured her until she told them what they wanted to hear. Once in their hands, they will force you to say what they want you to say."

Brushing him away, she gazed into the fireplace. "Then I will hide in the mine when I hear them coming."

"These people are stubborn, and when you let your guard down, they'll find you. The whole family will be charged for having hidden you," Jean replied.

However, Francisca's demeanor remained surprisingly calm. "Let me sleep on it. Come back tomorrow morning, Catherine, and I'll give my answer."

Martin searched Francisca's eyes but found no hint of fear. "I have been in your position before, madame, and I tell you, we must act quickly." Seeing her faraway gaze, he decided to change his tactics—he had to make her want to go. "Little Jean could use your wise guidance in Strasbourg."

Nodding, she said, "I will decide by tomorrow. Come alone at first light— only you, Catherine."

Numb, Martin surrendered. Francisca was stubborn, but he had thought she would listen to reason. She seemed in her own world now, listening to her own voices.

"Very well," Catherine said, kissing her cheek. "I'll be here when the sun rises."

That night, though her family wanted to keep her company, Francisca needed to be alone. Donning her shawl, she went outside. She knew what she had to do.

Her hands shook as she searched for a belladonna plant, hoping there would still be berries to harvest this late in autumn. She had searched for them once before—the day her mother had died. Back then, she had been hopeless and alone. This time would be different.

Sitting outside in the darkness, she closed her eyes and absorbed the night—the cool, moist air, the croaking frogs and singing crickets. Just before sunrise, when the chorus ceased, she woke Marie and waited at the door. When Catherine arrived, she said, "This is my favorite time of year—the leaves are changing color, the autumn flowers. I want to see Lac de la Maix one last time before I leave, but I'm too old to go alone, and I need the help of you and your mother."

Marie joined them with canteens.

Looking past them into the house, Catherine replied, "Are your things packed? Nicolas will be here momentarily to drive us."

"We will walk."

"But . . ." Looking at Marie for support, Catherine hesitated, but upon receiving none, she relented. "Well then, we must leave the moment we get back."

"I want to ask the help of the Virgin," Francisca said. "I'm not sure what she's thinking with all these people being massacred in her name."

The household was still asleep as they crept through the courtyard. The climb was long, and though Catherine kept pushing, Francisca and the trio stopped and reminisced many times about the happy moments they had shared over the years. At the lake, they sat side by side on one of the boulders in the shadow of the statue, silently absorbing the splendor.

Francisca broke the hush. "It is here that we will say goodbye."

"No, Mama," Marie said, crying.

"But I will come to visit you in Strasbourg, and we will remember," Catherine said.

"No, Lovey, I'll not leave this place. Go back to your children and those you love, and I will live in a small place in your heart. Today, I will close my eyes with all our memories here."

Catherine stared at her, confused.

"My life has been wonderful since I arrived at Le Petit-Courty, and I want it to end happily, not in horror. If you love me as I love you, you will understand."

Realization crept over Catherine's face, and she paled. "No, Mémé, we want you to go—"

"You want?" Francisca could not stop her anger, but the terrified look on her granddaughter's face forced her to soften. She swallowed hard and stared into the distance. Soon she would be with her daughter. Should she tell them about her? No, it would serve no purpose, and she forced her mind back to the present. Wiping the tears from her granddaughter's cheek, she removed her Gypsy cross pendant and slipped it over Catherine's head.

Marie said, "Mama, come home with us, please."

"No, daughter. If you love me, you will give me my last wish. I have always loved you as my baby." She squeezed Marie's hand. "And you as my grandchild." They clung to each other for a long moment before she broke away.

Weeping uncontrollably, Catherine begged, "Please, we will come with you to Strasbourg—we'll be merry; you can keep your eye on Little Jean for me."

"This is what I want to do. I have no desire to go to Strasbourg. I have lived a full life, and I'll not die without my pride. I want to die here, under my terms. Go now. Ask Jean-Baptiste to come tomorrow with the shovel to give me rest on this good land, and I will become part of this place that I love."

"Come now," Marie said, pulling Catherine away, but they lingered at the edge of the woods until Francisca stood, put her hands on her hips, and shouted, "Go home!"

She blew them a kiss, and they left her.

Nicolas paced beside Jean as Louis and his deputies stood by the path the women had taken that morning. By the time Catherine and Marie returned, it was late afternoon. Nicolas grabbed Catherine's arm and whispered, "Where were you? We've been searching for you all day. We must get Francisca out of here!"

He didn't expect their red-rimmed eyes, and he followed them into the house, Louis and Jean following them in too. Inside, Jean-Baptiste waited with Dimanchette, Beatrix, and Joseph.

Catherine started to cry, and though he was confused, Nicolas pulled her into his arms. Marie looked pale and dropped onto the bench. She lowered her gaze to her trembling hands and told them what had happened on the mountain. As the rest of the family fell to sobbing, Nicolas closed his eyes as numbness washed over him.

"That stubborn old woman," Jean-Baptiste said, wrapping his arms around his crying wife.

Realization crossed Jean's face. He glanced at Louis. "What happens now?"

"The deputies will fetch her body and bring it back for a wake. I will advise the bishop and allow him to confirm her death."

"No, Mémé will not be handled roughly by a bunch of strangers," Jean-Baptiste replied. "If she has to come back here, Joseph and I will fetch her."

"And I'll come too," Nicolas added.

Louis bowed to them. "I am sorry to intrude on this difficult time, but I must see her body. I will come back tomorrow. You have my sympathies."

Nicolas borrowed a horse and followed Joseph and Jean-Baptiste to the lake. When they finally stepped into the clearing, an eerie silence enveloped them—no wind, not a ripple in the water, not a bird singing—even the trees were still, as if flora and fauna were mourning.

At the foot of the Blessed Mother's statue, they found Francisca. Jean-Baptiste knelt beside her and stroked her cheek. With trembling lips, he said, "She looks peaceful."

As Joseph knelt beside his brother, Nicolas went around the other side and lifted her hand. She was still holding her rosary.

"She doesn't appear to have suffered," Joseph said.

Nicolas sighed. "Catherine was happy that she would stay with Little Jean. Why did she have to be so stubborn?"

Jean-Baptiste was curt. "Mémé didn't want to go to the city."

The words quieted them, and after a few moments with their thoughts, they wrapped her body in a blanket, tied it to a litter between two horses, and slowly made their way back to the farm.

The next day, Catherine went to greet Aunt Agnes and Uncle Sebastien's carriage and was surprised to see Anne inside. The sisters shared a long embrace. Anne said, "Martin sent a message two days ago. I received it yesterday and left immediately, but Aunt Agnes told me I was . . . too late." Anne choked out the last words.

The sight of her sister in tears brought on a new round of crying for both of them.

"I didn't realize Mémé was ill, or I would have come sooner."

"She wasn't sick," Catherine said before relaying the events.

Anne's shocked reply was a whisper, "Did Mémé drink something?"

"She made us leave, I—"

Behind them, Nicolas cleared his throat. Catherine spun and found Father Edmond with his eyes wide. She covered her lips with her hand as if that would take back her words, but it was too late.

Edmond's mouth dropped open. "Francisca did what?"

"Father!" Catherine slid her hand down to her neck. "Umm, Mémé asked us to leave without her—she probably didn't think she could make it back."

"Yes, Father," Nicolas added. "No one knows exactly what happened." He exchanged a guilty look with Catherine and turned to the priest, who shifted uncomfortably.

Thankfully, Marie joined them, breaking the tension. "Father, so nice of you to come."

The priest took her extended hand and sighed as if relieved for the change of subject. "I came to bless my good friend Francisca. Will we proceed to the church from here?"

"Mama wanted to be buried at the lake."

Edmond frowned. "Why not bury her beside Humbert, in consecrated ground?"

Marie swallowed hard before replying, "Father, they accused Mama of witchcraft. I never thought you would allow her in the graveyard."

"Well, Francisca was not convicted, and she saved my life."

"Dearest Father," Marie said, patting his hand. "Thank you, but Mama loved the lake, and I want to honor her last wish. You understand."

The priest's forehead puckered in confusion. "Of course. May I go with you to bless her final resting place?"

"Please join us."

At the lake, Jean-Baptiste chose a site near the statue. The ceremony and blessing were short; afterward, Martin played her favorite song on his violin.

That evening at the farm, as they waved goodbye and Catherine settled beside Nicolas on the carriage bound for home, emptiness weighed down on her. Mémé was gone. To hide her tears from her children, she turned her head. Her eyes stopped on the crest of the hill, and she remembered another time in her life when she'd had a similar hopeless feeling.

The night watchman.

The wind whispered, "I'm here, Lovey," and the calm of that night washed over her again.

"I have noticed you look up there almost every time we leave," Nicolas said. "What are you looking for?"

She folded her hands. "I'm being silly. Once, I woke in the middle of the night and went to the window for some fresh air. I saw a man on a white horse staring at the house. He sat there for a long time. It was strange, but he made me feel safe, as if he were watching over me. I have often thought he was an angel."

Puzzled, Nicolas studied her. "When was that?"

"The night you saved me from the troubadour. Why?"

He exhaled and rubbed his chin. "I ended the courtship with Salomé that night. I wanted to see you so badly, but I thought you hated me, and I figured your papa would shoot me if I knocked on your door in the middle of the night, so I just sat there, looking at the house."

Catherine stared at him, at the sadness in his eyes, and she was angry with herself for carrying a grudge for so long. Tears filled her own eyes, and he wiped her cheek with his finger. She had not let him near her in so long that a tingle raced down her spine at his touch, and she leaned toward him until their lips met. He brought his other hand up and cupped her face—the reins still in his grip scratched her cheek. He kissed her with urgency, as he had that day at the farm, then held her face in his hands, his hazel eyes searching.

Her heart pounded. *Should I apologize? Should he?*

She turned her head slightly and kissed his hands—his calloused, gentle hands. When she turned back, he was smiling, and she knew exactly what to say.

"I love you, Nicolas."

⚓

Though Nicolas felt drained upon their return, he needed to keep busy, so he went to his shop, but instead of going inside, he sat on the bench and watched the world go by. When the Angelus bells rang, the peddler packed his wares and placed a scrawny rosebush into his cart. Nicolas hurried over, bought it, and planted it beside the door of their house, finally bringing a smile to Catherine's face.

That night, while she rocked the baby to sleep, Nicolas lay on the bed and watched Catherine rubbing the child's head and singing to her, relieved to have his wife back. Just as he began to relax, she crawled under the blanket and laid her head on his shoulder, the first time she had done so since before—

Something pointy dug into his armpit. "Ouch, you're stabbing me. What is that?"

She leaned up on her elbow. "Oh, sorry."

In the dim light, he could clearly make out the shape of a pendant. His eyes bulged. "Where did you get that?"

"It was Mémé's," Catherine said, lovingly rubbing her thumb on the arms of the cross before taking it off and handing it to him. "Surely, you have seen it before. She wore it every day."

He jerked to sit up and flipped it over. "No, I had never seen her wear it."

"Well, she tucked it in when she was working, but—"

"Catherine, I made this." It came out louder than he had wanted, and he lowered his voice so as not to wake the children. "I mean, I made one like this—for that nun, remember?"

She lurched up beside him. "That one who resembled her?" She gasped and covered her mouth with her hand. "But what could this mean?"

A LONG, dismal winter followed Francisca's death. Once the snow began to melt, the coach started running again, bringing an influx of new customers into the tavern and forge.

Nicolas's first order of the spring, a new style of tongs for Beatrix, now running the Auberge du Cheval Blanc. Catherine's baby sister had started at the inn over the winter when guests were sparse, and as the customer load increased, she learned to handle it with ease.

When Nicolas delivered the order, he found Sebastien sitting at a table with the tanner. Though his health had deteriorated to the point where he walked with a cane, he continued coming to the restaurant daily, giving his opinion on every topic.

At Nicolas's wave, Sebastien boomed, "Ah, Nicolas, my boy. Have a drink with us."

Nicolas pulled up a chair.

"There is a new tavern on the other side of town—The Fidélité," Sebastien said to bring Nicolas into the conversation. "Owned by that one-eyed character, Laville. Have you seen him? His face is sunken and scarred, and he rarely covers it—he looks grotesque."

The tanner agreed. "And he claims he lived here, but I don't remember a one-eyed man."

Nicolas finished his ale and said, "I see Laville occasionally after Mass—which is strange because he never attends. He just mulls around outside afterward." He turned to Sebastien. "Maybe I should investigate that tavern one of these days."

"Don't be spending any money over there," Sebastien said, winking.

"Never think of it. See you later."

Sebastien must not have heard the rumors. The new establishment had grown and now employed maids wearing low-cut gowns with no partlets or barely laced kirtles over scanty bodices.

A few days later, Catherine's brother Joseph appeared at the forge. Nicolas had always been amused with Joseph, and at twenty-four, the young man still had tousled hair and mischievous eyes. Several girls flirted with him, but he could not limit his attention to just one of them.

Nicolas laid down his hammer and took off his gloves. "Joseph, how are you?"

"Bonjour, Nicolas, I came right away to tell you."

"Tell me what?"

"Don't tell Aunt Agnes, but I went to The Fidélité. I wanted to see the big"—Joseph held his hands in front of his chest and continued—"ideas."

Nicolas laughed. "Oh, the maids. How did you like their big ideas?"

"Nice." Joseph winked. "But has anyone from your family gone there?"

"No, Catherine wouldn't appreciate me looking at the ideas. Why?"

"That one-eyed proprietor is talking about your papa."

The mischievous air suddenly turned serious. "What did he say?"

Joseph lowered his head and kicked a stone. "Remember, these are his words, not mine. Laville said your papa is mayor only because your grandfather was mayor, and the people should ask where all the tax money has gone."

Shocked, Nicolas stiffened and stepped back. "What else did he say?"

"He said if there were an investigation, your papa would be arrested."

"Who is this man? Why would he say such things?"

"I think some townspeople believed him. I thought I should tell you."

"I appreciate that, Joseph. Come tell Papa what you have heard."

The color drained from Jean's face as Joseph retold the story. "I've never met this man. Why would he say these things about me?"

Joseph punched his palm repeatedly. "Do you want me to go back and—"

"Is he there now?"

"He was there a few minutes ago."

Jean slammed his apron to the ground, and the three of them stormed to the opposite side of town to The Fidélité.

Inside the dim, crowded interior, people stood in groups, some bleary-eyed and slurring their words, others singing roguish ballads to the maids and their ideas. If not so angry, Nicolas would have appreciated them, but now he followed his father to the bar, where Laville sat among a group of agitators.

"Now you're in trouble," one of them laughed.

Anger shot from Jean's eyes. "Do you have something to say to me?"

"Yes," Laville replied without hesitation. "Why is the road in front of your shop the best in town and nothing but mud in front of my hostel?"

"If you have a complaint, why not come to me instead of making insinuations?"

"Why not answer my question?" Laville sneered.

"Any day you want, you can look at the books." Jean turned and gestured to the crowd. "Any of you—come right now, and I will show you."

"Answer the question," someone called from the back of the room.

"The main street is maintained because of the coach, and it is no better in front of my shop than in front of the supply, the chandler, the bakery, or the inn. That coach brings business to this town."

"And benefits your family above all others!" someone else yelled.

"The coach made this community what it is today. My grandfather petitioned the count for the coach to stop here. He mortgaged his property to buy the horses and build the stable. Any of you could have done the same, but you didn't. You'll not dishonor his name."

Laville smirked. "We're not dishonoring his name. We're dishonoring yours."

Fury filled Nicolas, and he shouted, "How dare you!"

When Laville laughed, Nicolas lunged for him. Joseph stepped in and dragged Nicolas toward the door.

Several older patrons followed and wiped their feet as they left. One of them said, "Come, Jean. These idlers are here for the cheap ale. They cannot think for themselves and only know what they've been told to think."

Once outside, Jean fumed, "Who the hell is that man?"

Another replied, "He has to be getting money from someone. He gives out free drinks whenever he gets an audience. At first, I thought he only complained to get his road fixed, but he enjoys slandering your family—your entire family—and I doubt it has anything to do with the road."

Nicolas tried to remain calm. *Could this be Father Michel's revenge?*

Every year since Nicolas was a boy, he had accompanied his father in touring the area to remind the villagers of the annual assembly for ratification of community leaders called Le Plaid. Attendance was mandatory, with fines assessed on those who didn't attend and the money added to the municipality's budget.

At the meeting in the town hall, Nicolas took a seat in the front row while Jean stood before the room, answering polite questions and listing the expenses of the community. Murmurs in the crowd, though, turned to the issues of the accusations made last week by Laville, and then Laville entered with a rowdy group of followers.

"I demand to be considered for the position of mayor," he shouted.

"The count has to ratify any nominees," Jean said.

"The count has ratified my name," Laville answered, flinging a paper showing the official seal over his head.

The provost was the only person who could offer a name to the count, and Nicolas followed Jean's gaze to the back of the room, where Louis squirmed, eventually turning to look out the window. His father's oldest and dearest friend must have known. Why had Louis not warned them?

"Well, therefore, we have Le Plaid," Jean said after blinking several times in shock. "If you're not satisfied with my service, you have every right to vote for someone else."

With a deep bow, Jean offered the stage to Laville and disappeared out the door. Nicolas followed him. Outside, they paced, waiting while the voting took place. Soon, people filed out. A small group surrounded them, including Sebastien, Jean-Baptiste, Joseph, and eventually Martin and Quentin. Without anyone saying it, the uncomfortable silence confirmed the vote. Jean-Baptiste and Joseph patted Jean's back, tipped their hats, and left on horseback.

The rest of the group walked in silence. The crunching of their boots on the dirt road echoed. At the inn, Sebastien said, "Come in for a drink, Jean."

"Thanks," Jean replied, "but I think I'll just go home."

"I'll walk with you, Sebastien," Quentin said.

At the estate, Martin asked, "Jean, do you want to talk?"

"No, I think I'd rather be alone tonight. I'll see you tomorrow."

"Nicolas, I'd like some company," Martin said.

With a grateful nod, Nicolas followed Martin to his house, where embers still glowed in the fireplace, making the room comfortably warm. They hung their cloaks on hooks by the door, and while Martin retrieved the jug and poured them some wine, Nicolas threw a log on the embers and sat on the divan.

When Martin joined him, Nicolas asked, "Do you think Father Michel could be behind this?"

"Indeed, the thought has crossed my mind."

Nicolas leaned back and rubbed his eyes. "Or it could be Salomé."

"Couples separate before marriage all the time," Martin said, staring at the fire. "She thinks I am a heretic, but—"

Nicolas sighed heavily before confessing his involvement in Salomé's trip to Strasbourg. Without scolding him, Martin simply sat there, scratching his ear. Finally, he drew his eyes from the flames, turned to Nicolas, and said, "Whether Laville arrived with an agenda, his marriage to Salomé now certainly complicates matters."

"What are we going to do?"

The next day, there were no customers at the forge. While Martin and Quentin groomed the horses, Nicolas kept busy working on items to sell at the fair. He didn't see his father until the late afternoon, when Jean stuck his head in the door of his shop and said, "Son, can I talk to you?"

"Sure, Papa," Nicolas replied before moving his drawings aside to make room for his father to sit at his desk. "I wanted to see you, but I thought you might need some time alone."

Visibly upset, Jean rubbed his hands together and stared at them. "I wanted to say I'm sorry to you, son. I thought you would follow me as mayor one day."

"The truth will come out eventually. Perhaps I should take a trip to Nancy and investigate the rumors about Laville."

"Once spoken, lies cannot be taken back," he said with a sigh. "I'm just disappointed Louis didn't warn me."

Nicolas sat on the corner of his desk, his heart aching for his father, especially since he may have been responsible. "It seems so unlike Louis. And why did they say you used tax money? Makes you sound like a thief."

"Nobody likes to pay taxes. The mere mention of somebody stealing tax money gets everyone angry." He stared into the distance. "Maybe this is for the best." With a change in tone, he said, "We have no customers today. What do you say we close the shop and go fishing?"

Over the summer, customers were rare. While Nicolas and Jean kept busy making articles to sell, Quentin and Martin spent most of their time in the stable and Catherine and the girls planted a bigger garden. One evening as they sat before the fire, the weight became overwhelming, and Nicolas sighed heavily.

Catherine asked, "What's wrong?"

"No customers again today." He rubbed his tired eyes.

She laid down her sewing and joined him on the divan. "It's so unfair, but we'll be fine—we have no debts. Business is slow, but we have food on the table and clothes to wear."

"What about dowries? The girls are getting older, and we've not saved anything for months."

"Don't forget the money Mama saved for me from the wine."

Nicolas pulled away and gaped at her. "What money?"

Catherine looked confused. "Whenever Mama sells a barrel of wine, she splits the money by six, one for her and one for each of us children. She's kept mine for me."

"Why haven't you mentioned this before?"

Catherine hesitated and cocked her head. "Well, we've never needed money, and I thought Papa told you the day he showed you the mine."

Disbelieving, Nicolas stood and paced in front of the fireplace. "How much money?"

She shrugged. "I've no idea, but it should be plenty for three honorable dowries."

"Have you never wanted to spend any money? Buy pearls or something?"

Her eyes widened in dismay. "Pearls? I never thought I could own pearls."

"Well, you can't now." He embraced her with a half-hearted smile.

THE night air had been chilly for early autumn, causing Martin to close the windows when he retired for the evening. Now, hours later, he awakened, sweating. Too lazy to get up, he lay there for a while, but finally, he rolled out of bed and looked out the windows.

Smoke was billowing out the back door and the windows of the stable.

With a horrified gasp, he pulled on his pants, snatched his gun, and shot it out the window into the earth to alert Nicolas and the neighbors. He screamed, "Quentin! Fire!"

By the time he yanked on his boots and ran out the door, Quentin had disappeared into the flaming stable. The horses were pacing and snorting.

Quentin gripped the door of the nearest stall and pulled. It wouldn't open. When Martin tried another door, it wouldn't budge either. As the smoke thickened, Quentin grabbed the ax, and after three swings, the door fell from its hinges. Martin caught the horse's halter and Quentin's arm and yelled, "Come, Quentin, it is too late!"

But Quentin sprinted back into the flames.

Left to its own devices, a horse will run to its perceived safe place, which could be a burning barn, so Martin led it across the street, tied it beside the inn, and ran back toward the inferno.

Nicolas heard the shot and jumped out of bed. The eerie glow in the sky drew him to the window. "Oh my God! Catherine, stay here with the children. Marie, wake your grandfather and stay with your grandmother."

Nicolas raced down the slope in time to stop Martin from limping back into the flames. "Where's Quentin?"

"The doors will not open; he's trying—"

Without waiting for an explanation, Nicolas ran into the smoke. Flames licked the walls on their way to the roof as Nicolas found Quentin fighting to open a stall door. "Quentin! Come on; it's too late!"

Wild-eyed and half-crazed, Quentin shouted, "We must save them!" He swung the ax again. The door splintered and fell out of the way. The terrified horse reared, grazing Quentin's head, jumped over the shredded wood, and disappeared in the smoke.

Quentin fell, hitting the floor hard and knocking the wind out of him. When he didn't move, Nicolas grabbed him under the arms and dragged him toward the door. As the smoke thickened, he dropped to his knees, where he could breathe, and pulled Quentin behind him.

Voices rose above the roar. "Nicolas! Quentin!"

Thank God! Two figures appeared in the smoke—his father and Martin. They pulled Quentin from his grasp and stumbled to safety. Nicolas crawled on all fours and collapsed onto the street, gasping for air.

A deafening crash boomed through the valley as a sudden blast of smoke roared through the barn and rained embers and debris on the growing crowd outside the stable. The wind blew up the hollow, catching still-burning pieces of straw, flinging them toward the sky. The screams of the terrified horses still trapped in the barn echoed as the flames shot through the roof.

Catherine screamed, "Nicolas!"

"I'm all right," he coughed. "Quentin, help Quentin!"

Catherine followed Martin to the street, where Jean was kneeling beside Quentin with Beatrix crying over him. Blood smeared on the side of his head, shimmering in the light from the flames. Jean smacked his cheeks, trying to wake him.

"Give him some air," Sebastien grumbled, waving his cane from side to side as townspeople pressed in closer.

An ear-shattering crash blew out the windows of the stable as part of the roof collapsed. The crowd turned back to the spectacle.

"Maybe he breathed in too much smoke," Catherine whispered to Martin. "What did Vesalius say?"

To her surprise, Martin gasped, shook his head furiously, and mouthed, "No!"

She clutched his shoulders and shook him. Her lips tightened as she replied, "Quentin is going to die unless we do something!"

Martin whispered behind his hand, "Vesalius said the lungs need to be inflated to keep the heart beating, but we cannot do anything in front of this crowd."

"Auntie? Could we take him into the inn?"

"Of course!" Agnes cried. Beatrix ran ahead and cleared a table.

As Jean carried Quentin inside, Martin held the door, then closed and locked it behind them.

Catherine tried to remember Vesalius's words. "I thought it said to blow into a reed."

Martin rolled his eyes. "Where will we find a reed in the middle of the night?"

"Blow into his mouth," Catherine said, pointing to Quentin.

Shocked, Martin stepped back. "I cannot blow into his mouth!"

Catherine turned to Jean, who looked confused. He shook his head.

"Oh!" She threw her arms up in exasperation. "I will do it myself!"

She leaned over the boy. Not sure where to begin, she adjusted his head, took a deep breath, and blew, then stood, confused. "All the air came out his nose."

"Well, pinch his nose shut," Aunt Agnes replied as if Catherine should have known.

The others watched, but nobody offered any advice, so she tried again.

"His chest rose!" Martin shouted. "Keep going."

The words gave her confidence, and she repeated the procedure. The young man's chest rose and fell a third and a fourth time.

Martin put his ear by Quentin's nose, with his face toward the boy's chest. "He is breathing better. I cannot believe it."

Trembling, Catherine slumped into the nearest chair.

Sebastien grimaced and pointed to the lump on Quentin's head. "Probably had nothing to do with breathing. Whatever caused this bump probably just knocked the wind out of him."

"Give the girl some credit," Agnes scolded. She hugged Catherine's shoulders. "You did it!"

To everyone's surprise, Quentin sat up, glanced at the faces staring at him, and stammered, "What happened?"

"Good thing you have a hard head, boy," Sebastien replied.

"My head is splitting."

"But how is your breathing?" Beatrix said, touching his cheek.

His eyes sparkled as he looked at her. "I'm fine."

"Does your chest hurt?" Martin asked. "Breathe deeply. Does it feel heavy?"

"No, but I'm a little dizzy."

"Sit down and rest, and I'll get you some willow bark and chicory," Beatrix said.

The boy's eyes followed Beatrix, but before Catherine could say anything, pounding on the door startled them. Martin unlocked it to find Nicolas.

"How is he?"

Catherine ran to his embrace. "He seems fine."

Nicolas held her much longer than usual. "The forge is gone and all but two of the horses."

A few minutes later, Jean-Baptiste, Dimanchette, Joseph, and Marie arrived. As they approached the table where Quentin sat, Joseph said, "We saw the glow in the sky and knew it must be a big one."

Sebastien poured Jean an ale, which he took with a nod of thanks, but instead of drinking, he stared at it. He took out his handkerchief and wiped his forehead with shaking hands. "For some reason, Laville wanted to ruin me. And he has succeeded. Thank you for the drink, Sebastien."

With that, he returned to the street.

While Nicolas and Catherine followed Jean outside, Martin looked at the pensive faces of the group. "What will happen tomorrow when the coaches arrive, expecting fresh horses?"

Sebastien swung his cane in the air. "That one-eyed bastard probably has horses at his stable, all fresh and ready to take over."

"We rarely have customers since Laville started those rumors. Without the coach, there is no reason to rebuild," Martin replied.

The room fell silent when Beatrix's shy voice rose from the open kitchen door. "Why not buy horses?"

"*Vingt Dieux!*" boomed Sebastien. "Where do you suggest we find eight coach horses tonight?"

Agnes scowled. "Sebastien!"

With an exaggerated pout, Sebastien lowered his head. "Sorry, Beatrix." He turned to Joseph. "My nephew supplies the horses for the glassworks in Ribeauville. Perhaps he would have some for sale."

"Well, Nicolas saved my life, and I owe him," Joseph said. "Where is it?"

"That is a nice sentiment, Joseph, but one horse is a lot of money," Martin said. "Do you have any idea how much eight would cost?"

"Yes, Nicolas saved my life too, in more ways than one," Jean-Baptiste said with a nod. "I'll pitch in, and I'll come with you."

"What would have happened if Nicolas were not there the day Father Michel came for Mama?" Marie asked. "I want to help."

"After the attack, Jean gave me his horse," Aunt Agnes added. "Besides, if the coach moves to the other side of town, our business will suffer. Sebastien and I will help too."

Joseph jumped to his feet. "I'll go home and fetch the money."

While their intentions are good, it will be impossible to make it there and back before the noon coach tomorrow, but I have no money. What can I do to help?

"There might be horses for sale in Framont, and Le-Chêne will want to be here," Martin said. When he walked out the door and saw the burning building, the realization that his horse was lost in the flames hit him. The horse that Quentin had saved remained tied to the post in front of the inn. Martin scanned the darkness—everyone was focused on the fire. Though he didn't know whose it was, he planned to have it back before anyone missed it.

Outside the inn, Catherine sat on the bench beside Nicolas and his father and watched in horror as the final support beams fell with a deafening crash, shooting embers into the sky. The crowd slowly dispersed, some offering their condolences as they passed.

"I used to love to watch the flames crackle in the fireplace in the evenings," Catherine said. "Now the thought makes me sick."

She snuggled against Nicolas, and he wrapped his arm around her. "You should go home. The children are probably scared to death. Actually, I told you to stay there when I left." He kissed her forehead. "But I'm glad you didn't listen to me."

"Your mama is with the children. She probably has put them to bed by now."

A long silence followed until Jean mumbled, "I'm glad Little Jean took his apprenticeship in Strasbourg. Nothing is left for him here."

"We will rebuild, Papa," Nicolas said. "We'll rebuild everything."

38

As the sky lightened, ashes still glowed. The heat from the massive pile of embers warmed the chilly morning. With no wind to blow the smoke away, the morning mist mingled with soot, hanging heavy in the air.

On the bench, Nicolas awoke with a start. Catherine had fallen asleep on his shoulder, and he, in turn, slept against his father. Jean looked as if he hadn't slept and appeared to have aged overnight, his weary eyes glued to the sight before him.

"What do we do now, Papa?"

"I wish I knew, son."

The movement woke Catherine, and she sat up and yawned. "I'll fetch us something to drink." She disappeared inside the inn, where Aunt Agnes's voice rose. "Oh, you're awake." Agnes then came to the door. "Come in. I've kept the soup on all night, and the bread is done."

"Thank you, Agnes, but you shouldn't have gone to any trouble; we just live up the hill," Jean said without pulling his eyes from the wreckage.

"Oh, it's no trouble, but I didn't realize how chilly it is out there. I should have given you a blanket."

"Thank you, Auntie." Nicolas pulled on his father's arm until he stood and followed him. Inside, Beatrix and Quentin were eating at the bar. The bump on his head had swollen into a welt.

"You gave us a scare," Jean said. "You risked your life for a horse."

Quentin lowered sorrowful eyes. "I couldn't let them suffer. I just got carried away."

The horse's screams echoed in Nicolas's mind, but Quentin shouldered responsibility unnecessarily. "Yeah, but you're too heavy to get carried away. My back still hurts."

Quentin almost smiled. "That's the best you could do?"

Nicolas shrugged before pinching his brow. "Papa, should I go to the next stop and tell them not to expect a relay today?"

"There will be relays today, son," Jean replied with a somber voice. "I'm sure Laville is prepared, and once I cannot service the coach, my contract with the county will be broken and it will be his."

"Can he do that?"

"Who can stop him?"

"But we can buy more horses," Catherine cut in.

"No, Catherine, we cannot purchase horses and have them ready by noon. It's over." Jean turned to Agnes. "This soup is excellent. Thank you."

"But you've worked too hard to give up," Catherine pleaded.

His shoulders slumped, and he laid his spoon on the table. "I'm sorry, Catherine." He stood and walked out.

Not knowing what to do, Nicolas simply squeezed Catherine's hand and joined his father.

Agnes grabbed Catherine's shoulder when she stood to follow them. "Let Jean mourn, Lovey. He is a strong man, but he needs time. Maybe you should go home and give Elisabeth a break. The children need a hug from their mama."

In Framont, sunrise revealed the distant pillar of smoke. Martin and Le-Chêne searched the town for horses and returned to Vacquenoux as quickly as possible. The smell of the ruins permeated the air. After spending every day of the last twenty years in that stable, a great loss filled Martin. "I did not realize how the sight would affect me."

Jean was speaking to Father Edmond as they approached.

As they dismounted, Le-Chêne said, "I'm sorry, Papa, there were only three coach horses for sale in Framont. I rented this saddle horse for the week, figuring somebody would need one."

"Thank you, son." Jean gave a weary smile. "Surely, someone will need them, but we may as well use the coach horses to pull these dead ones out of here. Three horses are not enough for the coach."

Father Edmond said, "But four are."

"Thank you, Father, but I cannot take the church's horse."

"No, Jean, it was my father's horse. If not for Le-Chêne and that dear woman Francisca, I'd have starved. You can service the noon coach if nothing else."

"Thank you, Father. We'll borrow it for a couple of days."

When the noon coach came and Martin and Quentin completed the exchange, the drivers and the helpers applauded as the relay was completed.

The still-glowing embers were drenched with water. Martin put on heavy gloves and joined the others in the dismal work of sorting through the horrific tangle of charred horseflesh and ashes for anything of value. Throughout the morning, townspeople came, helped for a while, and left as others moved in to replace them.

Around midmorning, Martin stood to greet Louis Gauthier, then hesitated after remembering recent events. When Louis waved, Martin nudged Jean and Nicolas, who dropped the charred pieces of wood they were carrying and joined him.

Jean greeted Louis with a strained voice, "Bonjour, Louis."

Uncharacteristically humble, Louis lowered his gaze and clasped his hands in front of him. "I've wanted to speak with you since that day, but I—"

"What did I do to offend you, Louis?"

Martin shuffled uncomfortably. He nodded toward Nicolas and said, "We'll leave you alone."

"Stay, you two. I have something to say, and it'll be easier to say it once than leave unanswered questions."

The four of them moved to a quiet spot beside the wreckage, where Louis sighed heavily, alternating glances between them. "Laville came to see me soon after he moved here, saying he wanted to become mayor and . . ." Louis's voice trailed off. He cleared his throat and, without raising his eyes, said, "I may as well say it; Laville is extorting me. If I were the only one affected, I'd accept the scandal and resign, but this will affect my daughter's family." Louis cleared his throat again. "You see, Louise was . . . We concocted the story . . . They went to Strasbourg . . ."

Martin's heart skipped, and he glanced at Nicolas, whose expression was of horror. *Strasbourg!*

Finally, Louis looked up at Jean, frowning. "Jean, my son is not my son—he's Louise's son. They went to live with my sister during her confinement. Laville apparently lived next door and recognized her." Louis laughed dismally. "What were the chances of that?"

Embarrassed at what he had seen, Martin turned his attention away from Louis, who continued, "So when Laville noticed Louise married with only one child, a girl, and my son of the right age, he saw his opportunity. And now I have betrayed our friendship. Can you ever forgive me?"

"My good friend, I forgive you," Jean said. "Losing the election upset me, but the people have the right to choose. Losing our relationship was much worse, not to mention how Laville has tarnished our name. And now this."

The lines on Louis's face softened with relief, but then he frowned. "Do you think it was arson?"

Martin replied, "Someone wedged the stall doors shut. Quentin nearly died trying to break them with an ax."

"Have you found evidence? I am not sure what good that would do, but at least we could prove it to the community." Louis patted Jean's arm. "I will help you search."

As the afternoon wore on, Nicolas made a mental note of those who came to help or offer support so he could thank them later. Though Quentin wanted to help, he was told to rest, but he kept busy showing Catherine and the girls how to remove hardware from the charred wood. Marie and Dimanchette joined them, and eventually, a small clutch of women circled their chairs, removing and straightening the handmade nails and hardware. Even Elisabeth was there.

When an elegant coach stopped, the group of women paid little attention to the bejeweled, magnificently dressed woman who stepped out of the carriage and stood before Catherine. Nicolas gave a passing glance, stopped suddenly, and gasped.

Salomé!

What would she tell Catherine?

He dropped whatever he was holding and ran toward her, jumping from timber to timber.

Little Claudette pointed to the woman. "Oh, Mama, look, a princess!"

Catherine snatched her daughter's arm. "No, Lovey, it's not polite to point."

As Catherine gazed upward, she raised her hand to shade her eyes and left a black streak on her forehead. Black soot covered her apron and hands. Nicolas winced and stepped in front of her.

"Why are you here, Salomé? To see your handiwork?"

She pulled a handkerchief from her cuff, covered her mouth, and said over her shoulder, "Something smells foul."

"Yes, the stench is unbearable," Laville said, stepping beside her. Even though he wore an oversized hat covering his face, his notorious eye patch was visible. He took her elbow but stared strangely at Catherine. Le-Chêne must have noticed as well and stepped between them.

Salomé fanned herself with her handkerchief. "We're concerned about the horse my husband mistakenly entrusted to your care."

As his parents, Louis, the women, the workers—the entire village—gathered to watch the confrontation unfold, Jean asked, "Why are you here, Monsieur Laville?"

Standing on his tiptoes as if to appear taller, Laville shouted for all to hear. "As my lovely wife has stated, I've come to check on the horse I bought from the Bishop of Strasbourg—it is extremely valuable. I have the bill of sale right here."

Nicolas's stomach dropped, and he shot a look at Martin. *The Bishop of Strasbourg!*

"No, you have never brought a horse here to board." Jean took the bill of sale, but without glancing at it, he handed it off to Louis.

"Me? No, I do not do menial tasks." Laville nodded at his coach. "My driver brought it here two days ago."

Someone pushed Nicolas from behind. It was Quentin, who disappeared into the crowd.

Laville glanced at the ruin. "Where is my horse, monsieur?"

With an exaggerated gesture, Jean motioned toward the pile of rubble. "You know exactly where it is."

Laville stood on his toes to emphasize the statement. "In that case, I demand reimbursement for my loss."

"He is not responsible for an act of arson," Louis said, pointing to a pile of wood. "Show him what we have found."

Jean retrieved the piece of charred wood, clearly showing a wedge tied to the frame. "This is evidence of arson and will be presented in court."

"What does this filthy pile of ash mean to me? I certainly do not frequent stables—I think you are trying to divert the blame. All I want is reimbursement for my loss, which you are responsible for, and that request is not unreasonable." He swung his arms wide for the crowd. "These good people have worked hard to obtain their livestock and deserve reimbursement as well. If you cannot pay your debts, we will take goods of an equal amount."

A voice came from the crowd, "I can't afford to buy another horse."

"Neither can I," said another, "not to mention a saddle and bridle and—"

"This is not Jean's fault," interrupted a third. "How can a victim of arson be responsible? We should find the arsonist—make him pay."

"No, you're right." Jean turned to the crowd and shouted, "You trusted me with your animals and tack, and I will reimburse all of you."

244 • Juliette Godot

Meanwhile, Louis glanced at the bill of sale and held it up. "You did not pay this. Nobody would pay this much for a horse. This receipt is a forgery, and the count would never allow it."

Laville sneered. "My friend, you'll not scare me with threats of your heretic count as you did my friend Bishop Michel."

Nicolas's heart pounded. *That depraved bishop is behind this!*

Jean could hardly speak. "I will get you the money."

"I am not a banker, but I am not an unreasonable man. Your property will cover the debt."

"No court ever would uphold—"

"You seem to have forgotten, monsieur, I won Le Plaid. I am the judge in civil court in this area, and I will uphold reimbursement for negligence."

All the air left the mountain. Moments passed in complete silence until Father Edmond stepped up to face Laville, then flinched before saying, "Guillaume? Guillaume, is that you?"

When he received no response, he continued, "Guillaume, I know it is you. Nanny told me about your eye."

"Stay out of this, Edmond," Laville spat.

"Why did you hide from me? Why did you disguise yourself and use only Laville as your name?" Another silence followed. The priest continued. "Why are you mistreating these people, Guillaume? Your mother would be ashamed of you."

"My mama is dead! She died saving that bastard's life." Laville shouted, pointing to Le-Chêne.

Le-Chêne cringed and said, "Your mother was . . ."

The priest recoiled and slapped Laville's hand out of the air. "Guillaume! Le-Chêne had the plague. He did not kill your mother. Nounou went to him willingly, as she went to all the other victims. She helped so many; she was a saint." Softening his voice, Edmond continued, "I was with her when she died."

Spit flew from Laville's mouth, "She was my mother, and she is dead, and that bastard is alive!" He ripped off his hat and patch. "Look at my face! That little witch did this to me!"

"Sir Guy!" Catherine shrieked as the color drained from her face and her knees buckled.

Nicolas reached for her, but Le-Chêne had already wrapped his arms around her.

"This family has ruined my life! Ruined everything that I had!"

"Guillaume!" Father Edmond roared. "I don't know how you lost your eye, but you cannot blame them for everything that has happened to you. You are blessed with a new life and a beautiful wife—"

Laville pointed in the priest's face. "I can blame them, and I do blame them."

Through all of this, Salomé stood beside her husband with an evil smirk on her face. Nicolas shook with rage as he whispered, "Call your husband off, Salomé."

"Ha," she snarled. "You're finally paying for—"

"Call him off right now, or perhaps I will tell everyone what you did when you visited Strasbourg."

Her eyes narrowed, and her smile turned into a grimace. "You wouldn't dare."

Flinging his arms wide amid the devastation, he fumed, "I have nothing to lose." Turning to Laville, Nicolas raised his voice for the crowd, "Have you spoken to your lovely wife about *her* trip to Strasbourg?"

Louis stepped behind Nicolas. "Do you want to file a report?"

Putting his face inches away from Salomé's, Nicolas whispered through clenched teeth, "I swear to God, I will watch you burn."

"Master Jean!" Quentin called out. "I found it—I found his horse. It was tied beside the inn."

Laville whirled, and his face mottled red as he studied the animal. He replied in almost a whisper, "This horse means a lot to me."

After tying it to their coach, Quentin joined the others. Handing him the bill of sale, Louis motioned toward Laville, but Quentin glanced at it first, laughed aloud, and elbowed Jean. "He paid that much for this horse? Either he is the world's biggest liar or the world's biggest fool!"

A jingling sound arose from the west. The evening coach was coming a half-hour early.

Laville broke the momentary calm. "I would not celebrate if I were you, monsieur. You were able to complete the morning relay, but another coach is here, and you have no horses—your contract is broken. Luckily, I had the foresight to schedule replacements—"

"Here they come," Agnes shouted, pointing to the east. Marie added, "Thank God," as Joseph and Jean-Baptiste galloped into town, each leading four perfectly matched coach horses. The crowd opened for them to approach, and Agnes and Marie hugged them as soon as they dismounted. "Thank heaven you made it back on time," Agnes said.

"We were so worried," said Marie.

Nicolas realized his mouth was gaping and closed it. Tears filled his eyes as Joseph, wearing his usual wide grin, made his way through the crowd. "You should not have done this; Joseph, we cannot afford such fine—"

"Stop, Nicolas, I am repaying a debt to you. When I was a child, you saved my life and suffered my father's wrath. I'll not accept repayment."

"And two of those are from me for the same reason," Jean-Baptiste said.

From behind them, Marie said, "And those two are from Francisca and Humbert."

Agnes approached Jean and took his hand as tears filled his eyes. "You gave me a horse once. Consider these two replacements with a little interest, considering how long it has been. I'm glad the day came when I could repay you."

Drained, his body shaking and his stomach upside down, Nicolas struggled to find words. He and his family hugged their benefactors with such concentration none of them noticed Laville and Salomé's coach driving away from the scene.

With the spectacle over, the crowd dispersed, and the Cathillon family went to the inn for something to eat.

Jean dropped onto a piece of charred timber and put his head in his hands. When the rest of the family circled him, Catherine started to cry.

"I never meant to put his eye out. He attacked me—I swung my fist."

"He got what he deserved," Nicolas said, embracing her.

"Catherine, you simply defended yourself," Le-Chêne said, patting her shoulder. "This is my fault. His mother died saving me."

"No," Nicolas said, "I am afraid it is my fault." Catherine pulled back, and everyone stared at him. He lowered his gaze, sighed heavily, and began, "I started it when I went to Strasbourg with Little Jean . . ."

Nicolas retold the story with Martin chiming in now and then. Though they mentioned no names, Catherine's eyes widened, and she covered her mouth with her hand. As the story continued, it was clear to Nicolas that her tears were for the realization that he was talking about Jean-Baptiste. But when Martin explained the reason for Little Jean's sudden change of hairstyle and mannerisms, her tears turned into anger.

"You should've told me; he's not safe there."

"We knew he was not safe here, where the priest would expect him to be."

"But if he were here, we could protect him."

"Like we protected our livelihoods?"

Elisabeth shook her head. "Well, I cannot believe Father Michel would—"

"Mama, wake up!" Nicolas hissed.

"Louis arrested Michel," Jean said, touching Elisabeth's hand. "I saw it! Louis had a reason."

But then Nicolas's anger turned to remorse, and his eyes filled with tears. "I'm sorry, Papa. I didn't connect Laville to Michel. I'm not sure how they found each other, and now Salomé has joined them in their revenge."

Le-Chêne added, "I saw the look she gave you as she left—I doubt this is the last time we will hear from them."

A WEEK following the fire, the rubble had been cleared. Nicolas pooled his money with his father and Martin to purchase horses or tack for townspeople who had suffered losses. One evening over supper, they estimated the cost of building a new stable. Even without Nicolas's office, they could not pay for it without going into debt, and without customers, the income from servicing the coach was not enough to make the payments.

At a long lull in the conversation, Quentin spoke up, "Nicolas, would you make a ring for me? I'm going to ask Beatrix to be my wife."

After the eruption of congratulations, Nicolas patted Quentin on the back. "You're already a part of the family. Now it will be official."

"Thank you, Uncle."

"I'll be your brother."

"My brother . . ." Quentin whispered as a melancholic smile crossed his face. He cleared his throat. "Beatrix suggested you might need the dowry money to help rebuild, and then I could be a full partner."

"Quentin, you are already a partner," Martin said. "While I am thrilled that you and Beatrix will marry, since Humbert died, I imagine the Cathillon family is having as much trouble getting by as we are. You will need your small dowry to start your life together."

"No, I'll move into her room in the inn."

Nicolas chuckled at the look of pity on Martin's face. Martin must not be aware of the Cathillon family secret. "Martin, I suggest you visit Jean-Baptiste to discuss the contract."

By the following spring, the stable was completed and, a few weeks later, the forge, which Nicolas and Jean would share. Customers slowly trickled back.

Le-Chêne married a lovely girl, who gave him a son they named Humbert, and Quentin married Beatrix and moved into the tavern.

When the Le Plaid election came around again, Nicolas didn't want to attend but accompanied his father to avoid the fine and scandal their absence would cause. Once again, Laville stood in front of the town hall, describing a thriving community, though the city had fallen into disrepair.

Someone mentioned the half-burned wreckage of a house at the edge of town. Though months had passed since the fire, it was now a shelter for transients and rats. "That monstrosity would have been down the day after the fire if Jean were still mayor."

"The owners of that home are responsible for cleaning up that mess," Laville replied. "We will not spend tax money to—"

"But they left town when they lost everything in the fire!" yelled another.

"What do we pay our provost for?" Laville shouted.

Louis, who sat beside Jean, showed no expression.

Joseph punched his fist in the air and bellowed, "You can't get blood from a turnip!"

"People, people, enough of this." Laville raised his arms for silence. "It's time to vote, and I am ready to serve you once more, so let us see a show of hands."

When only a few people obliged, Laville raised his voice angrily. "Raise your hand!"

An egg hurled toward Laville caused Louis to stand. His booming voice hushed the crowd. "We have no choice. The count must ratify candidates, and nobody else has offered a name."

"We want Jean back!" boomed Sebastien's deep voice.

All eyes turned to Jean, who had remained silent during the melee, but then he stood, and his face reddened as he shouted to the crowd, "Wait just a minute! Do you think I can forget the things you said about me? You called me a liar and a thief! You made your bed; lie in it." And he stormed out the door.

Louis turned to the crowd. "Well, the count ratified Jean years ago, so he is still eligible."

"We want Jean back!" Sebastien boomed again.

40

A FEW months later, Nicolas received a letter via the coach from Strasbourg. He rushed home to open it with Catherine. Little Jean announced that two years of being an errand boy earned him an apprenticeship in the bindery.

Nicolas could finally relax. His wife was content, the stable and forge were profitable again, his son was safe and happy learning his chosen profession, and Salomé had apparently taken his threat seriously and convinced Laville to abandon his plot of revenge. Their children would have a bright future indeed.

We have achieved our drop of heaven.

A violent beating on the door woke them in the middle of that same night. Catherine jumped out of bed and grabbed her shawl from the rocking chair while Nicolas pulled on his pants and rushed out of the bedroom in front of her. In the main room, the door crashed open, and four men barged in, knocking Nicolas off his feet.

Catherine screamed and tried to catch him, but he staggered backward and fell, splintering a chair. The frightened girls ran out of their room and hid in the folds of her nightgown while he scrambled to his feet between them and the intruders.

The four men had unkempt beards and were clad in raggedy overcoats and big floppy hats. She could not make out their faces. One of them, taller than her husband, brandished a knife and shouted orders while the others toppled furniture.

"What do you want?" Nicolas yelled. "We have no valuables. Our only money is in that purse you have already found. Take it and go."

A fifth burly man burst in with a knife in one hand, dragging Elisabeth, whose eyes were wide in terror, with the other.

"*Ja*, she vas alone," he said to the one who must be the leader before throwing Elisabeth to the floor.

Jean is in Pierre-Percée with Louis!

Elisabeth's bare feet were covered in dirt, her nightgown slid up, showing her knees, and her skewed nightcap covered half her face.

"Oh!" she shrieked.

Nicolas lunged at him but halted when the man gripped her hair and shoved the knife perilously close to her face. When Nicolas straightened, the one shouting orders moved behind him, pressing the blade to his throat. The other one dropped Elisabeth, who wailed again. Catherine, fighting to maintain the shaking in her limbs, helped Elisabeth to her feet, and they clung to each other, sobbing.

Nodding toward their trunk, one of the men opened it and dumped out the books.

The leader laughed, deep and throaty, and said in a thick German accent, "*Mein guter freund*, you have many interesting things here."

"Those books are approved!" Nicolas shouted before the man pressed the blade tighter to his throat.

The pale moonlight through the window barely illuminated the pages, but the group leafed through the books as if looking for something, tossing them back into the trunk one by one.

"Zee von vith zee drawings is not here."

Catherine couldn't breathe. *They are looking for the Vesalius. How did they know? Where did Martin hide it?*

"No matter," the leader said.

Two lugged the chest from the house and dumped its contents in the courtyard, while another ignited a rag and shoved it in Nicolas's face, the glow revealing sopping sweat despite the cold night. The group cheered when the flaming rag was tossed and the pile of books caught and burned.

The burly one yelled, "Herr Heretic wants a heretic count to listen to his rhetoric and continue to spread his garbage against the pope!"

"The pope? We're Catholic! This has nothing to do with—" Nicolas shouted.

Before anyone realized what had happened, the one holding Nicolas pulled the blade across his throat.

"NO!" Catherine screamed and ran toward him as he dropped to his knees and reached for his neck. Glistening in the light from the roaring fire, blood sprayed out, soaking his bare chest. He let out a guttural moan and collapsed onto the ground, his muscles twitching.

"NICOLAS!"

"Catherine," he mouthed as she fell beside him. She looked into his terror-stricken eyes and placed her hand over the wound, but the men ripped him away from her grasp and tossed him into the fire. She watched in horror as embers billowed around his body, vaguely aware that Elisabeth had fainted and the girls were shrieking.

"Now he is burning in hell," one of them shouted as they ran to their horses and disappeared into the night.

Catherine ran to the fire, reached in, and dragged Nicolas onto the grass, slapping his legs with her hands to extinguish the flames.

She crawled up to his head. His eyes were partially open and staring.

"NICOLAS!" She fell onto his chest, wailing.

When Jean went to Pierre-Percée for meetings with community leaders, Nicolas usually opened the shop early, but the next morning when he didn't appear, Martin decided to investigate. Halfway up the hill, a burning odor made him accelerate his step. When he rounded the corner, he saw smoke in the distance, gasped, and ran the path toward Nicolas's house. There, near a pile of smoldering ashes, Catherine cradled Nicolas's blood-soaked body against her, whispering to him and rocking him back and forth, his charred legs blackened and still sizzling.

"Oh my God, Nicolas!" Martin ran to them and dropped to his knees beside Catherine. Tears flooded his eyes. "And the girls?"

Catherine raised a glazed look, but no sound came from her lips.

Elisabeth, barefoot and covered in mud, appeared in the doorway. "The girls are asleep in the house," she said in a shaking voice. When she looked at Nicolas, her knees buckled, and Martin jumped to catch her. He helped her to a backyard bench and searched her face.

"Who was it?"

"Five armed men." She touched her forehead with shaking hands. "They spoke German and said they were Catholics punishing heretics."

When the initial shock wore off, Martin gently pulled Nicolas's body from Catherine's grasp. Her blackened hands dropped like rags. He carried Nicolas into the house, laid him on the bed, and returned to the courtyard where she remained, crumpled, staring. The blood on her nightgown shimmered in the morning sun. He knelt before her and took her hand, which looked like burned meat.

"I will drive you to Le Petit-Courty, then go to Pierre-Percée to fetch Jean and Louis."

"If only Jean had been here," Elisabeth moaned in a weak voice.

"Elisabeth, had he been here, against five armed men, he inevitably would have been murdered too, but surely they took advantage of his and Louis's absence to act."

Martin sat beside Catherine as the reality sank in. He pulled her into his embrace and held her as they wept.

Nicolas is dead.

That night, Catherine awoke in the loft of her family's farm, her bandaged hands throbbing, her daughters in the bed beside her. She couldn't remember how she got there.

Darkness surrounded her, the beams of the roof pushed down on her, and all she could see were Nicolas's eyes, glazed, half-open, and staring. The smell of burning books tinged with charred flesh still filled her nostrils. She wiped away another tear, wondering what kind of life lay ahead.

As usual, the loft was too hot. She kicked off the blanket, then, remembering the Night Watchman, she jumped out of bed and ran to the window, but there was no moon, no stars, no crickets chirping, no frogs singing—nothing. Just silence.

Dead silence.

Nobody to watch over her.

She crumpled to the floor. She had been mad at Nicolas for so long. Now she was angry with herself. She had wasted so much time.

Martin took the next coach to Pierre-Percée for the grim task ahead, Joseph was off to notify Little Jean, and Jean-Baptiste would tell Le-Chêne. The driver offered to find a messenger to pass a note to Anne.

As Martin watched the passing valleys of the Vosges Mountains, he thought of his closest friend, whom he had considered his little brother, and he fought to hold back tears. At the top of the highest ridge, the coach stopped in the shadow of the ancient castle of Salm, still clinging to the rocks over the former

254 • Juliette Godot

capital city. He gathered his rucksack and took off toward the town square, hoping to find the venue where the community leaders gathered.

The brightly colored storefronts and bustle of the town only added to Martin's dread. What would he say to Jean? Would telling Louis everything Nicolas had confided to him help an investigation, or would it simply tarnish his memory? Martin turned a corner to find a group of men emerging from a building, and he waited. Louis was near the back of the line, followed by Jean. Cold sweat formed on Martin's forehead and palms when their eyes met.

As Martin relayed the tragedy, Jean paled, slid down the side of the building, and stared, as if unable to move. A long moment of shocked silence followed. Louis assured Jean that he would find the people responsible. While Jean fought to keep his composure, Martin took Louis aside and revealed all he knew about Salomé.

Nodding as if he had already known, Louis said, "I doubt Salomé would have done anything like this on her own, but I feel sure she knew of Laville's plans; perhaps she even helped him craft them." Red-faced and clenching his fists, Louis said, "I will find evidence. I will avenge Nicolas's death."

As they were speaking, a gangly boy about the age of Little Jean approached them, took off his cap, and handed Martin a note. "Sorry, monsieur, I am a friend of the coach driver. I was not able to find Madame de Puyloubier at this address."

Shocked, Martin took the letter and stared at it. He had sent a note to the same address when Francisca died. "Thank you," Martin said after the boy had already left.

When Martin turned back to Louis, Jean, pale and aged, approached them. "I have to go," he said in a weak voice.

Martin embraced him. "Go ahead without me. I must find Anne. I will be along shortly."

While Louis accompanied a devastated Jean home, Martin rented a horse and set off for Anne's countryside address. Outside the city, anglers dotted the lake, vineyards lined the slopes, and evergreens darkened the heights of the mountains. Manicured courtyards separated elegant stone houses and fit his vision of Anne's home. At the address, two small children played in a velvet courtyard under a nurse's watchful eye.

The boy must have been confused.

However, instead of verifying Anne's address, the nanny confirmed what the lad had said, and she knew nothing of the previous owners.

No one responded to Martin's knock on the nearest neighbor's door. A little farther down the road, a kindly elderly gentleman said from beneath an impressive gray mustache, "Did you not know Monsieur de Puyloubier was killed in Geneva? It has been almost two years. My wife and I used to visit that nice couple, and we enjoyed their little ones."

Anne never informed her mother? Astonished, Martin asked, "Two years ago?"

"Yes, our army went to support the Protestants against the Duke of Savoy. Those damned Catholics tried to climb the cursed walls of Geneva in the middle of the night." The old man punched his fist in the air. "They fortunately failed, but our army also suffered losses, and Captain de Puyloubier died with a dozen of his soldiers."

Martin rubbed his forehead. "What befell his wife and children?"

"As far as I know, she returned to her family." The man stepped back into the house.

Disbelieving, Martin stared at the closed door. Where could Anne be? No matter how long it took, he vowed to find her.

He went first to Badonviller, where Anne had spent many years working in the castle. For two days, he knocked on doors until he thankfully found Clauda, a woman who identified herself as Countess Chrestienne's childhood nurse. The old woman confirmed Henri's death, but she said sadly, "Despite my advice, Anne refused to tell her family. However, I will tell you what I know since you have come so far and with such horrible news."

Clauda led Martin to a chair and gave him a beer. She sighed and shook her head. "After Henri's death, Anne did not stay in Pierre-Percée, where she could have worked at the castle. She had told everyone she and Henri were married, and her pride would not permit her to ask for help. She found a job in our castle, but the fine ladies and gentlemen had all gone with Chrestienne to Nancy, and there was no need for embroiderers, only of washerwomen, working for a pittance."

Martin lowered his gaze to his clasped hands. "Pride."

"During the day, I care for her two little monsters." Clauda winked at the children, who had appeared in the doorway. Their wide smiles prompted one from Martin. "Anne gathers them in the evening to go to her room next door."

Stunned, Martin stayed with Clauda so he could speak with Anne, and when it was near time for her return, he took his leave. He waited for her by a small bridge in the shadow of the fortress, watching the sunset, remembering that evening so long ago when they had stood together. When at last a figure approached in the fading sunlight, he immediately recognized the shape of the beautiful girl who had never left his heart. As she neared, however, he saw how her features had changed. A cover of bitterness and wrinkles marked her tired eyes, which widened in astonishment when she saw him.

"Martin! How did you find me?"

"I had to find you," Martin said without hesitation, taking her hand.

She withdrew it abruptly. "My hands are hideous." She stepped back and raised her head proudly. "So Clauda told you. My life is here now. Did she also say I refuse to come home as a beggar?"

Their eyes met and held and after a moment he said, "I have missed you so much."

Anne squared her shoulders. "Why? I'm the same peasant I was all those years ago, Martin. Why the change in attitude now?"

Stung, Martin lowered his gaze. "Anne, you are so wrong. You were the most—you *are* the most beautiful woman I have ever known, and I knew I could never be enough for you."

Anne turned from him. "It is too late, Martin. I have two children and many more years that weigh heavily on me. I'm no longer the young girl awash with the joy of living that you once knew."

She walked away, but he followed her, trying to choose the words that would break through. "Anne, please." He caught up with her, and she turned to him with weary eyes.

"I must talk with you. Please, I came all this way."

With a heavy sigh, she followed him to the parapet of the bridge, where they sat together. He took her hand, and they sat in a long silence, watching the cold, dark water swirl and bubble over moss-covered rocks. A slight breeze blew, pulling a wisp of Anne's hair and brushing it against his cheek, just as it had that day in the burned-out barn.

"Come home with me," he said.

She stared straight ahead before responding. "I need time, Martin."

"There is no time. Catherine needs you now." Through tears, he relayed the events.

Trembling, she said, "Oh, poor Nicolas! Why didn't you tell me right away?"

"We cannot do anything until the coach tomorrow. Pack your things and come with me."

"Of course I will."

She pulled a handkerchief from her sleeve and dabbed her eyes but could not stop the flood. She buried her face in his chest, and they clung to each other and wept until no tears were left.

About a month later, Catherine awoke early. The household was still asleep when she walked into the courtyard and pressed her back against the sturdy trunk of a great oak tree as if to draw upon some of its energy. The past few weeks had turned her life upside down.

Though Jean had made it back for the requiem Mass, since then he had become frail. Martin had to close the forge—both forges. Elisabeth could not bring herself to attend the funeral, and neither had left the house since. The whole town of Vacquenoux felt the loss.

Louis interrogated everyone in town but could find no evidence. Nobody could testify; nobody had seen a thing.

Although Anne moving in with Catherine was a godsend, she needed to be alone with her memories. Now she stood quietly in the silence of the morning, the mist rising as the dew burned off the grass. A glimpse of crimson caught her eye, and she approached the rosebush Nicolas had planted beside the door. It had grown into a lush beauty. She broke a bloom off the stalk and a thorn pricked her finger. She imagined the bite of the flames on her beloved, but she closed her eyes against that pain and recalled the soft embrace of the man she had always loved.

"Mama, this is for you." The smile of her youngest daughter, Mougeotte, carrying a bouquet of weeds brightened Catherine's spirit. "Don't be sad. See how pretty?" She swung her arms in a wide circular gesture, encompassing where the grass had started to grow again, partly hiding the sinister black spot of the fire.

The wind whispered Nicolas's words. *If the rose is life, pick me.*

FTER a long, lonely winter, Catherine's life had turned routine. Anne was Catherine's constant companion, and their five children living in the small house kept them busy. Little Jean wrote often, but he still had several years left before he would finish his apprenticeship.

One evening, Catherine found herself, as she often did, in the forge, sitting behind Nicolas's desk. While she had kept some of his drawings containing doodles or musings, she'd sold the others, along with his unfinished projects and raw metals. A few shelves honored his memory, displaying the objects he had made. The large wood-and-leather bellows remained too, attached to the wall as a link between the air he breathed and the new air filling these places.

The door to the street stood ajar. The sound of a horse and cart and faraway laughter arose when a familiar voice interrupted her musings.

"Catherine, finally I will tell you how I sigh . . ."

She could not see the face of her agitator shadowed in the doorway against the late afternoon sun, but she recognized that voice out of a thousand—her emerald-eyed troubadour!

Ripping off his hat and patch, he revealed a sunken cheek and the notorious scar of a knife print that must have cauterized the wound. "Behold your handiwork!" His good eye narrowed, and he spoke through clenched teeth. "I have dreamed of ways to make you pay for my disfigurement."

Though her knees turned to jelly, it only took a second for anger to replace her remorse, and she stood tall. "You have no one to blame but yourself and your drunken friends. I thought you liked me."

"Oh, you poor little naïve child. *I thought you liked me*," he mocked in a silly voice.

With his hands clasped behind his back, he brazenly strolled in and studied the shelves holding her precious memories.

She tried to maintain her dignity and not burst into tears. "What do you want from me?"

"I just wanted to introduce myself as your new provost."

"New provost?"

"Your puppet provost has suffered an attack of some sort," Laville said, running his finger across her beloved bellows. "He can only move one arm. He can't walk, and he can't talk."

Oh, poor Louis . . .

"And I, your esteemed former mayor, have stepped forward, offering my service to all. Our small community will benefit, as I have stood before kings and am a friend of the Bishop of Strasbourg."

"Why are you here, Monsieur Laville?"

"I came to advise you of my first assignment: to arrest an herbalist accused of selling birth prevention powder. I have heard you have a long history as a witch—"

Catherine stiffened. "I am not now, nor have I ever been, an herbalist."

"Well, I guess we will determine that in the coming days."

He turned and laughed, but as he walked away, instead of fear or fury, she felt pity for the pathetic man who had once stood in the presence of kings.

A week later, a morning fog was slow to burn off the slopes as Catherine walked toward the inn to help Beatrix prepare for a wedding celebration at the tavern. The chance to break the monotony to work at the inn, which would be drudgery to others, seemed a luxury to her. Lost in thought, Catherine approached the street when shouts of a crowd jeering at a passing prison cart drew her attention.

The townspeople hurled insults, "Witch! Whore! Murderer!"

Catherine gasped in shock when she recognized the accused as none other than Salomé, disheveled and wild-eyed. With her face painted ghostly white, pink circles drawn on her cheeks, and blood-red lips drawn three times their size, she looked like a court jester.

She caught Catherine's gaze and shouted, "I will finally get you too, my dear. I'll not burn alone. Trust me!" The rest of her invective was lost in the noise of the cart.

Stunned, Catherine stumbled onto Nicolas's desk. Did Laville have his wife arrested? The woman looked mad. *Will she accuse me of witchcraft?* Surely, they would know she was lying.

Besides, the villagers would verify Catherine was not an herbalist. With the thought still burning in her mind, she continued to the inn.

A few days later, shouting and the jingling of a cart awoke Catherine, and that awful night of Nicolas's murder flashed in her mind. She grabbed her shawl and ran to the door before it crashed open.

Three men she didn't recognize wearing uniforms of the provost stood beside a prison cart. One of them with a red band on his arm—like the one Louis wore—stepped forward and asked, "Are you Catherine Cathillon de la Goutte de Paradis?"

Barely able to mouth the words, she whispered, "Who are you?"

His face was stone cold. "We are deputies of the provost."

But she knew all of Louis's deputies; Laville must have replaced them. Her breath caught in her throat, and she gasped, "Provost Laville?"

Without acknowledging her question, he said, "Answer the question, madame."

She whispered, "Yes."

He shoved a writ at her, but it fell to the ground when he seized her and tied her hands behind her back. Her heart pounded in her ears.

Shaking uncontrollably, she screamed, "NO!"

She fell onto the cart, he bound her ankles, and the men returned to their horses.

Anne appeared at the door. "Catherine!"

The cart began to move. In the early morning light, she watched her sister get smaller and smaller.

The children. What of the children?

The guards flung Catherine to the stone floor of the cell and departed without a word, plunging her into complete darkness at the close of the door. On her hands and knees, she waited for her eyes to adjust, but with only one small window, she could barely see anything.

Crawling on the rough, slimy stones, she touched spiders or something crawly under her fingers, but terror had weakened her so much she didn't care. She fingered her way to a wall where she sat, wrapped her shawl around her, and trembled until, after what seemed like hours, she finally fell into a fitful sleep.

Something brushed her arm, waking her with a start. She shivered at the unnerving sensation. How long had she slept? Outside the small window, another building distorted the light, blurring day and night. No one came to her cell except guards, who left a jug of water and tossed pieces of bread onto the floor.

At first, she stayed in her cocoon-like position—the thought of eating made her sick. As soon as the door closed, however, scurrying and chomping noises confirmed she was not alone. She put her head on her knees and cried at the thought of her little children as orphans.

All her life, she had worried about this happening to Mémé, and now . . . Catherine pulled the pendant from under her chemise and held it in her hand, trying to draw from its strength.

There was nowhere to relieve herself, but the need was inevitable. She groped along the wall to a corner where a squishy feeling under her feet and a reek that seemed to envelop her indicated others had the same idea. She was glad she couldn't see.

Time stood still—or flew, she was not sure.

Hunger and thirst became all-encompassing, and though she was afraid to leave her safe spot, she decided the next time the door opened, she would run for the food while she could still get to it before the rats did.

Finally, the guard came, and Catherine jumped up, but this one handed the bread and jug to her, and she ripped into the bread and downed the water like an animal. He also brought her a few shovelfuls of clean straw to sleep on and another to cover the dunghill in the corner. For a moment, she was embarrassed, but her situation overwhelmed her, and she felt nothing.

He raised an eyebrow at her pendant. "What is that?"

"It was my mémé's; it gives me solace."

He looked at her with pity. "Take it off and hide it until . . . after."

After . . .

Catherine shuddered but summoned the courage to ask him, "How long have I been here?"

"Four days."

"What are their intentions for me?"

"I'm not sure."

He set his lantern in the hall, allowing a little light to shine through a small crack in the door, breaking the terrible darkness. But the light also revealed her furry cellmates. One of them looked at her, wiggling its whiskers. Catherine should have been afraid, but that was the least of her worries.

Following the guard's advice, she removed the pendant and held it in her hand, terrified at the thought of what would happen in the days to come, though she had no fantasies about her chances of getting out alive. Death did not frighten her. Death would be simple, and she had considered it often when missing her beloved Nicolas, but for the children . . .

No, what terrified her was the suffering that would come first. Martin had discussed the confessions extracted through torture. Others before her had tried to invent names—Jeannon or Margot—but amid their torments, they mentioned real names, those that came most readily to their disturbed minds. This must have been how Mémé was incriminated.

She knew denying obedience to the devil would not protect her, and eventually, she would confess to end the torture no matter how ridiculous the charge. There, in the grim and terrible darkness, a small idea occurred to her, smaller even than the tiny beam of light from the guard's lantern, but it grew, replacing some of the horrors. Perhaps the torture itself could save her.

It was her only hope.

chapter

42

ORD spread quickly in Vacquenoux. The family gathered at the stable, debating what to do, who would drive, and who should stay. For the third or fourth time, Martin shouted, "Drop everything. We must go to Badonviller—now!"

As the discussion continued, a stranger approached. The man handed Martin a sealed missive. It was from the notary, and panic grew in his chest as he read it. "Oh my God!"

Everyone turned his way, and he read aloud:

"With great distress I write to you, my friend. Monsieur Laville came to my office yesterday, demanding title to La Goutte de Paradis as a reward for denouncing his wife as a witch, who, in turn, accused your loved one. Had the estate been in Nicolas's name, Laville would have had a case. He left highly agitated. Please take any necessary precaution."

The pale faces of the others stared back at him—angry, confused, despairing.

Le-Chêne flung his arms in exasperation. "Laville has the biggest mansion in the area. Why would he want La Goutte de Paradis, except to hurt me?"

The weight of the air pushed down on Martin. "He must be so blinded by hatred that he wants everything, but we cannot think about that now. We have to concentrate on Catherine."

Le-Chêne walked in circles, pinching the bridge of his nose. "My wife and children offered to stay with Mama and Papa to help with the little ones. Will they be safe?"

Beatrix had been crying uncontrollably, and Quentin kissed her atop her head. "I must stay and service the coach. Besides, Elisabeth and Jean are my grandparents too, sort of. I'll watch over everyone."

"The coach is loading," Martin said. "We will meet at the boardinghouse by the prison." Instead of Anne taking his outstretched hand, she pulled Beatrix from Quentin's embrace. They joined Martin and Le-Chêne in the coach.

The ride was somber, with everyone sharing ideas. Martin suggested Master Carolus might know someone who could help, but Strasbourg was too far away and in the wrong direction. Le-Chêne considered utilizing the power of the forge's guild, but the director and the Church were always at odds. "Perhaps Duchess Chrestienne will remember me," Anne said. "Perhaps I could speak with her."

"That might be our only hope, but you should not go to Nancy alone," Martin said. "I will come with you."

Anne frowned but nodded.

Beatrix looked at them with sorrowful eyes. "You will continue to Nancy? What will I do?"

"Come with me," Le-Chêne said. "We will try to find someone to bribe."

At the exchange station in Badonviller, Le-Chêne and Beatrix disembarked while Martin and Anne continued to the castle of the Duke of Lorraine.

Refused an audience with the duchess, they stood at the servants' entrance as Anne approached every employee, coming or going, trying to find someone who remembered her. Hours went by, darkness fell, and they spent the night sitting on the ground, leaning against the gate, hoping for a miracle.

After hundreds of confused looks and apologies, finally a friendly face.

Regnault Douvier, Chrestienne's personal driver and one of Anne's friends from Badonviller, appeared to take the duchess to her morning rituals. They quickly explained the situation, and Regnault agreed to arrange an impromptu meeting at the door to the duchess's private chambers. They waited outside, and when the coach returned, Anne jumped up. Though Martin held her back, the commotion caught the duchess by surprise, and she flew into a rage.

"Who allowed these people into my private entrance?"

Regnault bowed deeply. "Your Grace, they're friends of mine."

"Douvier! My husband handles disputes with his subjects, and I want no part of it!"

"There was no time," Regnault said, bowing again.

The duchess brushed them off and rushed down the hall, but Anne cried to her back, "I helped you once, please, Chrestienne!"

She spun, her eyes piercing. "Nobody has ever helped me without expecting something in return. And who are you to call me Chrestienne? I am the duchess!"

"I helped the little girl in the library of the abbey. I didn't know who she was, just a small girl who had cut her finger."

Anne wriggled away from Martin and ran toward Chrestienne. A guard seized Anne's arms and held a knife to her throat, yet she continued to struggle. "Let me go! Chrestienne, please!"

Those regal eyes studied Anne. The duchess motioned for the guard to release her. "I remember you. That was a long time ago. Why are you here now? For money?"

Throwing herself to the floor at the duchess's feet, Anne sobbed, hardly able to speak. To Martin's surprise, Chrestienne helped her up and led her down the hall and out of sight. He closed his eyes and whispered a prayer. This was the best outcome he could have imagined. Perhaps there was a glimmer of hope.

WHEN the cell door opened, Catherine slid the pendant under the straw and stood. Without a word, two guards escorted her to a dank chamber smelling of urine and vomit. Shackles hung from the walls, whips interspersed with small hooks were strewn on the floor, and a man dressed in a long black robe stood behind a large wheel rack, his bony fingers twirling in small circles in front of his lips—

The inquisitor. No matter the charge, I will confess.

His penetrating gaze bore into her. "Would you like to confess?"

Catherine awaited the charge, but none came. The man just stared at her, unwavering, his fingers twirling. Her heart pounded. What charges should she confess?

Allowing the tears to flow, Catherine pleaded, "Please help me. I have carnally known the Lucifer."

The inquisitor straightened and gave her a confused look, probably accustomed to receiving confessions only after breaking someone by torture. Then he scowled, leaned forward, and placed his hands on the rack. "Confess!"

Trying to keep her voice from wavering, Catherine cried, "He lives inside me. He made me deny God. Please give me an exorcism."

He studied her with piercing scrutiny. "Confess!"

But she didn't know what to say. "He carried me on his back to the Wild Hunt of the Hellequin and the Sabbat, where we danced and lay together to the sound of the lute."

Still, those evil eyes drilled into her, wanting more.

Desperately trying to think of Martin's discussions, she suddenly remembered other ridiculous charges. "I changed the bedding on Friday; I refuse to eat pork!"

The inquisitor's brow furrowed, his lips a thin line. No doubt he had a higher-than-average intelligence. How could he accept such nonsense—accept and blindly obey? He nodded to the guards.

I did it—I must have satisfied him! Relief washed over her at the thought of going to trial without being tortured, but then one of the guards ripped off her clothes. Naked and shivering but refusing to feel shame, she clenched her jaw, raised her chin, and squared her shoulders.

The other guard pulled out a razor and smiled wickedly. She squeezed her eyes shut, waiting for the bite of the blade, but he shaved her head and body. The priest examined every inch of her skin, carefully documenting every blemish and freckle as a mark of the devil.

Atop her forehead, he found the scar left when Sir Guy attacked her.

She forced herself to think of something else. Mémé's—loving arms around her, as always. *Lovey, don't be afraid. I am with you.* None of that comfort was here.

The inquisitor pricked the scar with a silver needle, found it didn't bleed, and noted the evidence of a diabolical sign. Added to her confession, Catherine knew he would submit this as evidence to the court.

Though she tried to remain calm, she trembled uncontrollably. The guards laid her on the rack and bound her wrists and ankles.

She struggled and screamed. "No! Please! I have confessed, and you've found the mark of the devil. What else do you need to send me to death?"

"Who accompanied you when you promised your allegiance to the Prince of Darkness?"

"Lucifer!"

The inquisitor turned the crank that stretched her body.

The pain was unbearable, yet Catherine focused on one word, "Lucifer!"

"This heretic, Martin—he served the devil with you! He taught you! This is his sole responsibility, not yours. We could be lenient with you."

"Lucifer!"

Another crank. Her wrists and ankles popped, and as the rope tightened, she thought they would snap off her body. She screamed in pain.

"Quentin is the son of a witch. He showed you how to practice the craft. He is responsible for your being here. You must tell us before he condemns your younger sister as well."

"Oh, Lucifer! Help me, Lucifer!"

"Simply nod; I will understand."

She fainted.

When she came to, darkness surrounded her again, and the cold stone floor dug into her. She dragged herself to the straw, frantically searching for Mémé's pendant. It was still there! Catherine forced her swollen hands to move it to her lap.

Every noise made her jump, fearing they were coming back.

The click of the lock. Someone was at the door. She closed her eyes, pretending to be unconscious.

"Madame, they have finished and are preparing for your trial," said the kind guard, who brought more bread and water.

"Would you please help me with my pendant?" she asked, nodding to it on her lap.

He glanced around before candidly slipping it over her head and tucking it inside her smock.

The cold metal against her skin warmed her. "Thank you."

He nodded and left.

Shivering in fear and soaked from the clammy sweat covering her body, she hardly had the strength to bring the pitcher to her lips. Her arms were leaden and quivering so severely that she spilled half of the water as she poured the rest onto her swollen wrists and ankles.

Far from weakening her, the torture infuriated her.

Why had this happened? Catherine had spent her life doing everything asked of her— attending ridiculous rituals simply because it was expected, keeping her opinions to herself, following her husband's wishes, and no longer trying to heal people—and still, here she was! She wished Francisca had taught her about poisons.

To take her mind off her plight, she focused on what she would say at her trial. No one would represent her or testify on her behalf. No one would hear her defense but the county prosecutor, the judge, and those representing the Church, and she had no illusions about their impartiality.

But she also knew there would be a transcript and hoped her words, once written in black and white, would pass beyond the walls of the court, and one day these innocent victims might receive justice.

She would give them an earful.

chapter
44

DOZEN jugs of water and pieces of bread later, two guards came to Catherine's cell. With her feet so swollen she couldn't stand, they pulled her up and tied her hands behind her back. When they pushed her toward the door, her ankles gave out. Grumbling, the guards gripped her under the arms and dragged her through the hall, where other prisoners shouted obscenities at them.

As the door to the street opened, sunlight burned her eyes. She winced and dropped her head just as they flung her toward the cart. Off-balance, she smashed into the rail and fell, landing face down on the platform. Pain reverberated up her spine, tears flooded her eyes, and she cried out, but the guards merely gathered her up again and pushed her. Every jolt of the wagon shot through her back as they drove to the Hall of Justice.

In all her life, she had never left Vacquenoux, and she would have loved to see a city the size of Badonviller under different circumstances. As it was, the brightly colored signs and storefronts passed by her unnoticed. People rushed here and there as if nothing was wrong, and she watched in dismay. Nobody cared about such a thing until it happened to them. How could they simply allow this?

The cart stopped, and the guards dragged her into a room the size of their church back home, with a similarly high roof, and propped her behind a podium before a long table where the tribunal sat. Above them, bright sunlight shone through a huge, strategically placed window, casting their faces in shadow. Lost in the glare, all she could see were a dozen forms dressed in red: red capes, red shoes, red caps. A man in a black cloak leafed through handwritten pages at another table, sometimes raising his head to glance at her. Behind him, clerics cut their feathers and opened their inkwells, preparing their transcription.

Entering the room and standing before the man in black, the inquisitor read his findings, raising his index finger for emphasis. Catherine held her breath in fear. "First—she confessed to all the charges. Second—there is no record of this woman's baptism, and she received the Sacraments. Third—I found a forensic brand of evil on her forehead where she has a scar in the shape of a toad leg, but the most damning . . . she admitted to having the devil inside her."

Amid gasps from those before her, the man in black said, "Thank you," and to her relief, the inquisitor left.

One of the clerks stood and read the testimony given by the villagers. Of course, Salomé Müller was most prominent, and she had expected Sir Guy, but the list was long and included friends that Catherine had known all her life.

"She caused violent deaths around her, including her father, Humbert Cathillon; her husband, Nicolas de la Goutte de Paradis, and even a Catholic priest."

The most disappointing testimony of all came from her dear sister Beatrix, who testified that, "she breathed life into a dead man." Even the court officials murmured among themselves at this.

What was Beatrix referring to—when she blew into Quentin's mouth after the fire? Beatrix understood what was happening. They must have twisted her words.

The room swirled, and Catherine's heart pounded in her ears so loudly that she thought they would explode, but she forced herself to pay attention; she had to hear everything so she could defend herself.

The room abruptly went quiet, and all eyes bored into her. It must be her turn to speak. Catherine took a deep breath, and though her voice was weak, she spoke with as much assertion as she could muster.

"In the name of God, you face the accused after having them shaved and tortured until they lose reason. Instead of guiding morality by your example, you use terror. Instead of serving the Church, you impose your will upon it. God is goodness and mercy, but you kill anyone who does not follow the dogma of the Church to the letter."

Her ankles gave way, and she shifted more of her weight onto the podium, stretching her neck to appear to stand tall. "John said: 'God did not send His Son into the world to condemn the world, but to save the world through Him.'"

The prelates leaned toward each other, whispering and making gestures of anger.

"Blasphemy!" one of them yelled.

The judge in black silenced them. "The accused has the right of justification and explains why she turned away from the faith to make a pact with the devil."

Taken aback by the interpretation, Catherine briefly lost her path of reasoning. The sun's glare battered her eyes and scattered her wits, but she must think!

She cleared her throat and continued. "You have made God in your own image: intolerant, violent, vindictive, and full of hatred, denying women any place in the world outside of birth. For good measure, you burn some men, allowing you to eliminate liberals, freethinkers, and those who speak out against your corruption."

"Enough!" thundered one of the men in red who was endorsed by those around him.

The judge again imposed silence with a single hand gesture. Catherine became hopeful. Could this man, named by the Protestant count, condemn the duplicity of the Church? Could he save her? Catherine chose her words carefully. "Have you never considered why everyone confesses to the same thing, word for word?"

One of the men in red stood, pointed angrily at her, and with spit flying, raged, "Peasants cannot read. How do they know what others have said before them?"

The judge banged violently on the table for silence and turned to Catherine. "Please hasten to conclude."

Catherine shivered under the pressure of the moment. *I am here, Lovey.*

"Your inquisitor will extract a confession at any cost, describing everything he needs to hear to the last detail. Did you fornicate with the devil as a sign of devotion? *No?* An additional stretch of the rack and the response is: *Yes!* Is he like Pan, covered in hair? Does he have hooves? A long tail? If the accused is too weak to respond, a simple gesture of the head, a single groan of pain is as good as an affirmation."

Another red-garbed man stood, pointing and glaring at her in condemnation. "The neighbors saw you flying on the back of the Hellequin. One watched you breathe life into a dead man, and one man said you removed his eye. They were not tortured and came to declare willingly."

Catherine inhaled deeply, filling herself with an unknown strength. She would not be silenced. "It is much easier to believe what someone tells you to believe than to think for yourself. The woman who accused me was mad. The man who lost his eye tried to rape me, and if I could breathe life into a dead man, I would have saved my papa and my husband."

Ignoring the murmur of outrage flowing from the men in red, Catherine stared directly at the judge. "I confessed to the charges everyone here pretends to believe because your inquisitor would have tortured me until I did. Under torture, the pope himself would confess to dancing with Satan."

The cardinals ranted at once, "We warned her! Nevertheless, she persisted!"

"Enough!" hissed the judge. "The court will deliberate."

As the tribunal left the room, Catherine collapsed onto the floor, exhausted, conscious of having played her trump card. Perhaps the man in black would convince those in red of the unfairness of conviction. Maybe she was dreaming. He might banish her. She could go to Strasbourg—be with Little Jean, perhaps help Master Carolus. She would even submit to an exorcism, anything but enduring the horrors at the stake. At any rate, the judge would have the last word.

The tribunal returned, and the man in black told her to stand. Catherine tried to get up but did not have the strength. The guard lifted her, and she clung to the podium.

"I, Judge . . . seeing that . . . because . . ." After repeating the long list of testimonies, confessions, and statements, he finally came to the ruling, which he read in the same neutral voice without glancing from his text.

"Catherine Cathillon, widow of the smith Nicolas de la Goutte de Paradis, I condemn you to be strangled and burned at the low pit of Badonviller for crimes of sorcery."

All the air escaped her lungs, and Catherine collapsed to the floor. Her strength drained, her mind was empty, and her hope for humanity had vanished.

chapter
45

GUARDS seized Catherine and dragged her outside onto the platform. While they awaited the cart to return to the prison, someone jumped out of the shadows below them.

It was Sir Guy. He pointed at her and laughed.

"What's he doing here?" one of the guards barked at the driver. He let go of Catherine's arm and swung his club at Laville's head. Not prepared for his action, the guard holding Catherine lost his balance and let go of her. Without support, her ankles gave out, and with her arms tied behind her back, she landed hard on the side of her face. Her pendant fell from inside her smock and landed right in front of Laville.

The troubadour laughed louder. "Finally getting what you deserve." His eyes widened when he saw her pendant. "That's mine!"

But then he pulled a replica from under his shirt.

Catherine stared at it. She had never seen another, though Nicolas had said he had made one for that nun.

Laville's eyes widened. "Where did you get that?" He reached for Catherine's neck, but the guard stepped on his hand. He squealed and pulled it away, shouting, "Please let me see—"

The guard unsheathed his sword. "Get out of here, you vermin!"

Sir Guy's shocked gaze remained on Catherine's necklace. "But it is exactly like mine!" He reached for his pendant.

"He has a weapon!" the driver shouted.

The guard swung his sword, striking Sir Guy on the side of the head. His patch and hat shot off, his head jerked back, and blood and spit flew as he screamed and fell. The guard watched over the side of the platform, and when there was no movement, he spit again and sheathed his sword.

The prison cart backed up to the platform, and the guards pulled Catherine up and tossed her in. It took a moment for the dizziness to clear, and when it did, she could see the troubadour lying motionless on the ground, his face sliced like a piece of meat, his eye socket empty.

Was he dead?

The thought should have brought her satisfaction, but she had no feelings left.

At an inn near the Hall of Justice in Badonviller, Martin waited with the family for the sound of the beat of a drum. Whenever he heard it, he hurried to the street to listen to the latest news from the crier. After several days of waiting, the dreaded verdict came.

Martin held Anne as she wept. "Chrestienne said she would try to contact her cousin Phillippe."

"Indeed, she said she would try."

"But if the duchess can't do anything, who can?"

"Anne, Count Philippe Otto might still be at the court of Emperor Ferdinand. As a reward for converting to Catholicism, he will become a prince of the Holy Roman Empire. Perhaps the duchess could not reach him, or he didn't want to bring attention to himself by offering clemency to a witch."

"She is the duchess!"

Martin enfolded her. "I know."

The next morning, reality weighed heavily on everyone when Clauda, Anne's friend from her days working at the castle, appeared at the inn.

"I came as soon as I heard the verdict." She embraced Anne. "Calm down and listen, dear."

"Thank you for coming," Anne said after blowing her nose and dabbing her eyes.

Martin led them to a bench, sat beside her, and held her hand until she quieted.

When Clauda glanced around the room as if looking for danger, Martin motioned for the rest of the family to encircle them. Once hidden, she whispered, "You cannot keep your sister from the stake."

A new round of sobs and wailing erupted, and Anne withered in her seat. Martin pulled her into his arms, and she clung to him. Despite the dreadful, unspeakable horrors to come, he would get her through this.

When the room again went silent, Clauda said, "I can help your sister."

A glimmer of hope? "What could you do?" Martin asked.

"I will find something for your sister—so she doesn't suffer." The old woman paused and looked at the faces of those surrounding them. "The only problem is getting it to her. My grandson is a guard at the prison, but he cannot give her anything, and the priest of Badonviller is not trustworthy."

"The priest of Vacquenoux might help us," Jean-Baptiste said. "Father Edmond said he would do anything to help, but he is in Vacquenoux."

"But he did not foresee helping someone commit suicide," Martin said.

"Oh no! A person would have to eat at least ten to kill her," Clauda interrupted. "Four dried mushrooms will only prevent someone's brain from feeling what's happening."

Martin and Anne exchanged worried glances.

"If your priest does not believe me, I will eat one for him."

"A dangerous proposition," Martin said. "If he is caught, who knows what would happen? There is no harm in asking, but we had better hasten."

"Your sister will have a day or two, so my grandson will have time to speak with her. She must ask for her parish priest, and they usually grant her last request. Tell me when he is in Badonviller. I will visit him at night, away from prying eyes."

Anne's eyes widened. "But Clauda, could your grandson help Catherine escape? We would hide him!"

"No, dear. My grandson does not have the keys to the dungeon. His overseer opens and closes the main doors. There are armed guards in the corridor, a drawbridge, and the garrison of the army outside the gate. He will tell her to request her parish priest." She wiped a tear from Anne's cheek and said, "I only wish I could do more. Go quickly to fetch him."

"I'll go," Jean-Baptiste said, and Joseph added, "Me too."

They kissed Anne's cheek and rushed out the door.

While Anne and the women went to their rooms, Martin joined the men in the tavern, but before they found a table, a man wearing a provost uniform approached them. Martin tensed. *Oh God, Catherine named me.*

The man bowed more deeply than usual. "Excuse me," he said. "I am Jean Idoux, Provost of Schirmeck. I could not help but overhear you. I would like to offer my sympathies."

Martin's breath caught. *What did he say?*

Le-Chêne said, "Thank you."

"I was tasked with interviewing witnesses, and I must tell you the evidence was thin."

Martin stared at him, incredulous, but he couldn't think of a reply.

"Someone powerful held a grudge." Idoux shook his head and pinched his brow. "I will never believe there are no baptismal records either." He bowed again. "Well, I just wanted you to know that not everyone involved is complicit."

He turned to walk away, but Martin touched his shoulder. "Could you help us?"

"I'm sorry, I've already spoken with the judge. The verdict cannot be overturned. I requested a copy of the transcript that I can give to you, although it might make you feel worse. I usually receive them in a day or two."

"Have you heard from the duchess? She said she would intervene."

A look of surprise crosse Idoux's face. "Duchess Chrestienne? I don't know anything . . ."

"I guess it is irrelevant now."

Le-Chêne's voice cracked. "Do you think we could see her one last time?"

"I'm sorry. Even I cannot see her."

Martin lowered his head, trying to hold back tears. "How long does she have?"

"Just a day or two," Idoux spoke with empathy. "Believe me, she will welcome death. That prison is horrific. I wish there were more I could do."

Le-Chêne bowed to Idoux. "Thank you for your effort."

There must be something that will give a little comfort. "Could we get her remains?" Martin asked.

"She cannot be buried in consecrated ground," Idoux said.

"I know. We would bury her at Lac de la Maix."

Idoux hesitated, then nodded. "I will need to speak to the judge immediately."

46

THREE days later, the click of the lock startled Catherine. She sat up and held her breath, dreading what would happen next. Two guards stepped into her cell, one who had shown her kindness, followed by Father Edmond.

Relieved to see a friendly face, she smiled weakly and tried to stand, but her ankles still refused to hold her weight. The priest rushed to her and fell to his knees alongside her. She clung to him, but with no tears left to cry, all she could manage was a whisper.

"Thank you for coming."

Father Edmond's eyes brimmed with tears. "Would you like absolution?"

At her nod, he turned to the guards and waited until they left.

She struggled to kneel before him, and the priest laid his hand on her head for the ritual, but as soon as they were alone, he stopped and slipped four mushrooms into her hand. Surprised, she glanced at them—she had seen them before, but Mémé had told Catherine to avoid them. Now she welcomed them and wordlessly shoved them all into her mouth at once. They tasted like dirt—chewy dirt—and she swallowed quickly.

When he finished the ritual, the priest said, "Catherine, I'm sorry. I failed to get a copy of your baptismal records. This could all have been avoided had I just . . ."

"The only thing I regret is leaving my children." Her voice cracked, and tears filled her eyes. "Would you please ask Anne to raise them?"

A sudden hot flush swept over Catherine, and she swayed and leaned against him. "I want Martin and Anne to marry and raise the children in their own house. Would you please . . ."

Catherine looked up at the priest but couldn't remember what she was saying.

"I will," Father Edmond said before giving her the Viaticum.

By the time the guards returned, her eyes wouldn't focus, and the pain was easing in her aching limbs. Edmond gave her a tearful final embrace. Though she expected words of wisdom to carry with her, he lowered his head and choked, "God be with you."

Should she feel something? Sadness? Regret? Her pain was gone, and she felt hollow—almost with a sense of relief. The guards took her arms, dragged her down the long hall, and stepped outside onto the same platform as the day of the trial. Again, after several more days in darkness, the bright sunlight burned her eyes, but she forced herself not to drop her head this time.

While there were people outside the building, most were used to the repetition of countless persecutions and went about their day without even stopping. The executioner tied her to a post outside the church, and the provost read the sentence.

When her eyes acclimated, she looked out at the square. The colors had never been so vivid—everything seemed to glow. Her eyes wandered about and alighted briefly on a small group huddled behind a guard who appeared to be preventing them from approaching.

One of them was Nicolas. "Nicolas, Nicolas!" *Can he see me? Why doesn't he come to me? But wait! This is not the great oak where we escaped the wolves; I am tied to this post for some reason. That's not Nicolas; it's our baby, Little Jean. He's a grown man, his arm wrapped around my mother.*

"Mama," she mouthed.

Beatrix was weeping. "Don't cry, little sister. I know they tricked you."

Martin was holding her dear sister, Anne, against him. Catherine smiled at them. "Take good care of each other. Play a song for me."

And Jean-Baptiste and sweet Dimanchette and Joseph . . . and there was Le-Chêne, a full head taller than everyone else, standing in the back, and he was not even trying to hide his tears. Catherine saw him say, "I love you." Perhaps she said it back.

Deep in her blurring mind, she said, "Francisca, where are you?"

I'm here, Lovey!

"Yes, I remember. You're waiting for me at the edge of Lac de la Maix. I'll see you soon."

Martin searched the platform for a second prisoner before he realized with horror that the bald, emaciated skeleton with bruises covering half her face was his beloved friend. In the thirty years since Claude, his professor, had been executed, nothing had changed. For all the advances made in the world, intolerance remained constant.

He had been forced to convince Anne to come, but Catherine needed to have a final vision of her loving family, and they couldn't let her die alone. Martin tried to prepare everyone for the spectacle he had witnessed in Geneva, but now, seeing Catherine like this, his tears flowed too.

Martin said, "I think Clauda's potion worked. She is smiling. Thank God!"

The guards untied Catherine from the post, carried her to the cart, and drove her to the pit. One helped her climb the pile of wood and straw and tied her hands behind her against the wooden pole. He spoke to her and pointed toward the family.

When she looked their way, Martin shouted and waved his arms. "She sees us!" His shout of "We love you!" was followed by the cries of those around him.

When the guard moved away from her, her body sagged against the post. A minute later, the executioner put a rope around her neck, pulling her head back.

Catherine was floating—no longer tired, nor weak, nor in pain. Her head was jerked back, bringing the tops of her beloved mountains into view.

It was so incredibly hot! Everything was fuzzy, like a dream.

It was early in the morning, still dark, and she had awakened in the loft of Le Petit-Courty. The skin had fallen over the window during the night, and she rose to reattach it to the nail. A fresh breeze blew in, and she slipped her head out the window to enjoy the crisp night air. There on the mountain was the man wearing a white shirt, riding a big white horse. Smoke blew across her face, blocking her view, and when it cleared, the man was standing before her—Nicolas. He slid forward on the saddle so she could mount the horse behind him.

She crossed her arms. "You know Papa yelled at me for straddling the horse."

He smiled; his eyes crinkled at the corners—she had missed that smile. He helped her climb sidesaddle in front of him. She felt his fingers in her hair, and that long-forgotten shiver raced up her spine. She melted into his kiss and laid her head on his chest as the horse moved through the smoke, and the sky became brighter and brighter . . .

s Martin watched Catherine's ordeal, he could barely stand the weight of the air pushing down on him. The sobs from the others had quieted. The suffocating silence blended with the echo of crackling wood as a sinister black cloud hid the brilliance of the sunny day.

Catherine never screamed, thank God. She simply looked toward the heavens and wilted. He couldn't bear to see her blackened body, so before the flames died down, he said, "She's gone. Let us go."

The group trudged to the inn and, without the strength to return home, decided to spend another night in Badonviller. The women went to their rooms while the men proceeded to the tavern, where they pulled tables around the fireplace.

That evening, Provost Idoux arrived. Martin introduced Idoux to the group and invited him to join them. He took a seat and handed Martin a box tied with a cross pendant secured to the top.

"I found this in the ashes," Idoux said. "I assumed it was hers."

Martin didn't realize Catherine also had a pendant, but when he turned it over and saw the name *Fran*, he simply stared at it.

Idoux also revealed two envelopes, jarring Martin from his reverie. "I was able to attain both Madame Laville's and Catherine's transcripts."

Little Jean pointed to his mother's transcript and said in a shaky voice, "I would like to read this alone." At Martin's nod, Little Jean took it and retreated to a quiet corner of the tavern.

"Does anyone mind?" Martin said as he picked up Salomé's transcript. When he received no response, he settled into a chair beside the fireplace. After reading a few lines, he glanced at Idoux. "Did you read this?"

"No, I brought them over as soon as I received them."

Martin sighed heavily and rubbed the crease in his forehead.

Le-Chêne said, "What is it, Martin?"

Martin adjusted his weight in the chair, frowned at Le-Chêne, and read aloud, *"Nicolas made me do the things that I have done."*

Le-Chêne's mouth dropped open, and he stared at the paper. "What kind of things?"

"She confessed to murdering Magdalena."

Jumping to his feet, Le-Chêne paced and punched into the air. "She blamed Nicolas for killing Magdalena?"

The room erupted with everyone talking at once, and the other family members gathered nearer. All eyes fell on Martin.

"No, not literally. She says, *'Nicolas reached out to me and pulled me into the flames.'"*

The image of Nicolas's partially burned body flashed in Martin's mind, and a lump formed in his throat. He lowered his head, swallowed hard, and turned back to the transcript, *"I bribed a guard with jewels."* He turned to Idoux. "Is that possible?"

Confusion filled Idoux's expression, and he shrugged. "Who's Magdalena?"

"She was accused of witchcraft," Le-Chêne replied. "But why would Salomé kill Magdalena? And what would Nicolas have to do with any of it?"

Though Martin knew, he would not sully Nicolas's name and acted as confused as everyone else. "Magdalena was arrested, and we had heard she killed herself in prison—supposedly threw herself on a knife." He paused and added, "But Louis was always suspicious of her suicide."

"Well, prisoners don't usually have access to knives." Idoux nodded.

Martin continued reading silently. When he winced, Le-Chêne said, "Martin."

They surely will read this. I may as well tell them. "She says, *'Nicolas forced me to cast an infant from my womb.'"*

With his hands on his head, Le-Chêne moaned, "Oh my God!"

The transcript felt like lead in Martin's hands, and he tossed it on the table.

"Remember," Idoux said, "this testimony was based on torture. She may have said whatever she needed to say to make it stop."

Martin rubbed his eyes, then leaned on the table while the rest of the group either remained silent or quietly discussed the unbelievable accusations.

Little Jean rejoined the group, his eyes visibly red. The boy had lost both his parents in a short span in as horrific circumstances as Martin had endured. He would make sure Little Jean didn't fall into the same self-pity trap as he had been wallowing in.

282 · Juliette Godot

Martin asked him, "Are you all right?"

Little Jean nodded. "Mama was strong." He laid the transcript on the table.

"Yes, she was. May I read this?"

"Of course."

The sunlight through the window had faded, and Martin turned slightly, holding the paper to optimize the light from the fireplace. He couldn't help but fill with pride when he read Catherine's testimony. "Well, they certainly did not break her spirit," he said over his shoulder.

The door of the inn crashed open, and everyone jumped to their feet. Instinctively, Martin folded Catherine's papers and tucked them into his shirt before he turned and stood with the rest of the group. Four guards surrounded them and demanded Catherine's transcript.

Idoux stood. Recognizing his uniform, the guards' expressions changed. "I received the transcript legally," Idoux said.

"Just doing my job, sir," the guard replied.

Salomé's pages still lay on the table. Martin grabbed them and said, "Her transcript is right here. May I finish reading it first?"

"You have one minute," the commander growled.

Martin crouched in front of the fireplace and pretended to scan the pages. Then he tossed them into the fire.

The pages blackened and curled. A guard leaped forward, reaching into the flames, then threw the smoldering pages on the stone floor, stomping on them. When he picked them up, the bottom sheets disintegrated, leaving only the top page intact. Charred and unreadable, the only visible marking was the justice seal at the top. The commander seized Martin's arm with an iron grip and dragged him to his feet. Martin struggled. "Wait, I thought you said you wanted to destroy the transcript. I must have misunderstood."

Stepping into the fray, Idoux said, "The judge willingly gave that to me, and it is now destroyed. If he wants to talk to me, I'm here with my friends, and he is welcome to join us."

The guards mumbled among themselves but released Martin and departed with the charred page. Martin breathed a sigh of relief and touched his chest, making Catherine's paper crinkle. "Today has been exhausting. I will see you tomorrow. I am going to my room."

But Idoux stood and placed his hand on Martin's back. "I'll walk with you."

"Of course." Martin cringed. *Idoux wants this transcript.*

When they were out of earshot of the others, Idoux stopped and said, "I have filed a formal complaint about Catherine's case with Count Philippe. A man named Douvier testified that he entrusted a letter from Duchess Chrestienne of Lorraine to a bishop, but the bishop testified that he did not recall receiving any letter."

Bishop Michel!

"The duchess is furious. The abbot has traveled to Nancy to apologize personally to her."

"Anne was right; Chrestienne did try to help," Martin said. "What will happen to the bishop?"

"The abbot will decide. Had the letter been from the duke, the bishop would be in real trouble. As it is, he will probably be reassigned."

Again! Martin scowled before nodding in appreciation. "Thank you. For everything."

The next morning, Martin joined the group assembled for the trip home. Before they got underway, Idoux approached him. Assuming he had changed his mind about the transcript, Martin slumped, but to his surprise, Idoux said, "I've been thinking about that charred piece of paper. I just wanted to reiterate that if the actual record is found in your possession, your entire family will suffer."

"Indeed." Martin nodded. "I will hide it well."

As Idoux turned to leave, Martin called to him, "Catherine loved Lac de la Maix. She would have loved our trip tomorrow and would not want us to be somber. Her mother is planning to make it memorable." He nodded toward Marie and the other women filing onto the coach. "Would you like to come, Monsieur Idoux? The lake is beautiful this time of year."

"I will consider it. Thank you."

"Bring your family; they will enjoy the trip."

He nodded and waved goodbye.

In the morning, with sunlight streaming over the Vosges Mountains, promising a beautiful day, Martin packed his violin and joined the family gathered at Le Petit-Courty. Quentin led every available horse from the stable to carry the children and older members of the family. As they prepared for the journey, Provost Idoux arrived.

Jean-Baptiste, who had made the trip many times, led the funeral procession on the long trek to the lake, passing through the fields and dense pine forest.

All were in awe at the size and quiet beauty of the mountain lake and surrounding valley. The water—rippled and black at the edges, slightly lighter in the center—took on multiple shades, reflecting the dark green hues of the pines. Dragonflies skimmed the surface, showing the translucent green of their wings. A deer bent to drink at the other side of the lake. Startled, it raised its head and disappeared into the forest in a few strides.

The group surrounded the statue of the Blessed Mother. As Martin played his violin, Father Edmond blessed Catherine's final resting place.

There was not a dry eye among them as Jean-Baptiste buried the box containing his sister's ashes beside Francisca and his stillborn son.

The walk back to the farm went on and on. The group took comfort in being together and stayed for a meal before returning to their respective lives. Marie waved Martin over to join her conversation with Father Edmond and Anne.

Marie took his hand. "Thank you, Martin, for playing so beautifully today. Catherine surely was happy."

Martin nodded and turned to the priest. "I wanted to thank you too, Father, for accepting the risk—"

"No." He lowered his eyes. "I bore such guilt about not having a copy of the baptismal certificate. I wanted to ask Catherine's forgiveness, but she wouldn't allow me to apologize. Her only thought was of her children."

"Did Catherine have any last wishes?" Marie asked, releasing Martin's hand to brush away a tear.

"Yes," the priest said, glancing at Anne. He wrung his hands nervously. "She asked me to . . . well, she wanted you two to get married and raise her children in their own home."

Martin's heart leapt. When Anne had returned as a widow, he'd hoped they could start over, but she had no interest in him. Now he looked at her hopefully, but she stiffened. Marie nudged Anne, though, and she dropped her gaze. Heat rose in his face. He was being a fool—an old fool. He let his shoulders slump and said, "Father, I am not—"

"Now just stop it, you two," Marie said sharply, sounding much like Francisca. "You love each other. I see it in your eyes. Anne, you are too proud for your own good, and Martin, you are a good catch—start acting like it."

Marie had never raised her voice in Martin's presence. The rest of the family also took notice and stopped what they were doing to watch. Embarrassed,

Martin turned to the priest, who nodded encouragingly and said, "It was Catherine's last wish."

Martin had never considered switching sides. In fact, he'd thought the Catholic hierarchy to be evil, but there were evil men in all religions. Protestants had murdered Humbert and Nicolas.

Everyone was staring at him, waiting. If he did not convert right now, he would lose Anne forever.

Henry of Navarre did it to end the Wars of Religion.

Count Phillippe did it to become a prince of the Holy Roman Empire.

His former professor was right about switching sides in a heartbeat, but there was another reason to do it—not for power or wealth, but for love.

Anne is worth a Mass, but will she accept me? He had been embarrassed before, and he'd survived. What did he have to lose?

He dropped to one knee and took Anne's hand. "Will you marry me, Anne?"

Anne looked down at him, then shook her head and exhaled, turning her gaze off into the distance. Marie nudged her again, and she turned back, her expression softening, and she nodded.

"I will."

Raising her hands above her head and gazing at the sky, Marie danced in a small circle, clapped, and hugged them both. "Finally."

Martin stood while the rest of the family gathered around, congratulating them.

"Father, could you marry us right now?" Anne asked. "Before Martin starts worrying . . ."

Martin turned to the priest. "Could you?"

Father Edmond's eyes widened. "Well, Martin, please understand that you would need—"

"To become Catholic." Martin nodded. "I will." He looked hopefully at Anne, whose sad eyes brightened a little. He could do this.

Four years later, Little Jean finished his apprenticeship with Master Carolus and, with Martin's help, converted the forge into a bindery that would receive pre-printed sheets to be custom bound per customers' specifications.

For his first project, Little Jean bound a family Bible in his mother's honor, with Martin's handwritten note about the events of Catherine's death hidden in the front cover and the transcript of her trial in the back.

For many years in April, family and friends gathered in remembrance of Catherine in the beautiful valley of Lac de la Maix. As part of the festivities, Martin played his violin. After a few years, the horror of Catherine's death waned and they remembered her life, the music became lively, and the family danced.

Furious that a celebration honored a witch, Bishop Michel started a new rumor about a devil playing the violin at the lake, and *The Legend of the Devil Fiddler of Lac de la Maix* was born. That legend lives to this day.

Epilogue

PROGRESSIVE religious tolerance in Salm only lasted until 1623 when Protestant Rhingrave, Philip Othon, Count Frédéric's son, was forced to bow to the Holy Roman Emperor Ferdinand II and convert to Catholicism.

In exchange for his conversion, Philip received the title of Prince of Salm. Immediately he banished Reformed pastors throughout the region. The entire Protestant population had one year to convert to Catholicism or be exiled. As a result, most of the Protestant community migrated to Saint-Marie-aux-mines where religious tolerance was still accepted.

On March 2, 1793, the French Republic annexed what was left of Salm, and the castles and princely estates were sold as national property.

Underlying Facts

The following are some of the underlying facts referenced in this novel:

- Catherine Cathillon de la Goutte de Paradis, born around 1570, was burned at the stake for sorcery in Badonviller on April 25, 1622.
- Nicolas de la Goutte de Paradis, born 1567 in Wackenbach, died in Vacquenoux in 1605.
- Nicolas and Catherine married around 1585.
- Humbert Cathillon was born about 1530 in Vacquenoux. There is no record of his date of death.
- Jean (Le-Chêne) de la Goutte de Paradis was born in Vacquenoux in 1560 and died on November 1, 1631. Records list him as *maréchal* (master) blacksmith at the forge of Framont for the years 1601, 1604, and 1626. His first wife, Rachelle, died in childbirth, and he married his second wife, Claudette, in 1601, the first year he served as master of record. Claudette died within one year. He married his third wife, Marie, in 1610 and fathered two additional children not mentioned, Louis and Dominique. Some members of his family took Le-Chêne as their family name.
- Jean Idoux, the provost of Schirmeck, was born in 1580 and died in 1669. His daughter Christine married Little Jean's second son, Jean-Toussaint de la Goutte de Paradis.
- The Saint Bartholomew Day Massacre occurred on August 24, 1572, in Paris, and other massacres occurred in various provinces of France during the following weeks. The death toll varies widely from five thousand to thirty thousand.
- Johann Carolus, Strasbourg printer, published the first weekly journal of European information in 1601, called *Communication of all important and memorable stories.*

- The inquisitor of Salm in this novel is based on the most notorious inquisitor of that period—Nicolas Remy, the attorney general of Lorraine. He boasted of sending nine hundred people to the stake in a single decade.
- The Council of Trent condemned the sale of indulgences in 1563, and Pope Pius V abolished their sale in 1567.
- In 1588, Pope Sixtus V issued a papal bull officially classifying abortion, regardless of the stage of fetal development, as homicide, but the only penalty was excommunication. Most ignored this penalty, and after Sixtus's death, Pope Gregory XIV rolled back the dictate, offering no permanent solution to the legal status of abortion.
- Between 1500–1600, an estimated fifty thousand to eighty thousand people suspected as witches, mostly women, were executed in Europe, especially in the Holy Roman Empire and Lorraine.
- During the sixteenth and seventeenth centuries, scattered cases of the plague were reported in France every three years.
- Henry III, the last French monarch of the Valois dynasty, ruled as King of France from 1574 until his death in 1589.
- Henry IV, the first French monarch of the House of Bourbon, ruled as King of Navarre from 1572 to 1610 and King of France from 1589 to 1610.
- The 1555 Peace of Augsburg allowed for both Catholic and Protestant princes to rule their respective territories while remaining loyal to the Holy Roman Empire.
- Chrestienne de Salm married Francois de Vaudemont, Duke of Lorraine, in 1597, and the bizarre split of the county, never seen before or since, happened the following year.
- Frédéric Sauvage, called Rhingrave, and his descendants ruled the other half of Salm until the French Revolution.
- Françoise Cordier, my distant cousin from France, greatly helped in the inception of this story, the translations of Ronsard and Rabelais, and researching the historical facts. Françoise is a direct descendant of (Little) Jean and Anne-Marie Chastillion's first child, Nicolas, and his wife, Zabeth Honion. Françoise's book, *Les Demons du Pays de Salm*, is her version of this story, based on the same historical facts. It is written in French.
- I am a direct descent of Little Jean and Anne-Marie's second child, Jean-Toussaint, and his wife, Christine Idoux.
- Catherine Cathillon de la Goutte de Paradis is my thirteenth-generation grandmother.

About the Author

Juliette Godot is a former software engineer for Carnegie Mellon University, but her passion is genealogy. After cataloguing over forty thousand ancestors, she wanted to know more than just names on the family tree. The quest to find her roots led her down the back roads of France to the unsung principality of Salm, where superstitions were part of everyday life. The myths and legends of the Renaissance and the grit of the people steadfast in faith as war surrounded them enveloped Juliette. Writing about it was the only way she could get it out of her mind.

Juliette's debut novel, *From the Drop of Heaven*, has won the 2021 Gold Medal in the Royal Palm Literary Awards for unpublished historical fiction.

Connect with her online.

JulietteGodot.com

Twitter: @JulietteGodot

Facebook: JulietteGodot

Made in the USA
Middletown, DE
11 December 2022

18030010R00177